ACOLYTES OF
CTHULHU

ACOLYTES OF CTHULHU

SHORT STORIES INSPIRED BY
H. P. LOVECRAFT

EDITED BY ROBERT M. PRICE

TITAN BOOKS

Acolytes of Cthulhu
Print edition ISBN: 9781781165263
E-book edition ISBN: 9781781165270

Published by Titan Books
A division of Titan Publishing Group Ltd
144 Southwark Street, London SE1 0UP

First Titan Books edition: June 2014

1 3 5 7 9 10 8 6 4 2

Introduction Copyright © 2014 by Robert M. Price
Cover Art Copyright © 2014 by Bob Eggleton. All rights reserved

Earl Peirce, Jr."Doom of the House of Duryea" © 1936 Popular Fiction Publishing Company for *Weird Tales*
Joseph Payne Brennan, "The Seventh Incantation" © 1963 by Joseph Payne Brennan for *Scream at Midnight*
Hugh B. Cave and Robert M. Price, "From the Pits of Elder Blasphemy" © 2014 by The Estate of Hugh B. Cave
Duane Rimel, "The Jewels of Charlotte" © 1935 by Duane Rimel for *Unusual Stories*
Manly Wade Wellman, "The Letters of Cold Fire" © 1944 by Popular Fiction Company for *Weird Tales*
Henry Hasse, "Horror at Vecra" © 1943, appears here by permission of Forrest J. Ackerman
Charles R. Tanner, "Out of the Jar" © 1940 by Albing Publications for *Stirring Science Stories*
Edmond Hamilton, "The Earth Brain" © 1932 by Popular Fiction Company for *Weird Tales*
James Causey, "Legacy in Crystal" © 1943 by Popular Fiction Publishing Company for *Weird Tales*
C. Hall Thompson, "The Will of Claude Ashur" © Popular Fiction Publishing Company for *Weird Tales*
David H. Keller, "The Final War" first appeared from Perri Press in 1949
Arthur Pendragon, "The Dunstable Horror" © 1964 by Ziff-Davis Publishing Company for *Fantastic Stories of the Imagination*
Arthur Pendragon, "The Crib of Hell" © 1965 by Ziff-Davis Publishing Company for *Fantastic Stories of the Imagination*
Steffan B. Aletti, "The Last Work of Pietro de Opono" © 1969 by Health Knowledge, Inc. for *Magazine of Horror*
Steffan B. Aletti, "The Eye of Horus" © 1968 by Health Knowledge, Inc., for *Magazine of Horror*
Steffan B. Aletti, "The Cellar Room" © 1969 by Health Knowledge, Inc. for *Weird Terror Tales*
John S. Glasby, "Mythos" as by Max Chartair, © John Spencer & Co. for *Supernatural Stories*
Jorge Luis Borges, "There Are More Things" © 1975 by The Atlantic Monthly for *The Atlantic Monthly*
Randall Garrett, "The Horror Out of Time" © 1978 by Mercury Press, Inc. for *Fantasy & Science Fiction*
S.T. Joshi, "The Recurring Doom" © 1980 first appeared in Kenneth Neilly, ed., *Lovecraftian Ramblings XV*
Dirk W. Mosig, "Necrotic Knowledge" © 1976 first appeared in Mosig, ed., *The Necrotic Scroll*
Donald R. Burleson, "Night Bus" © 1985 by Yith Press for *Eldritch Tales*
Peter H. Cannon, "The Pewter Ring" © 1989 by Cryptic Publications for *Tales of Lovecraftian Horror*
David Kaufman, "John Lehman Alone" © 1987 for *Alfred Hitchcock's Mystery Magazine*
Gustav Meyrink, "The Purple Death" translated by Kathleen Houlihan and Robert M. Price © 1997 by Robert M. Price
Richard F. Searight and Franklyn Searight, "Mists of Death" © 1999 for the present collection.
Neil Gaiman, "Shoggoth's Old Peculiar" © 1998 by Neil Caiman. First published in *The Mammoth Book of Comic Fantasy*

A CIP catalogue record for this title is available from the British Library.

Printed and bound in the United States.

Dedicated to Duane Rimel, Great Old One and
Arch-Acolyte of Cthulhu

CONTENTS

INTRODUCTION

*Lovecraft, since his death in 1937, has rapidly been becoming a cult. He
already had his circle of disciples who collaborated with him and imitated him.*
Edmund Wilson, "Tales of the Marvellous and the Ridiculous"
November 24, 1945

THE BIG CLUE IS THAT H. P. LOVECRAFT USED TO SIGN HIMSELF
sometimes as "Grandpa Cthulhu" or simply as "Cthulhu." Thus the
acolytes of Cthulhu are the acolytes of Lovecraft himself. The Cthulhu
cult is the literary cult of Lovecraft. In this fact I believe we have a large
part of the explanation for the power with which Lovecraft's writings
grasp many of his readers and captures their imaginations, never to let
go. All fiction, as Michael Riffaterre notes (*Fictional Truth*) gains depth
and resonance, manages in short to "ring true" to its readers only
insofar as the author has built in the sounding board of a subtext, some
apparently prior reality against which story images and developments
will seem to ring solid. A fiction built on sand will sound tinny,
hollow, when tapped by the reader. A classic example might be the Old
Testament proof texts adduced by the Gospel of Matthew in order to
demonstrate that various events in the life of Jesus fulfilled prophecy.
The supposed events require some sort of a credibility boost, since they
depict a man being conceived by the divine spirit in a virgin's womb,
miraculously healing the sick, etc., not exactly items that easily pass the
test of most readers' criteria of plausibility. But once Matthew narrates
them, then provides an apparently matching proof text from ancient

scripture, you think the miracles may be true after all. They all of a sudden appear to match ancient prophecy. They appear to be the other shoe falling, matching the one that Isaiah or Jeremiah or Zechariah let drop hundreds of years before.

To take a very different example, the horror in Stephen King's *Pet Sematary,* which the movie version cannot keep from looking cartoonish, strikes deep for the sensitive reader since a great length of the noose rope has been strung upon the gallows of an excruciatingly rendered family tragedy surrounding the gratuitous death of a beloved child. If not for the subtext of too-real tragedy, the text of dripping zombies could never convince.

And I am suggesting that one big reason Lovecraft's fiction is so hypnotically effective for many of us is that we see ourselves reflected in the mirror it holds before us. When we discover HPL we are likely to be adolescent bookish types, unathletic or at least uninterested in the hormone-driven lemming-existence of our peers. Thus we identify with the scholarly misanthropes populating Lovecraft's stories. We love books, and by the time we have discovered our favorite recondite authors, most of their works are probably out of print, so we, like the doomed bibliophiles in Bloch's "The Shambler from the Stars" and Howard's "The Thing on the Roof," learn what it is to covet unobtainable volumes and to go to what seem to us (and even more to others who do not share our love of books) to be fantastic, fanatical lengths to possess our treasures. Securing a copy of *The Outsider and Others* would scarcely be less of an event than stumbling upon a copy of John Dee's *Necronomicon.*

Some notice with an element of unease that fandoms tend to take on the overtones of a religious commitment. To those fans, the more mundane issue the challenge to "Get a life!" Ah, but you see, Montressor, we *have* a life! It's more a question of *where.* As Debbie Harry sang in her song "The Real World," "I'm livin' in a magazine [*Weird Tales,* in our case]... I'm not livin' in the real world... no more, no more, no more." Or if you prefer REM, "It's the end of the world as we know it, and I feel fine." There is no objective "real world." All lives are essentially scripted fictions running their course in the context of some fictive narrative universe or other. Everyone is a "creative anachronist," but we Lovecraftians, like our cousins in other Buddha-fields of fandom, have elected to live a minority, sectarian existence in what sociologists Berger and Luckmann (*The Social Construction of Reality*) call a "finite province of meaning." We are willing to bear the reproach of the walking dead around us, the same who persecute poor Dilbert. We are proud of HPL for not being able to hold down a worldly job, even if we ourselves are able.

Lovecraft has become our Christ, our God. In a dream an angel appeared to the erudite Saint Jerome to rebuke him for his love of the Classics: "Thou are not a follower of Christ, but of Cicero." Guilty as charged!

Some despise fandom-as-[a substitute for]-religion because they assume, as Paul Tillich did, that a religion must center about, and must symbolize, one's ultimate concerns, and that these concerns must be appropriately ultimate in their scope, dealing with issues of timely relevance and eternal significance. But this is a sad and Puritanical definition of religiosity. It gets the focus wrong and neglects the role of imagination in religion, i.e. in myth. I think religious sensitivity is essentially an aesthetic stimulation of the imagination contributing to an aesthetic apprehension of life and the world through whatever filters we may choose to view it, whether that, e.g., of the great salvation-epic of the Bible, or that of the cosmic history of Lovecraft. It is such living fantasies as these which valorize an otherwise dull and utilitarian life. Moral convictions which, admittedly, everyone needs, are a different matter, and it is a dangerous confusion to make them dependent on, a function of, religious convictions. If you make that confusion, morality will always be subject to dogmatic decree, and holy wars, heresy hunts will sooner or later come to pass. So we Lovecraftians, we acolytes of Cthulhu, do not pretend to derive our varied moral stances from Lovecraft (except insofar as we read his essays and letters where he treats of such matters and happen to find him convincing). And we don't think others should necessarily derive their moral compasses from their religions either. What a better world it would be if we could come together and derive our moral scruples from a common-sense, this-worldly set of considerations and agree to disagree on what choice will nourish our imaginations, generate the symbolic universes we will breathe the air of day by day.

But the Lovecraft cult, I fear, is on a more infantile level than the Baker Street Irregulars and the cult of Sherlock Holmes.

Edmund Wilson, "Tales of the Marvellous and the Ridiculous"

...the prisoners all proved to be men of a very low, mixed-blooded, and mentally aberrant type. Most were seamen, and a sprinkling of negroes and mulattoes, largely West Indians or Brava Portuguese from the Cape Verde Islands, gave a colouring of voodooism to the heterogeneous cult.

H. P. Lovecraft, "The Call of Cthulhu," 1926

Adolescence is a time when intelligent people have begun to attain enough independence from family-circle influences to place all inherited beliefs under severe scrutiny. If you are going to become a rationalist, a skeptic, an agnostic, adolescence is the prime time to do it. It is a rebellion mechanism. It is a way of standing up on your own, for yourself. That doesn't mean you are not correct in throwing out childhood catechism. You have also come into possession of critical reasoning skills for the first time. If there is something rotten in Dogma Denmark, you have the keen nose to smell it. And all this, too, primes one for HPL. One catches sight of Lovecraft's scientific, rationalist, cosmicist worldview, where the myth of human self-importance is overthrown by realization of the yawning eternity of (as William Jennings Bryan summed it up) universal dust.

Thus cut off from the common run of conservative sitcom watching parents and prom-attending contemporaries, the young Lovecraft reader clutches his secret lore gleefully to himself, contemptuous of the surrounding herd, even as Lovecraft himself was, and for the same reasons. Such a reader will see himself reflected just as truly in Stanley G. Weinbaum's novel *The New Adam*.

The trouble with Edmund Wilson, which led him to those blasphemous words about our God of fiction that we can never forgive, any more than Vietnam veterans can ever forgive Jane Fonda, is that he was getting frostbite and enjoying it. Unlike the Transactional Analysis theorists who urge us to keep the child inside us alive and well, Wilson belonged to a cigar-chomping, scotch-sipping generation addicted to the stale smoke and the bitter reek of "realism," of boring adulthood, and who thought literature should reflect that outlook, the pages of "good books" merely wallpaper sheets for the prison cell of adulthood. We come on the scene with a childlike second sight which enables us to see the roaring glories of the Zen initiate. Growing up applies cloudy cataracts to the soul, and we can see the magic no longer, though fans have found a way. We use Lovecraft's fiction (and other fan-idols) like the jaded Randolph Carter used the Silver Key, to return to that brilliant world of dream, which is meaning. And Lovecraft, like Proust, freely admitted it was a regression to childhood. But why put it so nastily? Why not choose another metaphor, say, turning about and becoming as a child to enter the kingdom of heaven, since only their like will gain it.

> *The time is right for a greater appreciation of this deeper, more serious aspect of Lovecraft's fiction... The ground is particularly ready in Europe, where his works are held in highest esteem.*
>
> Dirk W. Mosig, "The Prophet from Providence," 1973

> *Antediluvian-cyclopean ruins on lonely Pacific island. Centre of earthwide subterranean witch cult.*
>
> H. P. Lovecraft Commonplace Book #110, 1923

The exotic pungency of the secret cult of Cthulhu in Lovecraft's fiction arises from the curious paradox of it being both widespread, worldwide, on the one hand, and yet secret on the other. It is conterminous with history, the bequest of the sleeping Old Ones to their dupes the human race (not that this is any different from the traditional Near Eastern religions, since in both the Babylonian *Enuma Elish* and in Genesis, humanity is created to serve as a slave race of grounds keepers). It covers the earth as the waters cover the sea; if one learns too much about it, "nautical-looking Negroes" will appear out of thin air to bump you off, and yet Western scholars seem never to have heard of it. The cultists of Cthulhu ply their rituals in lonely places, far from the ken of civilization.

And so with Lovecraft's acolytes: we identify with the vague net of Lovecraftians spread abroad somewhere else, and though we would relish fellowship with kindred spirits, we dread it, too, lest we be forced to profane our dearest treasures by bringing them forth into the open air. The friendly interest of another Lovecraft fan well met is at once a relief (we're not crazy—at least someone else suffers from the same obsession!) and a threat, since for us Lovecraft's fiction is a Holy of Holies into which only the solitary soul may step. The gathering of the coven should be a sacred convocation, and yet it is somehow a trespass.

And perhaps this fact explains a shocking and horrifying feature of many fan conventions (even in those microcosms of the same known as comic book stores). When those who by themselves are esotericists as they tread the solitary path nonetheless come together periodically, they magically transform into a bunch of obnoxious, profane, mundane Racoon Lodge conventioneers. Their odd costumes, which seemed the mark of solitary devotion to Darker Mysteries, now by virtue of simple public accumulation, have become a new and public mundanity, like geeks in the audience of *Let's Make a Deal*. Attending such a function one suddenly feels the force of the old joke that you wouldn't want to be a member of any club that would have someone like you as a member. The Mysteries become pathetically profane by mutual revelation. Thus the esotericist requires secrecy even should one some day become the majority (and for the moment, in a convention, one *is*). As Macrobius said with reference to the ancient Greek Mysteries: "only an elite may know about the real secret... while the rest may be content to venerate the mystery, defended by... figurative expressions from banality." In my estimate, the wonderful Necronomicons have perfectly walked the tightrope I am describing. No costumes are allowed, no weapons, except acid critical tongues.

Similarly, the lover of what is despised by the run of lesser mortals must think twice before seeking respectability among the mundanes for what one loves. Some Lovecraftians are urgent that Lovecraft gain the same anesthetic acceptability among mousy schoolmarms and blockheaded academics that has sunk Poe into the soporific sea. One wonders if their goal can be to return to mundane existence and yet not have to leave Lovecraft behind. But this is all misguided: if one must leave Shangri-La behind, don't drag HPL kicking and screaming through the enchanted portal with you, for Yog's sake!

We may be tempted likewise to defend Lovecraft against those who can never appreciate him (like the unregenerate mundane Wilson) by using the favorite trick of the freshman Anthropology major who embraces the ways of alien cultures only to gain a strategic position from which to take pot-shots at his own. In the case contemplated here, we must think of the intimidated Lovecraft fan who counters the criticism of the soulless mundane that Lovecraft must not be worth much if windbags like Wilson don't like him. (This is like Lucy telling Schroeder that Beethoven can't be so great or he'd be featured on bubblegum cards.) What is the response? The Lovecraftian apologist may reply that Lovecraft is more highly esteemed in Latin America and Europe, especially in France. But then, come to think of it, so is Jerry Lewis.

> *The possibility of imitation proves, as it were, that every idiosyncrasy is subject to generalization. Stylistic singularity is not the numerical identity of an individual but the specific identity of a type-a type that may lack antecedents but that is subject to an infinite number of subsequent applications. To describe a singularity is in a way to abolish it by multiplying it.*
>
> Gerard Genette, *Fiction and Diction*, 1993

> *"I am His Messenger, " the daemon said*
> *As in contempt he struck his Master's head.*
> H. P. Lovecraft, "Azathoth," *Fungi from Yuggoth XXII*

Perhaps the greatest black mark against Lovecraft's cults, Cthulhu's acolytes, is that they try too hard (or is it not hard enough?) to follow the Old Gent in his writing. Their many pastiches smell like the seafood Lovecraft himself could not stand. So great is their enthusiasm, that, granted, many go off half-cocked to the fight. But have a little patience. Consider it a learning exercise. In fact, in the ancient Hellenistic world, it *was* a school exercise. Students would prove their understanding of Socrates, Diogenes, whoever, by composing anecdotes and sayings summing up what the great man would have said. That's what pasticheurs are doing, and many of them are cutting their teeth doing it. They may one day go on, like Brian Lumley, Ramsey Campbell, and Robert Bloch, to discover their own style.

But it's also entirely possible that the result may be a mature Lovecraft pasticheur, someone who will actually carry on the old legacy. Perhaps like the Theosophists ready to anoint Krishnamurti, we must still wait for the One Who Is to Come, though I think we have found him incarnated in Thomas Ligotti and a few others.

But there remains something to learn from the youthful pastiches which constitute something of a right of passage for Lovecraftians (see S.T. Joshi's "The Recurring Doom" in this volume). Suppose one reads such derivative tales and finds them wanting—do you blame HPL? As if only a poor magnet attracts such filings? Mustn't a god who allows his servants to clobber him in this way be an idiot?

I think not. It is important to keep in mind that parody and pastiche are kept separate only by a razor's edge, like love and hate. The pasticheur seeks to grasp the distinctive marks of his model's style, so to emulate it. The more deeply he grasps the original, the better the result. But if the would-be pasticheur sees no farther than the most obvious surface features (e.g., the Lovecraftian book titles and monster names, or the italicized story endings) one is going to lean too heavily upon them, ignoring the rest, the more complex texture of style and structure that works its magic subtly enough to bewitch even the adolescent reader yet without him being able to put his finger upon precisely what does the trick. It does the trick, all right, but like the amazed audience of Houdini, the adolescent pasticheur cannot figure out how to reproduce the feat, and if he tries, the result will be embarrassing. But eventually, this way, the kid may learn the tricks himself, if we will be patient with him.

In what sense may the contributors to this volume be considered "acolytes" either of Lovecraft or of Great Cthulhu? A few were among the elite number to whom Wilson referred, disciples of Lovecraft during his lifetime, apprentices who sought his advice and wrote in his mode. Duane Rimel is one such. His "The Jewels of Charlotte" is an adjunct to his better known tale "The Tree on the Hill," as well as to his poem sequence "Dreams of Yith," both of which Lovecraft had a hand in. With the former story this one shares the protagonist Constantine Theunis, and like the latter, it mentions the far-flung planet Yith, his creation, along with Lovecraft. Likewise, Richard J. Searight was another correspondent of Lovecraft and accepted his ideas eagerly. Searight left two unfinished draft fragments of a story he planned to call "Mists of Death," and his son, Franklyn Searight, a gifted weird fictioneer of the old school, has woven the dangling threads into a complete tapestry his father would have been proud of.

Other writers, without consciously seeking to write in the Lovecraftian vein, nonetheless may be numbered among the acolytes of Cthulhu in that they seem to have been, like the mad sculptor Wilcox, sensitive to the R'lyehian Dreamer's urgings. They were on the same wavelength as Lovecraft, even if they wrote independently of the Providence recluse. One such was Gustav Meyrink, whose novel *The Golem*, Lovecraft highly praised. But I am thinking of a different work by Meyrink, "Der Violette Tod." An English version of the story, "The Violet Death," appeared in the July 1935 issue of *Weird Tales*. Anyone familiar with the original German of Meyrink will recognize that the *Weird Tales* version is only a kind of loose adaptation, not strictly a translation of "Der Violette Tod." Thus I have commissioned a new, faithful translation by Kathleen Houlihan, called "The Purple Death." You will find it most revealing to compare the two English versions. Thanks to Professor Daniel Lindblum for locating the original for me.

Earl Peirce was something of a literary grandchild of the Old Gent, being a protege of Lovecraft's protege Robert Bloch. In "Doom of the House of Duryea," Peirce takes a leaf from Bloch's book. Which book, you may ask? A little volume you may have heard of: *De Vermis Mysteriis*.

Henry Hasse was another *Weird Tales* contemporary of Lovecraft who, like Wellman, found the *Necronomicon* too fascinating a book not to check out of the Miskatonic Special Collections Room. He refers to the dreaded tome in "The Guardian of the Book" (in my anthology *Tales of the Lovecraft Mythos*) and in the present, admittedly more fannish tale, "Horror at Vecra," which appeared, appropriately enough, in that premiere Lovecraftian fan magazine *The Acolyte* for Fall 1943.

In his intriguing essay "Some Notes on Cthulhuian Pseudobiblia" (in S.T. Joshi, ed., *H. P. Lovecraft: Four Decades of Criticism*), Edward Lauterbach tried to call attention to a neglected Mythos text devised by scientifictionist Charles R. Tanner in his tale "Out of the Jar" (*Stirring Science Stories*, February 1941), the *Leabhar Mor Dubh*, or "Great Black Book," a volume of Gaelic blasphemy. Lauterbach's voice somehow failed to gain for Tanner the attention he deserved. I hope reprinting the story itself may help remedy that. My thanks to William Fulwiller, who doesn't miss much, for directing me to the tale.

Another case of novel Mythos tomes which remained obscure despite their inherent juiciness is Steffan B. Aletti's hellish *Mnemabic Fragments*, which made a too-brief debut in Aletti's "The Last Work of Pietro of Apono" (*Magazine of Horror* #27, May 1969). Aletti's early work, a quartet of tales all appearing in Doc Lowndes's magazines, made quite a stir among readers, who readily recognized and acclaimed him as a new standard bearer in the Lovecraft tradition. Until very recently, however, Aletti dropped out of the field, and it is high time his early tales be made available again, lest they become as rare as the *Mnemabic Fragments* themselves. Three occur here, while the fourth, "The Castle in the Window," appears in my Chaosium anthology *The Necronomicon*. I am indebted to Mike Ashley for introducing me to Steffan Aletti's work.

Another Lovecraftian writer whose reputation is narrower than it ought to be is Arthur Pendragon. This relative anonymity is easily understood, however, for two reasons. First, as far as I know, he wrote only a pair of tales, "The Dunstable Horror" and "The Crib of Hell" (which appeared in *Fantastic*, April 1964 and May 1965, respectively). Second, he hid behind a transparent pseudonym. As the learned Darrell Schweitzer points out, Pendragon's secret identity was most likely Arthur Porges, who wrote for the magazine under his own (noticeably similar) name during the same period. Sounds good to me. Let me thank Fred Blosser for putting me onto the two tales of Pendragon/Porges.

In a letter to his friend Lovecraft, Clark Ashton Smith griped as follows: Edmond "Hamilton, consarn him, has ruined an idea somewhat similar to one that I had in mind, for a tale to be called 'The Lunar Brain', based on the notion that there is a vast living brain in the center of the Moon" (March 1932). Does Smith mean that Hamilton, a favorite whipping boy for both CAS and HPL, had ruined the idea by a hackneyed development of it? Or that he had merely ruined the prospect for Smith's using it, since now it might seem he was copying Hamilton? In any case, Hamilton's story, included here, has much to commend it, especially from the standpoint of Lovecraftian cosmicism.

Among the acolytes of Cthulhu we must certainly count Professor Dirk W. Mosig and his brilliant disciples S.T. Joshi, Donald R. Burleson, and Peter H. Cannon. All followed Mosig's lead in their innovative scholarship and critical reinterpretation of Lovecraft's philosophical outlook, as well as in his experimental attempts to write genuinely Lovecraftian fiction uninfluenced by the Derlethian tradition, some of it tongue-in-cheek, some deadly serious. And then there's the delightful Derlethian pastiche "The Recurring Doom," a youthful indiscretion perpetrated by the 17-year-old Joshi in 1975 and reprinted here from Ken Neilly's premiere fanzine *Lovecraftian Ramblings* XV (1980).

Robert M. Price
Halloween 1997

DOOM OF THE HOUSE OF DURYEA

BY EARL PEIRCE, JR.

ARTHUR DURYEA, A YOUNG, HANDSOME MAN, CAME TO MEET HIS father for the first time in twenty years. As he strode into the hotel lobby—long strides which had the spring of elastic in them—idle eyes lifted to appraise him, for he was an impressive figure, somehow grim with exaltation.

The desk clerk looked up with his habitual smile of expectation; how-do-you-do-Mr.-so-and-so, and his fingers strayed to the green fountain pen which stood in a holder on the desk.

Arthur Duryea cleared his throat, but still his voice was clogged and unsteady. To the clerk he said:

"I'm looking for my father, Doctor Henry Duryea. I understand he is registered here. He has recently arrived from Paris."

The clerk lowered his glance to a list of names. "Doctor Duryea is in suite 600, sixth floor." He looked up, his eyebrows arched questioningly. "Are you staying too, sir, Mr. Duryea?"

Arthur took the pen and scribbled his name rapidly. Without a further word, neglecting even to get his key and own room number, he turned and walked to the elevators. Not until he reached his father's suite on the sixth floor did he make an audible noise, and this was a mere sigh which fell from his lips like a prayer.

The man who opened the door was unusually tall, his slender frame clothed in tight-fitting black. He hardly dared to smile. His clean-shaven face was pale, an almost livid whiteness against the sparkle in his eyes. His jaw had a bluish luster.

"Arthur!" The word was scarcely a whisper. It seemed choked up quietly, as if it had been repeated time and again on his thin lips.

Arthur Duryea felt the kindliness of those eyes go through him, and then he was in his father's embrace.

Later, when these two grown men had regained their outer calm, they closed the door and went into the drawing-room. The elder Duryea held out a humidor of fine cigars, and his hand shook so hard when he held the match that his son was forced to cup his own hands about the flame. They both had tears in their eyes, but their eyes were smiling.

Henry Duryea placed a hand on his son's shoulder. "This is the happiest day of my life," he said. "You can never know how much I have longed for this moment."

Arthur, looking into that glance, realized, with growing pride, that he had loved his father all his life, despite any of those things which had been cursed against him. He sat down on the edge of a chair.

"I—I don't know how to act," he confessed. "You surprise me, Dad. You're so different from what I had expected."

A cloud came over Doctor Duryea's features. "What *did* you expect, Arthur?" he demanded quickly. "An evil eye? A shaven head and knotted jowls?"

"Please, Dad—no!" Arthur's words clipped short. "I don't think I ever really visualized you. I knew you would be a splendid man. But I thought you'd look older, more like a man who has really suffered."

"I have suffered, more than I can ever describe. But seeing you again, and the prospect of spending the rest of my life with you, has more than compensated for my sorrows. Even during the twenty years we were apart I found ironic joy in learning of your progress in college, and in your American game of football."

"Then you've been following my work?"

"Yes, Arthur; I've received monthly reports ever since you left me. From my study in Paris I've been really close to you, working out your problems as if they were my own. And now that the twenty years are completed, the ban which kept us apart is lifted for ever. From now on, son, we shall be the closest of companions—unless your Aunt Cecilia has succeeded in her terrible mission."

The mention of that name caused an unfamiliar chill to come

between the two men. It stood for something, in each of them, which gnawed their minds like a malignancy. But to the younger Duryea, in his intense effort to forget the awful past, her name as well as her madness must be forgotten.

He had no wish to carry on this subject of conversation, for it betrayed an internal weakness which he hated. With forced determination, and a ludicrous lift of his eyebrows, he said, "Cecilia is dead, and her silly superstition is dead also. From now on, Dad, we're going to enjoy life as we should. Bygones are really bygones in this case."

Doctor Duryea closed his eyes slowly, as though an exquisite pain had gone through him.

"Then you have no indignation?" he questioned. "You have none of your aunt's hatred?"

"Indignation? Hatred?" Arthur laughed aloud. "Ever since I was twelve years old I have disbelieved Cecilia's stories. I have known that those horrible things were impossible, that they belonged to the ancient category of mythology and tradition. How, then, can I be indignant, and how can I hate you? How can I do anything but recognize Cecilia for what she was—a mean, frustrated woman, cursed with an insane grudge against you and your family? I tell you, Dad, that nothing she has ever said can possibly come between us again."

Henry Duryea nodded his head. His lips were tight together, and the muscles in his throat held back a cry. In that same soft tone of defense he spoke further, doubting words.

"Are you so sure of your subconscious mind, Arthur? Can you be so certain that you are free from all suspicion, however vague? Is there not a lingering premonition—a premonition which warns of peril?"

"No, Dad—no!" Arthur shot to his feet. "I don't believe it. I've never believed it. I know, as any sane man would know, that you are neither a vampire nor a murderer. You know it, too; and Cecilia knew it, only she was mad.

"That family rot is dispelled, Father. This is a civilized century. Belief in vampirism is sheer lunacy. Wh-why, it's too absurd even to think about!"

"You have the enthusiasm of youth," said his father, in a rather tired voice. "But have you not heard the legend?"

Arthur stepped back instinctively. He moistened his lips, for their dryness might crack them. "The legend?"

He said the word in a curious hush of awed softness, as he had heard his Aunt Cecilia say it many times before.

"That awful legend that you—"

"That I *eat* my children?"

"Oh, God, Father!" Arthur went to his knees as a cry burst through his lips. "Dad, that—that's ghastly! We must forget Cecilia's ravings."

"You are affected, then?" asked Doctor Duryea bitterly.

"Affected? Certainly I'm affected, but only as I should be at such an accusation. Cecilia was mad, I tell you. Those books she showed me years ago, and those folk-tales of vampires and ghouls—they burned into my infantile mind like acid. They haunted me day and night in my youth, and caused me to hate you worse than death itself.

"But in Heaven's name, Father, I've outgrown those things as I have outgrown my clothes. I'm a man now; do you understand that? A man, with a man's sense of logic."

"Yes, I understand." Henry Duryea threw his cigar into the fireplace, and placed a hand on his son's shoulder.

"We shall forget Cecilia," he said. "As I told you in my letter, I have rented a lodge in Maine where we can go to be alone for the rest of the summer. We'll get in some fishing and hiking and perhaps some hunting. But first, Arthur, I must be sure in my own mind that you are sure in yours. I must be sure you won't bar your door against me at night, and sleep with a loaded revolver at your elbow. I must be sure that you're not afraid of going up there alone with me, and dying—"

His voice ended abruptly, as if an age-long dread had taken hold of it. His son's face was waxen, with sweat standing out like pearls on his brow. He said nothing, but his eyes were filled with questions which his lips could not put into words. His own hand touched his father's, and tightened over it.

Henry Duryea drew his hand away.

"I'm sorry," he said, and his eyes looked straight over Arthur's lowered head. "This thing must be thrashed out now. I believe you when you say that you discredit Cecilia's stories, but for a sake greater than sanity I must tell you the truth behind the legend—and believe me, Arthur; there is a truth!"

He climbed to his feet and walked to the window which looked out over the street below. For a moment he gazed into space, silent. Then he turned and looked down at his son.

"You have heard only your aunt's version of the legend, Arthur. Doubtless it was warped into a thing far more hideous than it actually was—if that is possible! Doubtless she spoke to you of the Inquisitorial stake in Carcassonne where one of my ancestors perished. Also she may have mentioned that book, *Vampyrs*, which a former Duryea is supposed to have written. Then certainly she told you about your two younger brothers—my own poor, motherless children—who were sucked bloodless in their cradles…"

Arthur Duryea passed a hand across his aching eyes. Those words, so often repeated by that witch of an aunt, stirred up the same visions which had made his childhood nights sleepless with terror. He could hardly bear to hear them again—and from the very man to whom they were accredited.

"Listen, Arthur," the elder Duryea went on quickly, his voice low with the pain it gave him. "You must know that true basis to your aunt's hatred. You must know of that curse—that curse of vampirism which is supposed to have followed the Duryeas through five centuries of French history, but which we can dispel as pure superstition, so often connected with ancient families. But I must tell you that this part of the legend is true:

"Your two brothers actually died in their cradles, bloodless. And I stood trial in France for their murder, and my name was smirched throughout all of Europe with such an inhuman damnation that it drove your aunt and you to America, and has left me childless, hated, and ostracized from society the world over.

"I must tell you that on that terrible night in Duryea Castle I had been working late on historic volumes of Crespet and Prinn, and on that loathsome tome, *Vampyrs*. I must tell you of the soreness that was in my throat and of the heaviness of the blood which coursed through my veins… And of that *presence*, which was neither man nor animal, but which I knew was some place near me, yet neither within the castle nor outside of it, and which was closer to me than my heart and more terrible to me than the touch of the grave…

"I was at the desk in my library, my head swimming in a delirium which left me senseless until dawn. There were nightmares that frightened me—frightened *me*, Arthur, a grown man who had dissected countless cadavers in morgues and medical schools. I knew that my tongue was swollen in my mouth and that brine moistened my lips, and that a rottenness pervaded my body like a fever.

"I can make no recollection of sanity or of consciousness. That night remains vivid, unforgettable, yet somehow completely in shadows. When I had fallen asleep—if in God's name it *was* sleep—I was slumped across my desk. But when I awoke in the morning I was lying face down on my couch. So you see, Arthur, I *had* moved during the night, *and I had never known it!*

"What I'd done and where I'd gone during those dark hours will always remain an impenetrable mystery. But I do know this. On the morrow I was torn from my sleep by the shrieks of maids and butlers, and by that mad wailing of your aunt. I stumbled through the open door of my study, and in the nursery I saw those two babies there—lifeless, white and dry like mummies, and with twin holes in their necks that were caked black with their own blood...

"Oh, I don't blame you for your incredulousness, Arthur. I cannot believe it yet myself, nor shall I ever believe it. The belief of it would drive me to suicide; and still the doubting of it drives me mad with horror.

"All of France was doubtful, and even the savants who defended my name at the trial found that they could not explain it nor disbelieve it. The case was quieted by the Republic, for it might have shaken science to its very foundation and split the pedestals of religion and logic. I was released from the charge of murder; but the actual murder has hung about me like a stench.

"The coroners who examined those tiny cadavers found them both dry of all their blood, but could find no blood on the floor of the nursery nor in the cradles. Something from hell stalked the halls of Duryea that night—and I should blow my brains out if I dared to think deeply of who that was. You, too, my son, would have been dead and bloodless if you hadn't been sleeping in a separate room with your door barred on the inside.

"You were a timid child, Arthur. You were only seven years old, but you were filled with the folklore of those mad Lombards and the decadent poetry of your aunt. On that same night, while I was some place between heaven and hell, you also heard the padded footsteps on the stone corridor and heard the tugging at your door handle, for in the morning you complained of a chill and of terrible nightmares which frightened you in your sleep... I only thank God that your door was barred!"

Henry Duryea's voice choked into a sob which brought the stinging tears back into his eyes. He paused to wipe his face, and to dig his fingers into his palm.

"You understand, Arthur, that for twenty years, under my sworn oath at the Palace of Justice, I could neither see you nor write to you. Twenty years, my son, while all of that time you had grown to hate me and to spit at my name. Not until your aunt's death have you called yourself a Duryea... And now you come to me at my bidding, and say you love me as a son should love his father.

"Perhaps it is God's forgiveness for everything. Now, at last, we shall be together, and that terrible, unexplainable past will be buried forever..."

He put his handkerchief back into his pocket and walked slowly to his son. He dropped to one knee, and his hands gripped Arthur's arms.

"My son, I can say no more to you. I have told you the truth as I alone know it. I may be, by all accounts, some ghoulish creation of Satan on earth. I may be a child-killer, a vampire, some morbidly diseased specimen of *vrykolakas*—things which science cannot explain.

"Perhaps the dreaded legend of the Duryeas is true. Autiel Duryea was convicted of murdering his brother in that same monstrous fashion in the year 1576, and he died in flames at the stake. Francois Duryea, in 1802, blew his head apart with a blunderbuss on the morning after his youngest son was found dead, apparently from anemia. And there are others, of whom I cannot bear to speak, that would chill your soul if you were to hear them.

"So you see, Arthur, there is a hellish tradition behind our family. There is a heritage which no sane God would ever have allowed. The future of the Duryeas lies in you, for you are the last of the race. I pray with all of my heart that providence will permit you to live your full share of years, and to leave other Duryeas behind you. And so if ever again I feel that presence as I did in Duryea Castle, I am going to die as Francois Duryea died, over a hundred years ago..."

He stood up, and his son stood up at his side.

"If you are willing to forget, Arthur, we shall go up to that lodge in Maine. There is a life we've never known awaiting us. We must find that life, and we must find the happiness which a curious fate snatched from us on those Lombard sourlands, twenty years ago..."

Henry Duryea's tall stature, coupled with a slenderness of frame and a sleekness of muscle, gave him an appearance that was unusually gaunt. His son couldn't help but think of that word as he sat on the rustic porch of the lodge, watching his father sunning himself at the lake's edge.

Henry Duryea had a kindliness in his face, at times an almost sublime kindliness which great prophets often possess. But when his face was partly in shadows, particularly about his brow, there was a frightening tone which came into his features; for it was a tone of farness, of mysticism and conjuration. Somehow, in the late evenings, he assumed the unapproachable mantle of a dreamer and sat silently before the fire, his mind ever off in unknown places.

In that little lodge there was no electricity, and the glow of the oil lamps played curious tricks with the human expression which frequently resulted in something unhuman. It may have been the dusk of night, the flickering of the lamps, but Arthur Duryea had certainly noticed how his father's eyes had sunken further into his head, and how his cheeks were tighter, and the outline of his teeth pressed into the skin about his lips.

It was nearing sundown on the second day of their stay at Timber Lake. Six miles away the dirt road wound on toward Houtlon, near the Canadian border. So it was lonely there, on a solitary little lake hemmed in closely with dark evergreens and a sky which drooped low over dusty-summited mountains.

Within the lodge was a homey fireplace, and a glossy elk's head which peered out above the mantel. There were guns and fishing tackle on the walls, shelves of reliable American fiction—Mark Twain, Melville, Stockton, and a well-worn edition of Bret Harte.

A fully supplied kitchen and a wood stove furnished them with hearty meals which were welcome after a whole day's tramp in the woods. On that evening Henry Duryea prepared a select French stew out of every available vegetable, and a can of soup. They ate well, then stretched out before the fire for a smoke. They were outlining a trip to the Orient together, when the back door blew open with a terrific bang, and a wind swept into the lodge with a coldness which chilled them both.

"A storm," Henry Duryea said, rising to his feet. "Sometimes they have them up here, and they're pretty bad. The roof might leak over your bedroom. Perhaps you'd like to sleep down here with me." His fingers strayed playfully over his son's head as he went out into the kitchen to bar the swinging door.

Arthur's room was upstairs, next to a spare room filled with extra furniture. He'd chosen it because he liked the altitude, and because the only other bedroom was occupied...

He went upstairs swiftly and silently. His roof didn't leak; it was absurd even to think it might. It had been his father again, suggesting that they sleep together. He had done it before, in a jesting, whispering way—as if to challenge them both if they *dared* sleep together.

Arthur came back downstairs dressed in his bath-robe and slippers. He stood on the fifth stair, rubbing a two-day's growth of beard. "I think I'll shave tonight," he said to his father. "May I use your razor?"

Henry Duryea, draped in a black raincoat and with his face haloed in the brim of a rain-hat, looked up from the hall. A frown glided obscurely from his features. "Not at all, son. Sleeping upstairs?"

Arthur nodded, and quickly said, "Are you—going out?"

"Yes, I'm going to tie the boats up tighter. I'm afraid the lake will rough it up a bit."

Duryea jerked back the door and stepped outside. The door slammed shut, and his footsteps sounded on the wood flooring of the porch.

Arthur came slowly down the remaining steps. He saw his father's figure pass across the dark rectangle of a window, saw the flash of lightning that suddenly printed his grim silhouette against the glass.

He sighed deeply, a sigh which burned in his throat; for his throat was sore and aching. Then he went into the bedroom, found the razor lying in plain view on a birch table-top.

As he reached for it, his glance fell upon his father's open Gladstone bag which rested at the foot of the bed. There was a book resting there, half hidden by a gray flannel shirt. It was a narrow, yellow-bound book, oddly out of place.

Frowning, he bent down and lifted it from the bag. It was surprisingly heavy in his hands, and he noticed a faintly sickening odor of decay which drifted from it like a perfume. The title of the volume had been thumbed away into an indecipherable blur of gold letters. But pasted across the front cover was a white strip of paper, on which was typewritten the word—INFANTIPHAGI.

He flipped back the cover and ran his eyes over the title page. The book was printed in French—an early French—yet to him wholly comprehensible. The publication date was 1580, in Caen.

Breathlessly he turned back a second page, saw a chapter headed, *Vampires.*

He slumped to one elbow across the bed. His eyes were four inches from those mildewed pages, his nostrils reeked with the stench of them.

He skipped long paragraphs of pedantic jargon on theology, he scanned brief accounts of strange, blood-eating monsters, *vrykolakas*, and leprechauns. He read of Jeanne d'Arc, of Ludvig Prinn, and muttered aloud the Latin snatches from *Episcopi.*

He passed pages in quick succession, his fingers shaking with the fear of it and his eyes hanging heavily in their sockets. He saw vague references to "Enoch," and saw the terrible drawings by an ancient Dominican of Rome...

Paragraph after paragraph he read: the horror-striking testimony of Nider's *Ant-Hill*, the testimony of people who died shrieking at the stake; the recitals of grave-tenders, of jurists and hangmen. Then unexpectedly, among all of this munimental vestige, there appeared before his eyes the name of—*Autiel Duryea*; and he stopped reading as though invisibly struck.

Thunder clapped near the lodge and rattled the window-panes. The deep rolling of bursting clouds echoed over the valley. But he heard none of it. His eyes were on those two short sentences which his father—someone—had underlined with dark red crayon.

...The execution, four years ago, of Autiel Duryea does not end the Duryea controversy. Time alone can decide whether the

Demon has claimed that family from its beginning to its end...

Arthur read on about the trial of Autiel Duryea before Veniti, the Carcassonnean Inquisitor-General; read, with mounting horror, the evidence which had sent that far-gone Duryea to the pillar—the evidence of a bloodless corpse who had been Autiel Duryea's young brother.

Unmindful now of the tremendous storm which had centered over Timber Lake, unheeding the clatter of windows and the swish of pines on the roof—even of his father who worked down at the lake's edge in a drenching rain—Arthur fastened his glance to the blurred print of those pages, sinking deeper and deeper into the garbled legends of a dark age...

On the last page of the chapter he again saw the name of his ancestor, Autiel Duryea. He traced a shaking finger over the narrow lines of words, and when he finished reading them he rolled sideways on the bed, and from his lips came a sobbing, mumbling prayer.

"God, oh God in Heaven protect me..."

For he had read:

As in the case of Autiel Duryea we observed that this specimen of *vrykolakas* preys only upon the blood in its own family. It possesses none of the characteristics of the undead vampire, being usually a living male person of otherwise normal appearances, unsuspecting in inherent demonism.

But this vrykolakas cannot act according to its demoniacal possession unless it is in the presence of a second member of the same family, who acts as a medium between the man and its demon. This medium has none of the traits of the vampire, but it senses the being of this creature (when the metamorphosis is about to occur) by reason of intense pains in the head and throat. Both the vampire and the medium undergo similar reactions, involving nausea, nocturnal visions, and physical disquietude.

When these two outcasts are within a certain distance of each other, the coalescence of inherent demonism is completed, and the vampire is subject to its attacks, demanding blood for its sustenance. No member of the family is safe at these times, for the *vrykolakas*, acting in its true agency on earth, will unerringly seek out the blood.

In rare cases, where other victims are unavailable, *the vampire will even take the blood from the very medium which made it possible.*

This vampire is born into certain aged families, and naught but death can destroy it. It is not conscious of its blood-madness, and acts only in a psychic state. The medium, also, is unaware of its terrible role; and when these two are together despite any lapse of years, the fusion of inheritance is so violent that no power known on earth can turn it back.

The lodge door slammed shut with a sudden, interrupting bang. The lock grated, and Henry Duryea's footsteps sounded on the planked floor.

Arthur shook himself from the bed. He had only time to fling that haunting book into the Gladstone bag before he sensed his father standing in the doorway.

"You—you're not shaving, Arthur." Duryea's words, spliced hesitantly, were toneless. He glanced from the table-top to the Gladstone, and to his son. He said nothing for a moment, his glance inscrutable. Then, "It's blowing up quite a storm outside."

Arthur swallowed the first words which had come into his throat, nodded quickly. "Yes, isn't it? Quite a storm." He met his father's gaze, his face burning. "I—I don't think I'll shave, Dad. My head aches."

Duryea came swiftly into the room and pinned Arthur's arms in his grasp. "What do you mean—your head aches? How? Does your throat—"

"No!" Arthur jerked himself away. He laughed. "It's that French stew of yours! It's hit me in the stomach!" He stepped past his father and started up the stairs.

"The stew?" Duryea pivoted on his heel. "Possibly. I think I feel it myself."

Arthur stopped, his face suddenly white. "You—too?"

The words were hardly audible. Their glances met—clashed like dueling-swords.

For ten seconds neither of them said a word or moved a muscle; Arthur, from the stairs, looking down; his father below, gazing up at him. In Henry Duryea the blood drained slowly from his face and left a purple etching across the bridge of his nose and above his eyes. He looked like a death's-head.

Arthur winced at the sight and twisted his eyes away. He turned to go up the remaining stairs.

"Son!"

He stopped again; his hand tightened on the banister.

"Yes, Dad?"

Duryea put his foot on the first stair. "I want you to lock your door tonight. The wind would keep it banging!"

"Yes," breathed Arthur, and pushed up the stairs to his room.

Doctor Duryea's hollow footsteps sounded in steady, unhesitant beats across the floor of Timber Lake Lodge. Sometimes they stopped, and the crackling hiss of a sulfur match took their place, then perhaps a distended sigh, and, again, footsteps...

Arthur crouched at the open door of his room. His head was cocked for those noises from below. In his hands was a double-barrel shotgun of violent gage... thud... thud... thud...

Then a pause, the clinking of a glass and the gurgling of liquid. The sigh, the tread of his feet over the floor...

"He's thirsty," Arthur thought—*Thirsty!*

Outside, the storm had grown into fury. Lightning zigzagged between the mountains, filling the valley with weird phosphorescence. Thunder, like drums, rolled incessantly.

Within the lodge the heat of the fireplace piled the atmosphere thick with stagnation. All the doors and windows were locked shut, the oil-lamps glowed weakly—a pale, anemic light.

Henry Duryea walked to the foot of the stairs and stood looking up.

Arthur sensed his movements and ducked back into his room, the gun gripped in his shaking fingers.

Then Henry Duryea's footstep sounded on the first stair.

Arthur slumped to one knee. He buckled a fist against his teeth as a prayer tumbled through them.

Duryea climbed a second step... and another... and still one more. On the fourth stair he stopped.

"Arthur!" His voice cut into the silence like the crack of a whip. "Arthur! Will you come down here?"

"Yes, Dad." Bedraggled, his body hanging like cloth, young Duryea took five steps to the landing.

"We can't be zanies!" cried Henry Duryea. "My soul is sick with dread. Tomorrow we're going back to New York. I'm going to get the first boat to open sea... Please come down here." He turned about and descended the stairs to his room.

Arthur choked back the words which had lumped in his mouth. Half dazed, he followed...

In the bedroom he saw his father stretched face-up along the bed. He saw a pile of rope at his father's feet.

"Tie me to the bedposts, Arthur," came the command. "Tie both my hands and both my feet."

Arthur stood gaping.

"Do as I tell you!"

"Dad, what for—"

"Don't be a fool! You read that book! You know what relation you are to me! I'd always hoped it was Cecilia, but now I know it's you. I should have known it on that night twenty years ago when you complained of a headache and nightmares... Quickly, my head rocks with pain. *Tie me!*"

Speechless, his own pain piercing him with agony, Arthur fell to that grisly task. Both hands he tied—and both feet... tied them so firmly to the iron posts that his father could not lift himself an inch off the bed.

Then he blew out the lamps, and without a further glance at that Prometheus, he reascended the stairs to his room, and slammed and locked his door behind him.

He looked once at the breech of his gun, and set it against a chair by his bed. He flung off his robe and slippers, and within five minutes he was senseless in slumber.

He slept late, and when he awakened his muscles were as stiff as boards, and the lingering visions of a nightmare clung before his eyes. He pushed his way out of bed, stood dazedly on the floor.

A dull, numbing cruciation circulated through his head. He felt bloated... coarse and running with internal mucus. His mouth was dry, his gums sore and stinging.

He tightened his hands as he lunged for the door. "Dad," he cried, and he heard his voice breaking in his throat.

Sunlight filtered through the window at the top of the stairs. The air was hot and dry, and carried in it a mild odor of decay.

Arthur suddenly drew back at that odor—drew back with a gasp of awful fear. For he recognized it—that stench, the heaviness of his blood, the rawness of his tongue and gums... Age-long it seemed, yet rising like a spirit in his memory. All of these things he had known and felt before.

He leaned against the banister, and half slid, half stumbled down the stairs...

His father had died during the night. He lay like a waxen figure tied to his bed, his face done up in knots.

Arthur stood dumbly at the foot of the bed for only a few seconds; then he went back upstairs to his room.

Almost immediately he emptied both barrels of the shotgun into his head.

The tragedy at Timber Lake was discovered accidentally three days later. A party of fishermen, upon finding the two bodies, notified state authorities, and an investigation was directly under way.

Arthur Duryea had undoubtedly met death at his own hands. The condition of his wounds, and the manner in which he held the lethal weapon, at once foreclosed the suspicion of any foul play.

But the death of Doctor Henry Duryea confronted the police with an inexplicable mystery; for his trussed-up body, unscathed except for two jagged holes over the jugular vein, *had been drained of all its blood.*

The autopsy protocol of Henry Duryea laid death to "undetermined causes," and it was not until the yellow tabloids commenced an investigation into the Duryea family history that the incredible and fantastic explanations were offered to the public.

Obviously such talk was held in popular contempt; yet in view of the controversial war which followed, the authorities considered it expedient to consign both Duryeas to the crematory...

THE SEVENTH INCANTATION

BY JOSEPH PAYNE BRENNAN

"Of these black prayers or incantations there be seven, three for ordinarie charmes and aides, and the like number for the unholie and compleat destruction of alle enemies. But of the seventh the curious in alle these partes are warned. Let not the last incantation be recited, unlesse ye desire the sight of moste aweful deamon. Although it be said the deamon shews not unlesse the wordes be spake by the bloodie altar of the Olde Ones, yet it were well to beware. For it be knowne that the Saracene sorcerer, Mai Lazal, dide wantonlie chante the dire wordes and the deamon dide come—and not finding a bloodie offering did rage at the wizard and rende him exceedinglie. The life bloode of a childe or chaste maid be best, yet a beaste, a goode ox or sheep, is said sufficient. But beware lest the beaste be dead when the bloode be taken, for then shall the deamon's rage be dire. If the offering be well, the deamon shall give unholie power, so that the servant grow riche and reache above alle his neighbors."

FOR THE THIRD TIME, AND WITH GROWING EXCITEMENT, Emmet Telquist read the faded words. They were contained in a crumbling and curious and probably unique bound manuscript book which he had discovered quite by accident some days before while shuffling through the dust-laden packing crates which held his deceased uncle's library.

The book was entitled simply *True Magik*, and the writer signed himself "Theophilis Wenn." Quite possibly the name was a pseudonym; certainly, judging by the contents, the rash author must have had reason to keep secret his real identity.

The book was a veritable encyclopedia of devil's lore. There was everywhere manifest a genuine and erudite scholarship which had been lavished on a vast variety of esoteric and forbidden subjects. There were detailed discussions on enchantments and possession, paragraphs on vampirism and ghoul legends, pages devoted to demonology, witch worship, and eldrich idols, notes on holocaust rites, unspeakable maculations and fearsome full-moon sacrifices to the powers of pristine darkness.

Evidently the writer had been a necromancer of note. The style in general was arbitrary and assured, betraying egoism and not a little arrogance. There was no faint note of humor. Theophilis Wenn—or whoever it was that disguised his true identity under that name—had written in dire earnest. Of that there could be no doubt.

Emmet Telquist, the village outcast, the bitter misanthropic issue of an infamous father and a mother who had died insane, regarded the book as a sudden treasure, a secret storehouse of knowledge and power which would enable him to compete with his more successful neighbors.

He had always been an outsider, a misfit, the subject of vindictive local gossip and criticism. He had always felt himself more or less allied to inhuman laws and agencies.

His uncle, the only relative he ever remembered, had been a sour, black-hearted, brooding old man who tolerated him only because of the chores and errands which he performed. He never had had the slightest doubt that his uncle would have disowned him utterly had he not been a useful drudge. The bond of blood would have been meaningless to the old man.

As a matter of fact, had it not been for his sudden and somewhat mysterious death, the scoundrel probably would have seen to it that his nephew inherited only black memories. But since no will had been located, Emmet Telquist had gained possession of his uncle's rambling farmhouse and such meager chattels as it contained.

But as he squinted eagerly at the quaint faded hand-writing of the necromancer Theophilis Wenn, Telquist began to believe that the manuscript book was by far the most valuable item which his evil relative had unintentionally put into his hands.

Furthermore, a number of matters which had always puzzled him in the past became less baffling. He had often wondered about the peculiar behavior of his uncle—his long absences from the house, especially at night, the muttering and mumbling which frequently came from his room, his unexplained sources of income.

With a sense of mounting suspense and expectation, he turned the pages whereon the seventh incantation was inscribed. It was written in a peculiar bluish-grey ink which seemed faintly phosphorescent. He did not dare to read the words; he merely glanced at them, ascertaining that they were what appeared to be merely a jumble of meaningless vowel sounds frequently interspersed with the name "Nyogtha."

Grinning slyly to himself, he turned back the pages and reread the paragraph which served as an introduction and explanation of the incantations. Well he knew what Theophilis Wenn had in mind when he referred to the "bloodie altar of the Old Ones"! He, Emmet Telquist, had seen such an altar.

Although that had been years before when the swamp was not as nearly impassable as it had since become, he had no doubt that he could locate the accursed sacrificial cromlech. How well he remembered crawling along the faint raised pathway which wound through the swamp! The sudden, unexpected knoll, dark somehow, even in the midday sunlight, the circle of huge monoliths, the mound in the center, the enormous flat slab on its top, rusty red with an unspeakable eldrich stain which even the rains and winds of centuries could not blot out!

He had never spoken of his discovery to anyone. The swamp was a forbidden place—ostensibly because of rumored quicksands and poisonous serpents. But on more than one occasion he had seen old-time villagers cross themselves when mention was made of the area. And it was said that even hunting dogs would abandon the pursuit of game which fled into its fastnesses.

Already anticipating the power which would ultimately be his, Emmet Telquist began to formulate plans. He would not make the mistake of the unfortunate Saracen sorcerer, Mai Lazal. Although he did not quite dare to take the necessary steps to secure a human sacrifice, "a childe or chaste maid," a sheep should be relatively easy to obtain. He could steal one at night from any of the several village flocks. He knew all the woods and lanes and would be safely away with his prize long before the loss was discovered.

The night before the advent of the full moon, he slipped into a nearby pasture where sheep were grazed and made away with a fine fat ewe, shoving and dragging it over a stone wall and then leading it off along circuitous back roads and grass-grown lanes.

The next day he paid a stealthy visit to the environs of the forbidden swamp, exploring the rank underbrush until he discovered the start of the faint trail down which he had stolen years before. Although it was partially obliterated by a thick growth of sedge, vines and lush swamp grass, there were indications that deer used it occasionally. Probably patience would be required to force a way through, but at least the path should not be impassable.

Carefully noting its location, he returned home and completed his preparations for the evening.

Shortly before eleven o'clock he crept into the shed where he had tethered the ewe and led it forth into the moonlight.

The countryside was steeped in a bewitching silver light. He experienced no difficulties in reaching the swamp and after some little searching located the narrow trail.

But as he plunged into the shoulder-high grass, the tether tightened in his hand. The ewe strained against the rope, its eyes suddenly wild with fright.

Cursing, he scrambled around and kicked it brutally. It bolted forward a few yards and stopped. Grimly determined, he tightened the tether until it cut through the ewe's wool into its hide.

He made progress by the foot and by the inch. The ewe had to be dragged and shoved at regular intervals. And as he penetrated toward the heart of the swamp, the increasing height and thickness of the lush undergrowth made passage more difficult.

Moonlight filtered down eerily among the trees and on all sides treacherous pools gleamed silver-black in the shadowy darkness. Occasionally hidden watchers stared at him out of the depths and quite often enormous toads hopped into the path and regarded him with their amber eyes. They seemed to be devoid of fear, almost as if they considered the swamp their special domain and deemed him incapable of harming them. He began to imagine there was something vaguely malignant about them. He had never seen them so large before, nor in such numbers. But probably that was merely because they were left unmolested in the swamp to breed and develop without encountering the artificial obstacles which would inevitably prevail in any less shunned area.

As he pushed into the heart of the swamp, the gathering silence became oppressive. The ordinary night sounds ceased altogether and only his own strained breathing broke the silence. The ewe became more obstinate than ever; all his strength was required to drag it along. It appeared, he imagined, to sense the fate which awaited it.

Suddenly, so suddenly that he nearly cried aloud in astonishment, the underbrush ended and he was standing at the base of the unhallowed knoll.

It was just as he had remembered it—huge menhirs standing in a rough circle about a central mound upon which lay a large flat slab of a dark hue which did not match the color of the surrounding monoliths. Over all a shadow seemed to fall, and yet when he glanced upward he saw that the full moon stood directly overhead.

Shaking off the sense of dread which closed upon him, he started up the lichen-covered slope. But now the ewe sank upon its forelegs and he was obliged to drag it inch by inch toward the circle of megaliths. He rather welcomed the exertion however, for it freed his mind of the nameless fear which the cromlech aroused in him.

By the time he had dragged the sheep alongside the ring of boulders, he was nearly exhausted, but he dared not pause to rest, for he knew that delay would be his undoing. He already had a wild desire to leave the ewe and rush back through the toad-infested swamp to the familiar outer world.

Quickly slipping off the sheep's tether, he bound its legs firmly together and with a tremendous heave shoved it onto the rust-colored sacrificial slab.

Rejecting an almost uncontrollable impulse to flee, he unsheathed the hunting knife which he carried and drew from his pocket the curious bound manuscript book, *True Magik* by Theophilis Wenn.

He had no difficulty in locating the strangely sinister seventh incantation, for in the bright moonlight the unusual bluish-grey ink in which the characters were inscribed seemed actually luminous.

Holding the book in one hand and the knife ready in the other, he began to repeat the jumble of unintelligible sounds.

As he read, the syllables appeared to exert some unearthly influence upon him, so that his voice rose to a savage howl, a high-pitched inhuman ululation which penetrated to the farthest depths of the swamp. At intervals his voice sank to low gutturals or a thin sibilant hiss.

And then, at the last enunciation of the oft-repeated word, "Nyogtha," there reached his ears as from a vast distance a sound like the rushing of a mighty wind, although not even a leaf stirred on the surrounding trees.

The book suddenly darkened in his hand and he saw that a shadow had fallen across the page.

He glanced up—and madness reeled in his brain.

Squatting on the edge of the slab was a shape which lived in nightmare, a squamous taloned thing like a monstrous gargoyle or a malformed toad which stared at him out of questing red eyes.

He froze in horror and a sudden rage flamed in the thing's eyes. It thrust out its neck and an angry hiss issued from its mottled beak.

Emmet Telquist was galvanized into action. He knew what the thing wanted—life blood.

Raising the knife, he advanced and was about to plunge it downward into the sheep when a new horror seized him.

The ewe was already dead. The unspeakable presence which squatted beside it had already claimed it. It had died of fright. Its eyes were glazed and there was no indication that it still breathed.

Remembering Theophilis Wenn's warning, "beware lest the beaste be dead," Emmet Telquist stood like a stone statue with the knife still unraised in his hand.

Then he dropped it and ran.

Darting between two menhirs, he plunged down the knoll and raced toward the swamp trail.

Lifting its scaly neck, the presence on the slab looked after him and finally, hissing in fury, bounded off the stone and leaped in pursuit.

One terrible shriek rang out and presently the thing hopped back onto the slab, holding in its bloody beak a dangling lifeless form, a fitting sacrifice.

FROM THE PITS OF ELDER BLASPHEMY

BY HUGH B. CAVE & ROBERT M. PRICE

THERE WERE DRUMS TONIGHT—OR WAS IT THUNDER, SO FAR off he couldn't yet tell the difference? But then he could hardly hear them. Not only too far off, but suddenly drowned by something closer at hand, something admittedly less ominous, but with more raw irritation—the barking of dogs. It started, his bedside clock documented, at precisely 3:15 in the morning, putting an end to any hope of slumber. One dog would bark somewhere in that part of Port-au-Prince in which he had rented a room at the Pension Etoile. Half a dozen others would follow, scattered throughout the city, at first with an almost tentative note, as if a great canine orchestra were tuning up for a concert. But when they started in earnest, it was more like a shouting match, each bark answered by challenging rejoinders until the whole city was set ahowl. Dismissing the momentary urge to add his own barked "Quiet!" to the melee, a weary Peter Macklin gave up in disgust and got out of bed. Shrugging himself into his clothes, he opened the verandah door to let in any breeze that might be passing by. It was July, and Haiti—this Caribbean land of *vodun* and poverty—was as savagely hot as its people were gentle in their unspoken surrender.

He had expected the city to be hot in July, of course. As a graduate student of anthropology, that fascinating study of man's veiled origins, struggling development, and kaleidoscopic cultures, he had twice before visited Haiti to write about *vodun* and its believers. By now he could speak enough French to carry on conversations with the country's elite, as well as sufficient Creole to communicate with the masses. And he had had ample occasion in his work to do both. His studies had evidenced enough early promise to merit a modest travel stipend included as part of his scholarship, but it was close to exhausted, and he had comparatively little to show for it. After all, *vodun*, "voodoo," had long attracted researchers, both serious and sensationalist, because of its inherent exoticism, and his academic advisors warned him of delving into a dried-up well. He was beginning to fear they had been right. What else was there to say about it?

This time he was here on little more than a hunch, based on a rumor he had heard in Miami's Little Haiti while visiting his parents in Florida. He had once heard of something similar in hushed whispers among the Rasta communities of Jamaica, too. The rumor involved certain of the magicians, or shamans, as anthropologists were careful to call them nowadays, *bocors* and *houngans*, belonging to a secret cult whose members were in touch with unknown deities, terrible gods from the sound of it, who might be called upon to do terrible things. The infamous zombie legends went back to such people. They existed as religious outlaws on the margins of *vodun* society and theology, operating much as contract killers who claimed magical means to do dirty jobs. But until now no one had ever heard of them banding together in a religious society of their own. Was it something new? Or perhaps something very, very old, only now becoming known for the first time? In either case, here was a new wrinkle, a new aspect of the matter. And his research took on a whole new relevance. Here was his chance not only to avoid reploughing a depleted field, but even to gain a precocious reputation among his peers by a major discovery. If, that is, he could make it more than a rumor. There would have to be interviews, participant observation, and before that, some actual, personal contact.

And here he was in luck, for it turned out that the brother of a young Haitian in Florida, who did odd jobs for Peter's family, claimed association with this mysterious cult, and Peter was awaiting the arrival of this man, one Metellus Dalby, who would bring him news of the group's latest meeting. He did not have long to wait. It almost seemed as though the barking of the sleepless dogs had been prophetic, an oracle wrung from them by some supernatural influence on their keen other-than-human senses. Within fifteen minutes there came a knock on the rickety door of his room.

Leaving the little verandah where he had gone for a breath of air, only to find more of the crowded city's suffocating heat, Peter advanced the short distance to the door and opened it. The man confronting him was a Haitian, tall, slender, and very black.

"You're back already?" asked Peter, startled, in Creole. It came out almost like a rebuke.

"With good news, *m'sieu*." Nodding briskly, Metellus Dalby stepped past him into the room, then spun about to face him. "There is to be a big meeting of the cult this very night. You must accompany me to it!"

The bright gibbous moon illuminated the scene of two men, one white, one black, staring at each other. Then the Haitian spoke again, more slowly. "But there is something we must do first, *mon ami*." From a pocket of his baggy trousers he withdrew a pint bottle of some dark liquid.

Peter nodded. "How long will it take?"

"I will apply the first coat now, another about noon, and a third before we begin the journey." His smile broadened into a shining crescent moon. "You will look like one of my people when I finish, I promise you that. And while it will itch, a little, it will not inconvenience you."

"What about my sharp nose, my thin lips?" For the first time, Peter saw them as he feared a non-Caucasian might see them, not handsome, but marks of alien origin.

"Haitians come in all shapes, my friend. Some of our ladies on the Mardi Gras floats could win prizes anywhere in the world. You've seen them."

The Pension Etoile was on the Champ de Mars, and, that being part of the Mardi Gras route, Peter involuntarily glanced out the window, as if half-expecting to see the marching bands and gaudy floats in full force. His companion smiled again, showing those whiter than white teeth.

"It may burn a little, this vegetable dye," Metellus warned. "But not for long. You'll be comfortable again soon, I promise." Peter wondered what sort of errands had made Metellus so familiar with the stuff and its use. Whatever they might have been, they only made

Metellus exactly the sort of person who would know how to help him on a gambit such as he contemplated. Like the CIA, anthropologists sometimes had to deal with people who could get things done when there were only dubious ways to get them done.

Peter took the two or three steps to the bed, removed the top part of his pajamas, and lay down on his back. Pulling the cork from the bottle and leaning like a masseuse over his client, this man he looked on more and more as a friend, Metellus began the process of darkening those parts of the white man's body that would be revealed by short-sleeved attire. As he did so, he talked.

"What is to happen tonight, *m'sieu*, will interest you, I am certain. These people plan a special meeting in which they will call upon the Old Ones to present themselves. There is a line you will hear, and you must be ready to join in the first time you hear it. That is not dead which can eternal lie, and with strange eons, even death may die. I heard it from Tiburon, on the Southern Peninsula, who told me it was not for the ears of just anyone. You do not want to sound like it is new to you. That is not dead," he repeated, coachingly, "which can eternal lie, and with strange eons, even death may die."

"Meaning?" Peter asked with a frown.

The Haitian shrugged. "Who knows, exactly? But they know its meaning, never fear. And perhaps after tonight we, too, shall know." He fell silent, giving the white man the chance to repeat the formula to himself silently till he knew it.

When the bottle was empty, Metellus stepped back from the bed to look Peter over, then nodded. "We should plan on being there before dark, so we can show my work off to best advantage, eh? We can use my Jeep to take us as far as Furcy, then we'll have to walk a few miles. Those mountain trails are not easy, as I believe you know."

Paying as little mind as he could to his tingling skin, Peter looked at the mirror while speaking to his partner. "What time did you leave there tonight?"

"Just after midnight."

Peter glanced at an alarm clock on his chest of drawers, subtracting the minutes it was off by. Its lazy hands now stood at five minutes to five, and Metellus had been here how long? Forty-five minutes? A little more? "So we want to be there when?"

"I should plan on picking you up about three o'clock this afternoon, I think."

Nodding matter-of-factly, Peter opened the top of the chest of drawers, a storage place with absolutely no security, to take out his billfold. From it he handed the Haitian some gourd notes. "Fill up the gas tank, Metellus. Better put some food in the Jeep as well. There's no telling what we may be getting into, eh?"

"Thanks, boss," he answered with a note of irony, noticing that there was more there than needed for the tasks Peter had stipulated. He left, and Peter's sole companion was once again the humidity, which by now seemed to have gotten the better of the dogs, who had fallen silent. Maybe he'd be able to get some sleep now. When the dye on his skin seemed to be dry enough, Peter returned to his bed and dozed till mid-morning, knowing he would probably not sleep at all in the night ahead of him. Who or what, he wondered, were the "Old Ones" his Haitian friend had talked about? Old gods, older than the conventional Obeah pantheon, to be sure. But which gods? What kind? It later seemed vaguely to him that his dreams that morning tried to give him some hint, but he could not remember.

Come five minutes to three that afternoon, Metellus turned his Jeep into the Pension driveway, and Peter, standing ready, stepped right into it. Several of the little hotel's other guests had stared unabashedly at Peter as he had descended the staircase from his second-floor room and walked through the downstairs hall to the door. No doubt they were startled at a white man having becoming a black one, but none questioned him, perhaps feeling it safer not to. As he slid onto the seat beside the driver's, his Haitian friend nodded approval and said, "The dye worked well, I see. If I were you, I might be wondering how long it will take to wear off."

"I have thought about it, now that you mention it." Peter smiled as he made himself as comfortable as possible. The Jeep was an old one, open, with a fabric top to shield its two occupants from rain or sun.

"You may continue a Haitian for three or four days," said Metellus, with the air of a doctor, showing his white teeth again in a grin.

"I can think of things I'd less rather be."

"Eh?"

Peter realized he probably hadn't phrased the remark properly in

Creole. "Just so long as it works tonight," he amended.

"Yes," replied Metellus with surprising and sudden gravity, as he backed out of the Pension's drive. "Just so long as the Old Ones don't know who and what you really are." Peter thought about that remark from time to time as the two of them traveled up the winding road to Petionville, where so many of the country's wealthier citizens lived to escape the heat and squalor of Haiti's capital. It lingered in his mind on the even longer climb over a narrow blacktop road to the mountain village of Kenscoff. And it jabbed at his mind now and then as Metellus, a skilled and careful driver, took the little vehicle up the final twisting climb to the end of the driving road at Furcy. At various times during the journey Peter had turned in his seat to peer down through the heat-haze hanging over the roofs of the capital, as if trying to penetrate the opaque mists of antiquity. He wondered why he was doing what he was doing. Did all anthropologists live dangerously? It was only missionaries who wound up in cooking pots, wasn't it?

His companion brought the vehicle to a stop in front of a peasant cottage, and Peter snapped out of his reverie. "We leave the Jeep here," Metellus announced. "These people know me." He glanced at the watch on his wrist. Peter had earlier observed that he wore a Rolex or some such, which one would think out of the range of any legitimate income. But he had wisely traded it for a more modest Timex for the occasion. "Are you hungry, my friend?"

His eyes concluding a sweep of the cottage and what lay beyond it, Peter barely caught the words but replied, "I hadn't given it a thought. The heat takes away my appetite. But perhaps we ought to eat something, eh?"

Metellus slid from his seat and leaned into the back of the Jeep to lift out a bag of food. It turned out to be a strange mixture of fruit, vegetables, and the worst sort of greasy junk food. More of all of it than they could expect to eat. And there was alcohol. Metellus opened the bag and gave him his choice. Peter grabbed a couple of apples and a roll. Metellus took even less. Just then the cottage door opened, and it was an attractive, middle-aged black woman who greeted them both with a smile and a happy "Bon jour!" Metellus handed her the rest of the provisions. Trust him to think of everything, Peter thought.

From there they walked. And Peter soon discovered and appreciated why Metellus had judged it wise to arrive at their destination before dark. The trail was a footpath. It was a snake twisting through the forest. At times it would be blocked by fallen tree-limbs, mostly pine, and by boulders that must have come crashing down the mountain. Peter hoped there were no more like them at home. It seemed endless.

Peter was tired, his companion scarcely less so, when the pair finally arrived at a cluster of huts in a clearing that, mercifully, turned out to be their destination. But there was to be no rest for them. People came striding from the huts—men, mostly—and Peter had to be introduced to them by Metellus. Had to smile and remain standing while his companion explained that Peter was a Floridian, a friend of Metellus's brother, and that he was deeply interested in the Old Ones. Also that he was eager to participate in the night's proceedings, at least as an observer. Peter momentarily started at hearing the exact truth from the other's lips. He had expected more pretense than this, though he could think of no real reason it should be necessary.

By the time the newcomer had been introduced all around, it had grown dark enough for lanterns to be lit and hung in the surrounding trees, and *vodun* drums began to throb. No one seemed suspicious of him, and the only looks in his direction that he noticed appeared to be polite and friendly. He returned the smiles he saw and hoped for the best. He asked if he might do anything to help prepare, was told that he was a guest and should not busy himself with such tasks. This he took for permission to nod off for a brief nap.

Once he felt Metellus nudging him awake, he realized he had slept for at least three hours. The moon was high, and the clearing was now crowded with eager figures darting to and fro, creating almost a strobe effect as they passed rapidly before the blazing lamps and lanterns. He got rapidly to his aching feet and looked nervously to make sure his sleeping posture had not revealed any pink flesh. Metellus's grin anticipated him and let him know all was well. The two of them hurried into the circle and looked for good seats, close to the action, whatever action there should be, yet not too obtrusive, lest any surprise or reluctance on their part be noticed. Here at the scene itself, Peter wondered for the first time how much of the celebrations of this sect Metellus had actually seen? He spoke enigmatically about it, as if he knew little, and yet he appeared to be well enough known to those gathered. Perhaps he had received only a preliminary degree of initiation and could only guess, as Peter had heard him do, at the real secrets of the cult. But didn't that imply he himself, an outsider, could not hope to see anything much out of the ordinary? Well, there was nothing to do but wait now.

He scanned the close-packed crowd. The scene was familiar, as were the expressions of adventurous expectancy on the black faces gleaming with sweat and firelight. Then with a start he hoped no one noticed, he saw faces of a more ominous cast, weathered and haughty visages whose peculiar lines betrayed habitual emotions and exaltations of a kind he could not guess. Some bore ritual scars, others faded tattoos and paint. There were ear-hoops of strange workmanship, too, some suggesting the forms of strange sea creatures. Here was something new. Might he perhaps interview these old men, who were certainly those curiously allied *bocors* and *houngans* rumor had described as improbably coming together for some frightful purpose? He sensed somehow his chances of that were slim.

His eagerness dulled to disappointment once the congregation hushed as if by some tacit signal and the service began. The celebrant, an aged fellow with a wrinkled face and a voice little more than a fatigued whisper, droned out the singsong of the usual introductory prayers. He drew the usual *veves* around the base of the central pole or *poteau mitan*. Still droning, as if wearily reciting a child's nursery rhyme, he called upon the usual string of *vodun* deities: Legba, Ogoun, Erzulie, Damballah, and the rest. Peter had seen and heard all this too many times before. And yet the gathered cultists appeared to be all the more eager, as if their favorite part were on its way.

At once the rote character of the display vanished. The preliminaries, perfunctory, were over. Gestures in the crowd became rapid, even violent, aimless jabs, striking heads and torsos oblivious of the impact. Eyes rolled up, people blindly rising, shrilly chanting, joining a frenzied follow-the-leader snake-dance. At Metellus's urgent signal, Peter joined in as best he could. He strained to make out the words being sung, and because of the number of voices, twenty-five or so, it was difficult. Especially difficult for one to whom Creole was not a primary language. Yet he understood some of it. And to his surprise, these black bacchantes were calling not on the traditional gods of vodun, whose names he had heard mere moments before, but on someone, something, far more ancient. The names were altogether new to him, and he realized this was why it was so difficult to understand. Some of the... names? were so bizarre, and were barked and screamed past comprehension. *Tulu... Nigguratl-Yig... Nug and Yeb...* And the cacophony was rapidly giving way to some alien language, perhaps speaking in tongues. Less and less Creole.

An intuitive flash told him what must be going on here. Old Ones. He knew, anyone knew, that the nominal Christianity of Haitians and other Caribbean peoples thinly masked the African religions of their pre-slavery ancestors. They might call the object of their ecstatic devotion Saint This or That, but they were really invoking Damballah, Baron Samedhi and the others, gods of ancient Africa. But what he was beholding here was something else—these Old Ones had to be the unthinkably archaic gods and devils to whom screaming sacrifices had been offered in the dawn ages before Zimbabwe and Benin and Opar, deities whose worship had at length been banned and driven underground to take refuge under the names of the more wholesome gods of Zulu, Ashanti, Shona, and other tribes. Behind their myths the Things of Elder Blasphemy still lurked and ravened, as the benign spirits of African faiths would later hide behind the haloes of Catholic saints. In a moment he knew.

The chanting and the drumming continued. So did the dancing, as the cultists formed a rough circle and continued to move their feet—some in flat-soled sandals, others quite bare—in a shuffling processional. The celebrant, whose torpor had long since vanished, hopped into the center of the circle and began to rotate, his glazed eyes following the crowd as it spun round him. He shouted something once, twice, stabbing a finger in the direction of two of the entranced mob. One of these, who could hardly have even been aware of the summons, a teenaged girl, broke from the group and fell to the ground. She was instantly followed by a second, this one an old hag. Further uncouth vocables erupted from the voodoo priest's raw throat, and the two females obediently threw off all restraint, their faces still strangely vacant, and began a savage death-struggle. Gouts of blood and torn-off flesh flew everywhere, and Peter's stomach roiled. Fistfuls of human meat, an eye, another, scattered into the air. Blood somehow splashed over him from the direction of the two women as if thrown from a paint can. The young anthropologist found his consciousness tottering. Rousing a moment later, he realized he had fallen into the arms of Metellus. He prayed no one else had noticed this failure of nerve, but a quick glance told him no one was paying any attention to him, nor would they.

Parts of the two ragged forms surrounded the old priest, who now sank to his bony knees and began to scoop up the blood and apply it to himself, a gory baptism, finally falling down and rolling in the crimson pool. The others grew silent, watching intently, Metellus and Peter no less than the rest. The old man regained his knees and remained in a posture of supplication, his blank eyes showing only their whites, intoning some throat-kinking chant.

Peter knew that in an ordinary vodun ritual, one would next expect the ecstatic possession trances to begin, nothing very sinister, not far removed from the goings-on in any Appalachian Pentecostal ceremony. But he was in for a surprise. From one of the nearby huts a strange figure appeared. The crowd wheeled as one to face it. The drummers poised motionless with hands upraised over their drumheads. Into the clearing there slowly advanced, on clawlike feet each some fifteen inches long, a body like that of a chicken but as big as a barrel, with the head of a human male. And it did not seem to be a costume. Behind it in single file came half a dozen other monstrosities. In absolute silence (Peter absently noted the distant cacchinations of forest insects) the cultists widened their circle to give the summoned newcomers enough room.

Then came another, all by itself. A creature anthropologist Peter Macklin recognized from his reading, or thought he did. What was its name? He could not remember. His mind was in too much of a turmoil to function properly. But the thing was like an octopus. A huge one. You couldn't see all of it because it seemed to sprout a number of weaving, waving tentacles. They moved with supreme ease despite the lack of any fluid medium. Everything about it seemed to be in motion, hypnotic motion. Some of the tentacles moved it forward; others writhed and trembled above its bulbous body, glistening greasily in the lantern light that illumined the whole clearing. Then as it came closer Peter saw that he had been wrong; in truth it was more like a huge sea-serpent, with ugly-looking big claws on some of its arms—or were the arms really feet? All he knew for sure was that a name for it came into his mind.

The monstrous Thing joined those that had preceded it. Peter was no longer certain what was or was not hallucination. It somehow appeared that he was looking at a line of gigantic creatures seen from a great distance. But then they seemed to be standing here, with their human worshippers, in this Haitian hilltop clearing. Metellus, beside Peter, now on his left, leaned toward his companion, who was plainly paling beneath the dye. He said in a low voice, "That last one is the dreaded *Tulu*, my friend."

The name which had come into Peter's mind was different. It was Cthulhu. But he only nodded. And then he felt two pairs of strong hands take his elbows and guide him quickly out of the circle and into one of the huts, not that from which the entities had emerged. Momentarily, amid his sudden panic, it occurred to Peter to wonder how any of the tiny huts could have contained the great creatures he saw. A familiar voice spoke in the intelligible accents of Creole. It was Metellus.

"Do not worry. The ceremony has reached a point which we may not see. Here, take your rest." Metellus indicated a soft straw mat on the ground. Peter felt himself sinking fast into sleep. Perhaps he had in truth been hypnotized, or perhaps the emotional shocks he had experienced were proving too much for him. He put up no resistance. He did not notice whether Metellus lay down beside him or returned to the festivities.

Peter slept dreamlessly, or at least he remembered no dreams, and this with a strange sense of relief. He was awakened by the hand shaking his shoulder. He was led wordlessly by a couple of big Haitians into another of the huts. There, cross-legged and completely cleansed of the previous night's defilements, sat the wizened priest, who silently motioned him to sit on the ground opposite him. His two retainers assumed waiting positions on either side of the structure, seeming to blend in with the barbaric figures depicted on hangings that draped the circular walls. Peter felt no fear, only a sense of nervous anticipation, much as he had felt defending his Master's thesis before his committee.

The old man's Creole was clear, his voice steady. "Young sir, I think you would like to join us. Have you not come among us for that purpose? A simple initiation will be required. Don't worry. No harm will come to you, despite what you perhaps think that you witnessed last night. Then, and only then, can our true secrets be revealed to you."

Peter did not hesitate. Indeed, this was more than he could have hoped for! He had seen something disturbing the previous night, at least he thought he had. But he could not remember what. Maybe he had dreamed after all. At any rate, this would be an unparalleled opportunity for participant observation. This was his chance to do original research into a virtually unknown Afro-Caribbean religion! His academic career would be off to a flying start!

"It would be an honor, Grandfather. I must tell you, though, I must eventually return to the States where I have obligations. I would not be able to be present as regularly as I would desire. May I still join you?"

"Your friend Metellus has told us you would divide your time between here and the United States. That poses no difficulty. You bring to us new blood. I believe your coming to be a boon both to yourself and to our divine lords. Indeed, I have no doubt but that it is they who guided your path to us."

Peter smiled and answered, "I'm sure you are right, Grandfather." He secretly wondered how delighted the old man or any of the others would be when he published his research on their cult. He hated to betray a confidence in that way, but it was sometimes necessary if knowledge were to be shared with one's colleagues, and with the world.

"Go and rest now, young Peter, till tonight, when you shall swear the First Oath of Damballah. Remain in your hut until the sun sets. Then these brethren," (indicating the two giants who still stood silently like sculptures) "will pick you up for the ceremony, when you will become one with us." He smiled. Both men rose. Which man was concealing more from the other?

When he returned, Peter was glad to see Metellus waiting for him.

"Tonight I'm to be initiated, Met!"

"Me too," the Haitian replied, making his friend's eyes widen.

"I half-suspected you were already a member, the way everybody knows you here."

"The truth is that I took the First Oath when a young boy. I took the Second when I reached manhood, at age thirteen. I learned more then than you know now. But the Deep Things, as they call them, are revealed only to those who take the Third Oath of Damballah. That is what I'm to take tonight. I hoped I would. But now I'm beginning to wonder, to worry. I think maybe I've already seen too much."

"You mean, last night?"

"Yes, that's exactly what I mean. Except that I don't know what I mean. I can't remember much, except for some nightmares afterwards. I don't know what was dream and what wasn't. Do you?" Peter shook his head, a frown settling across his stained face.

"I'm not sure I want to go through with it, Peter. And I'm even less sure you ought to go through with it."

"But why not, Met? It seems like a once-in-a-lifetime opportunity!"

"Oh, it is—for them!"

"I don't follow you."

"About the only thing they don't know about you, *mon ami*, is that you are white. I doubt they would care about that any more. You see, I think they want to use you, your position in society back in the States. They know that you will have connections they could never get, influence they wish they had."

"For what?"

"Oh, the cult is very old. They once had power and influence on a scale you can't imagine. They would love to get it back. At least that's what the Old Ones are telling them in dreams. I know, because since the Second Oath, I share in some of those dreams. And they think you can help them get their old power back again. And I'll tell you something else—I'm quite sure they'll never let you publish the facts of what's really going on here. Only a kind of toned-down version. I'm sorry to upset you, Peter. I'll leave now. I want to scout about the camp a bit. I'll see you tonight before the ceremony. Till then, you think about what I've said, okay?" Metellus left without giving Peter a chance to respond.

Peter did give the matter some thought, though nothing he could think of persuaded him to change his mind. He had too much invested in the thing now. And what harm could come of it? Metellus seemed to have survived it with no difficulty. And what was he worried about all of a sudden? It was dark in the hut, and, while not quite as hot as in the countryside below, the place was still pretty sweltering. So Peter did what he often did on such days. Without actually deciding to, he slept.

He dreamed. In his dream, Metellus returned earlier than he had said he would. He had a sense of great urgency about him, said he had managed to remember something. But the more he pleaded with Peter to get up and leave the compound with him, the deeper Peter seemed to sink into slumber. It was a strange dream, and Peter began to forget it as soon as he felt hands shake him awake. They were black hands, Metellus's he thought at first, but no. The priest had sent him the two unspeaking escorts as he had promised. Peter was happy to join them and surprised, once the door opened, to see that it was already dusk. And no sign of Metellus. Well, probably he was on his way to the ritual area where the crowd was beginning to reassemble. Metellus, too, he remembered, was due to undergo an initiation this night.

Smiling faces greeted the outsider, about to become an insider. The throng parted like a curtain to let him penetrate to the center, where the old priest, in ceremonial finery, stood holding a ceramic cup. He was already chanting. It did not sound like Creole. The postulant met the old man's glance, smiling and, he hoped, reverent. But he could not help stealing a glance here and there to check on Metellus's presence. Still he did not appear.

Peter was made uneasy by the strange language, filled with gutturals and grunts, yet also with tongue-twisting, liquid-sounding accents, almost melodious, and yet somehow bestial. It became clear, as the priest neared a crescendo, that he was reciting the conditions of an oath, the Oath to Damballah. Peter knew he should shortly have to assent to whatever it was they were requiring of him. If only Metellus were here to help him make some sense of it all. But then, he thought ruefully, he was the anthropologist! He should be able to figure it out. Well, there was nothing for it now but to go on with the drama. When the priest stopped, looking expectantly at Peter, the latter nodded and bowed, hoping that would suffice. It must have, for the old man said something else unintelligible to his congregation, and they broke into wild applause and joyful shouting. Women and children came forth to place flower wreathes around his neck, a laurel wreath upon his sweating brow. Several dipped their fingers in the cup the old priest held, then made crosses on Peter's face and forehead with the red substance contained in the cup. After all had their chance, the old man offered the cup to Peter and bade him, this time in clear Creole, to take a drink. Peter knew by now that it must be sacrificial blood. But he was not one to be shocked or disgusted at alien mores, much less alien diet. As a field anthropologist, he could never afford such scruples. So he took the cup and drank of the salty beverage. More cheering followed. He guessed he had successfully taken the First Oath of Damballah. Now he need only wait to discover what secrets the initiation entitled him to. It was a cross-cultural constant: initiates into any cult received catechism about the inner truths, though still deeper secrets might well remain pending further degrees of initiation, degrees he dearly hoped might not take him too long to attain. It was all a matter of research, and of making friends with these people. And that shouldn't be too hard. Like all Haitians he had met, they were plainly good-natured and friendly.

The drums began to throb, and his pulses involuntarily picked up the pace. The priest gestured toward one of the huts, and Peter realized the ritual was not over after all. He looked at his initiator, then in the direction he had pointed. Shrugging, he decided he was game, and started for the hut. Now he noticed the drummers were moving into a circle around the small structure. As the shaman walked beside him, Peter ventured to whisper to him, "Grandfather, you do me great honor. But where is my friend? Was not, he, too, to receive initiation tonight?"

The oldster smiled and bobbed his head enthusiastically. "So he was. And so he did, less than an hour ago. You will see him soon enough. And now, my son, you will learn the secrets of life and death. First life. The Second Oath of Damballah." So saying, he pushed open the flimsy door. Peter went through it and gazed around the close quarters. There was room for a pad on the ground, and it was not unoccupied. Her black flesh gleaming in the light of banks of candles, the very incarnation of Haitian female vitality stretched out invitingly. His pulses hammered, his hormones surging. The drums outside did his thinking for him, though thinking had little to do with a situation like this! She was naked, and in a moment, he was, too. As he mounted her, as impatient as she of preliminaries, he got a good look at her face and saw two things with a gasp. He recognized her as the woman at whose cottage they had left Metellus's car. And her eyes were completely vacant, whites showing, lost in a rapture that was at least as spiritual as sexual, probably more. Peter understood that she was in the midst of a possession trance, no doubt believing herself to be indwelt by the spirit of the love-*loa* Erzulie. He had never imagined making love to a woman in such a state. As he entered her, pumping madly, he found she was like a volcano, a bucking mustang. It was all he could do to hold on, to gain purchase and drive himself home again and again till explosive release came. It was glorious!

He was winded, rolled over, felt her lithe limbs shuddering, shivering, coming to a gradual relaxation. Still she said nothing. And in the post-coital silence Peter could detect the low tones of an antiphonal chant. On one side of the hut, he could make out male voices. They repeated an invocation, *Nigguratl!* Then the female voices responded, *Yig!* He wondered what it meant specifically. He knew what it meant generally: he had just participated in a holy rite older than Baal and Asherah, the *Hieros Gamos*, or sacred marriage between god and goddess, between heaven and earth. It was supposed to be a magical guarantee of fertility for the fields. As this went through his mind, he realized for the first time he had exposed his piebald, half-dyed flesh! But the woman had been past noticing.

He had barely managed to wipe himself down and replace his clothes when the old priest swept the door open, exposing him to the laughing, eager faces of as many of the cultists as could get a view inside. The old man beckoned him to come out, while a couple of older women rushed past him to see to the woman, who was beginning to rouse from her trance. He was still reeling with ecstasy and exhaustion, but there was evidently to be no break. Eager hands ushered him into a smaller hut, this one with smoke ebbing from the door corners. He dimly observed that it was no doubt a sweat lodge, part of the universal pattern of the rites of passage. You could find them in preliterate cultures the world over: Amerindians, Siberians, Melanesians, Amazonian rain forest dwellers. All of them did it. In Peter's preconscious mind rested the knowledge that the smoke hut symbolized the womb of the second birth, birth unto a higher plane. It would be an ordeal, designed, through oxygen starvation and sensory deprivation, to produce visions, usually visions mirroring the traditional totem-masks of the tribe. What would he see, if anything?

Half-stumbling, partly due to the shoving of his escort, partly to his residual light-headedness, Peter fell to the ground inside the fire-lit hut. The ground was plain but not hard. The light flickered with its source.

He felt a great urge to surrender to sleep. When had he slept so much? He could not remember. He drifted, drifted. He supposed he was asleep again, because now there appeared to be a row of figures stooping and sitting before him, too long a line for the small space to accommodate. He thought that he ought to know them. There was surely something familiar about them. And then he remembered he had marked their faces the previous night, at that ceremony he had largely forgotten. Maybe he would remember more of it now that they were here again, the *bocors*, the *houngans*, the tattooed and branded sorcerers of the cult. The firelight did strange things to their outlines, that was for sure, but it seemed to Peter that it was their shadows that were strangest of all. They did not seem remotely to correspond with the bodies casting them. The man in the middle, with the hoop ear rings and the worst scars along his neck: the shadow that loomed above him reminded Peter vaguely of the outlines of Great Tulu, the pincers attached to rolling necks and appendages. The others were all different but equally ill-fitting. Yes, the Old Ones... He was beginning to remember...

The spokesman for the group opened his eyes, and Peter saw no iris or pupil, only an empty expanse of glowing green, as when a ray of sunlight penetrates the sea water above a diver. The figure started to speak. It seemed as if he had been speaking for some time, as if someone had turned on a radio in the middle of a speech. But the content was definitely directed to him. "We know it is knowledge that you seek. The true seekers come to us sooner or later, as you have come. Here they learn the higher path, the path to the past. Which can come again. But you are special, Young Sir. The Old Ones have sent you to us for a purpose. You can help us to bring back the past of the Old Ones."

Peter felt he should be sitting in a posture of respect or veneration to these old saints, these elders of the community. But he was utterly empty, barely able to grasp what was being said. He lay there like a limp doll, hoping they would take no offense.

"We know you want to learn our secrets so you may gain fame by betraying them to the outside world. That you cannot do. But you will gain your fame. You will write your book. We will tell you what you may say. Others will even be able to verify what you say. And when you have your fame, we will have it. And then we will send one to you with something else you may tell your world. It is a world that loves the drugs. Substances." A ripple of laughter followed this.

"In that day, maybe two, three years down the road, when you are the so-famous professor, you will tell them you have discovered something great among us. You will tell them the old island witch doctors are not so stupid. That they have chemical secrets from the rain forests. Powders that can lift the spirit, than can extend the manhood, that will shrink the fat from the white man's ass. And it will. And it will do other things their tests will not show. And in this way, you, my son, will open their hearts to love the past of the Old Ones. And in that day you white men will sing as we sing: That is not dead which can eternal lie. And with strange eons, even death may die!"

He didn't see them leave. Maybe he had blacked out, lost consciousness even within the dream. But at length he roused again, sure by this time that he had been secretly drugged, even before being brought here to the sweat lodge. Now the fumes were making him cough. That's it—he had coughed himself awake. There was something in the smoke that was playing hell with his sinuses, that kept him confused, too. But that, of course, was part of the regimen. It didn't worry him unduly. But it entered his head to wonder about Metellus. Was he elsewhere in the camp, undergoing something similar?

And then: there he was! Peter flinched with shock, as welcome as the sight of him was.

"Peter! I made a big mistake bringing you here!" The image of his friend hovered nearby. The man must be kneeling to look into Peter's sodden face. Peter smiled and reached out to touch the other's shoulder in reassurance, but he could not reach him somehow.

"No, no, Met. It's all going well! Better than I could have... Say, that's quite a scar you've got there... How'd you...?"

The black visage, curiously dim and gray in the smoky interior of the hut, waited for Peter to compose himself, to get his thoughts straight.

"Hear you passed your initiation rite, or test, or.. Give me a minute..."

"Yes, *mon ami*, I took the Third Oath of Damballah, all right. With the Third Oath one renders oneself entirely to the Old Ones."

"Well, I can tell you, buddy, the Second Oath's not s'bad! I never had such a..."

"What about the First Oath, my friend? Did you taste the drink? The salty cup?"

"Yes, it was blood, I know. I knew it would be. Very common in these things. Probably one of their goats."

"I think it was a goat named Metellus," the black man said, closing the mouth in this face and opening the new lips of his throat into a horrible grin. "It is no mere scar. You now have my blood in you. That is why I may come to you in this manner, while your mind has been opened to the influences. I have little time left. You have little time left."

Peter was shaking himself awake, shruggingly gathering himself into a sitting position. His wide eyes looked on the face of his dead friend, and the greater his sobered clarity became, the dimmer the features of Metellus became. "No, Metellus, I..."

The words came as a sourceless whisper: "You dare not leave and disobey the Old Ones now. They will not permit it. Do not openly defy them. But do not serve them. I will..." And there was no more. But Peter was now very definitely awake. His head pounded without benefit of drums. The smoke was about dispersed, which, he figured, was probably what allowed his head to clear. He lay down for a second, found that this only made his head hurt worse. So he rolled over to kneel and stand, but as he rolled, he encountered a supine form and recoiled. At first, his memories mixed up, he imagined it was the woman from a few hours before. But it wasn't.

He sprang backwards away from the machete-butchered carcass of Metellus. It hadn't been just his throat. That must have been only the beginning. He hadn't looked like this in the dream Peter had just awakened from. But he could no longer begin to guess, in this place, what was a dream and what was waking reality, or even what the difference was supposed to be. Anything was equally real, it seemed.

He flung open the fragile door and staggered out. A semicircle of the cult elders, a couple of their musclemen, and a few little boys awaited him. His dramatic appearance caught some by surprise, awakened others. The little fellows scattered, their interest in the stranger at an end for the time being. The others, rising to meet him, seemed subtly to come too close, their chests hoisted as if to signal threat, forming a cordon around him. A strange way to treat a guest and a new brother in the faith! But they must have a pretty good idea what was going through his mind. Mustn't he be weighing his old loyalties against his new ones? He would in a short time seal off the past and identify fully with the cult. That would be easier, of course, the longer they could keep him here among themselves, isolated from his professional colleagues and family members back home.

He met their polite questions as to his welfare with equally empty answers. He knew he was meant to see the corpse of Metellus. It must somehow be part of the ritual experience, "the secrets of life and death." It also no doubt stood for a warning that the same thing could happen to him should he have second thoughts. Peter thought better of expressing his sorrow and rage at the ritual murder of his friend. It could only increase their suspicion. Better for the moment to let them think, as they no doubt did, that as a white man (oh yes, they knew all right: "you white men"), he regarded Metellus merely as an expendable hireling.

"I... saw great things. Heard great words. Words of destiny..." The older men smiled and looked at one another. He knew they had been waiting to hear something like this.

During the long afternoon, Peter listened and took extensive shorthand notes as the oldest of the cult elders fulfilled the promise made to him, that initiation should carry the privilege of disclosure. He got an earful of the lore of the cult. There was very little about the history of the group. Life changed very little in their tiny world from year to year, even from century to century, with the exception of the disruption of slavery. But the faith could go on and did go on, with only the temporary lack of sacrifices, in the slave quarters. And occasionally they had been able to get to the swamps on certain nights. By far most of their lore concerned the Old Ones, old gods, as he already knew, but now he sat entranced with morbid fascination at tall tales and weird theogonies unlike any he had encountered in his wide study of folklore and mythology. It was a treasure trove, and a genuine ancient tradition. There was far more here than he had dreamed of when he first dared hope there might exist in remote Haiti an untapped trove.

Most of what they told him, he was made to understand, he would be permitted to communicate to the outside world in the form of scholarly monographs. It was a sacrifice of traditional secrecy, to be sure, but even that was necessary to pave the way for the past of the Old Ones to come again. All men must know their Masters so that they might render them a fitting welcome when the great day came. Peter understood that there were yet greater arcana to which his two degrees of initiation did not yet entitle him, and of these he dared not ask, nor were the elders likely to permit them to be spread abroad.

Nor was Peter especially eager to advance farther along on the cult's path of discipleship, given what he knew had happened to poor Metellus at the climax of his initiation. He kept thinking of those last words his friend's shade had uttered in the dream vision. He had left him a dilemma, a riddle. He dared not give any sign of resisting or renouncing his role in their insane conspiracy, yet neither could he afford to become their accomplice, really their puppet, in it. He waited, as if for a signal he knew could never come: a signal from a dead man.

The catechism went on for days and then weeks. He could hardly imagine there was so much to the religion! It must be ancient indeed for the legendry to have become so complex, so fulsome, so baroque! There was no way of knowing how old the belief was. Their own lore said that it went back, of course, to the Old Ones themselves, and that they had come to this planet from somewhere else entirely. But here history had shaded off into mythology. The true story would never be known. Peter found he was beginning to think like an anthropologist again. He found himself, as he looked over his notes by firelight each evening, musing over possible methodologies to make sense of the seemingly confused symbols and myths. He felt even Levi-Strauss would find himself outwitted by these old myth-mongers! Well, one thing anyway: if he managed to get out of here alive and unharmed, he had more than enough for a monograph, no, a series of them that would make Victor Turner's famous studies of the Ndembu look like a kid's description of a birthday party!

If only he could leave it at that. But a dark pall hung over him. There was little chance, he now realized, that they would hinder his return to the outer world (he once would have called it "the real world," but who knew what that was anymore?). Indeed, his role in their plan depended on that. But how many more atrocities must he be implicated in before he left? Back home, he could put that part of it out of his mind. Cultural relativism and all: who was he, a Westerner, to judge their ancient customs? And so on. But there was a ritual tonight in which the Old Ones would be invoked, and believers would receive their expected foretaste of the ecstasy of the past of the Old Ones, a past which now looked closer than ever to returning, thanks to their new brother. He knew he could not stand seeing any more of the poor wretches picked out of the crowd to die in a bloody holocaust as part of the ritual. Yes, he now remembered all too well what had transpired on that first night.

He had a seat of honor alongside the ranks of shamans and *bocors* inside the circle. Behind him gathered a number of children, whom he hated to contemplate seeing what he feared they would see, though he knew they must be hardened to it by now. Peter was a favorite of the children, especially as his skin, free of the dye, had begun to lighten and lighten, until it approached very nearly its original hue. This fascinated the children, who followed him around like baby ducks.

The time came, and soon, as he feared, one of the priests began to intone the familiar invocations. He was interested to note that, even though they no longer had to be judicious in the presence of outsiders, the crowed persisted in the ancient formula, calling on the names of the *vodun* deities that masked the terrible entities they actually served. He knew that traditions endure even absent their original rationale. So here came the names: Legba, Ogoun, Erzulie, Damballah, Samedhi...

As before, the crowd's enthusiasm was pent and building. But suddenly something surprised them. Something was going on at the rear of the circle. Peter craned his neck, trying to see over the shoulders of the old men. In a moment he could tell that the same thing, whatever it was, was going on all around the outer perimeter. Instinctively, he turned to his young entourage, gathered behind him, and sternly told them in his clearest Creole to get out, go to their homes, even out of the village, now.

The commotion was building. He could hear numerous physical impacts—bodies falling? Crowds clashing in battle? Was a riot beginning? Were some already intoxicated? Screaming began, and not just screams of alarm or of pain. There were shrieks of holy terror that ripped through the cotton humidity of the jungle night. Peter was on his feet, moving around aimlessly, uncertain what to do. If it was a fight, what side should he be on? How could a company of men approach the compound undetected? He began to slip on skids of blood on the packed ground, then to trip over bodies. A bloody harvest was progressing with amazing speed. He guessed that he, too, would momentarily fall under the scythe. Lanterns swung wildly and were extinguished. Torches bobbed and some went out. Some were swung as weapons, but ineffectively.

Suddenly, in the midst of the melee, Peter was sure that his sweat-stinging eyes glimpsed the impossible visage of Metellus, his livid gash gaping. But the gross wound did nothing to impede his prowess with the machete. He hacked and hacked without the fatigue of the living. Dead, he had himself become the Grim Reaper. But he did not fight alone. Like a gang of laborers chopping down jungle growth to clear a field or the path for a road, there was a whole crew of forms wielding knives, clubs, machetes. All silent. None of their faces was visible given the bad lighting. But the nearest one seemed incongruously to be sporting a top hat and sunglasses over a gaunt form one would not have thought sturdy enough to inflict the blows he was dealing.

The *bocors* and cult priests, taken by surprise, began to rally. They had no earthly weapons, but Peter could see their hands and arms flailing as if they bore deadly cudgel and sword. He knew they must be conjuring. It looked like superstitious pantomime, but Peter could tell something was happening because of what he heard, or thought he heard. He seemed to catch the echoes of explosions without the explosions themselves. Aftershocks of invisible eruptions. Something was occurring on a plane he could not see. But whatever it was, it had little effect on the invaders. One or two seemed to vanish, not to fall smitten, but just to disappear. But then perhaps they were leaving of their own accord now that the massacre was near its end. In the hacking fury of Metellus's vengeance, with the aid of his mysterious hosts, tattooed heads flew like coconuts in a windstorm. Blood rained down, and Peter found himself spitting it out as he could not prevent a good deal of it entering his nose and mouth. Indeed, there seemed a red fog which made him gag and cough till he thought his lungs would burst.

He made for the edge of the clearing, where he could see the terrified yet curious young faces following the whole ghastly business. Their eyes grew even wider, if possible, as he approached, a wild and terrifying sight, he knew. But once he was upon them, and they kept looking past him, he knew another was the object of their gaze, and he turned to face it. It was Metellus. He gave a look to his dripping machete and cast it away, into the trees. He extended an arm toward

Peter, but when the latter made a move to join him, Metellus waved him off. He tried to say something, but there was no sound, and Peter could not read his lips. He knew it was a final parting gesture, though. And then there was no one.

Peter's ears felt the pressure of sudden and total silence. None of the adults could have survived. But neither were their conquerors anywhere to be seen. Yet he knew where they were: wherever Metellus was. The true *loa* had taken their revenge, and Metellus had shared in it. As for him, Peter knew what he must do next. He would round up the newly orphaned children of the village and, with them in tow, begin the long journey back down the mountainside to the cottage. A few could return with him to town in the Jeep; the rest could be picked up by the authorities. He hoped they could all find homes, and anything would have to be an improvement.

He paused for a moment, looking in the direction of his hut. His papers and notes were there, even a tape recording or two. His book, yet unwritten, was there. His career was there. But now who would believe any of it? The myths and rituals of a small community—now all dead in a massacre? A massacre he alone had survived? How would any of that look? He turned his back on the village, counted the children, and started for the foot path.

THE JEWELS OF CHARLOTTE

BY DUANE RIMEL

"YOU WILL PERHAPS QUESTION MY STORY OF INCIDENTS which occurred in the mouldering old town, but I think they will be of interest nonetheless." Constantine Theunis leaned back in his chair luxuriously.

We were seated in his elaborate parlor before a crackling fireplace blaze. The lights were extinguished, and a chill autumn wind howled eerily about the house, giving a threat of snow. But the flickering shadows and austere atmosphere were secondary to Theunis himself. Lighting his pipe, he gazed steadily at the roaring flames, clearly deep in thought. He had asked me over to hear a story of some sort—the exact nature of which he had not yet explained.

"You remember my vacation in July, Single?"

"Of course," I replied, recalling that the old town he spoke of must be Hampdon, where he had for a week visited in search of solitude and antiques.

"While there, a peculiar train of events occurred which I've been keeping quiet all this time. Two federal agents, a sheriff and myself were the only ones who dug into the whole thing—they from duty and I from curiosity; and we found—but first I must go back a bit.

"As you know, Hampdon is a most curious mixture of the new and the old; that being one reason for my sojourn there. It is an isolated place, stuck down between forbidding hills and inhabited by natives who believe every bit of gossip that comes to their ears. They do not exactly welcome strangers, and my arrival at the hotel was not a very pleasant occasion. But I wished to look over some of the stone carvings near the village and explore a bit in the nearby caverns. For five days I had a splendid time, absorbing an abundance of good mountain air, peering into the hillside caverns and soaking in some local gossip as well. On every hand I heard mutterings of varied description, subdued whispers which seemed to occupy the whole time of the village wits and loafers. My efforts to persuade some of them to confide in me met with failure—in fact, at times, they appeared to resent even my presence. The landlord was noticeably sullen, and never seemed to care whether the meals were served or not.

"Finally I found that most of their everlasting mutterings centered about some sort of fabulous gems known as the jewels of Charlotte. Nothing more concerning them, however, reached my ears. It was amusing to watch how a group of villagers would suddenly cease their talking at my approach. Toward the last I grew more and more inquisitive about the strange gems and longed for someone to whom I could at least venture my opinions; for my interest had gradually shifted from the dark hillside caverns to the disjointed jargon of the miserable townspeople.

"Imagine my surprise when, on the sixth day, upon entering my hotel, I found two responsible-looking gentlemen whom I had met several times in Croydon. They were the agents I spoke of. We exchanged greetings, they seeming as pleased as I to find an acquaintance among these surroundings. They had parked their car in the rear, and I had not seen it in approaching the place. Luckily, they had arranged for a room adjoining mine.

"We immediately became confidential—that is, so far as their professions would allow. I knew that a man-hunt or something equally important was brewing, since two seemed so large a force for so small a hamlet. They had not confided in anyone but the county sheriff, they said, and explained that their purpose must not leak out.

"Both men were about forty; the eldest, Sargent, doing the most talking. His companion, Roberts, seemed less inclined to speak. They were dressed in civilian clothes, and I doubt if any villager suspected their true identities or purpose. It was only by chance that I learned of their mission at all, and this chance led up to the most unexplainable jumble I've ever run into. But I'm getting ahead of myself again.

"At dinner that evening the two were strangely quiet. At the same table sat a rough-looking individual whom I took to be the sheriff. I was seated in one corner partaking slowly of the meal placed in front of me by the disheveled waiter. The three had not ordered. An unaccountable tenseness reigned over the room. The other occupants went on about their business. A window close by was open, and the distant croaking of frogs came faintly to my ears. The two agents half-faced me while the sheriff was turned squarely in the opposite direction. I bring out these details in view of what subsequently happened. As I said, the frogs were chorusing and the air seemed loaded with an unknown, malign quality.

"Suddenly, from out of nowhere, there sounded a golden mellow chime. The air was filled with a momentary flood of sweet, sinister music that rang like the voices of woodland nymphs on the cool mountain air. It made my flesh creep. There was a distinct element of the unknown and forbidden in that one elfin-like tone. For an instant the air seemed charged with a vibrant, tangible force—elusive as a rainbow, yet startling and chilling in its utter unearthliness. To say where it came from would be impossible. Simultaneously it seemed to spring from the dark hills and from the very air of the room. I know I must have been startled, for my fingers trembled on the table-top.

"The effect on the natives was startling. Every one of them froze in attitudes of intense listening. The rugged sheriff cursed under his breath and rose quickly to his feet. The faces of the two marshals showed nothing but awed surprise, and my own must have reflected the same emotion. My God, Single, I can hear that chime ringing yet! A mellow echo; breathtaking in its suddenness, and inherently evil and unreal. I could make nothing of it. About me the few occupants seemed somehow to recognize that note—and to fear it. The sheriff grasped his hat and hurriedly left the ill-lit room, followed by the federal officers, who glanced now and then out the open windows. I heard them pass around to the back, start their powerful automobile, and roar away into the night. I wondered if their destination concerned the haunting, sinister note. I left the dining room, unable to take my thoughts from the thing. I need not describe the utter terror and fear that lined the faces of the people in that room. There was something altogether horrifying in the effect which the one sound had upon them—something that was dimly echoed in my own uneasiness.

"That night in my room I was awakened by the sound of voices. The strange chime had filled my thoughts before retiring, and I must have slept lightly. The conversation was coming from the adjoining room, the thin walls permitting the words to filter through very distinctly, though, I assure you, I never intended at any time to eavesdrop. My bed was close to the wall. I rubbed the sleep from my eyes and saw that a shaft of moonlight played on the bare floor. Then I listened closely to the talking, which originated from the three who had left so mysteriously earlier in the evening.

"It finally became apparent that they were trailing two suspicious characters who had arrived in Hampdon under great secrecy. I thought it strange that I had neither seen nor heard of their coming, but, as you know, the townfolk had told me absolutely nothing. I expected them to say something concerning the lone chime, and, finally, many moments later, the conversation indeed turned in that direction. I was, of course, wondering why they had not referred to it so far. To my astonishment, the two outsiders knew nothing about it and confessed they were greatly puzzled at the sound. I listened, fairly holding my breath, as they plied the sheriff with questions. He seemed reluctant to talk of it. Some time later, though, after a long interlude of whispering, the fellow began an unusual story. As I remember it, his guttural words told a tale something like this:

"A long time ago, when Hampdon was nothing but a settlement, a strange man and his daughter Charlotte came there from God-knew-where and built a house over by the hills. No one could say just how long ago this was, but the man—now very old—still lived in the same dwelling. People had long since quit going near the rotting place, which crouched under those overhanging cliffs. At any rate, his beautiful daughter Charlotte fell from the high mountains to her death, as the legend went, and the old fellow—his name was Cruth—never recovered from the shock.

"Some said he built an enormous tomb in the fastness of the hills where he laid his beloved child. Others said he had spirited her away to other places. Most people believed in the hidden tomb. About two years after her death, there arose rumors to the effect that there were gems of uncountable wealth buried within the tomb of Charlotte. No one knew just what they were, though some said diamonds, others pearls, and others opals. An intense longing grew among some of the younger people to subdue Cruth, hunt up the hidden tomb and loot it of its enormous fortune. There was, of course, much uncertainty about the matter, but for years it had been the talk of the townspeople— especially after the occurrence of a certain incident.

"In the fervor of the new gossip, a group of young men—five in all— decided to explore into the hills in quest of the mysterious sepulcher. This was, of course, nearly twenty years ago, and at the time most of the people had laughed when anyone mentioned the mysterious jewels. No one asked old Cruth about the affair or even cared to. The marauders started out one morning and did not reappear till late evening. They told strange, disjointed tales of finding the hidden place, but of fearing to enter at the last moment for some vague, unstated reason. No person could elicit anything concrete from the five. They seemed reluctant to reveal the incidents of the previous day, and very little was learned of the mysterious tomb.

"The next day they were off in fevered haste, neglecting to tell anyone just where their find had been made. The townspeople waited another day, still tolerantly amused at the antics of the young men. But that night they did not make an appearance. And they never came back! Not a trace of them was ever found! Dozens of expeditions were sent into the hills, but none of them ever solved the riddle of the missing five. After that, people did not laugh when anyone mentioned the Jewels of Charlotte, as they eventually came to be known. Some doubted the existence of the jewels; the sheriff did himself. But here is the strangest and most significant part of the whole thing. That night when the five were expected back—about eight o'clock—a very peculiar thing occurred. From somewhere in the hills there came a golden, mellow chime! And now that accursed ringing had been heard again— for the only time since then—and people were counting their families.

"But that wasn't all. About a month before, two ragged-looking men had come into Hampdon and settled in a decrepit shack near the place where old man Cruth lived. From the first, the sheriff had not liked their actions; but there was nothing he could pin on them, so he just bided his time. At length, he saw them call on the old man—which was extremely singular, since Cruth had never cared for strangers. The sheriff had hidden in the brush, and when they came out of the house he saw that there was dark hate and anger on their faces. He could hear the old man's hoarse voice ordering them to take their accursed proposition and get out of his shack. When they had moved off a ways, Cruth stepped out and yelled so loudly that the words were clearly audible to the sheriff—and he never forgot them. The aged man, as he tottered on his feeble legs, had cried: '—and if you monkey with those stones, the chime will ring again!' The sheriff hadn't known whether they actually read any significance in the phrase, but their faces surely looked as if they had. That had only been two days ago. Then the marshals arrived. 'Do you wonder,' concluded the sheriff, 'that I jumped up and beat it for those fellows' shack this evening when we heard it? But it was empty—and tonight the thing rang again...'"

"I did not sleep well that night.

"Upon rising the next morning I decided to make a clean breast of my eavesdropping. At breakfast I told the two marshals what I had heard. At first they were displeased, but in the end they seemed glad to confide in me. The story had affected them fully as much as it had me—indeed, they believed that a sinister element hovered over the whole region and the whole affair. It was an idea that had bothered me a great deal as well. We were talking the matter over when the sheriff arrived and I was introduced to the man to whom I had listened the night before. He was an interesting individual, once one became acquainted with him. Sargent and Roberts explained my interest in the affair and the chance eavesdropping that had occurred. He was more than willing to have another man in the swing.

"We set out immediately for Cruth's house to investigate the matter of the two missing men. My own interests centered around the strange sound, and I think the sheriff's did too. But it was all so hopelessly jumbled that none of us knew just where to start. As the car roared down the road toward the ancient abode I happened to glance at the local officer. His gaze, instead of resting on the rapidly approaching house, was fastened longingly on the forbidding wooded slopes. He had not mentioned that a brother of his had been among the missing five...

"When we pulled up at the ramshackle dwelling, the only sign of life was a thin ribbon of smoke rising from the leaning chimney. Far above loomed the dark hills and rugged outcroppings of black rock. About the place were tall, moss-covered pines which seemed to shroud the house in a blanket of perpetual gloom.

"We approached the house and the sheriff rapped on the door. For several moments no sound came from within—then a hobbling movement and the door creaked open. An age-wrinkled face glared out at us. Cruth's eyes were sunken and bloodshot, and he braced himself feebly against the warped door jamb.

"'What do you want?' he asked weakly, his lined hands clasped tightly around his cane.

"Sargent stepped forward. 'We want to know if you have seen your two neighbors this morning.'

"'My neighbors,' he croaked, 'those damned thieves aren't no neighbors of mine! I haven't seen 'em and I don't want to!'

"'Why not?' queried Sargent.

"'Why?' wheezed the old man. 'Because they wanted me to tell them how to get to the tomb of my girl—my little girl—and her pretty stones!' His voice grew weaker and trailed off. Then suddenly: 'But I told 'em! I told 'em!—and last night—last night...' His breath was failing. '...the chime—rang—again! The chime! The golden chime! My...'

"'Come on, let's go!' the sheriff whispered.

"We complied, but the old fellow still stood in the doorway gibbering, half to himself. We heard his last words faintly, and I shall never forget them.

"'—and I think soon the chime will ring—again, for—I know the way well... Through the ancient gate—and beyond—where... in Yith my Charlotte will not—be broken—and I shall pass...'

"The roar of the motor drowned out further words—words I wish we had listened to—words which might have been the key to the whole thing. As the faded dwelling passed from sight around a curve in the road, I felt a queer tinge of sorrow course through me. The sheriff stared straight into the weaving road. He, too, had heard.

"We stopped momentarily at the shack where the two fugitives had lived, but found it completely empty, with signs of recent habitation quite evident. The decrepit hut seemed too empty and suggestive after the visit with the old man, and we left hurriedly. It soon disappeared from sight as the car sped down the winding road, and I was relieved to be gone from the mouldering thing that hinted at something wholly alien and sinister; something that should be left undisturbed. It was strange how I felt, for some unexplainable reason, that the former occupants would never return to their lowly dwelling.

"I left that evening on an outgoing stage—I don't know whether they ever solved the secret or not; at least nothing ever appeared in the papers. So far as I'm concerned it can stay hidden. The look in old man Cruth's eyes still lingers hauntingly with me. There was a deep wisdom behind that ancient voice—a wisdom which perhaps should not be discussed.

"That night as the stage swung up and around the many turns of highway which leads out of Hampdon, I watched the flickering lights of the tiny city fade away in the distance. Far to the west, the afterglow bathed the beetling hills in rosy splendor, and below, deep shadows were gathering in ravines and gulleys. And as the panorama faded slowly from view, I heard, above the roar of the motor, a single haunting, and never to be forgotten, chime that echoed and reechoed faintly in the gathering dusk."

THE LETTERS OF COLD FIRE

BY MANLY WADE WELLMANN

THE EL HAD ONCE CURVED AROUND A CORNER AND ALONG THIS block of the narrow rough-paved street. Since it had been taken up, the tenements on either side seemed like dissipated old vagabonds, ready to collapse without the support of that scaffolding. Between two such buildings of time-dulled red brick sagged a third, its brickwork thickly coated with cheap yellow paint that might well be the only thing holding it together. The lower story was taken up by the dingiest of hand laundries, and a side door led to the lodgings above. Rowley Thorne addressed a shabby dull-eyed landlord in a language both of them knew:

"Cavet Leslie is—" he began.

The landlord shook his head slowly. "Does not leave his bed."

"The doctor sees him?"

"Twice a day. Told me there was no hope, but Cavet Leslie won't go to a hospital."

"Thanks," and Thorne turned to the door. His big hand was on the knob, its fingertips hooked over the edge. He was a figure inordinately bulky but hard, like a barrel on legs. His head was bald, and his nose hooked, making him look like a wise, wicked eagle.

"Tell him," he requested, "that a friend was coming to see him."

"I never talk to him," said the landlord, and Thorne bowed, and left, closing the door behind him.

Outside the door, he listened. The landlord had gone back into his own dim quarters. Thorne at once tried the knob—the door opened, for in leaving he had taken off the night lock.

He stole through the windowless vestibule and mounted stairs so narrow that Thorne's shoulders touched both walls at once. The place had that old-clothes smell of New York's ancient slum houses. From such rookeries the Five Points and Dead Rabbits gangsters had issued to their joyous gang wars of old, hoodlums had thronged to the Draft Riots of 1863 and the protest against Macready's performance of *Macbeth* at Astor Place Opera House... The hallway above was as narrow as the stairs, and darker, but Thorne knew the way to the door he sought. It opened readily, for its lock was long out of order.

The room was more a cell than a room. The plaster, painted a dirt-disguising green, fell away in flakes. Filth and cobwebs clogged the one backward-looking window. The man on the shabby cot stirred, sighed and turned his thin fungus-white face toward the door. "Who's there?" he quavered wearily.

Rowley Thorne knelt quickly beside him, bending close like a bird of prey above a carcass. "You were Cavet Leslie," he said. "Try to remember."

A thin twig of a hand crept from under the ragged quilt. It rubbed over closed eyes. "Forbidden," croaked the man. "I'm forbidden to remember. I forget all but—but—" the voice trailed off, then finished with an effort:

"My lessons."

"You were Cavet Leslie. I am Rowley Thorne."

"Rowley Thorne!" The voice was stronger, quicker. "That name will be great in hell."

"It will be great on earth," pronounced Rowley Thorne earnestly. "I came to get your book. Give it to me, Leslie. It's worth both our lives, and more."

"Don't call me Leslie. I've forgotten Leslie—since—"

"Since you studied in the Deep School," Thorne finished for him. "I know. You have the book. It is given to all who finish the studies there."

"Few finish," moaned the man on the cot. "Many begin, few finish."

"The school is beneath ground," Thorne said, as if prompting him. "Remember."

"Yes, beneath ground. No light must come. It would destroy what is taught. Once there, the scholar remains until he has been taught, or—goes away in the dark."

"The school book has letters of cold fire," prompted Thorne.

"Letters of cold fire," echoed the thin voice. "They may be read in the dark. Once a day—once a day—a trap opens, and a hand shaggy with dark hairs thrusts in food. I finished—I was in that school for seven years—or a hundred!" He broke off, whimpering. "Who can say how long?"

"Give me your book," insisted Thorne. "It is here somewhere."

The man who would not be called Cavet Leslie rose on an elbow. It was a mighty effort for his fleshless body. He still held his eyes tight shut, but turned his face to Thorne's. "How do you know?"

"It's my business to know. I say certain spells—and certain voices whisper back. They cannot give me the wisdom I seek, but they say that it is in your book. Give me the book."

"Not even to you, Rowley Thorne. You are of the kidney of the Deep School, but the book is only for those who study in buried darkness for years. For years—"

"The book!" said Thorne sharply. His big hand closed on the bony shoulder, his finger-ends probed knowingly for a nerve center. The man who had been in the Deep School wailed.

"You hurt me!"

"I came for the book. I'll have it."

"I'll call on spirits to protect me—*Tobkta*—"

What else he may have said was muddled into a moan as Thorne shifted his hand to clamp over the trembling mouth. He prisoned the skinny jaw as a hostler with a horse, and shoved Cavet Leslie's head down against the mattress. With his other thumb he pried up an eyelid. Convulsively the tormented one freed his mouth for a moment.

"Ooooooooh!" he whined. "Don't make me see the light—not after so many years—"

"The book. If you'll give it up, hold up a finger."

A hand trembled, closed—all but the forefinger. Thorne released his grip.

"Where?"

"In the mattress—"

At once, and with all his strength, Thorne chopped down with the hard edge of his hand, full at the bobbing, trembling throat. It was like an axe on a knotted log. The man who had been Cavet Leslie writhed, gasped, and slackened abruptly. Thorne caught at a meager wrist, his fingers seeking the pulse. He stood silent for a minute, then nodded and smiled to himself.

"Finished," he muttered. "That throat-chop is better than a running noose."

He tumbled the body from the cot, felt quickly all over the mattress. His hand paused at a lump, tore at the ticking. He drew into view a book, not larger than a school speller. It was bound in some sort of dark untanned hide, on which grew rank, coarse hair, black as soot.

Thorne thrust it under his coat and went out.

John Thunstone sat alone in his study. It was less of a study than a lounge—no fewer than three chairs were arranged on the floor, soft, well-hollowed chairs within easy reach of bookshelf, smoking stand and coffee table. There was a leather-covered couch as well. For Thunstone considered work of the brain to be as fatiguing as work of the body. He liked physical comfort when writing or researching.

Just now he sat in the most comfortable of the three chairs, facing a grate in which burned one of the few authentic fires of New York. He was taller than Rowley Thorne and quite as massive, perhaps even harder of body though not as dense. His face, with its broken nose and small, trim mustache, might have been that of a very savage and physical-minded man, except for the height of the well-combed cranium above it. That made his head the head of a thinker. His hands were so large that one looked twice to see that they were fine. His dark eyes could be brilliant, frank, enigmatic, narrow, or laughing as they willed.

Open on his lap lay a large gray book, with a backing of gilt-lettered red. He pondered a passage on the page open before him:

Having shuffled and cut the cards as here described, select one at random. Study the device upon it for such time as you count a slow twenty. Then fix your eyes on a point before you, and gaze unwinkingly and without moving until it seems that a closed door is before you, with upon its panel the device of the card you have chosen. Clarify the image in your mind, and keep it there until the door seems to swing open, and you feel that you can enter and see, hear or otherwise experience what may happen beyond that door...

Similar, pondered John Thunstone, to the Chinese wizard-game of Yi King, as investigated and experimented upon by W. B. Seabrook. He was glad that he, and not someone less fitted for such studies, had happened upon the book and the strange cards in that Brooklyn junk-shop. Perhaps this was an anglicized form of the Yi King book—he said over in his mind the strange, archaic doggerel penned by some unknown hand on the fly-leaf:

This book is mine, with many more,
Of evilness and dismal lore.
That I may of the Devil know
And school myself to work him woe.
Such lore Saint Dunstan also read,
So that the Cross hath firmer stead.
My path with honor aye hath been—
No better is than that, I ween.

Who had written it? What had befallen him, that he sold his strange book in a second-hand store? Perhaps, if the spell would open a spirit-door, Thunstone would know.

He cut the cards on the stand beside him. The card he saw was stamped with a simple, colored drawing of a grotesque half-human figure, covered with spines, and flaunting bat-wings. Thunstone smiled slightly, sagged down in the chair. His eyes, narrowing, fixed themselves in the heart of the red flame...

The illusion came sooner than he had thought. At first it was tiny, like the decorated lid of a cigar-box, then grew and grew in size and clarity—shutting out, it seemed, even the firelight into which Thunstone had stared. It seemed green and massive, and the bat-winged figure upon it glowed dully, as if it were a life-size inlay of mother of pearl. He fixed his attention upon it, found his eyes quartering the door surface to seek the knob or latch. Then saw it, something like a massive metal hook. After a moment, the door swung open, as if the weight of his gaze had pushed it inward.

He remembered what the book then directed: Arise from your body and walk through the door. But he felt no motion, physical or spiritual. For through the open door he saw only his study—the half of his study that was behind his back, reflected as in a mirror. No, for in the mirror left would become right. Here was the rearward part of the room exactly as he knew it.

And not empty!

A moving, stealthy blackness was there, flowing or creeping across the rug between a chair and a smoking stand like an octopus on a sea-bottom.

Thunstone watched. It was not a cloud nor a shadow, but something solid if not clearly shaped. It came into plainer view, closer, at the very threshold of the envisioned door. There it began to rise, a towering lean manifestation of blackness—

It came to Thunstone's mind that, if the scene within the doorway was faithfully a reproduction of the room behind him, then he could see to it almost the exact point where his own chair was placed. In other words, if something dark and indistinct and stealthy was uncoiling itself there, the something was directly behind where he sat.

He did not move, did not even quicken his breath. The shape— it had a shape now, like a leafless tree with a narrow starved stem and moving tendril-like branches—aspired almost to the ceiling of the vision-room. The tendrils swayed as if in a gentle wind, then writhed and drooped. Drooped toward the point where might be the head of a seated man—if such a thing were truly behind him, it was reaching toward his head.

Thunstone threw himself forward from the chair, straight at the vision-door. As he came well away from where he had sat, he whipped his big body straight and, cat-light despite his wrestler's bulk, spun around on the balls of his feet. Of the many strange spells and charms he had read in years of strange study, one came to his lips, from the *Egyptian Secrets:*

"Stand still, in the name of heaven! Give neither fire nor flame nor punishment!"

He saw the black shadowy shape, tall behind his chair, its crowning tendrils dangling down in the very space which his body had occupied. The light of the sinking fire made indistinct its details and outlines, but for the instant it was solid. Thunstone knew better than to retreat a step before such a thing, but he was within arm's reach of a massive old desk. A quick clutch and heave opened a drawer, he thrust in his hand and closed it on a slender stick, no more than a rough-cut billet of whitethorn. Lifting the bit of wood like a dagger, he moved toward the half-blurred intruder. He thrust outward with the pointed end of the whitethorn stick.

"I command, I compel in the name of—" began Thunstone.

The entity writhed. Its tendrils spread and hovered, so that it seemed for the moment like a gigantic scrawny arm, spreading its fingers to signal for mercy. Even as Thunstone glared and held out his whitethorn, the black outline lost its clarity, dissolving as ink dissolves in water. The darkness became gray, stirred together and shrank away toward the door. It seemed to filter between panel and jamb. The air grew clearer, and Thunstone wiped his face with the hand that did not hold the whitethorn.

He stooped and picked up the book that had spilled from his lap. He faced the fire. The door, if it had ever existed otherwise than in Thunstone's mind, had gone like the tendril-shape. Thunstone took a pipe from his smoking stand and put it in his mouth. His face was deadly pale, but the hand that struck a match was as steady as a bronze bracket.

Thunstone placed the book carefully on the desk. "Whoever you are who wrote the words," he said aloud, "and wherever you are at this moment—thank you for helping me to warn myself."

He moved around the study, peering at the rug on which that shadow image had reared itself, prodding the pile, even kneeling to sniff. He shook his head.

"No sign, no trace—yet for a moment it was real and potent enough—only one person I know has the wit and will to attack me like that—"

He straightened up.

"Rowley Thorne!"

Leaving the study, John Thunstone donned hat and coat. He descended through the lobby of his apartment house and stopped a taxi on the street outside.

"Take me to eighty-eight Musgrave Lane, in Greenwich Village," he directed the driver.

The little bookshop looked like a dingy cave. To enter it, Thunstone must go down steps from the sidewalk, past an almost obliterated sign that read: BOOKS—ALL KINDS. Below ground the cave-motif was emphasized. It was as though one entered a ragged grotto among most peculiar natural deposits of books—shelves and stands and tables, and heaps of them on the floor like outcroppings. A bright naked bulb hung at the end of a ceiling cord, but it seemed to shed light only in the outer room. No beam, apparently, could penetrate beyond a threshold at the rear; yet Thunstone had, as always, the non-visual sense of a greater book-cave there, wherein perhaps clumps of volumes hung somehow from the ceiling, like stalactites...

"I thought you'd be here, Mr. Thunstone," came a genial snarl from a far corner, and the old proprietress stumped forward. She was heavy-set, shabby, white-haired, but had a proud beaked face, and eyes and teeth like a girl of twenty. "Professor Rhine and Joseph Denninger can write the books and give the exhibitions of thought transference. I just sit here and practice it, with people whose minds can tune in to mine—like you, Mr. Thunstone. You came, I daresay, for a book."

"Suppose," said Thunstone, "that I wanted a copy of the *Necronomicon?*"

"Suppose," rejoined the old woman, "that I gave it to you?" She turned to a shelf, pulled several books out, and poked her withered hand into the recess behind. "Nobody else that I know would be able to look into the *Necronomicon* without getting into trouble. To anyone else the price would be prohibitive. To you, Mr. Thun—"

"Leave that book where it is!" he bade her sharply. She glanced up with her bright youthful eyes, slid the volumes back into their place, and turned to wait for what he would say.

"I knew you had it," said Thunstone. "I wanted to be sure that you still had it. And that you would keep it."

"I'll keep it, unless you ever want it," promised the old woman.

"Does Rowley Thorne ever come here?"

"Thorne? The man like a burly old bald eagle? Not for months—he hasn't the money to pay the prices I'd ask him for even cheap reprints of Albertus Magnus."

"Good-by, Mrs. Harlan," said Thunstone. "You're very kind."

"So are you kind," said the old woman. "To me and to countless others. When you die, Mr. Thunstone, and may it be long ever from now, a whole generation will pray your soul into glory. Could I say something?"

"Please do." He paused in the act of going.

"Thorne came here once, to ask me a favor. It was about a poor sick man who lives—if you can call it living—in a tenement across town. His name was Cavet Leslie, and Thorne said he would authorize me to pay any price for a book Cavet Leslie had."

"Not the *Necronomicon?*" prompted Thunstone.

Her white head shook. "Thorne asked for the *Necronomicon* the day before, and I said I hadn't one to sell him—which was the truth. I had it in mind that he thought Cavet Leslie's book might be a substitute."

"The name of Leslie's book?"

She crinkled her face until it looked like a wise walnut. "He said it had no name. I was to say to Leslie, 'your schoolbook.'"

"Mmmm," hummed Thunstone, frowning. "What was the address?" She wrote it on a bit of paper. Thunstone took it and smiled down. "Good-by again, Mrs. Harlan. Some books *must* be kept in existence, I know, despite their danger. My sort of scholarship needs them. But you're the best and wisest person to keep them."

She stared after him for moments following his departure. A black cat came silently forth and rubbed its head against her.

"If I was really to do magic with these books," she told the animal, "I'd cut years off my age—and rake John Thunstone clear away from that Countess Monteseco, who will never, never do him justice!"

There was not much to learn at the place where Cavet Leslie had kept his poor lodgings. The landlord could not understand English, and Thunstone had to try two other languages before he learned that Leslie had been ill, had been under treatment by a charity physician, and had died earlier that day, apparently from some sort of throttling spasm. For a dollar, Thunstone gained permission to visit the squalid death-chamber.

The body was gone, and Thunstone probed into every corner of the room. He found the ripped mattress, pulled away the flap of ticking and studied the rectangular recess among the wads of ancient padding. A book had been there. He touched the place—it had a strange chill. Then he turned quickly, gazing across the room.

Some sort of shape had been there, a shape that faded as he turned, but which left an impression. Thunstone whistled softly.

"Mrs. Harlan couldn't get the book," he decided. "Thorne came—and succeeded. Now, which way to Thorne?"

The street outside was dark. Thunstone stood for a moment in front of the dingy tenement, until he achieved again the sense of something watching, approaching. He turned again, and saw or sensed, the shrinking away of a stealthy shadow. He walked in that direction.

The sense of the presence departed, but he walked on in the same direction, until he had a feeling of aimlessness in the night. Then again he stood, with what unconcern he could make apparent, until there was a whisper in his consciousness of threat. Whirling, he followed it as before. Thus he traveled for several blocks, changing direction once. Whatever was spying upon him or seeking to ambush him, it was retreating toward a definite base of operations... At length he was able to knock upon a certain door in a certain hotel.

Rowley Thorne opened to him, standing very calm and even triumphant in waistcoat and shirtsleeves.

"Come in, Thunstone," he said, in mocking cordiality. "This is more than I had dared hope for."

"I was able to face and chase your hound-thing, whatever it is," Thunstone told him, entering. "It led me here."

"I knew that," nodded Thorne, his shaven head gleaming dully in the brown-seeming light of a single small desk lamp. "Won't you make yourself comfortable? You see," and he took up a shaggy-covered book from the arm of an easy chair, "I am impelled at last to accept the idea of a writing which, literally, tells one everything he needs to know."

"You killed Cavet Leslie for it, didn't you?" inquired Thunstone, and dropped his hat on the bed.

Thorne clicked his tongue. "That's bad luck for somebody, a hat on the bed. Cavet Leslie had outlived everything but a scrap of his physical self. Somewhere he's outliving that, for I take it that his experiences and studies have unfitted his soul for any conventional hereafter. But he left me a rather amusing legacy." And he dropped his eyes to the open book.

"I should be flattered that you concentrated first of all in immobilizing me," observed Thunstone, leaning his great shoulder against the doorjamb.

"Flattered? But surely not surprised. After all, you've hampered me again and again in reaping a harvest of—"

"Come off it, Thorne. You're not even honest as a worshiper of evil. You don't care whether you establish a cult of Satan or not."

Thorne pursued his hard lips. "I venture to say you're right. I'm not a zealot. Cavet Leslie was. He entered the Deep School—know about it?"

"I do," Thunstone told him. "Held in a cellar below a cellar—somewhere on this continent. I'll find it some day, and put an end to the curriculum."

"Leslie entered the Deep School," Thorne continued, "and finished all the study it had to offer. He finished himself as a being capable of happiness, too. He could not look at the light, or summon the strength to walk, or even sit. Probably death was a relief to him—though, not knowing what befell him after death, we cannot be certain. What I'm summing up to is that he endured that wretched life underground to get the gift of this text book. Now I have it, without undergoing so dreadful an ordeal. Don't reach out for it, Thunstone. You couldn't read it, anyway."

He held it forward, open. The pages showed dull and blank.

"They're written in letters of cold fire," reminded Thunstone. "Letters that show only in the dark."

"Shall we make it dark, then?"

Thorne switched off the lamp.

Thunstone, who had not stirred from his lounging stance at the door, was aware at once that the room was most completely sealed. Blackness was absolute in it. He could not even judge of dimension or direction. Thorne spoke again, from the midst of the choking gloom:

"Clever of you, staying beside the door. Do you want to try to leave?"

"It's no good running away from evil," Thunstone replied. "I didn't come to run away again."

"But try to open the door," Thorne almost begged, and Thunstone put out his hand to find the knob. There was no knob, and no door. Of a sudden, Thunstone was aware that he was not leaning against a doorjamb any more. There was no doorjamb, or other solidity, against which to lean.

"Don't you wish you knew where you were?" jeered Thorne. "I'm the only one who knows, for it's written here on the page for me to see—in letters of cold fire."

Thunstone took a stealthy step in the direction of the voice. When

Thorne spoke again, he had evidently fallen back out of reach.

"Shall I describe the place for you, Thunstone? It's in the open somewhere. A faint breeze blows," and as he spoke, Thunstone felt the breeze, warm and feeble and foul as the breath of some disgusting little animal. "And around us are bushes and trees. They're part of a thick growth, but just here they are sparse. Because, not more than a dozen steps away, is open country. I've brought you to the borderland of a most interesting place, Thunstone, merely by speaking of it."

Thunstone took another step. His feet were on loose earth, not on carpet. A pebble turned and rattled under his shoe-sole.

"You're where you always wanted to be," he called to Thorne. "Where by saying a thing, you can make it so. But many things will need to be said before life suits you." He tried a third step, silently this time. "Who will believe?"

"Everybody will believe." Thorne was almost airy. "Once a fact is demonstrated, it is no longer wonderful. Hypnotism was called magic in its time, and became accepted science. So it is being achieved with thought transference, by experimentation at Duke University and on radio programs in New York. So it will be when I tell of my writings, very full and very clear—but haven't we been too long in utter darkness?"

On the instant, Thunstone could see a little. Afterwards he tried to decide what color that light, or mock-light, actually was. Perhaps it was a lizardy green, but he was never sure. It revealed, ever so faintly, the leafless stunted growths about him, the bare dry-seeming ground from which they sprang, the clearing beyond them. He could not be sure of horizon or sky.

Something moved, not far off. Thorne, by the silhouette. Thunstone saw the flash of Thorne's eyes, as though they gave their own light.

"This country," Thorne said, "may be one of several places. Another dimension—do you believe in more dimensions than these? Or a spirit world of some kind. Or another age of the world we know. I brought you here, Thunstone, without acting or even speaking—only by reading in my book."

Thunstone carefully slid a hand inside his pocket. His forefinger touched something smooth, heavy, rectangular. He knew what it was—a lighter, given him on an occasion of happy gratitude by Sharon, the Countess Monteseco.

"Cold fire," Thorne was saying. "These letters and words are of a language known only in the Deep School—but the sight of them is enough to convey knowledge. Enough, also, to create and direct. This land is spacious enough, don't you think, to support other living creatures than ourselves?"

Thunstone made out blots of black gloom in the green gloom of the clearing. Immense, gross blots, that moved slowly but knowingly toward the bushes. And somewhere behind him a great massive bulk made a dry crashing in the strange shrubbery.

"Are such things hungry?" mused Thorne. "They will be, if I make them so by a thought. Thunstone, I think I've done enough to occupy you. Now I'm ready to leave you here, also by a thought—taking with me the book with letters of cold fire. You can't have that cold fire—"

"I have warm fire," said Thunstone, and threw himself.

It was a powerful lunge, unthinkably swift. Thunstone is, among other things, a trained athlete. His big body crashed against Thorne's, and the two of them grappled and went sprawling among the brittle twigs of one of the bushes. As Thorne fell, undermost, he flung up the hand that held the book, as if to put it out of Thunstone's reach. But Thunstone's hand shot out, too, and it held something—the lighter. A flick of his thumb, and flame sprang out, warm orange flame in a sudden spurting tongue that for a moment licked into the coarse shaggy hair of the untanned hide that bound the book.

Thorne howled, and dropped the thing. A moment later, he pulled loose and jumped up. Thunstone was up, too, moving to block Thorne off from the book. Flame grew and flurried behind him, into a paler light, as if burning something fat and rotten.

"It'll be ruined!" cried Thorne, and hurled himself low, like a blocker on the football field. An old footballer himself, Thunstone crouched, letting his hard knee-joint come in contact with Thorne's incharging bald skull. With a grunt, Thorne fell flat, rolled over and came erect again.

"Put out that fire, Thunstone!" he bawled. "You may destroy us both!"

"I'll chance that," Thunstone muttered, moving again to fence him off from the burning book.

Thorne returned to the struggle. One big hand made a talon of itself, snatching at Thunstone's face. Thunstone ducked beneath the hand, jammed his own shoulder up under the pit of the lifted arm, and heaved. Thorne staggered back, stumbled. He fell, and came to his hands and knees, waiting. His face, upturned to Thunstone, was like a mask of horror carved to terrorize the worshipers in some temple of demons.

It was plain to see that face, for the fire of the book blazed up with a last ardent leap of radiance. Then it died. Thunstone, taking time to glance, saw only glowing charred fragments of leaves, and ground them with a quick thrust of his heel.

Darkness again, without even the green mock-light. Thunstone felt no breeze, heard no noise of swaying bushes or stealthy, ponderous shape-movement—he could not even hear Thorne's breathing.

He took a step sidewise, groping. His hand found a desk-edge, then the standard of a small lamp. He found a switch and pressed it.

Again he was in Thorne's hotel room, and Thorne was groggily rising to his feet.

When Thorne had cleared his head by shaking it, Thunstone had taken a sheaf of papers from the desk and was glancing quickly through them.

"Suppose," he said, gently but loftily, "that we call the whole thing a little trick of imagination."

"If you call it that, you will be lying," Thorne said between set teeth on which blood was smeared.

"A lie told in a good cause is the whitest of lies... this writing would be a document of interest if it would convince."

"The book," muttered Thorne. "The book would convince. I whisked you to a land beyond imagination, with only a grain of the power that book held."

"What book?" inquired Thunstone. He looked around. "There's no book."

"You set it afire. It burned, in that place where we fought—its ashes remain, while we come back here because its power is gone."

Thunstone glanced down at the papers he had picked up. "Why talk of burning things? I wouldn't burn this set of notes for anything. It will attract other attentions than mine."

His eyes rose to fix Thorne's. "Well, you fought me again, Thorne. And I turned you back."

"He who fights and runs away—" Rowley Thorne found the

strength to laugh. "You know the rest, Thunstone. You have to let me run away this time, and at our next fight I'll know better how to deal with you."

"You shan't run away," said Thunstone. He put a cigarette in his mouth and kindled it with the lighter he still held in his hand.

Thorne hooked his heavy thumbs in his vest. "You'll stop me? I think not. Because we're back in conventional lands, Thunstone."

"If you lay hands on me again, it'll be a fight to the death. We're both big and strong. You might kill me, but I'd see that you did. Then you'd be punished for murder. Perhaps executed." Thorne's pale, pointed tongue licked his hard lips. "Nobody would believe you if you tried to explain."

"No, nobody would believe," agreed Thunstone gently. "That's why I'm leaving you to do the explaining."

"I!" cried Thorne, and laughed again. "Explain what? To whom?"

"On the way here," said Thunstone, "I made a plan. In the lobby downstairs, I telephoned for someone to follow me—no, not the police. A doctor. This will be the doctor now."

A slim, gray-eyed man was coming in. Behind him moved two blocky, watchful attendants in white jackets. Silently Thunstone handed the doctor the papers that he had taken from the desk.

The doctor looked at the first page, then the second. His gray eyes brightened with professional interest. Finally he approached Thorne.

"Are you the gentleman Mr. Thunstone asked me to see?" he inquired. "You—yes, you look rather weary and overwrought. Perhaps a rest, with nothing to bother you—"

Thorne's face writhed. "You! You dare to suggest!" He made a threatening gesture, but subsided as the two white-coated men moved toward him from either side. "You're insolent," he went on, more quietly. "I'm no more crazy than you are."

"Of course not," agreed the doctor. He looked at the notes again, grunted, folded the sheets and stowed them carefully in an inside pocket. Thunstone gave a little nod of general farewell, took his hat from the bed, and strolled carelessly out.

"Of course, you're not crazy," said the doctor again. "Only—tired. Now, if you'll answer a question or two—"

"What questions?" blazed Thorne.

"Well, is it true that you believe you can summon spirits and work miracles, merely by exerting your mind?"

Thorne's wrath exploded, hysterically. "You'd soon see what I could do if I had that book!"

"What book?"

Thunstone destroyed it—burned it—"

"Oh, please!" begged the doctor good-naturedly. "You're talking about John Thunstone, you know! There isn't any book, there never was a book. You need a rest, I tell you. Come along."

Thorne howled like a beast and clutched at his tormentor. The doctor moved smoothly out of reach.

"Bring him to the car," said the doctor to the two men in white coats. At once they slid in to close quarters, each clutching one of Thorne's arms. He snarled and struggled, but the men, with practiced skill, clamped and twisted his wrists. Subdued, he walked out between them because he must.

Thunstone and the Countess Monteseco were having cocktails at their favorite rear table in a Forty-seventh Street restaurant. They were known and liked there, and not even a waiter would disturb them unless signaled for.

"Tell me," said the countess, "what sort of fantastic danger were you tackling last night?"

"I was in no danger," John Thunstone smiled.

"But I know you were. I went to the concert, and then the reception, but all the time I had the most overpowering sense of your struggle and peril. I was wearing the cross you gave me, and I held it in my hand and prayed for you—prayed hour after hour—"

"That," said Thunstone, "was why I was in no danger."

HORROR AT VECRA

BY HENRY HASSE

...an ancient evil that will not die,
but draws men, soul and brain,
The pale stars peering fearfully down
remember whence it came.
The very darkness where *They* wait
doth shudder at the Name...

—*Monstres and Their Kynde*

NOW, AFTER TWELVE YEARS, VAGUE REPORTS ARE ISSUING
again from the vicinity of Vecra. As yet they are little more than rumors,
but they have served to awaken the remote horror in my brain—horror,
for I now realize I must have failed, a dozen years ago, when I stood
there on that brink of madness for a few hell-filled seconds.

I used dynamite then—enough of it, I thought—and believed that
was the end. Now I can only wonder if this is the same evil, or some
spawn of it that will never die. Perhaps even now it is not too late. I
have kept silence, but now I shall tell my story and if I cannot then
enlist aid, I will myself... But lest I become too incoherent, I had best
begin on that day a dozen years ago.

Bruce Tarleton and I were returned to Boston from a two-week
camping trip. Bruce was driving, and before very long I began to suspect
that he had taken the wrong fork back at North Eaton; though he
maintained a stolid silence as the dirt road became gradually narrower

and ruttier. I had a disquieting feeling that it was luring us on and on into this strange New England back-country.

Our way twisted through gloomy stretches of forest where limbs hung low over the road—they seemed strangely gnarled and misshapen. Queer patches of colorless vegetation pressed in upon us. We crossed narrow wooden bridges whose loose planks rumbled beneath us as the car rolled slowly over them. We dipped into shallow valleys where the evening sunshine seemed oddly depressing and not as bright as it should be.

For the most part these valleys seemed barren and rock-strewn, but after a while we came upon occasional poorly tilled fields and square, ungainly, unpainted farmhouses. These were set upon slopes far back from the road, reminding me of nothing so much as dead things sprawled there in that unhealthy sunshine.

Neither of us had spoken much since leaving North Eaton, but I somehow got the impression that Bruce was secretly enjoying all this. At last we rumbled across a rickety wooden bridge, followed the turn of the road to the right, and with startling suddenness found ourselves in a little village. My first impression was one of surprise that it should be there at all; then, without exactly knowing why, I knew that I loathed the place.

"I guess this is Vecra," Bruce said, almost to himself.

"How do you know that?"

He turned and looked at me queerly. "Huh? Why, the sign—at the other end of the bridge back there. Didn't you see it?"

I looked at him suspiciously. No, I hadn't seen it; and I thought that was strange, because for the last twenty miles I had been watching for some such sign of a town. But I didn't say anything—instead, I looked about me. Vecra had evidently been at one time a more prosperous town than present indications showed. A score of frame houses lined each side of the road that was the main street; but now most of them were desolate, empty and weather-beaten, long since fallen into a state of sad decay. Only in a scattered few did we see pitiful enough signs of habitation, as oil lamps gleamed meagerly in the approaching dusk. Those lamps seemed no more meager than our own gloomy situation. Apparently the only way out of this forsaken country was back along the road we had traveled, and the prospect of retracing that route at night did not appeal to me!

We stopped at what appeared to be the general store, to inquire where we might stay overnight. A small, bent, leathery old man shuffled toward us as we entered. I took an immediate dislike to him. Maybe it was his suspicious black eyes that peered from beneath a tangle of dirty white hair. Maybe it was his quaint old dialect, and the way he seemed to be secretly enjoying something at our expense.

"Lost yur way, hev ye, young fellers? I seed ye drive up out there, an' I reckoned as haow that war the case; ain't many outside uns has call ter come thissaway, ceptin' them as takes the wrong rud back at Naorth Eaton." He peered closer at us and chuckled. "Them as does, alius comes cleer on ter Vecra, acause thur ain't no other way they *kin* come." I glanced nervously at Bruce, but saw that he was listening with intense interest to the old man's archaic speech. After another evil chuckle, he went on:

"Naow, as I war sayin', folks as gits up ter Vecra in daylight most alius goes back to Naorth Eaton. An' them as gets up here by dark... they be mostly skeered ter travel back afore mornin'." He leered at us with yellowish, bloodshot eyes. "Which be ye?"

"I guess we'll stay over for the night," I said hurriedly, "if there's someone who will be kind enough..."

"Yep! Reckon Eb Corey kin fix ye up fer the night. His place be easy ter find—the big haouse daown't end o' the rud. Tell Eb thet Lyle Wilson sent ye."

As we went out the door I looked back and saw the old man still leering at us. Although I couldn't hear him, I imagined he was chuckling evilly again.

"I don't like him," I said to Bruce.

Bruce chuckled, and it didn't sound much better than the old man's. "I do. He's certainly a queer old bird. I think I'll come down here tomorrow and have a longer talk with him."

We found the Corey place without any trouble. Eb Corey, a tall, gaunt, slow-speaking man, received us stolidly. However, I imagined his wife was vaguely perturbed. There was something tragic about her, especially in her eyes, as though she had been haunted a long time ago and had never quite forgotten. She served us a plain but substantial meal, and we ate appreciatively. The room was large and appeared to me as definitely nineteenth century, including the smell; it was lighted by only two or three oil lamps, and shadows clung to the far corners. The room seemed full of dozens of children of all sizes, though we learned later there were only five. As their mother sent them upstairs to bed, they peered back at us curiously through the stair banister.

"Many outsiders up this way?" Bruce asked at last, when we had finished the meal.

"Last was a few months ago," Corey replied. He seemed reluctant to talk.

Bruce lit his pipe and blew a wreath of smoke at the ceiling. His next words were so abrupt and inventive they startled even me.

"I hear you've got some mighty queer land hereabouts. I'm a government soil inspector—sent up from Boston." I gaped at the lie, knowing he was nothing of the kind; but he sent me a silencing look.

About land, especially about his land, and most particularly about what was *wrong* with his land, Eb Corey was more than willing to talk. For an hour or more they talked, while I smoked cigarettes in silence and listened amazedly to the technical knowledge of soil that Bruce displayed. He was a professor of languages at Boston College, a far cry from an expert in soil conditions; but then, I had learned always to expect the unexpected from Bruce Tarleton.

Before retiring, we went out to move the car. We came back in time to hear Mrs. Corey remonstrating with her husband; it seemed to have something to do with our sleeping quarters. Corey was shaking his head stubbornly, and Mrs. Corey retired from the argument as we entered.

"It's that room in the back wing upstairs," Eb explained as he led the way up the worn wooden stairs, lamp in hand. "There's been some tale about it for more'n fifty years—Martha's made me keep it locked lately. My grandfather built this place, added the wing later."

"Not haunted, is it?" Bruce asked with a show of jocularity. I noticed the falseness of his tone, the suppressed excitement, but Eb Corey did not.

"Naw!" he said. "The story's got something to do with a funny kind of dream people sometimes have when they sleep in that room; I don't know what it is. Martha says she does, but she won't talk about it. I slept in there a couple of times, but I never had any dream."

"That's all right," Bruce said. "I don't dream either."

"I knew a scientific man like you wouldn't put up with such stock. There's only a small cot in there that one of you can use—and then there's another small room across the hall. Sorry I can't offer you better."

I looked about me dubiously as we passed along a narrow hall toward the rear of the old house. The lamplight made a pale, moving pattern on the papered walls that were worn smooth and brown from the contact of generations. I stopped at my door, and Bruce went along to his, which directly faced the length of the hall. Eb unlocked that door and said, "I'll be out in the south field tomorrow, Mr. Tarleton; hope you'll come out and take a look at the soil."

I saw Bruce nod, and I waited until Eb Corey made his way expertly back downstairs in the dark. Then I quickly crossed the hall to where Bruce stood with the lamp in his hand. "I don't like this at all," I began. "What's this business about you being..."

"Come on in here, and I'll tell you."

Everywhere in this house I had been aware of that dank, age-old, peculiar odor. I might almost call it a *yellow* odor. I had smelled it in other old houses. But the moment we entered this upstairs room it seemed magnified, became almost tangible. The place seemed half bedroom and half store room. One side was piled haphazardly with trunks, boxes, broken tables and chairs. Bruce held the lamp high, looked around, and grinned most delightedly.

Already he had espied a tall, clumsy bookcase in the far corner. He strode over to it, and examined the faded tomes. Quickly he pulled one out, then another, and another. I groaned. I might have known this. Bruce had had this detour planned all the time; he had come up here deliberately. I sat down on a rickety chair and watched him. Finally I said, "All right, what is it this time? And don't give me any more of that *Necronomicon* stuff, for I know that's a myth." Bruce was an authority on certain terrible lores and forbidden books dealing with such lores, and he had told me things from a certain *Necronomicon* that literally made my flesh crawl.

"What?" he said in answer to my question. "Why look at these! Not *Necronomicons*, but most interesting!" He thrust a couple of worn, leather-bound volumes into my hands. I glanced at the titles. One was *Horride Mysteries* by the Marquis of Grosse; the other, *Nemedian*

Chronicles. I looked up at Bruce, and saw that he was genuinely excited.

"Do you mean to say," I said, "that you really didn't expect to find these?"

"Of course not! I'll admit I came up here deliberately because I've heard certain rumors..."

"Something to do with a dream?"

"No, nothing to do with a dream. And I'm as surprised as you are to see these books. These two I've seen before in expurgated editions. But *this* I've never seen before, although I've heard vaguely of it." He looked fondly at a third book he held, and I could see that his eyes were aglow with a sort of wild anticipation.

I reached for the tome, and he relinquished it almost reluctantly. It was huge, heavy, and the pages were brittle and brown. There was no title on the spine or cover, but on the first page I read in a delicate, faded script: M-O-N-S-T-R-E-S A-N-D T-H-E-I-R K-Y-N-D-E. Each word was in script capital letters, free of each other. No author was mentioned. I placed the book on my knees and saw that the edges of the leather binding were well worn, frayed in places. As I turned a few pages at random, a powdery brown dust blew out and lodged in my nose. I sneezed.

"Hey, be careful how you handle that!" Bruce took the volume back solicitously as a mother with her child. I took one more look around the room, sniffed the air distastefully, and said, "I'm getting sleepy. Good night."

I don't think he even heard me. When I left him there, to cross the hall into my own room, he was sitting hunched over the table by the oil lamp, opening *Monstres and Their Kynde* tenderly, peering down into it.

The next morning I was downstairs early only to be informed by Mrs. Corey that Bruce had preceded me. He had eaten hastily and said he was going down the road to see Lyle Wilson. She pronounced the name distastefully, and I could see that she didn't like the old man. I didn't blame her.

I waived breakfast, my only concern being to get out of this morbid town as soon as possible. I was doomed to disappointment, however. Upon reaching Lyle Wilson's store, I saw that Bruce and the old man had been talking in what appeared to be a mutual earnestness, if not eagerness. I came up in time to hear the latter say:

"I'm sartinly glad yew intend ter stick araound a mite. Ain't many outside uns hankers ter do thet. I've heerd more nor one o' 'em calc'late as haow the sunshine, an' the land, an' all araound here be sorta unhealthy like..." He stopped a moment when I came up; then went on with renewed eagerness, as if he didn't often have such an audience. "An' leave me tell ye suthin', young sirs–they may be *right*. Thur be sartin things I could tell abaout the cause o' it, tew–things sech as ye'd never b'lieve. But mark ye this: they be more in this waorld nor meets the eye, an' they be other things asides them as walks on top th' graound..." He looked from one to the other of us, grinning, and I moved back a pace to avoid his obnoxious breath.

But Bruce, to my surprise, said, "You mean things such as..." And he pronounced a word that I wouldn't even attempt. Lyle Wilson's eyes popped out in amazement. He looked at Bruce with a sudden startled suspicion.

"I read about it," Bruce hurried to explain, "in a book called *Monstres and Their Kynde.*" He regarded the old man carefully, to see the effect his words would have.

The effect was one of relief. "Oh, *thet* book. It aren't much. Belonged to old Hans Zickler–Eb Corey's grandfather–he thet built the haouse. But d'ye know, I got a better book than thet..." He chuckled in a way that sent a cold chill up my spine. He paused and peered at Bruce as though waiting for him to exhibit some curiosity, but Bruce wisely did not.

"I'll tell ye anyway. I got old Zick's *diary!* Eb Corey, he used ter hev it, but real suddint one day he told me as he war goin' ter burn it. I reckon as haow he had been readin' inter it. I asked Eb fer it, an' I guess he war more'n glad ter give me it as payment fer some things he war owin'. Said he didn't keer what become o' it, ceptin' as *he* wouldn't have it in his haouse no longer."

Now I could see Bruce's curiosity surge up, and his voice bordered almost on excitement. "You say you still have this diary?"

"Yep. Reckon I be the only person thet's ever seed inter it, ceptin' Eb Corey hisself, and I dun't think he read *much* o' it. He thought 'twar only the old man's crazy ravin's." Wilson's voice became confidential. "D'ye know, I'm kinda glad you fellers dropped by. Folk here-abaout wun't lissen ter me. Acause they be *scairt* to, thet's what; they be scairt o' what I could tell 'em abaout ol' Zickler an'–an' sartin things I seed 'im do. Things thet–thet warn't jest right. But sometimes when I gets ter ponderin', an' rememb'rin', an' readin' in the diary agin, thur comes a kinda *hankerin'* like; an' I wanta try, so's I kin know them things too, like ol' Zick did. An' sometimes the hankerin' gits too strong like..."

He stopped suddenly, as though afraid he would go too far, and a wild light died slowly out of his eyes.

"O' course," he went on more calmly, "I war jest a young un then, when I spied on ol' Zick, but I remembers right enough. An' even ef the land *dew* be gittin' better every year, an' things araound here ain't so bad as they used ter be, they's *still* suthin' abaout an' active oncet in a while. Look't the young Munroe boy, he as they claim wandered off an' fell daown in the ravine. But I knows a heap better. Ef he fell daown the ravine whyn't they ever find the body?" He moved his stool closer to Bruce, leered at him and repeated almost defiantly: "Eh? Whyn't they ever find the body?" The old man chuckled delightedly at the sensation he had made.

I was becoming considerably annoyed at all this crazy gibberish. I told Bruce I was going back to the house. He nodded absently. As I left, he hunched forward, listening intently as Lyle Wilson started on another wild trend.

At noon Bruce showed up for lunch, seemingly preoccupied and puzzled about something. I wondered what further stories he had succeeded in getting out of Lyle Wilson. I suddenly remembered, too, something I had intended to ask Bruce, but had forgotten. So, half facetiously, I asked: "Well, did you dream last night?"

Eb Corey, who had come in from the fields, looked at me curiously but not angrily. Mrs. Corey, however, shot me a look that made me wish I hadn't asked the question. Nevertheless we all awaited Bruce's answer—she most anxiously of all.

"Yes," he said, "I did. And that's peculiar, because I usually never dream. Maybe it was because I was up pretty late reading in those books..."

At the mention of the books Mrs. Corey looked at Bruce quickly, quizzically.

"Oh," Bruce said. "I'm sorry if I wasn't suppose to look at them, but you see I'm interested in that kind of lore."

"It's all right. Please go on."

"Sure," I reminded him, "what about the dream? But I suppose you don't remember it. Most people don't..."

"But I do. It was just a fragment of a dream really, but too vivid for me to forget. It seemed that I was walking somewhere in a sort of mist. Down a narrow dirt road. There was a rusty wire fence to my right, and I came to a gap in it. Automatically I turned and passed through it, and walked down a path behind a large house..." Bruce turned to me and smiled, as though he were reciting a fairy story to a child. "All this while, mind you, something was drawing me—I wasn't walking of my own volition. I knew I should make an effort to run back, but at the same time, paradoxically, I seemed very anxious to get to whatever was drawing me. Well... the path was tangled with coarse grass and weeds, and suddenly I saw where I was walking: in a graveyard. All around me were tombstones, but not stones really, for most of them were ancient nameboards of wood, inclining at all angles and overgrown with weeds and brambles. Then—right before me—I saw a low cement tomb. It was cracked and moss-covered, but the wooden door was still solid, and the huge iron hinges, though rusty, were still intact. I stood a moment before that door; now I felt a very strong attraction, almost an *affinity*, to—to whatever lay beyond. I don't doubt that I would have entered—in fact, I was just about to—but at that moment I awoke. I was lying on my cot upstairs and a cool breeze was coming in the window at my head. I closed the window and went back to sleep, but I didn't dream any more."

I glanced at Mrs. Corey. She had sat there taut and silent as Bruce talked. Now she was biting her lips as though to keep from screaming, but the scream showed in her eyes. She rose in sudden agitation and left the room.

Her husband continued eating for a moment in silence. Then he looked up, unperturbed, and said: "Martha's easy upset. But maybe there's good reason. You see, she had a sister that slept in that room once, and she dreamed that same dream, and then—she just disappeared. No trace ever found of her. Before that, it was the Munroe boy—I remember it like it was yesterday."

"Yes, Lyle Wilson was telling me about the Munroe boy's disappearance," said Bruce. "Do you know anything about it?"

"Nothing except he was playing out in the fields near the ravine, and he disappeared. We searched, but no trace of him. Then—it must have been all of a week later—his younger brother came running home and said he'd seen Willie's face, with a lot of others."

"His face!" Bruce sat bolt upright. "Is that what he said?"

"Yep, that's all he could say. He'd seen his brother's face, with a lot of others. Said he'd been playing down in the ravine, but he didn't know just where."

Bruce looked at me, and he wasn't smiling now. Corey seemed to take everything stoically. "Of course," he went on, "it used to be horses and cattle that disappeared—no trace. This all happened some few years ago. The land was pretty bad, then, too, but hasn't been so bad since. Not 'til just recent."

"What do you think of all this, Eb?"

Eb Corey looked at Bruce stolidly. "Mr. Tarleton, you're a scientific man. I'm just trying to make a living here off of land that—that ain't right, somehow. You said that books like them upstairs is a kind of hobby of yours. Then you oughta know more about all of this than I do. I looked into one of them books once—just once. I can say this: I didn't understand much of it, but I know such studyin' won't bring you to no good end. But that's your affair. Me—I just try not to think too much about it." That's the longest speech I ever heard Eb Corey make, and it seemed definite enough. Bruce apparently thought so, too, for he said, "I think I'll come out there a little later this afternoon and take a look at your soil."

"Wish you would, Mr. Tarleton, wish you would. You'll find me down on the south end."

I had listened to all this in silence, but something was bothering me, almost haunting me. I couldn't get it out of my mind. *Bruce's dream.* I arose from the table and left them there, still talking; and went upstairs, wondering just what it was about that dream that bothered me. The path across the old graveyard... the ancient tomb... something drawing him on...

On a sudden impulse I entered that room where Bruce had slept. A faded green blind was still drawn over the single window. I raised the blind. Even before I looked, I knew. Then I looked and saw. The scene swept across my brain like a dash of icy water. As I stood there momentarily paralyzed, I felt the first hint of the cosmic horror that was soon to engulf both Bruce and myself, and come near to blasting my mind.

There was the narrow dirt road, to the left. There was the rusty wire fence. The broken gap. There was the grass-tangled path, and the fallen tombstones in the ancient graveyard just behind this house. And there was the cracked cement tomb, just as Bruce had described it from his dream, only a short distance away from this window...

A few hours later, as we walked across the fields, I told Bruce what I had discovered—the graveyard behind the house, and the exact parallel to his dream. He wasn't surprised, said he'd seen it, too.

"I suppose you're beginning to think that what I experienced wasn't a dream at all—that I actually walked down that path toward the tomb. Well, you're wrong. It was nothing but a dream; I know I never left my room..." He seemed for a moment about to tell me more, then changed his mind.

But I was, by now, very curious; not with the avidity of a student of the ancient lores such as Bruce displayed, but with a certain skepticism. "Did Lyle Wilson tell you any more stories? What about that diary—I know you were dying to see it?"

"I saw it—but not enough of it. He brought it out and read me certain parts. Remember his saying he had a certain *hankerin'* sometimes? Well, I told him I often had a sort of *hankerin'*, too. Then he brought out the diary."

"A hankerin' for *what*, in heaven's name?"

"I don't know—but I'm afraid it isn't in heaven's name. Whatever *he* was talking about. That's what I wanted to find out."

"And did you?"

"Very little. I got too curious, I guess, and Lyle got suspicious. Still, he read me quite a few passages from that diary of Hans Zickler's, and I'm beginning to piece things together. Remember Corey saying his grandfather built this house, and added the back wing later? Well, that's right. Maybe you noticed the wing brings that room pretty close to the edge of the graveyard?"

"What about the diary?" I insisted.

"Well, I learned this much. Old Zickler used to sit at the window of that upstairs back room, in the late evenings, and mumble a kind of gibberish. That window's easily visible from the road; neighbors passing by soon got the idea that Zickler was crazy. Lyle Wilson says that he was just a young man then, but he remembers seeing old Zick sitting there—could hear him, too—and he was certainly a wild sight. Well... it seems that there was something in that tomb, and Zickler suggested that it had *answered* him—but in a strange way. Not audibly, but mentally. A sort of unearthly telepathy, I guess. Old Zick couldn't explain it quite right. All I can gather is that it was *teaching* Zickler something, and that occasionally it *thanked* him for something. I'd certainly like to read more in that part of the diary, but old Lyle is too shrewd.

"Along about that time, a lot of livestock was disappearing. And a few children. It seems that Zickler had them all carefully recorded, but it's hard to place any of these circumstances consecutively; as Lyle read to me he kept skipping about in the diary haphazardly, looking up every once in a while to see what impression it made.

"There was one place where Zickler hinted at being dissatisfied and restless and wanting to learn more, but to do that he would have to look up a certain passage in the *Necronomicon*. He mentioned saving his money so he could take a trip over to Arkham, to look into the copy of the *Necronomicon* it is rumored they have hidden away in the Miskatonic University there. But evidently he never did make the trip. At least, there's no mention of it, and Lyle tells me that Zick never left Vecra. Died a natural death here, though he was mumbling bizarre things on his deathbed."

We walked on to the south field, where we found Eb Corey busily plowing. He stopped for a while and watched Bruce poking around in the ground at various spots.

"I'll bet you never saw any soil like that before," Eb said grimly as Bruce straightened up with a sample.

"You'd win that bet all right. Look at this stuff, will you?" And Bruce handed a clod to me. It was the most peculiar looking soil I had ever seen—a queer grayish color, almost powdery, though it wasn't dry. More like slightly damp ashes. It seemed tainted somehow, and evil—even felt tainted to the touch, not like fresh clean earth should. I dropped it, repressing a shudder, and wiped my fingers clean.

Bruce looked at Eb in amazement. "Do you mean to say that things grow in this?"

"Oh, sure. Tain't near so bad down on this end as it is closer to the house."

"Closer to the old graveyard, you mean?"

Eb looked at Bruce, then shrugged. "Well, same thing. Not as bad as it was in my grandfather's day, either. Only thing is, stuff don't quite get to normal size somehow; and often as not, I raise some things that are might—well, queer, distorted like. But it all seems eatable enough."

"I wonder what your grandfather thought about this land. He must have had some idea about it..."

Eb shrugged again. "No telling what grandfather Zickler thought, especially in his last years. He was half crazy then, everybody knew that. All I can say is, he was drove to it—or drove hisself to it. I remember him saying once that the land didn't belong to us nohow. And the way he said it, he didn't mean just this little piece of land—he meant all the land everywhere, I guess. It give me the creeps the way he used to talk. Said something about we was here just temporary, like, and someday *They* would wake and claim the land that was rightfully theirs. He used to mention *They* sort of reverent like."

There was an awakened light of interest in Bruce's eyes as he tried to press this point. "He didn't say how or when this was to happen? He didn't mention certain names, such as—Lloigor? Or B'Moth? Or Ftakhar?"

But Eb didn't seem to remember. Old Zickler had spoken too many queer words. Bruce put a sample of that evil soil in an envelope, and before we left he asked one more question, "Eb, do you remember Lyle Wilson taking a trip to Arkham fairly recently? Maybe he said something about visiting the Miskatonic University library...?"

"Nope," Eb shook his head. Then he seemed to remember something. "Maybe you mean that time a little more than a year ago; Wilson made a trip then, was gone two or three days, but he never breathed a word to anybody where he'd been."

"Thanks." Bruce seemed deeply immersed in thought. Corey resumed his plowing, and Bruce and I cut across a field toward the ravine. It was quite steep where we reached it, full of small trees and scrub bushes. In the direction of the house, however, a quarter of a mile away, it shallowed into a little gully that ended by the edge of the old graveyard. Bruce looked intently down into the ravine for a moment, then turned away.

"What did you mean by those names you asked Corey?" I said, as we walked back to the house. "And what do they mean? Lord knows I won't attempt to pronounce them the way you did!" And I laughed.

Bruce didn't laugh.

"What do they mean?" he repeated. His voice was different than I had ever heard it. "I had come almost to believe that they meant nothing, that they were only names. But now—my god, I'm beginning to believe again. Do there really exist embodiments of those names? Perhaps old Zickler knew. And others, from time to time. After all, those names and the rumors and the books *do* persist through the years, and where there is legend there is a basis of fact, if only it could be traced back through the eons."

That was all I got from Bruce. But he didn't need to tell me more. For a long time I had been aware, disinterestedly, of his study of ancient lores. I knew he had in his library a certain shelf of old books, besides scores of fiction pieces on the subject. I had read a few of the fiction pieces, and was amused. Deep in my mind was the safe and comfortable knowledge that they *were* fiction and nothing more.

But now I wasn't so sure, and I didn't feel so safe. Perhaps all that fiction, after all, *had* been based on—on something I didn't like to think of. My vague perturbation was enhanced by the way Bruce had said those words: "But now—my god, I'm beginning to believe again!"

Just how much Bruce believed, I don't know. Nor what he was trying to learn, nor why he left his room that night. I doubt now if I could have acted in any way to stop him, even if I had known. The one fact I see clearly now is that neither of us then realized how slowly and insidiously everything was building up to that tragic climax...

That night after supper, Bruce went upstairs to his room—intending, he said, to look more carefully into those ancient books. I stepped outdoors to smoke my pipe; somehow I always enjoy it more outdoors and at night—it helps me to think, and that's what I needed to do. In a muddled sort of way I was trying to decide how much of this "ancient lore" business I dared, and how much I feared, to believe. I only knew that I liked this place less and less, and if Bruce didn't want to leave in the morning, I would take the car myself.

Finding I was nearly out of tobacco, I walked down to Lyle Wilson's store. The place was dark. I stepped onto the porch and was about to try the door, thinking perhaps he hadn't locked up yet; but then

I decided he must be in bed, and I had better wait until morning. I stepped off the porch and was almost out to the road again, when I heard his front door open. I turned and was about to call out to him... when something stopped me.

It may have been partly intuition, but mainly it was Lyle's actions. I could see him only dimly, and apparently he did not see me at all. But the way he closed his door ever so softly, and crept furtively across the porch interested me. He disappeared around the corner of his store, and I followed.

He passed through a gate at the rear of his property, crossed a field, climbed a low fence into another field. I stayed a safe distance behind him, just keeping him in sight. I could barely make out something that he carried under his arm—apparently a thick book; undoubtedly the diary that both he and Bruce seemed so interested in.

I soon saw that he was heading for the ravine. Undoubtedly he had traveled this route before, because he seemed very sure of his direction and seemed to be heading for a certain point. I lost him in the dark for a moment, hurried forward, bumped into the low-hanging branches of a tree and scratched my face. When I reached the ravine he had disappeared entirely, but I could hear him faintly as he climbed down some path near by. I searched for a few minutes; finally finding it, I descended.

Rather, I skidded, rolled and tumbled down that steep path in the dark, arriving at the bottom by the simple expedient of plunging head first the last five feet. I arose and brushed off my clothes. By that time, Lyle Wilson had disappeared entirely. I couldn't hear a sound, couldn't even guess which direction he'd taken. And if the night were dark before, it was positively Stygian at the bottom of this ravine.

As disgruntled as I was puzzled, I tried to climb back up the path. But I couldn't. I stood there for a minute, nursing my bruises and cursing myself for a fool. Then I remembered that the ravine became shallower until it led out by the edge of the graveyard a quarter of a mile away. The only thing to do was to follow it in that direction. After all, I decided, I might come upon Wilson again.

But I didn't see him. Once I stopped, thinking I heard the sound of metal striking on metal, but I didn't hear it again. I proceeded in the dark, avoiding small clumps of bushes and trees as best I could. It wasn't until I was almost at the graveyard that I remembered—

suddenly, disturbingly—something Eb Corey had said; about the youngest Munroe boy who had been playing in the ravine, and had run home to tell his mother he'd seen his lost brother's face, "with a lot of others."

At the thought of it, I hurried my steps. I cut across a corner of the graveyard to the house. Looking up at the window of the rear room, I saw no light there. Thinking Bruce must be asleep, I went around the house, entered the front door a bit breathlessly, and hurried upstairs.

I had intended to waken Bruce, if necessary, to tell him of Lyle Wilson's nocturnal excursion, for it might mean something to him. I pushed open the door and entered his room, and moved through the darkness to the table and the dimly-seen oil lamp. I searched in my pocket for a match, while with the other hand I fumbled for the lamp.

"Damn!" My searching fingers had found the lamp all right, and I had burned them on the still hot glass chimney. Bruce must have turned it off no more than a few minutes before. I finally managed to light it again, and as the shadows flickered about the room, I saw that Bruce wasn't there at all, nor had his bed been slept in. Perhaps he had stepped out for a breath of air.

On the table one of the heavy tomes lay open, which I recognized as *Monstres and Their Kynde*. Beside it was a soft-leaded pencil. Then I noticed that Bruce apparently had been checking certain passages with the pencil, very lightly on the crisp yellowish pages.

I decided to wait for him, so drew up a chair and began to read those passages which Bruce had so painstakingly marked. Now, after twelve years, I cannot precisely remember those excerpts; but I do know they were in a quaint old English spelling, and the first paragraph to strike my eye was almost as follows:

These be nott manifest, but They do wait in patience for a tyme that ys nott yet. Of a hydeous potency be ye blackeness wherein They dwell, for They do nott always sleep. They be remote one from another; nonetheless They do have a devious yntercourse. Beneath that far Northe, in ye ancient tymes yclept Hyperborea, do They wait. Afar in ye East, beneath vaste plateaus, They be rumoured. In ye new darke lands across ye seas They surely be. Men of ye sea have whispered of unspeakable manifestations on strange islands. Indeede there be fearfulle rumour of ye fate of men who go down with doomed shippes. These Creatures be nameless, but assuredly must They be spawned of ancient B'Moth and Ftakhar, Lloigor and Kathuln and ye others. In silence do They await ye call of those Elder Ones...

I stopped reading there, aware that this all sounded vaguely familiar. I must have read similar things in other old books of Bruce's. I turned a few pages to see if he had checked other passages. He had.

"Some mortals there do be who revere Them, and some fewe also whom They instruct in a certain wyse. One of these was ye Eybon of that ancient Hyperborea, and there have been others." Suddenly startled, I remembered old Zickler sitting at that very window talking a sort of gibberish to something in the tomb, which he hinted had *answered* him. Now I read on, suddenly eager, seeking out those passages which Bruce had marked:

There be divers ways, mostly forgotte, in whych They may be awakened; and it ys *then* that They become resteless and impatient for ye tyme, and provoke Their powers. One of ye ways, as sette down by Eybon in hys Booke, doth follow...

Here there was only the beginning of a long incantation of indistinguishable words. Most of it had faded away, as though from constant reference to this page. As I thought again of old Zickler sitting mumbling at this window, my interest surpassed all previous bounds. I turned back a few pages, to where Bruce had first begun marking.

So evyl They be, that ye lande whych under They lie doth become strangely polluted, and ye very soil dothe crawle, and strangely be ye thynges whych growe thereon... Alhazred in hys chronicle hath avowed: that whomesoever be attracted unto Them (by ye nefarious ynfluence whych They project when invoked), doth remain forever a *parte* of Them, nott dead, but newe and oddly bodied, instructing ye very grounde and adding to ye power of Them... also hath Alhazred said: evyl ye Mynde whych ys helde by no Hedde, and dyre ys ye grounde whych...

For the moment I stopped reading there, and my eyes skipped over to the next page where Bruce seemed to have underlined several of the statements, as if they were of the utmost importance. I read that passage carefully.

But Some there be amonge Them, whych wait resteless and impatient for ye tyme. 'Tis said these fewe do inherit ye Elder Power to attracte unto Them small animals; then ye cattle and smalle children; then ye weake and ye sycke; then whychever men who sleepe close to Them, upon ye whom They do project a kynde of Dreame. 'Tis also said, that whom-so-ever be thusly attracted unto Them, doth become a Part of Them (thate ys to saye, ye All-in-One whych ye Elder Ones await), and doth instruct ye Creatures and ye very grounde in whych They be. In thys wyse (when ye tyme doth come) shall They enjoy ye ultimate consummation; thusly shalle They inherit ye lande again whych once was Theirs.

That is as much as I read. I remembered old Zickler's statement about the earth not belonging to us. I remembered Mrs. Corey's vague hintings of people who had slept in this room, and who had dreamed and then disappeared. I remembered Bruce's dream the previous night, of the graveyard and the tomb behind this house. For perhaps five minutes I sat there in the flickering lamplight, remembering these and other things. Suddenly I leaped to my feet, shuddering, an icy-cold wave of horror sweeping over me. Here I had been sitting waiting for Bruce to come back!

In that moment I knew what I must do. I went leaping down the stairway out into the dark night, and around to the side of the house where we had left the car. The .45 automatic that Bruce usually carried in the glove compartment was gone. So was the flashlight. Anyway, it made no difference now. I found another flashlight in my kit; the batteries were very weak, but I was thankful for it.

I went through the gap in the fence, and down that path behind the house toward the tomb. I remembered Bruce's description of his dream, wherein something had drawn him here against his will. Nothing was drawing *me*, of that I was certain.

How true is the saying, "Fools rush in..."

Not until I was standing right before the tomb did I see that Bruce had indeed been there. The heavy plank door was pulled slightly ajar, making a little arc in the dirt. The iron chain which had held it was now broken. It was a tight squeeze, since the door would open no further, but I finally managed to enter. Flashing my light around, I saw a few mouldering wooden coffins at one side. I scarcely glanced at them. Instead, I examined the cement walls that were damp and musty.

Then I gave a start of surprise. Without quite knowing what I was looking for, I had found it! At the rear of the tomb, I saw a roughly rectangular hole in the cement. Quickly I crossed to it. I flashed my light into a passage that led slightly downward for about ten feet, then seemed to level off. Determined now to go where Bruce had gone, I bent low and squeezed into the passage.

At the bottom of the slight incline, I again flashed my light ahead. Then my heart pounded in excitement and amazement. The passage was narrow, but high enough for a man to stand erect—and it extended far beyond the feeble beam of my flashlight! I moved slowly ahead. Soon I began to distinguish what seemed to be other smaller passages branching off, but what struck me so forcibly was that this main passage seemed to extend *straight toward the ravine*!

There was a stagnant, loathsome stench that seemed to roll over me in tangible waves. I touched the earth walls, and recoiled. It was the same dampish, grayish kind of soil Bruce had examined, but much worse. It was slimy; it seemed to crawl under my touch as though it were alive. I came near then to giving up and going back; but, gritting my teeth, I went on.

My foot struck something hard. I bent, fumbled, and picked it up. It was Bruce's automatic. It still felt faintly warm. I knew it had been fired. Now there was no more doubt—only a vague fear and foreboding. I stood there in that noisome passage, holding the gun that had been fired, wondering what I should do next.

It was decided for me. Just then I heard the sound. Quickly I snapped off the flashlight and stood there in the dark, tense and listening. My heart pounded blood into my ears so that I could hardly hear the sound when it came again. But I heard it all right—faint and far away, not close as I had first thought.

The sound was a voice. A blurred and mumbled voice that seemed to chant, and the chant was a thing obscene and alien for all its vagueness—of that much I was sure. Quite still I stood and listened, and still the sound came, faintly from far away down that passage toward the ravine. It seemed jubilant and joyous; now uttering paeans of praise, now again descending to a garbled undertone of obscene implications that made my flesh crawl, despite that I could distinguish none of the words.

I knew, as I stood there listening to that loathsome ritual, that there were things I should piece together—something to do with Lyle Wilson—but somehow I couldn't remember any more; my thoughts were becoming jumbled and uncertain. Not daring to use the flashlight, I moved warily forward a few more paces.

"Bruce!" I called softly, and listened. Then a bit louder: "Bruce! Can you hear me? You must be in here!"

Then—oh god!—then I heard a sound that was not the chanting, a sound much closer, just ahead of me. I stopped and listened and didn't breathe. Something a few yards away was moving toward me in the darkness.

"Bruce, is that you?" I called again.

And suddenly I knew those were not footsteps nor anything resembling footsteps, nor anything I had ever heard before.

I never used to have nightmares, I never used to feel an awful fear of an enclosed room. I never used to wake in the middle of the night with a dread of a monstrous unclean thing coming toward me out of the dark, so that I must fumble frantically for the light cord, and lie sweating afterwards, and fear to sleep again.

I wish I had never clicked on my flashlight, there in that passage behind the tomb. Something stopped there, half revealed at the end of my pale beam of light. I know only that it wasn't human. I fired the gun and I didn't miss. There were only three bullets left, and I remember hearing every one of them hit with a soggy, sucking sound like pebbles thrown into thick mud. It could not have been more than ten seconds, but it was ten eternities. I suddenly knew that it did not fear the light, but was only momentarily confused.

And then—it came just a little nearer into the beam of light and stood fully revealed. I didn't hear myself scream, but I know I must have, for my throat was raw afterward. I felt my mind slipping slowly away into a chaos of vertiginous horror. I knew it was I that moved, and I must have screamed again. Yes, it was I who moved steadily, slowly closer; and I could not help myself! I knew I must move closer still, until...

Until what, I never knew; for at that moment, strangely, I seemed touched with a surging wave of coolness that beat down my rising panic. It no longer seemed I that moved; it was another part of me—a part that had been eons ago, that was trying now to go back to the soft, safe warmth of the primordial. It was the kind of ecstatic feeling I'd had as a child when I squeezed thick black mud between my hands—but this was magnified a thousandfold, cozy and dreamy and logical.

And yet there was something wrong, vaguely disturbing. There was another I, unimportant and far away somewhere, but persistently imploring... imploring me not to succumb, not to go back... to remember. Remember what? That tiny faraway me was so pitifully amusing, as it tried with a feeble sort of intensity to burst the surrounding comfortable darkness. It was trying to tell me... something to do with...

A dream? Was that it? Seemingly eons ago I remembered a dream a friend had told me... of something irresistibly drawing... an affinity...

How swiftly did comprehension flee back to me then, through a newly rising panic, as I remembered! How quickly I was back in that passage again as the ancient part of me and the present part of me merged with a frantic rush, and I saw...

Then it was that I screamed, for the third and final time, an articulate scream: "Bruce!..."

I was very near now to that thing that was drawing me, and I saw it quite clearly—but with that last articulate scream, something about me abruptly shivered, wavered, and I felt a sudden surge of power. I could feel *something* trying to help me tear my mind away; something softly, subtly, urgently aiding me; something whispering, "Do not come! Do not move! Go back! Now! Quickly!"

And that urging was the greatest horror of all, for I knew Bruce was there...

By what supreme effort I did tear my eyes and mind away, I shall never know. I do not remember it. I only remember the frantic escape up that last ten feet of slope... of something surging soundlessly behind, something that touched my ankle as I squeezed through the broken rectangle into the tomb... and the awful sodden sound of it hitting, seconds too late, with a sort of *squish* like a heavy wet sponge against a wall...

There remained one more thing to be done. Out of the tomb I fled, across the graveyard and into the ravine. I knew now what I was searching for, and I found it despite the darkness. I found it, well concealed in a little gully behind masses of bush and vine—*the other end of that passage.*

I saw the iron-barred gate across the tiny entrance, probably placed there by Lyle Wilson himself. It now stood open with a snap-lock hanging from it. Just inside the gate I could dimly see Lyle Wilson, a crouching figure, rapt and listening. He had heard my revolver shots, he had heard my screams—and then silence. Now he began another of those low chants that gradually rose in volume to a jubilant paean of praise. I could not have remembered the words even if I had wanted to. They were hardly even articulate words. I saw him accompany it with an unholy little ritual and dance that ordinarily would have sickened me to the soul; but already I was beyond that.

He didn't hear or see me until I had leaped forward to swing that gate shut upon him and snap the lock. The most horrible part of it was that his chant didn't even stop as he rushed at me, clawing, with a whitish sort of foam around his mouth. He crashed into the gate, tugged furiously at it... and then his chant turned into a sickening gurgle of terror as he quite suddenly realized what was going to happen. He sank down just within the tunnel, groveling in stark fear. I think his mind snapped, for soon his cries reverted again to an incoherent gibberish, like the memory of a horrible language long dead.

I waited there until I was very sure I heard—coming swiftly nearer down the tunnel—that surging primordial horror.

I have destroyed, of course, the book which Bruce was reading on that last night. And I, myself, may someday forget most of those excerpts at which I glanced. But never the one which read: "...whomsoever be attracted unto Them (by ye nefarious ynfluence wych They project when invoked), doth remain forever a *part* of Them, nott dead, but new and oddly bodied, instructing ye very grounds..."

I have said it was ten seconds that were ten eternities, there in the darkness of that passage, but my mind was numbed then. It is the horrible remembering later...

If there be gods, I pray to them to set my brain at rest. And as surely as there be things of evil, I pray to them to let me forget. But neither prayer is answered, so I must still remember that writhing, surging thing of iridescent evil, all shapes and yet shapeless... that primal, quasi-amorphous thing that moved as worms move... that sightless mass, not complete of itself, but with the power to draw men to it.

That much I could forget. *That* much would not make me dream, or wake up screaming with an awful fear of the dark.

But those dim faces that peered from out of it; that were now eternally part of it, still horribly alive and wide-eyed with the terrible anguish of knowing... those human faces that could not speak, could only implore in silent agony that I destroy them and this thing that should not be... those distorted faces enmeshed and enfolded in the confluent parts of that blasphemous thing, those faces among which I saw, dimly but surely, that of my friend, Bruce Tarleton...

OUT OF THE JAR

BY CHARLES R. TANNER

WE ALL HAVE FRIENDS WE WOULD LIKE TO SEE STUFFED INTO a jar... don't deny it... it has been that way since time began... So be a little careful next time you pick up a little jar at the knickknack counter at your hospital bazaar... be sure it's empty...

I am presenting here, at the insistence of my friend, James Francis Denning, an account of an event or series of events which, he says, occurred to him during the late summer and early fall of 1940. I do so, not because I concur in the hope which Denning has that it may arouse serious investigation of the phenomena he claims took place, but merely that a statement of those phenomena may be placed on record, as a case history for future students of occult phenomena or— psychology. Personally, I am still unpersuaded under which head this narration should be placed.

Were my mind one of those which accepts witches, vampires and werewolves in the general scheme of things, I would not doubt for a moment the truth of Denning's tale, for certainly the man believes it himself; and his lack of imagination and matter-of-fact mode of living up until the time of the occurrence speak strongly in his favor. And then too, there is the mental breakdown of the brilliant young Edward Barnes Halpin, as added evidence. This young student of occult history and the vague lesser known cults and religions was a fairly close acquaintance of Denning's for years, and it was at Denning's home that he suffered the stroke which made him the listless, stricken thing that he is today. That much is fact and can be attested to by any number of people. As to Denning's explanation, I can only say that it deserves a thorough investigation. If there is any truth in it at all, the truth should certainly be verified and recorded. And so, to the story.

It began, Denning says, in the summer of last year, when he attended a sale disposing of the stock of one of those little secondhand stores that call themselves antique shops and are known to most people as junk shops. There was the usual hodge-podge of Indian curios, glassware, Victorian furniture and old books; and Denning attended it as he did every event of this kind, allowing himself to indulge in the single vice which he had—that of filling his home with a stock of cheap and useless curios from all parts of the world.

At this particular sale he emerged triumphantly with a carved elephant tusk, an Alaskan medicine man's mask and—an earthenware jar. This jar was a rather ordinary thing, round-bodied, with a very short cylindrical neck and with a glazed band around its center, blue glaze, with curious angular characters in yellow that even the rather illiterate Denning could see bore a certain relation to Greek characters. The auctioneer called it very old, said it was Syriac or Samaritan and called attention to the seal which was affixed to the lid. This lid was of earthenware similar to the jar and was set in the mouth after the manner of a cork and a filling of what seemed to be hard-baked clay sealed it in. And on this baked clay, or whatever it was, had been stamped a peculiar design—two triangles interwoven to form a six-pointed star, with three unknown characters in the center. Although the auctioneer was as ignorant as Denning as to the real significance of this seal, he made a mystery of it and Denning was hooked. He bought the thing and brought it home, where it found a place, in spite of his wife's objections, on the mantle in the living room.

And there it rested, in a questionable obscurity, for a matter of four or five months. I say questionable obscurity, for as near as I can gather it was the bone of contention, during most of that time, between Denning and his wife. It was but natural, I think, that this estimable lady should object to having the best room in their little home filled with what were to her a mass of useless objects. Yet nothing was done about it. In the light of Denning's story of subsequent events, it seems almost incredible that that frightful thing could sit there, day after day, in that commonplace living room, being taken down and dusted now and then, and carelessly placed back.

Yet such was the case, and such remained the case until the first visit of young Halpin. This young man was an acquaintance of Denning's of long standing, and their friendship had been slowly ripening during the last year, owing to the fact that Halpin was able to add much to Denning's knowledge of the curios which he accumulated. Both of them worked for the same company and seeing each other every day, it was not unusual that they had become quite friendly in spite of the fact that neither had ever visited the other's home. But Denning's description of certain carvings on the elephant's tusk which he had bought interested young Halpin sufficiently to cause him to pay a visit to Denning's home to make a personal examination of the tusk.

Halpin, at this time, was still under thirty, yet he had become already a recognized authority in this country of that queer borderland of mystic occult study that Churchward, Fort, Lovecraft and the Miskatonic school represent. His articles on some of the obscure chapters of d'Erlette's *Cultes des Goules* has been accepted favorably by American occult students, as well as his translations of the hitherto expurgated sections of the Gaelic *Leabhar Mor Dubh*. In all, he was a most promising student and one in whom the traits of what now seem to have been incipient dementia praecox were conspicuous by their absence. Indeed, one of his strongest characteristics, Denning tells me, was a pronounced interest in almost everything about him.

"He was like that, the night that he first visited me," says Denning. "He looked over the tusk, explained all the curious carvings that he could and made little sketches of the remaining figures, to take away and study. Then his eyes began roving about the room and pretty soon they noticed some other little thing, I don't remember just what, and he began talking about that. I had a couple of Folsom points—those curious flints that are supposed to be much older than any other American artifacts—and he spoke about them for nearly twenty minutes.

"Then he laid them down and was up and around the room again; and presently he picked up something else and was talking about that. I used to learn an awful lot from Ed Halpin, but I think I learned more that night than I ever did at any other one time. And at last his eyes lit on that jar."

Yes, his eyes lit on the jar and started the series of happenings that at last made this story necessary. For Halpin was stricken with a sudden curiosity, picked up the jar and glanced over it, and then suddenly became wildly excited. "Why, it's old!" he ejaculated. "It's ancient Hebrew, Jim. Where in the world did you get it?"

Denning told him, but his curiosity was unappeased. He spent several minutes trying to extract from Denning a knowledge which it became obvious that the latter did not possess. It was easy to see that Halpin already knew more concerning the jar than did Denning, and so his questions ceased.

"But surely you know what it is supposed to be, don't you?" quizzed Halpin. "Didn't the auctioneer tell you anything about it? Didn't you see the previous owner? Lord, Denning! How can you find interest in these things, if you don't learn all you can of them?"

Denning was rendered apologetic by his evident exasperation, and Halpin suddenly relented, laughed and started to explain.

"That six-pointed star, Jim, is known as Solomon's seal. It has been a potent sign used in Hebraic Cabala for thousands of years. What has me interested is its use in connection with Phoenician characters around the body of the vase. That seems to indicate a real antiquity. It might just be possible that this is actually the seal of Solomon himself! Jim," his attitude suddenly changed, "Jim, sell me this thing, will you?"

Now, it seems incredible that Denning saw no slightest gleam of light in this guarded explanation of Halpin's. The young student certainly was aware of much of the importance of the jar, but Denning insists that the explanation meant nothing whatever to him. To be sure, Denning was no student, he had probably never heard of the Cabala, nor of Abdul Alhazred or Joachim of Cordoba, but surely, in his youth he had read the "Arabian Nights." Even that should have given him a clue. Apparently not—he tells me that he refused Halpin's offer to buy the vase, simply because of a collector's vagary. He felt that, well, to use his own words: "If it was worth ten dollars to him, it was worth ten dollars to me."

And so, though Halpin increased the offer which he first made, Denning was obdurate. Halpin left with merely an invitation to come back at any time and examine the vase to his heart's content.

During the next three weeks, Halpin did return, several times. He copied down the inscription on the blue band, made a wax impression of the seal, photographed the vase and even went so far as to measure it and weigh it. And all the time his interest increased and his bids for the thing rose higher. At last, unable to raise his offer further, he was reduced to pleading with Denning that he sell it, and at this, Denning grew angry.

"I told him," says Denning, "I told him that I was getting sick and tired of his begging. I said I wasn't going to sell it to him and that, even if it cost me our friendship, that vase was going to stay mine. Then he started on another line. He wanted to open it and see what was inside.

"But I had a good excuse for not complying with that plea. He himself had told me of the interest that attached to the seal on the clay and I wasn't going to have that broken if I knew myself. I was so positive on this score that he gave in and apologized again. At least, I thought he gave in. I know different now, of course."

We all know different now. Halpin had decided to open the vase at any cost, and so had merely given up the idea of trying to buy it. We must not think, however, that he had been reduced to the status of a common thief in spite of his later actions. The young man's attitude was explainable to anyone who can understand the viewpoint of a student of science. Here was an opportunity to study one of the most perplexing problems of occult art, and obstinacy, combined with ignorance, was trying to prevent it. He determined to circumvent Denning, no matter to what depths he had to stoop.

Thus it was that several nights later Jim Denning was awakened, sometime during the early morning hours, by a slight, unusual noise on the lower floor of his home. At first but half awake, he lay and listlessly pondered the situation. Had his wife awakened and gone downstairs for a midnight snack? Or had he heard, perhaps, a mouse in the kitchen? Could it be a sleeping sigh from his wife's bed made him realize that it wasn't she and at the same moment came a repetition of the sound—a dull "clunk" as of metal striking muffled metal. Instantly alert, he rose from his pillow, stepped out of bed, fumbled for robe and slippers and was tiptoeing down the steps, stopping only long enough to get his revolver from the drawer in which he kept it.

From the landing he could see a dim light in the living room, and again he heard the "clunk" that he had heard before. By leaning far over the banister, he was able to look into the living room, where he could see, by the light of a flashlight lying on the floor, the dark form of a man; his long overcoat and hat effectively concealing all his features. He was stooping over a round object, and as Denning looked, he raised a hammer and brought it down sharply but carefully on a chisel which he held in his hand. The hammer's head was wrapped in rags and again Denning heard the dull noise which had awakened him.

Of course, Denning knew at once who the dark form was. He knew that the round object was his vase. But he hesitated to make an outcry or even to interrupt the other for several seconds. He seemed a little uncertain as to the reason for this, but I am convinced, from what I know of Denning's character, that curiosity had gotten the better of him. Half consciously, he was determined to find out just why Halpin was so interested in the vase. So he remained silent, and it was only after several seconds that some slight noise he made caused Halpin to turn in a panic. As he did so, the last bit of seal crumbled from the jar, and rising, he still clung unconsciously to the lid. The jar turned over on its side and lay there for a moment unnoticed. Halpin was almost horror-stricken at the realization that he had been caught, as the lawyers say, in *flagrante delicto*. He burst into chattering, pleading speech.

"Don't call the police, Jim! Listen to me. I wasn't going to steal it, Jim. I'd have been gone with it long ago if I had intended to steal it. Honest! Let me tell you, Jim. It's one of Solomon's jars, all right. I was only going to open it. Good Lord, man, haven't you ever read about them? Listen, Jim, haven't you ever heard those old Arabian legends? Let me tell you about them, Jim—"

As he spoke, Denning had descended the stairs. He stepped into the room and seized Halpin by the shoulders and angrily shook him.

"Quit babbling, Halpin. Don't act like a damned fool. I guess the jar and its contents are still mine. Come on, snap out of it and tell me what this is all about."

Halpin swallowed his panic and sighed.

"There are old Arabian and Hebrew legends, Jim, that speak of a group or class of beings called Jinn. A lot of the stuff about them is claptrap, of course, but as near as we can make out, they were a kind of super-being from some other plane of existence. Probably they were the same things that other legends have called the Elder Ones, or the Pre-Adamites. Perhaps there are a dozen names for them if they are the same beings that appear in myths of other countries. Before the time of man, they ruled the world; but fighting among themselves and certain conditions during the Glacial Period caused them to become almost extinct, here on this earth. But the few that were left caused damage enough among men until the time of King Solomon.

"Arabian legend says that Solomon was the greatest of all kings, and from an occult standing I guess he was, in spite of the fact that the kingdom he ruled over was little more than a jerk-water principality, even in that age. But Solomon's occult knowledge was great enough to enable him to war on the Jinn and to conquer them. And then, because it was impossible to kill them (their metabolism is entirely different from ours), he sealed them up into jars and cast the jars into the depths of the sea!"

Denning was still dense.

"Halpin, you're not trying to tell me that you expect to find a Jinn in that jar, are you? You're not such a superstitious fool as to believe—"

"Jim, I don't know what I believe. There's no record of such a jar as this having ever been found before. But I know that the Elder Ones once existed and from an examination of the jar an occultist might learn much concerning—"

While Halpin had been speaking, Denning's eye had fallen on the jar, lying where it had tumbled at Halpin's sudden rising. And the hair on Denning's neck quivered with a wave of horripilation, as he stammered suddenly: "For the love of God, Halpin, look at that jar!"

Halpin's eyes turned at Denning's first words and he, too, stared, unable to take his eyes off the thing that was taking place. From the mouth of the jaw was flowing, slowly, sluggishly, a thick, viscous mass of bluish, faintly luminous stuff. The mass was spreading, oozing across the floor, reaching curious curly pseudopods out in all directions, acting, not like an inert vicous body should, but like—like an amoeba under a microscope. And from it, as though it were highly volatile, curled little streamers of heavy smoke or vapor. To their ears came, almost inaudibly at first, and then more loudly, a slow deliberate "cluck—cluck—c-lu-uck" from the mass, as it spread.

The two had forgotten their differences. Denning stepped toward Halpin and clasped his shoulder fearfully. Halpin stood like a stone statue but his breath was like that of a winded runner. And they stood there and looked and looked as that incredible jelly spread and streamed across the floor.

I think it was the luminous quality of the mass that horrified the men the most. It had a dull bluish glow, a light of a shade that made it absolutely certain that it was not merely a reflection from the light of the flashlight which still threw its beam in a comet's-tail across the floor. And too, it was certain properties, in the mist, for that behaved not like a normal mist, but with a sentience of its own. It floated above the room, seeking, seeking, and yet it avoided the presence of the two men as though it feared their touch. And it was increasing. It was quite apparent that the mass on the floor was evaporating, passing into the mist, and it was evident that it would soon be gone.

"Is it—is it one of those things, Halpin?" whispered Denning, hoarsely; but Halpin answered him not at all, but only gripped his hand, tighter and tighter and tighter.

Then the mist began a slow twirling motion and a deep sigh came from Halpin. It seemed that he was assured of something by this, for he leaned over and whispered to Denning with what seemed a certain amount of confidence: "It's one of them, all right. Stand back by the door and let me handle it. I know a little something from the books I've read."

Denning backed away, more than a little fearful of Halpin now, seeing that the young man seemed to know something of this terrible thing, but nevertheless grateful for the suggestion. Standing there by the doorway, hoping vaguely that his traitorous legs would obey him if it became necessary to flee, he watched the dread process of materialization take place. And I think he has never quite recovered from the effects of it; for surely, at that moment, the entire philosophy of his life was changed.

Denning, I have noticed, goes to church quite regularly now.

However, as I say, he stood there and watched. Watched the smoke, or vapor, or whatever it was, whirl and whirl, faster and faster, snatching up the vagrant wisps and streamers that had strayed to the far corners of the room, sucking them in, incorporating them into the central column, until at last that column, swirling there, seemed almost solid.

It was solid. It had ceased its whirling and stood there quivering, jelly-like, plastic, but nevertheless, solid. And, as though molded in the hands of an invisible sculptor, that column was changing. Indentations appeared here, protuberances there. The character of the surface altered subtly; presently it was no longer smooth and lustrous, but rough and scaly. It lost most of its luminosity and became an uncertain, lichenous green. Until at last it was a—thing.

That moment, Denning thinks, was the most horrible in all the adventure. Not because of the horror of the thing that stood before him, but because at that very moment an automobile driven by some belated citizen passed by outside, the light from its headlights casting eerie gleams across the walls and ceiling; and the thought of the difference between the commonplace world in which that citizen was living, and the frightful things taking place in this room almost overcame the cowering man by the doorway. And, too, the light made just that much plainer the disgusting details of the creature that towered above them.

For tower it did. It was, apparently, about nine feet tall, for its head quite reached the ceiling of Denning's little room. It was roughly manlike, for it had an erect body and four limbs, two upper and two lower. It had a head and a sort of a face on it. But there its similarity to man ceased. Its head had a high ridge running from the forehead to the nape of the neck—and it had no eyes and no nose. In the place of these organs was a curious thing that looked like the blossom of a sea-anemone, and beneath that was a mouth with an upper lip that was like a protruding fleshy beak, making the whole mouth take on the semblance of a sardonic letter V.

The front of its body had the flat, undetailed plainness of a lizard's belly, and the legs were long, scaly and terribly scrawny. The same might be said of the arms, which terminated in surprisingly delicate, surprisingly human hands.

Halpin had been watching the materialization with the eagerness of a hawk, and no sooner was it complete, no sooner did he notice the tautening of the creature's muscles that indicated conscious control, than he burst out with a jumble of strange words. Now, it happens that Denning was so keyed up that his mind was tense and observant of every detail, and he clearly remembers the exact words that Halpin uttered. They are in some little-known tongue and I have failed to find a translation, so I repeat them here for any student who may care to look them up:

"*Iä, Psuchawrl!*" he cried. "'*Ng topuothikl Shelemoh, ma'kthoqui h'nirl!*"

At the cry, the horror moved. It stooped and took a short step toward the uncowering Halpin, its facial rosette rose just as a man lifts his eyebrows in surprise, and then—speech came from its lips. Halpin, strangely, answered it in English.

"I claim the forfeit," he cried boldly. "Never has one of your kind been released that it did not grant to whoever released it one wish, were it in its power to grant it."

The thing bowed, actually bowed. In deep—inhumanly deep—tones it gave what was manifestly an assent. It clasped its hands over what should have been its breast and bowed, in what even the paralyzed Denning could tell was certainly mock humility.

"Very well, then!" the heedless Halpin went on. "I want to know! That is my wish—to know. All my life I have been a student, seeking, seeking—and learning nothing. And now—I want to know the why of things, the cause, the reason, and the end to which we travel. Tell me the place of man in this universe, and the place of this universe in the cosmos!"

The thing, the Jinni, or whatever it was, bowed again. Why was it that Halpin could not see its mockery! It clasped those amazingly human hands together, it drew them apart, and from fingertips to fingertips leaped a maze of sparks. In that maze of brilliant filaments a form began to take shape, became rectangular, took on solidity and became a little window. A silvery, latticed window whose panes were seemingly transparent, but which looked out upon—from where Denning stood, it seemed nothing but blackness. The creature's head made a gesture and it spoke a single word—the only word which it spoke that Denning recognized.

"Look!" it said, and obeying, Halpin stepped forward and looked through that window.

Denning says that Halpin stared while you might have counted ten. Then he drew back a step or two, stumbled against the couch and sat down. "Oh!" he said softly—very softly, and then: "Oh, I see!" Denning says he said it like a little child that had just had some problem explained by a doting parent. And he made no attempt to rise, no comment, nor any further word of any kind.

And the Jinni, the Elder One, demon or angel or whatever it was, bowed again and turned around—and was gone! Then, suddenly, somehow or other, Denning's trance of fright was over, and he rushed to the light switch and flooded the room with light. An empty jar lay upon the floor, and upon the couch sat one who stared and stared into vacancy with a look of unutterable despair on his face.

Little more need be said. Denning called his wife, gave her a brief and distorted tale which he later amplified for the police, and spent the rest of the night trying to rouse Halpin. When morning came, he sent for a doctor and had Halpin removed to his own home. From there Halpin was taken to the state asylum for the insane where he still is. He sits constantly in meditation, unless one tries to arouse him, and then he turns on them a sad, pitying smile and returns to his musings.

And except for that sad, pitying smile, his only look is one of unutterable despair.

THE EARTH-BRAIN

BY EDMOND HAMILTON

LANDON I HAD NOT SEEN FOR TWO YEARS BEFORE THAT DAY when New York knew fear. That day is remembered yet, with its sudden and unexpected earth-tremor that shook the island shortly after noon, swaying proud towers and shaking windows to fragments and loosing a storm of panic-stricken cries that could not drown the long, grinding roll of the shifting earth beneath.

I was in the midtown section that noon, and had been struggling through the hurrying crowds when the shock and quivering of the ground turned them suddenly into a white-faced, hoarse-voiced and terror-smitten mob. For five minutes they and all New York's millions tasted fear as the streets quivered beneath them. Then the tremor subsided and I saw Landon.

He was standing almost against me in the throng and his face was so strange that for a moment it held me without recognition. For Landon's face was a mask of fear, not the panic that was passing from those about me but a fear beyond fear, a deep and alien dread. His dark eyes looked out of that white and twisted face as though into vistas of hell. And then I recognised him.

"Clark Landon!" I cried. "Why didn't you let me know you were back? I didn't even know you were in the country!"

His dark eyes surveyed me with a fixedness that chilled me. "I landed only two hours ago, Morris," he said. "Two hours ago, and you see what has happened already."

"What's the matter, Landon?" I asked anxiously. "This earth-tremor hasn't upset you? I shouldn't think it would bother you after the polar quake you went through—I read about it at the time."

"Yes, that polar quake," he said softly. "You read that Travis and Skeel were killed in that but I wasn't? I wasn't killed, no; but I've been in all the quakes that have been racking earth since then, in Norway and Russia and Egypt, in Italy and England and now here in New York."

I was amazed. "Why, one would think earthquakes are following you!" I exclaimed. "But they say all these tremors and quakes are due to the big polar cataclysm you went through—they say it touched off things in some way and so caused the quakes that have been going on all over earth ever since that one."

"Ever since that one," Landon repeated slowly. "Yes, they've been going on ever since that one."

He was looking beyond me, lost in a strange abstraction. By then the streets about us were near normal, the city's millions losing their brief panic and taking up again the swift routine that even a near-earthquake could not disturb for long. Hurrying passers-by were already shouldering against the two of us.

"Look here, Landon," I said, "You don't look half well at the moment. My rooms are only a few blocks from here—come up and sit a while and you'll feel better."

"I'm afraid it will take more than that to make me feel better, Morris," he said.

Yet he came, and when we were seated at a window of my apartment with the mill-race of a cross-town street's traffic below, he seemed to relax a little. Sitting opposite him, I strove to analyse the strange dread that still seemed holding him, but was unable to do more than to say to myself that that dread was real and that Landon had apparently changed completely.

The Clark Landon I had known had hardly known the meaning of fear, a lithe dark fellow to whom danger spelled delight. His twin and equal interests had been geology and adventure. His inherited money had enabled him to combine the two in expeditions in which he and his inseparable comrades in science and adventure, David Travis and Herbert Skeel, had investigated the world's far corners.

Landon and Travis and Skeel had departed over two years before, on another such expedition, one intended to take them into the north polar region. Landon had announced their purpose as the investigation of certain geological oddities believed existent not far from the pole, but all knew that it was the lure of a new adventure that drew him and his companions as much as any hope of adding to geological knowledge.

The three had sailed in a special ice-breaking schooner Landon had chartered, which had taken them as far as the northern shores of Grant Land. From there Landon and Travis and Skeel had started north with two dog-sledges and two Eskimos, believing that with their equipment they could reach their objectives a few hundred miles south of the pole, and return without difficulty.

Ten days after Landon and his party started north from the ship there occurred that terrific earthquake that shook the whole polar region with unprecedented violence, and was registered by the world's seismographs as centring not far south of the pole itself. The waiting schooner was almost destroyed, but escaped the shifting ice and continued to wait, though with scant hope, for the party.

That first awful quake was followed in the next two weeks by a succession of less violent upheavals and tremors, trending southward. Then Landon and one of the Eskimos reappeared. The latter died the next day. Landon himself was far gone but was revived and could tell those on the ship that the great quake had indeed centred where they had been and that Travis and Skeel and the other Eskimo had perished in it. He was brought back to strength during the voyage south, and after a few narrow escapes from glacial fragments the ship reached Halifax.

While Landon was at Halifax had come the sudden quake that destroyed half of the city, though he had escaped. In the succeeding two years Landon himself was forgotten, but the great polar quake he had gone through was often referred to, for earth had been torn ever since by a succession of violent quakes and upheavals. They seemed to progress from one locality to another, from Newfoundland to Norway, to Russia and Egypt and Italy and England. It was the theory of many scientists that these succeeding quakes were caused by a series of faults in earth's structure, that had been touched off by the great polar quake Landon had gone through.

Of Landon himself, though, I had heard nothing after his leaving Halifax, and now I was amazed at his changed appearance as he sat opposite me. He must have guessed my thoughts.

"You think I've changed, Morris?" he asked. "Don't deny it, man—I know that I have. I know what's stamped on my face."

"Travis and Skeel—" I began awkwardly.

"Travis and Skeel are dead and they're lucky," he said somberly. "It's not their death that has changed me, though they were the best pals a man ever had. It's the way they died.

"There were three of us who went up there," he said, gazing darkly past me. "And the third still lives. I wonder for how long?"

"Landon, you've brooded too much," I told him. "I can understand what an appalling experience that polar quake must have been to go through, but—"

"You can't understand!" he lashed out. "No one can! Morris, you saw me panic-stricken a little while ago when that tremor shook the city. Did it surprise you?"

"Frankly, it did," I said slowly. "But I can understand how that first quake would have unnerved you—and the ones you've chanced to be in since."

"It wasn't chance that I was in them," he said astonishingly, and then leaned to clutch my arm. "Morris, can you conceive of such a thing as earthquakes following one person across the face of this earth, seeking him out no matter where he may go, riving the earth and razing cities and killing tens of thousands, to kill that one fugitive? Earthquakes that deliberately pursue one fleeing man with deadly purpose?"

"Earthquakes following a man?" I repeated. "Why, the idea's mad! You surely don't think because you have been by coincidence in all these quakes of the last two years—"

"I don't think," he said, "I know. I know that the quakes you speak of have pursued me across earth in the last two years with deadly purpose! Even today, two hours after I landed in this city, they have shown me that they are still after me!"

"Landon, you can't believe this!" I expostulated. "Be reasonable, man—an earthquake is simply a movement of the earth's mass. How could such movements follow you deliberately?"

"I know how," he said, his eyes strange. "Travis and Skeel knew, too, before they died. But I know and I still live, if only for a time.

"And I am going to tell you the thing, Morris. I know before the telling that you will find it impossible to believe, just as I would have two years ago. But in your unbelief remember this—that of all things in the universe the one we men know least really of is this earth we live upon.

"It has been over two years since Travis and Skeel and I started north on that trip of ours. We left St. John's in a sturdy Canadian schooner built for arctic work, with a Canadian crew. The ship was to take us as far as northern Grant Land, and from there we three were going to work north ourselves on the last lap. Our objective was a great ice-mountain, its rock visible through openings in its icy sides, that was supposed to exist in the polar region some three hundred miles or more this side of the pole.

"We had heard of this polar mountain from several sources. It had been a matter of minor dispute between two different aeroplane expeditions that had flown over the pole. One claimed to have sighted the big ice-clad peak and the other claimed that it didn't exist. Travis and Skeel and I were going north to see if it did exist.

"If you know anything at all of geology you will know what such a polar mountain—a mountain in that icy desolation at the earth's top— would mean to geologists. It would prove beyond doubt the existence of a polar continent beneath the ice and might throw a flood of light on things that have puzzled geological science. The three of us were afire to find out if such a peak did exist in the north polar region.

"The north pole, you know, like the south one, is more a region than a point. The earth is oblate, flattened at top and bottom, and that flat region around the northern pole is in fact the top or forefront of earth. In that great icy expanse the mountain was supposed to exist, and Travis and Skeel and I were bent on finding it. So we sailed north from St. John's with our schooner loaded with equipment.

"The schooner crept northward for two months through icy channels toward the northern tip of Grant Land. Travis and Skeel and I were busy making ready our equipment. At North Devon we picked up two Eskimos who were to make the final trip with us, two sturdy fellows named Noskat and Shan. Our sledges and dogs were ready, and when the ship reached the icy coast of Grant Land we were ready to start north on the final lap as soon as the freeze came.

"It came soon, and we started. Travis and Skeel and I, and Noskat and Shan, with the two sledges and dogs, headed north over the frozen wastes. We carried felt tents, special chemical fuel of small bulk and weight, food and instruments, and an automatic apiece. Travis and Skeel and Noskat took the lead-sledge, Shan and I the other.

"For ten days we pushed north over endless ice-fields, making thirty miles a day. Ten days—three hundred miles—it doesn't sound so much, does it? Well, it was a cross-section of icy hell. Can you imagine a world in which all has turned to glittering ice that stretches to the horizon in eye-aching whiteness? A world in which the sickly polar day never ceases to shine? A world in which the polar cold closes down upon you like a hand, gripping through your numbed flesh to your bones?

"That was the kind of world we were moving through. Ten days— and they each seemed weeks long. We would wake, would eat half-warmed food and limber our stiffened muscles, then fold the tent and harness the dogs. And then north again, north over the ice desert's hummocks and ridges like pigmies traversing that vast white expanse. North, until on the tenth day we sighted the mountain.

"At first we could not believe our eyes. We had been pushing onward so mechanically that in the sheer struggle we had almost forgotten our mission. Then as our eyes took in that huge peak towering into the steely sky far ahead, ice-sheathed and with the dark openings in its sides, our exclamations came with a rush.

"We pushed on, little heeding difficulties then. In another day we were at the mountain's foot, a thousand feet below the lowest of the dark openings in its icy bulk.

"We camped there that night, exultant at reaching our goal. And there trouble began. The dogs had been whining strangely as we approached the mountain, needing the lash to make them go forward at all, and our two Eskimos had been muttering to themselves. Then no sooner had we pitched camp than there came a slight earth-tremor, a shock as of earth stirring underneath that made our tent quiver and the ice-fields round it crackle.

"To us it was somewhat surprising to encounter an earth-tremor in this region, but that was all. But on Noskat and Shan, the two Eskimos, the tremor's effects were tremendous. Their swart faces grew positively livid with fear, they jabbered in their tongue for minutes, looking fearfully up toward the mountain's huge icy bulk, and then approached us in panic. By then the dogs had begun yelping strangely as though in terror.

"'We cannot stay here!' Noskat told us excitedly. 'This is the forbidden mountain at the earth's top—shunned by all our race! We knew not that this was your goal!'

"'Forbidden mountain?' repeated Travis. 'Forbidden by whom?'

"'Forbidden by the earth!' was Noskat's answer. 'The earth is living as we are living—it cares not how men move upon its vast living body as long as they do not approach this mountain!'

"'The earth living? What the devil is all this about?' Travis demanded. Skeel intervened.

"'It's an Eskimo belief, Travis,' he said. 'I've heard of it before—they think earth is a great living thing and that we humans are mere insects or the like living on its body.'

"'What a crazy belief!' Travis commented. He turned back to Noskat. 'Why does your living earth forbid anyone to come near this mountain, then?'

"'Because this mountain holds earth's mind—earth's brain,' said Noskat solemnly, Shan nodding corroboration. 'Earth likes us not to come this near its brain, and so it has moved its great body beneath us to warn us away.'

"'Rot!' said Travis. 'That tremor just now wasn't any warning, but a slight earthquake like any other earthquake.'

"'All earthquakes are but movements of earth's great body,' asserted Noskat stubbornly. 'Earth can move its body as it wishes.'

"'That sounds logical enough, Travis,' I said, grinning.

"He turned toward me. 'Don't encourage them, Landon,' he said sharply. 'We'll have trouble enough with them as it is.'

"He swung back on Noskat and Shan. 'That tremor was just an ordinary tremor and this stuff about a living earth is nonsense,' he said forcibly. 'We are going to stay here two days at least and you two are going to camp down here while we explore and examine this mountain.'

"'But you must not try to explore the mountain!' Noskat said excitedly. 'You dare not approach earth's brain! If you do—'

"'That's enough!' snapped Travis. 'You and Shan are going to wait here while we do explore the mountain, and there'll be no more talk about it!'

"When Noskat and Shan had gone to their own tent Travis turned to us with a disgusted expression.

"'This would be just our luck,' he said, 'to have those two, just as we get here, break loose with their superstitions.'

"'I wonder if they're only superstitions,' said Skeel thoughtfully.

"We stared at him. 'What the devil!' I exclaimed. 'Do you believe that stuff about earth being a living and intelligent being?'

"Skeel's face was serious. 'I've heard of stranger things, Landon. Why couldn't earth be a living organism instead of just a mass of inanimate matter? It seems an inanimate mass to us, it is true, but so must a human being seem an inanimate mass to the microbes that live on and in that being. Earth might be a living organism, all the planets might be organisms, of scale and nature so different from us that we mites who swarm upon it cannot even comprehend it. And if it is living it could possess consciousness and intelligence, perhaps intelligence operating on planes and for ends entirely alien to us.'

"'And you think, then, that, as Noskat said, earth's brain is somewhere in this mountain?' Travis demanded incredulously.

"Skeel smiled. 'I don't say that. Though as a matter of fact if earth were a living and intelligent organism it would have to have the seat of its intelligence somewhere, and as likely up here at earth's top as anywhere.'

"'I'll say you're a cuckoo geologist!' I exclaimed. 'You're as bad as those two Eskimos!'

"Travis stretched. 'Well, whether or not earth's brain is inside that mountain, we're going to do some climbing on it tomorrow morning.'

"'And some climb it's going to be,' I told him. 'If we can get up far enough to get a look at that uncovered rock we'll be lucky.'

"We turned in, huddling in our furs, and though the dogs were still whining in a panicky fashion now and then, we fell almost instantly to sleep.

"We were awakened when our watches told us it was morning by a sensation of someone shaking us, and found that it was another earth-tremor that was rocking the tent, one as strong as or stronger than that of the night before. It was over almost before we were awake, the grinding crackle of ice dying away.

"We struggled rapidly into our outer clothes and heard the dogs, who had yelped with terror when the tremor began, become silent as though cowed by utter fear. The tent still quivered from the tremor's last vibrations.

"Travis cursed. 'Another damned tremor! This will make those two swarthy sons of perdition harder than ever to handle, if I'm right.'

"His surmise proved correct, for we had not emerged from the tent into the polar cold and glare when Noskat and Shan were upon us. They were quite evidently in an extreme state of terror.

"According to them, the tremor was another and stronger sign that the earth was uneasy at our presence near its brain, and a warning for us to turn and head southward at all possible speed before earth destroyed us. They even went so far in their panic as to say that if we did not they would start south without us with one of the sledges.

"Travis's cold voice whipped to them through their terror. 'You'll stay here, all right,' he told them. 'You know too well what would happen to you if you showed up back down there at the ship without us.'

"'But if you try to explore the mountain, earth's brain will be very wroth!' wailed Shan. 'All earth will be wroth against you!'

"'I've had enough of this crazy talk about earth and its brain,' Travis told them impatiently. 'You two will stay here until we come back, or you'll go with us.'

"At that alternative both Noskat and Shan became silent out of sheer terror. I told them to see to the dogs, which were still acting strangely, and then with Travis and Skeel prepared for our climb up the icy mountain's side.

"As we could not hope to bring back any specimens, even if we succeeded in reaching one of the openings in the mountain's ice-sheath, we took only our ice-axes and a single rock-axe. We wore our automatics in our belts with the idea of impressing the two Eskimos if they still harboured ideas of flight, and we were roped together.

"With a final admonition and warning to Noskat and Shan from Travis, we started up the icy mountainside. A thousand feet above us was the dark circle in the ice we wanted to reach, an opening through the peak's frozen sheath, we were sure, to its inner rock. If we could make even a cursory examination of the mountain's rock-strata, we felt our trip would be worthwhile.

"From the first our climb was tremendously difficult. Travis led, cutting steps where needed with his ice-axe, taking advantage of ledges and cracks in the ice, moving tortuously up with Skeel and me close behind. Our heavy fur clothing was a hindrance to us in climbing, though even through it the polar cold penetrated.

"We were forced to rest every few yards, clinging against the icy slope like three strange furry animals. At such halts I looked down and for a time could see Noskat and Shan, down by the tents and sledges, watching our progress. Then an inward slant of the icy slope hid them from view for a time.

"This slant inward made climbing a little easier, and now we could plainly see the round opening in the ice above, and could make out that it opened through the ice to the dark bare rock of the mountain itself. That was a spur to our efforts and we struggled on, Travis's axe chipping, steadily ahead of us, until at last Travis pulled himself up into the opening in the ice and then jerked us up beside him.

"We were hardly in that opening, lying panting for the moment, when there came another earth-tremor, much more violent.

"It seemed that the whole mountain and the ice-fields around it were swaying and shaking, and there came as though from far beneath a crackling roar. We lay still and in a moment it ceased.

"'Good Lord!' exclaimed Travis as we stood up then. 'If that had happened a moment ago when we were climbing it would have been bad for us.'

"'Damn these tremors anyway!' I said, 'If that one has succeeded in scaring off Noskat and Shan I won't be surprised.'

"We peered down and saw them on the ice near the tents. They were on their knees, gesticulating in terror up toward us and the mountain. They made frantic motions for us to return.

"We shook our heads and Travis gestured sharply to them, ordering them to remain where they were. Their terror subsided a little, and he turned to us.

"'They'll stay there, I think—they're more afraid to go back to the ship without us than to stay. But we'd best not stay up here too long ourselves.'

"Skeel had turned and was staring into the opening in the mountain's side, at whose edge we stood. 'Lord, look at this!' he exclaimed.

"We looked and were petrified with astonishment. The opening in which we stood was the mouth of a round tunnel that slanted straight back and downward into the mountain's mighty mass.

"This tunnel was thirty feet in diameter and ran inward toward the mountain's centre in a slight downward grade, as straight as though it had been gouged by a huge punch.

"There was no ice in the tunnel, though a steady current of air rushed down it. We examined the black rock of its walls quickly, then again with mounting excitement. It was a geologist's nightmare. This mountain's rock was stratumless, a smooth black rock that might have come from earth's innermost mass!

"'I'll say we've found something here!' cried Travis excitedly. 'Why, this rock is pre-igneous even—it's a kind of rock geology's not even heard of!'

"'But this opening, this tunnel leading down into the mountain?' I asked. 'What could have formed it?'

"'God knows, Landon. But the other openings we saw in the mountain's ice-sides must be the mouths of similar tunnels! And they must lead down to some central opening or space, for there are air-currents in this one!'

"Travis unhooked from his belt his flat metal electric torch and sent its ray down the dark tunnel's length. The quivering little beam wavered down through the next few hundred feet of the tunnel but showed only the same smooth, black rock sides.

"'The only way we'll find out what this tunnel leads to down there is to follow it and see,' said Travis. 'Come on, you two.'

"We started down the tunnel. Its grade was not steep enough to make it perilous, though its floor, like its sides, was so smooth as to make footing difficult. We had a hard time to keep our footing when, a moment or so later, there came another tremor that swayed the mountain so that the tunnel's floor seemed to pitch beneath us.

"By then we were too excited over the geological strangeness of the tunnel and the black rock and the whole mountain to mind the tremor. We pressed on, Travis's quivering beam preceding us, with the circle of white light that was the tunnel's mouth dwindling and disappearing behind and above us. We paid no more attention to another tremor that shook us a few moments later, or to still another that followed that one closely.

"Within a quarter of an hour we had followed the tunnel downward for a half-mile and had found that it curved slightly now instead of running straight as heretofore, but led still in a general direction down toward the mountain's centre. By then, too, the tremors and quakings of the mountain and earth around it had become practically continuous.

"The tunnel's walls were swaying unceasingly around us, not violently but noticeably, and the sound of these continued earth-movements was now a tremendous monotone of rumblings and mutterings from far beneath. The strangeness of these continued tremors penetrated through even our excitement and we stopped in the tunnel's curve we were passing through, Travis flashing his beam ahead and behind.

"'Damn queer, all these tremors at once!' he exclaimed. 'They seem to be getting worse, too.'

"'I'm beginning to think this whole mountain is queer,' Skeel said. 'Tell me, have you two *felt* anything?'

"We stared at him. We *had* experienced with increasing strength a sensation so strange that neither Travis nor I had mentioned it. It was a sense of a tangible and powerful force that flooded out over and through us from ahead, a tingling force that had a strange effect upon my will.

"I cannot describe that effect better than by saying that the farther down into the tunnel we went, the more did my own will and personality seem shared or usurped by some will or force utterly alien and different. In other words, that as I went on I was not only Clark Landon but something or a part of something vast and strange, whose will partly replaced Clark Landon's will in me.

"'I've felt it, yes,' I told Skeel. 'But I didn't know you had. You too, Travis?'

"Travis nodded puzzledly. 'I've felt it also. There must be some centre of radioactive or electrical force down in this mountain and the closer we get to it the more it affects us.'

"'But what about the tremors?' Skeel asked. 'Can we go on in the face of them and this other thing?'

"'The devil with the tremors,' said Travis impatiently. 'There's something tremendous down inside this mountain and I say we go on, tremors or no tremors.'

"'What do you think, Landon?' Skeel asked me. I looked doubtfully from him to Travis.

"'After all, we've been in worse tremors than these,' I said, 'and I think Travis is right when he says there must be something tremendous down in this mountain.'

"'I think there is, myself,' said Skeel, 'and I think that with these tremors it's warning us back!'

"'Oh, rot!' said Travis. 'Are you going to start that silly notion of Noskat's about earth's brain being down here?'

"'No, I'm with you two if you want to go on,' Skeel said.

"'Then on it is!' I said. 'We can't go a great deal farther, anyway, for we can't spend too long a time down here.'

"We resumed our interrupted progress. The tunnel curved on downward, toward the mountain's heart. The currents of air still rushed down it unceasingly, making me wonder, as we went on, whether what thing of force was down here somehow drew or attracted those air-currents, through this and the other tunnels leading up to the mountain's sides.

"The tremors were somewhat more violent and it was evident that the whole mountain must be shaking. We moved on without commenting on them, though. It was hard work to keep our footing on the smooth, swaying floor of the tunnel and we were thrown continually against its sides, sometimes with force. But we held to our downward progress, drawn by the mystery we were now sure this mountain held.

"For the strange force that beat upon us from ahead with increasing strength as we went on could only be mysterious and unheard of to our science, so strange it seemed. The sensation as of the impact of a colossal will was stronger and stronger. Can you imagine a will so mighty that mere nearness to it makes one feel its power as tangible force? That is what this alien force inside the mountain felt like to us.

"Skeel's face was becoming grave and even Travis seemed troubled as we went doubtfully on. The tremors by then had become really terrible, great roarings and shakings that swayed the tunnel's walls about us. But now so strange was everything, so dazing that vast, enigmatic force that beat stronger upon us from ahead, that we paid small attention.

"We rounded another long curve in the downward-slanting tunnel and saw ghostly, glowing light ahead in it, heard a soft roar of steady sound over the grinding crash of shifting rock. Like puppets drawn by forces outside us, we pressed onward toward the light. As we neared it the impact of strange forces from ahead was almost stunning. There came a great last tremor that almost flung us from our feet. But even Skeel did not mind it, since in the moment it came we had reached the glowing light, had emerged suddenly from the dark tunnel into a great, glowing-lit space.

"We halted in it, stupefied. The tremors stopped altogether at that same moment, but only our subconscious minds registered the fact. We three were gazing across the great cavernous space into which the tunnel opened.

"It seemed in that first stunned glance that this strange cavern must occupy most of the interior of the mountain, so huge was it. It must have been a half-mile in diameter, and was like the interior of a hollow cone.

"The mountain's dozen tunnels all opened down into it. It was lit by a quivering, glowing light which came from what was beyond doubt the most awesome and stupefying thing that ever man dared to look upon. I cannot, even now, describe to you with one-tenth of its real terrible splendour, the thing that poised at the centre of this cone-like cavern over the rock floor, the thing at which Travis and Skeel and I gazed.

"Can you imagine a great ovoid of pure light, like a huge egg in shape and a hundred feet high, poised upon its smaller end? That was what we three looked upon, a giant ovoid of light or force that towered there at the cone-cavern's centre, emitting the light that illuminated it and also the enigmatic force that had beat upon us and the soft roar of sound we had heard.

"This ovoid was of all colours, it seemed. Its colours changed with incalculable swiftness like those of a racing cinema film. And those racing tints seemed to reproduce all the colours of the earth.

"The ovoid would flame for an instant with a red like that of devouring volcanic fires, of flowing flame. Then the red would be gone and instead would be a thread of blue, serene as the blue of mountain lakes. The blue would pass into brown like the warm brown of fresh-turned soil, and that in turn into green like that of ocean's depths or yellow of earth's fantastic rocks.

"These colours changed and spun and swam in the great ovoid of light constantly, unceasingly. And just as in them seemed represented every natural colour of earth, so in the soft roar of sound that came from the ovoid, there seemed merged and mingled all the natural sounds of earth.

"The crash of avalanches and thunder of slow-moving glaciers were in that roar, and the splitting of tortured rocks. One heard the howl of winds and the caressing whisper of soft breezes, the gurgling of small brooks and the hiss of rain and the smash of hurricanes and tidal waves. That roar of merged sound seemed issuing from a whispering gallery open to all the sounds of earth.

"From the lower end of this huge poised ovoid of light branched scores of great tentacles of light, glowing arms that ran down into the rock floor of the cavern. They did not run into openings in that rock but into the rock itself, interpenetrating it as light interpenetrates glass. Somehow it seemed to me even in that first stunned moment that those light-tentacles branching down from the ovoid were of inconceivable length, that from where it poised here at the frozen top of the earth those arms of force or light penetrated down through all earth's mighty mass!

"As Travis and Skeel and I gazed now at the mighty ovoid, there shot suddenly from its lower end a new light-tentacle, as though forming suddenly. It darted across the cavern and encircled us three. Its grip was like that of solid steel rather than of glowing light, and with us in its grasp it darted back toward the great ovoid.

"We were held by this tentacle a score of feet from the ovoid. The scene was incredibly weird—the mighty cavern, the huge ovoid of light with its kaleidoscopic colours and roar of merged sounds and downward-branching tentacles, the arm of light that held Travis and Skeel and me in remorseless grip!

"It held us beneath the ovoid as though that immense thing of light from which it branched was contemplating us. And somehow in my mind then I knew without shadow of doubt that the ovoid *was* contemplating us, was examining and inspecting us by means of strange senses somewhere inside its glowing mass of light, senses having nothing to do with any senses we knew but operating on planes entirely different. Its vast will, mind, beat out on us tangibly.

"Skeel's cry came thinly to my ears over the soft roar of the towering ovoid. 'The brain of the earth! The Eskimos were right—it's the brain of the earth!'

"'The brain of the earth! The Earth-Brain!' Travis and I mouthed the cry in stupefaction.

"For somehow we knew, knew absolutely, that it was the brain of the living earth that towered here and that held us, this awful ovoid of light poised in its mountain-chamber at the top of earth. This stupendous intelligence which saw and heard and somehow represented all the colours and sounds existing in its body, the earth! And whose light-tentacles ran down like animating sinews through its great earth-body!

"The Eskimos had been right. Their legends had told truth when they said that this mountain at the frozen top of earth held the brain of earth, and that it cared not how men moved upon its mighty earth-body so long as they approached not that body's brain, its self!

"For earth was but body to this great brain! And just as microbes move upon a human body without even knowing that it is a living thing and not a great inanimate mass they exist on, so had men moved and lived upon its body, the earth, without ever dreaming that the huge body was animated by a vast kind of life so different from their own that they had deemed it lifeless!

"Men had moved and lived so upon the living earth for ages, generation after generation of tiny parasites upon it, but now three of those parasites in the person of ourselves had had the audacity to approach the earth's brain, here at earth's top; had disregarded the Earth-Brain's warning tremors of uneasiness at our approach and had penetrated despite them to its inmost chamber, here to the Earth-Brain itself that now had seized us and was examining us!

"'Those tentacles of light!' Travis was yelling thinly in my ear. 'They must run down from this Earth-Brain like muscles through all earth!'

"'Yes—we know now what caused those tremors, what causes earthquakes!' I cried.

"The light-tentacles drew us closer to the Earth-Brain! Can you picture that scene? The great ovoid of light holding us with one of its tentacles, inspecting us? Yes, the Earth-Brain was examining us as a man might take and examine three tiny parasites or insects whom he had not noticed upon his body until they became too bold!

"And still upon us, through us, beat the Earth-Brain's will! The impact of that will was tangible, overwhelming. It seemed partly to replace, to usurp, my own will and mind. It seemed that I was not only Clark Landon, but also part of the Earth-Brain that held me. By the strange, unhuman expressions of Travis and Skeel I knew they experienced the same thing.

"I felt a withdrawal of interest from Clark Landon's petty affairs and viewpoints. My mind seemed to leap beyond his little concerns to infinitely vaster things. And yet I knew somewhere in my consciousness that it was not my own mind that leapt thus, but the mere reflection or echo in my mind of the Earth-Brain holding me.

"How can I tell what I seemed to feel? It was as though for the time I was part of that great Earth-Brain, was thinking as it thought and seeing things as it saw them. It was as though, like it, my mind was cased not in any tiny body of colloids and bones and blood-compounds, but in a vast body endowed with a totally different sort of life. As though my great body was a planet, its stupendous frame of stone and its circulating life-fluid the cataracts of flowing fire in its interior! As though all the multitudes of land and water forms of life that swarmed upon my vast body were as unnoticeable and unimportant to me, intent on my own vast affairs, as microbes to the human upon whose body they live.

"It seemed that I, the Earth-Brain now and not Clark Landon, sat here in this brain-chamber at the top of my earth-body. Poised here, I was as aware of all my great body as a man is of his arms and legs. For down into my earth-body ran the tentacles of light that extended to the uttermost parts of earth, the muscular system by which I moved my earth-body at will.

"I moved one of those mighty muscles of light and the answering movement of my earth-body was a great quake on the other side of earth! Another of my muscles twitched and an avalanche crashed somewhere else on earth! I paid no attention whatever to the verminous tiny things dwelling upon my body, often annihilated in hordes by my earth-body movements.

"And I, the Earth-Brain, and my great earth-body, were not stationary but moving! My great body was racing at awful speed through vast leagues of infinite space! Far off across those immensities of space I was aware of other living earths, other planets, some larger and some smaller than I, but each living in the same vast way as I lived, each with its own great Brain!

"Yes, and from those other living earths there came to me across the void messages, communication. I, Clark Landon, could not even dimly comprehend the nature of that communication which I, the Earth-Brain, carried on. But it was constant and unbroken, a strange speaking of living earth to earth across the void, an exchange of thoughts, of purpose—

"For purpose there was in the way in which I and those other mighty Brains moved our planet-bodies through space. It was not by mere blind chance, haphazardly, that we moved, but consciously, deliberately, carrying out together some vast purposeful design. Circling and moving with superhuman exactness, a colossal, geometrical march of vast living earth-things through space!

"And even as I, Clark Landon, thus seemed to share the superhuman viewpoints and purposes of the Earth-Brain that held us, so did I share dimly its attitude toward ourselves. In one part of my intelligence I was still Clark Landon, held with Travis and Skeel helpless by a thing of mystery and terror. But in another part of my mind I was the Earth-Brain, inspecting these three tiny parasites who had dared penetrate my brain-chamber.

"For I, the Earth-Brain, had never bothered in one way or another with the numberless verminous parasites that dwelt on my earth-body, except that when any had dared approach the mountain at my body's top that held encased myself, I had warned and driven them back by movements and tremors of my body.

"But these three had not been driven back but had come on with insane temerity until they had penetrated this dwelling-chamber of mine where none of their kind ever had penetrated before. And I, the Earth-Brain, had found their audacity so unprecedented and unexpected that I had grasped these three insect-things, was examining them!

"In so much did I, Clark Landon, share somehow the Earth-Brain's thoughts as those thoughts beat like tangible force through us. And I was aware, even as Travis and Skeel and I struggled vainly against the light-tentacle's grip, of the Earth-Brain's desire to inspect one of us more closely. I was not surprised when another light-tentacle whipped out from its base and grasped Skeel, raised him high in the air close beside the Earth-Brain, Travis and I still held by the first tentacle on the floor.

"Travis and I ceased our struggles, watched in a sort of paralysis of terror as Skeel was raised high beside the Earth-Brain. The glowing light of the great ovoid seemed to beat out through him as the tentacle turned him this way and that like a helpless puppet.

"The Earth-Brain was examining him, I knew, for there still held me that curious duality of mind in which I was at the same time Clark Landon and the Earth-Brain. Even as I, Landon, watched from below my comrade Skeel I, the Earth-Brain, was inspecting curiously this tiny thing I held and concerning which I was casually interested.

"It was I, the Earth-Brain, who shot forth from myself another light-tentacle to grasp this tiny living thing. And then suddenly with a red crash of horror I was no longer the Earth-Brain at all but was Clark Landon, screaming wildly with Travis and shaking impotent little hands up at the Earth-Brain. For with those two tentacles it had casually torn Skeel's living body into halves!

"The tentacles held the two torn red things of broken flesh and bone that a moment before had been Herbert Skeel closer to the Earth-Brain's towering ovoid. The Earth-Brain was inspecting them, as calmly and dispassionately as a man might tear apart an insect and examine its interior structure.

"'Skeel!' Travis was screaming raggedly over the unceasing soft roar. 'The thing's killed Skeel!'

"'It's vivisected him!' I cried. 'I'll kill the damned thing—I'll kill it!'

"I was struggling insanely to reach the automatic in my belt, but held in the light-tentacle's grasp with Travis, I could not move my arms an inch.

"The Earth-Brain still was examining the broken body of Skeel. The great ovoid's changing colours still raced and swam, its roar of merged sounds unceasing and its mighty will still flooding tangibly through us and giving us that queer sense of identity with the Earth-Brain. But that sense was overwhelmed in me now by my wild fury at seeing Skeel, the comrade of Travis and myself for so long, slain so terribly before our eyes.

"Travis and I were mouthing wild threats at the towering ovoid. The Earth-Brain paid no more attention to us than might a man to the waving antennae of ants beneath his feet. It broke the halves of Skeel's body into smaller pieces. After a moment's inspection it dropped these red fragments, and the two tentacles that had held them shot down towards Travis and me!

"They grasped Travis and swung him up toward the Earth-Brain's side as Skeel had been swung, to vivisect him as Skeel had been vivisected. The other tentacle of light still held me on the floor. But in the moment Travis had been taken by the two, the grip of it upon me had perforce for an instant loosened, and in that instant I had ripped my pistol from my belt. Now as Travis was raised toward the Earth-Brain I aimed in a flash and fired a stream of steel-jacketed bullets up into the Earth-Brain's mighty ovoid of light.

"It was in the sheer madness of insane fury that I shot thus into the Earth-Brain, for I had no conscious hope of hurting in the least that terrific thing of tangible light and force in which its intelligence was embodied. But certain it is that even unconsciously I had no expectation of the cataclysmic reactions that took place the instant after my bullets tore into the Earth-Brain's ovoid of light.

"The Earth-Brain flamed pure crimson instantly, the crimson of leaping hell-fires and raging holocausts, the red of a superhuman, stupendous wrath. Colossal anger emanated from it at the same moment like a wave of destroying force, and as that cosmic wrath swept through me I knew that I had committed blackest sin against the universe in daring to attack the brain of the living earth-body upon which dwelt I and all my tiny race!

"And as the Earth-Brain blazed blinding crimson in rage, all its great tentacles or light-muscles whipped and twisted in a wild convulsion of insensate wrath! Travis was flung against the cavern's wall and smashed into red pulp by the impact; I was hurled as wildly and struck not the cavern wall but the mouth of the tunnel down which we had come, and all earth seemed shaking with a tremendous grinding roar of shifting rock as the tentacles running down from the Earth-Brain into it convulsed.

"The Earth-Brain had for the moment gone mad with sheer rage and its earth-body was shaking and quaking in that mad spasm. I staggered to my feet. The mountain, the great cavern and the tunnel in whose mouth I was standing, were rocking about me like a leaf in the wind. The Earth-Brain, in its mad excess of rage at having been attacked, had for the moment even forgotten me, who had dared make that attack, and was reacting in an insensate convulsion of fury that was shaking the whole upper part of its earth-body, the whole polar region!

"I stumbled away from that awful spectacle of the Earth-Brain's crimson-flaming ovoid of light, up into the tunnel. It was mindless terror that made me struggle up the tunnel whose terrific shakings flung me this way and that. I knew that in a moment when the Earth-Brain's first wild rage subsided it would remember me and its vengeance would crash upon me.

"I cannot tell now for how many minutes I fought my way up that tunnel, thrown from my feet each time I staggered erect by the wild pitchings of the mountain around me; crawling crazily upward on hands and knees with the terrific grinding of rock-masses beneath and around me like the last roar of doom in my ears. I saw ahead the white circle of light that was the tunnel's opening just as the first awful quakes began to subside, as the Earth-Brain's first convulsive rage began to calm.

"I knew the Earth-Brain would now remember me and I flung myself forward, out of the dark tunnel into the daylight on the mountain's side. Below and far away stretched the glittering ice-fields but now they were heaved and rumpled like waves of a mighty sea, piling here and there in mountainous ridges and attesting the violence of the great quake that had just shaken them.

"Down the mountain's icy side I started by the path Travis and Skeel and I had cut in ascending. There came a roar from above and an avalanche of ice and rock poured down on me from the mountain's upper side. I flattened myself beneath the angle of the slant in the side and it roared over and past me. The Earth-Brain had indeed remembered, knew where I was upon its body and was seeking to slay me!

"Thrice it tried to destroy me as I struggled down the mountain's side. Twice other avalanches were shaken loose upon me, each almost annihilating me, and once the whole mountain shook violently as though to dislodge me and send me tumbling to death. God, what a weird progress was that of mine down the mountain, with the Earth-Brain, with earth itself, trying to destroy me!

"I do not know yet by what chance I evaded those tremendous attacks and got to the ice-field at the mountain's bottom, bruised and terror-dazed. I looked to where our camp had been and there was but Noskat and one sledge and three dogs. Shan and the other sledge and dogs had been caught and annihilated by the shifting ice. Noskat ran toward me.

"He was babbling madly of the vengeance of the Earth-Brain, of the mighty quake that had killed Shan and the dogs and shaken terribly the earth itself. I cut him short, and we fled southward from the mountain over the ice-fields. Before we had travelled two hours a strong quake shook violently the ice over which we were travelling. A crevice opened suddenly ahead of us that we almost fell into.

"Noskat cried to me that we might as well die, that we had offended the Earth-Brain and that wherever we went upon its body, the earth, it would know and would try to kill us. But I pressed on, motivated only by the insane desire to put more and more distance between myself and that towering ice-mountain in whose heart the Earth-Brain poised.

"The next week was like one in a strange inferno, an icy hell of cold in which we pushed south with the Earth-Brain's vengeance ever following closely. Nine times during that week we were menaced by violent quakes that shook the ice over which we travelled. How we escaped those suddenly opening crevices and marching ice-ridges and terrific shocks, I cannot now dream. Terror, a terror not of the quakes but of the Earth-Brain causing them, drove us on.

"It came to me during that week of hell that Travis and Skeel had been luckier in being slain outright by the Earth-Brain than had I, with this remorseless vengeance of that mighty ovoid of light and intelligence pursuing me. Yet with that mad persistence that still actuated me, I pushed on. Toward the week's end Noskat's strength failed. With him in the sledge, dying and babbling of the Earth-Brain, I struggled south and at last reached the ship.

"To the ship's officers, who talked excitedly of the great cataclysm that had almost destroyed the vessel and that had seemed to centre where Travis and Skeel and I had been, I lied. I said that there had been a terrific quake and that Travis and Skeel and Shan had been killed in it. Noskat died without regaining consciousness and there was none to contradict me. The ship started south.

"I prayed as we sailed southward that the Earth-Brain would pursue me no farther, but I feared—I feared. My fear was justified, for as the ship passed close to the shore of Grinnell Land, a projecting glacier broke and hurled out a huge mass of ice that barely missed the ship. Two days later an undersea disturbance almost swamped us. The ship's crew talked of unsettled conditions, of earth-faults caused by the great polar quake; but I knew the truth, knew that my prayer was not answered and that still the Earth-Brain's vengeance followed me.

"We finally reached Halifax, and there I saw that the Earth-Brain would not reck of killing all my race if it could slay me, who had dared attack it. For, two days after we reached Halifax, came a terrible quake that destroyed half the city and killed thousands of its people. I escaped again, by the mere chance of being in an open park when the quake began.

"The newspapers quoted the scientists as saying, like the ship's men, that the great polar quake I had gone through had somehow caused faults in earths's interior structure which had resulted in this quake. I knew how far they were from the truth, knew the Earth-Brain had moved its vast earth-body and caused that quake solely to kill me.

"I fled from Halifax, whose dead seemed to point accusingly at me who had brought the Earth-Brain's death upon them. I took a boat to Norway and the day I arrived there came a quake that did great damage. By then I knew enough to stay out of buildings that might crash upon me, even sleeping in the open air. I went on from Norway to Russia.

"Russia had a series of three devastating quakes, the third one of which almost got me despite my precautions. When I fled on to Egypt it was worse, for my presence in Alexandria brought a quake and tidal wave that killed more innocent thousands. When I headed north again to Italy, the peninsula was racked by unprecedented quakes and landslides during my stay. And when I went on to England the quakes followed me.

"I knew that sooner or later, despite my carefulness to stay out of buildings and away from mountains and hills that might loose avalanches on me, one of these quakes would get me, the Earth-Brain's vengeance would find me. But I fled on, took a boat home. I arrived in New York today, and you, Morris, saw what happened.

"You saw that when I had not been in New York more than a few hours there came an earth-tremor. To the people here it seemed only a tremor. But to me it was warning and knowledge, knowledge that the Earth-Brain knew of my presence here, that it was still seeking to slay me with the movements of its great earth-body.

"Yes, following me still with deadly purpose! And that is why I dare not stay here in New York, Morris. If I did stay, sooner or later the

Earth-Brain would again attempt to kill me with an earthquake or tidal wave that might kill more innocent thousands or tens of thousands here. I have the blood of enough people now on my head without wanting more killed on my account. So I must go on, must leave here now before I bring doom on New York from the Earth-Brain's endeavours to take my life."

That was the story Clark Landon told me in my New York apartment the morning of the tremor. He left the city despite all I could say, a few hours afterward. I parted from him at the station where he took a train to New Orleans. I never saw Landon again but I followed his movements from that time until the end, and will summarise them briefly here.

The train Landon took to New Orleans was derailed by a sudden earth-tremor when a few hundred miles from its destination. Landon escaped, according to the newspaper casualty lists, though a score of people were killed and more injured. There were several earth-shocks of varying violence while Landon was in New Orleans, but they ceased after he took a banana boat to Mexico.

Ten days later I read of a violent quake that had destroyed the town of Tegulcipan, in northern Mexico, and the neighbouring villages of Causo and Santlione. The newspaper dispatches estimated the dead at fifty and mentioned the escape of an American staying in Tegulcipan, Clark Landon.

Landon went southward and a more or less continuous series of earthquakes followed him. At Progreso, in Yucatan, a double quake laid practically every structure in ruins and slew three-fourths of the population. Again I saw Clark Landon mentioned as one who had escaped, and it was said he had started for Guatemala.

At Guatemala came the end. The day after Landon arrived came the first terrifying rumblings of an earthquake of tremendous violence. The radio and cable stories told of the unexpected suddenness with which the earth heaved violently and with which vast crevices began opening in it. They told also of the curious suicide of an American named Clark Landon, which took place as the quake started.

According to these dispatches, Landon, when the quake started, had rushed into the street along which crevices were opening and had shouted madly as though adjuring someone or something to stop the quake. The shocks becoming each moment more violent, Landon had shouted something about surrendering himself and stopping these quakes devastating earth, and had rushed to the nearest crevice and thrown himself into it. According to those who saw, the crevice closed instantly upon him.

With Landon's death the quake stopped almost at once, the tremors subsiding. Though a few of Guatemala's buildings were shaken down and much glass shattered, there was no other damage and so Guatemala had cause for rejoicing. It was only after the first sensational stories of the quake and its sudden stop had filled the papers that they carried the minor detail of Landon's strange suicide.

The quake at Guatemala was the last of the series of earthquakes that for almost two years had wrought destruction over earth's surface. There have been minor tremors and movements since, of course, but no such succession of cataclysms as that which began with the great polar quake and moved here and there over earth until it ended at Guatemala.

That is all of the story, and I, Morris, intend to attach to it no explanation or attempt at explanation. It must end not with explanations but with questions, questions that may have their answer in known natural causes or that can be answered, perhaps, only by the incredible tale Clark Landon told me that morning.

Was the tale the literal truth? Did Landon and Travis and Skeel actually penetrate that icy mountain at earth's top to find there the Earth-Brain, the vast mind that has this earth for body? Was it because Landon attacked that Earth-Brain that for two years earth was racked by quakes?

Certain it is that that terrible series of quakes did follow Landon over earth's surface. Whether that was by coincidence only, or whether those quakes were the deliberate movements of its huge earth-body by which the Earth-Brain was striving to kill Landon, as he believed, there will be different minds.

And what of that last quake at Guatemala, where Landon flung himself into the crevice after madly adjuring the Earth-Brain to stop its destruction? There can be no doubt that Landon saw himself as bringing endless death and destruction on innocent cities and peoples by his mere continued living, and that he felt at last that only by sacrificing himself would the Earth-Brain's vengeance be satisfied, and the quakes cease.

Here again it is certain that no sooner had Landon flung himself into that crevice in the Guatemala street than the quake there stopped, the whole series of quakes stopped. Was that, too, by chance only? Or was it that Landon's sacrifice was not in vain, that with his death the Earth-Brain's revenge was accomplished?

It is with such questions and not with explanations, as I said, that the story must end. We cannot say whether up in its mountain-chamber at earth's top sits that mighty ovoid of sentient light that Landon called the Earth-Brain, whether we who consider ourselves masters of all are not but a race of microscopic parasites dwelling upon the vast and strangely living body of that Earth-Brain. It may be that we shall never be able to say, and I think that that is best. I think it is infinitely best that we, who know so much so certainly, do not know this thing.

THROUGH THE ALIEN ANGLE

BY ELWIN G. POWERS

"I'm sorry, but that's all the books the library has on that subject." I started to protest to the librarian, but knew at once it would do no good. I should have realized the folly of venturing out on a stormy night to try to get some information from this mausoleum of knowledge, and would have done better to go directly to the University. And with the time the girl had spent in vain searching for my material, the University Library had certainly closed. My final paper on the prehistory of man, due in class tomorrow, was in a sadly incomplete state.

I turned away, wondering whether I dared attempt to find a bookstore which might have remained open this late. But it was unlikely that any ordinary bookstore would have the books I needed. As I stood there, I felt a touch on my arm.

I turned, and looked at an old man who stood there. He came barely to my shoulder, and his white hair and beard made me think that he was a teacher from some local school. But his eyes were what arrested my attention. They were deep-set and dark, and seemed to hold in their depths some hint of dark and forbidden knowledge. I was tempted to rebuff him, but he smiled at me disarmingly.

"They are hopelessly materialistic here," he said, in a quiet voice. "I heard you asking about certain books. I may be able to help you, and my own small collection is at your disposal if you wish."

I thanked him. Scorn not the gifts that the gods provide, and I remembered that uncompleted class paper.

"I live a little way from here," he said, as I nodded my assent. "Is it still raining, as it was? Yes? Well, we will take a cab."

Almost before I could protest, he had hustled me from the library and into a taxi. He muttered something to the driver, and we whirled away into the dark.

I was almost inclined to withdraw from this singular venture, but I was confident of my ability to take care of myself, and so relaxed, and spent the time watching my companion as the cab sped along.

He seemed to have an indefinable air of antiquity about him, and I observed that he wore a cape—this incongruous garment had previously escaped my notice.

I grew more and more uncomfortable as the minutes passed. But suddenly the cab pulled up before a row of old brownstone houses, and the caped man paid the driver and we alighted.

That part of town was unfamiliar to me, and I stared at the residence with misgivings. But I suddenly caught sight of a police prowl car under a distant street light, and, reassured that help was near if I should need it, I mounted the steps behind my companion.

The room into which we stepped made me gasp, for it was luxuriously furnished, in contrast with the plain exterior of the house. In every corner stood relics, antiques from every corner of the globe. There was a saturnine statuette from Easter Island, a gorgeous Egyptian mummy-case, carved jade figurines, miniature Indian totems, Mayan tablets—and many others.

"Interesting, aren't they?" the old man said, breaking his silence. I wish I could give his name, but for some reason it never occurred to me to ask it. And I have never been able to find that house again, though I have combed the city several times, looking for it.

The antiquarian in me aroused, I examined several pieces more closely. They were undoubtedly genuine, and worth a small fortune.

"Collected every one myself," he said. "But come. In the library is what you wish to know."

He ushered me into another room, and here my astonishment was redoubled. For the walls were lined with books—books of every nature and description. But in spite of my enthusiasm, I could not help feeling that there was something amiss. And after a searching look around, I discovered what it was.

The room was not square. Two walls, the floor, and the ceiling, seemed to come together at an angle—a puzzling angle. And it seemed as if a person could walk into that peculiar conjunction, and walk right on—into, or through, or beyond our normal plane of things. But my attention was diverted from this odd phenomenon by the books about me.

I was standing before a shelf which seemed to hold all the forbidden books about which I had heard strange and disquieting whispers. The *De Vermis Mysteriis* of Ludvig Prinn, the *Nightbook* of Jacques Mosquea, several volumes by von Junzt, Perre Ereville, and Dirkas. Others were labeled simply by name, and I saw the *Song of Yste*, the *Book of Eibon*, and many others I had never heard of before. And, set a little aside, were two black-bound tomes—one was the *Necronomicon* of Abdul Alhazred, and the other was stamped simply *Cthulhu*—but that dread connotation sent chills down my spine.

"I think this will help you," said my host, as he drew out a volume. "*The Stanzas of Dzyan* are reliable. Sit down, and I'll read."

For half an hour he read aloud, drawing me a vivid picture of a prehistoric world—of creation itself, of strange races that had inhabited the earth before the Aryan race. But it was information that I could not use for fear of being laughed out of class, and I told him so when he had finished.

"Hopeless materialists, all of them!" he snorted. "Well, you at least will know about it, anyway. Do you want to hear more?"

I assented, and he took down a volume, the name of which I could not see. "I would like to light some incense," he said, and suited action to the words. "It may help you to listen."

I doubted it, but agreed. He sat down and began to read again—this time in a language unknown to me, though I am somewhat of a linguist. And as he read, and the pungent incense wafted through the room, I became drowsy.

But I do remember rising, through no volition of my own, and walking—walking toward the angle of the room that had so intrigued me earlier. And to my horror—and amazement—I seemed to pass through the solid walls. There was a moment of blackness, of unbearable chill—and then I opened my eyes on a vista which I am sure no mortal man had ever seen before.

It was a city—but what a city! Great domes rose all about me.

Graceful minarets sent their spires toward the sky. But all about me was a feeling of an alien presence. And my shadow—my shadow was two! I faced about—and two suns hung in a cold, brassy sky.

Terror gripped me, but I forced it aside. I was somewhere in a strange universe—but the main concern of returning to my own planet drove all other thoughts aside—even scientific interest in this monstrous place.

As I began to prowl through the deserted streets, I noticed many things. The city was undoubtedly of great antiquity, and had been deserted for many years—perhaps centuries, for the great columns and balustrades had crashed down in many places.

And then, as I approached one building more stately and imposing than the others, I saw—it.

I have since learned that the thing is a shoggoth—a globular mass of protoplasm, fifteen feet in diameter—able to take any form it desires—created as a servant of certain races of the universe—strong—tenacious—indestructible—and worst of all—intelligent!

It must have been a guardian of that building, untold eons ago. For as I stood in paralyzed horror, it rolled toward me—throwing out tentacles as it did so.

It was almost upon me, pseudopods lashing out, before I could move. And as I leaped back, turned and fled, it followed—and its speed was a match for my own.

Where I ran, and for how long, I do not know. Time lost all meaning as I dodged and hid in that accursed city—with the thing dogging my heels. And it was sheer luck that led me finally onto that street of ruins.

A building had collapsed, and strewn its skeleton to the winds. But some trick of fate had flung pillars and walls in an arrangement that made my heart leap—an angle, the angle that had thrust me into this bizarre world!

The shoggoth was close behind me, and I had to act. The angle might not be the same, but I was trapped anyway—so I charged blindly at it.

There was the blackness, the cold—and I struck ground with a thud. I rolled, picked myself up—and then—oh god!—the shoggoth came crashing through, not five yards from me!

I was on a road leading to the city, and I ran with all my strength toward the friendly lights, with the thing not far behind me. But as I came under the first streetlamp it slowed its pursuit, and then turned and withdrew.

But it will track me down. In that strange other world, it had a job to do—to protect a certain place. I invaded that place, and must die—and it will carry out its task, though in another universe. Even now, I know that it is lurking somewhere near—disguised by its amazing ability of mimicry, waiting for me. It will search me out, even on top of the building where I am writing this.

I am resigned to death. But—after I am slain, what then? The monster is here—here! It cannot return to its own world. What will it do? What terror will it spread? What inconceivable, awful horror faces mankind? I shall never know.

LEGACY IN CRYSTAL

BY JAMES CAUSEY

AGATHA SIMMONS LEANED FORWARD EXPECTANTLY.

"How long, Doctor?"

The man at the bedside looked up in brief distaste. He consulted his watch professionally.

"I really can't say," he whispered. "Perhaps another half hour. Perhaps ten more minutes—" He blinked at her and recommenced fumbling in his bag.

Agatha was silent. She looked at Jonathan's closed eyes. His breathing was barely perceptible now. She smiled.

So long. She had waited so terribly long for her cousin's estate. He must be well past eighty. In the past, she had been dimly afraid he would outlive her as he had all his other relatives.

But now—

"I must get some water." The doctor's voice intruded upon her thoughts. "For the solution—"

He went to the door, fumbling with his hypodermic needle.

Agatha did not hear him. She was gazing around the great gloomy bedroom. At the shades, drawn.

Behind the doctor, the door closed. The prone figure in the big four-poster bed stirred.

"Impatient, Agatha?"

She gave a little start. Jonathan Miles had raised himself on one elbow, with an effort.

He was staring at her, his thin, dark face mocking.

"Why—no, Jonathan. I was only hoping you'd get well soon."

"*Hah!*" The old man cackled with laughter. "Me get well soon! You know, you remind me of a buzzard, Agatha. Waiting for me to die. A pity, too. That auto accident. Mashed ribs... complications. I bet I would have outlived you, too—"

He broke off, lips still moving. Agatha frowned, then as she noted his breathing become slower, more fluttery, she restrained a smile.

No one knew how Jonathan Miles had acquired his vast fortune. He had always been a scholar, delving into out of the way places in far-off lands. A dabbler in archaeology. Suddenly, in his middle years, he had struck it rich. Now, in the declining years of his life, he had lived all alone, a gloomy old recluse in a dark old house, spurning all efforts of his relatives to visit him.

Agatha's gaze flicked avidly around the room. This old house—everything, would be hers soon.

She glanced at a ring on Jonathan's finger. A rather big diamond, that. Jonathan Miles followed her avid gaze keenly. He chuckled.

"Ah, but you're a greedy woman, Agatha."

"Why, I—"

"I don't *like* greedy women."

Agatha was silent. For the fortune soon to be hers, she could well endure a few insults.

Then she blinked. For Jonathan was fumbling with the ring on his finger, and he was handing it to her.

"Here, Agatha." His smile was vaguely mocking. "Take this. A little token of my esteem. No, don't thank me—"

He made a feeble gesture and sank back on his pillow.

"You'd take it after I'm dead, anyway—so I give it to you now."

"Jonathan! Really, I had no idea of—"

"Keep the ring," Jonathan said softly. "It has helped me—a great deal." His shoulders rippled with silent laughter.

Agatha stared at the ring. It was not a diamond. A large rosy crystal, gleaming lambently in the dim light. Set in a massive base of silver with strange symbols carven on it.

"What do you mean, Jonathan—helped you?"

Her cousin did not seem to hear her. He was staring at the ceiling. His lips were trembling. "My soul," he whispered. "I'm afraid the bargain wasn't... quite... just."

"What?"

No answer.

Agatha looked at him. Jonathan's eyes were closed.

He was not breathing.

Agatha drew a deep breath and went to the door.

Walter Simmons, standing in the parlor, saw his wife emerge from the bedroom. He blinked guiltily, and quickly hid his cigar.

"Walter! He's dead. Dead, you hear? This house—his money. All ours." She was jubilant.

"Uh—fine," said Walter, though inwardly he flinched at his wife's callousness.

The doctor came back from the kitchen, his hypodermic filled. "What's this? Did you say he was—"

"Dead," said Agatha, and hardly could restrain her morbid pride in possession of the house until the doctor had completed the necessary formalities and departed.

Walter Simmons heard the front door slam behind the physician and felt quite sorry for him, having to deal with Agatha in her present mood.

"Walter!" His wife's voice was shrill.

"Yes, dear."

His wife sniffed suspiciously. "Cigar smoke. How often have I told you—"

"I'm sorry," Walter said nervously.

"Well, let's see. There's this living room—ghastly old place. Gloomy. We'll have chintz curtains put in instead of those dreadful black drapes. The whole place needs remodeling. Maybe we'll sell it... later."

"Yes, dear."

"Of course you'll quit your bookkeeping job," mused Agatha. "We'll live here for the time being."

Walter Simmons nodded meekly. Ever since their marriage ten years ago he'd led a dog's life. Do this. Do that. Don't smoke cigars in the house. You know they're bad for my asthma. Now Agatha would have all the money. His life would be worse than ever...

He saw her tall, ungainly figure move about from doorway to doorway, criticizing, exclaiming, planning.

Walter sighed and went into the study. It was a huge dark place, with queer paintings on the walls. Near the center of the room was a dusty desk piled high with books.

Walter looked at these books. Old they were, crumbling with mildew. He paused, fascinated. He opened one book which was lying on the desk, closed. He frowned.

"Greek," he murmured disgustedly. He'd had four years of it in college. Squinting, he tried to decipher some of the words sprawling blackly across the pages...

Walter Simmons turned very pale. He shut the book quickly, and moved away from the desk where he stood for a moment, rubbing his hands suspiciously as if something had contaminated them.

Presently, fascination overcame his horror, and he stepped forward, looking at the book. But he did not touch it. His lips moved as he tried to decipher the faded dark words on the cover.

"The Nec—Necro—" he blinked. Cautiously, he turned the cover and looked at the first page.

Small and precise, the scrawl read:

Greek Trans. Abdul Alhazred.

Walter Simmons did not look into the book again. He remembered what he had read, and shivered.

He glanced at the other books. One caught his eye.

De Vermis Mysteriis. Prinn.

There was a little slip of white paper thrust in the middle as a bookmark. Gingerly, he opened it. He frowned. It was in Latin, of which he knew little, and there were penciled translations upon the sides. On the piece of paper was scrawled:

Trans. E103—

Never accept a gift from a necromancer or demon. Steal it, buy it, earn it, but do not accept it, either as a gift or legacy.

The word *legacy*, was circled in red pencil.

Walter Simmons stared at some of the strangely shaped hieroglyphics just beneath the notation. He licked his lips.

He looked around the huge dark study, and suddenly got out of there—fast.

* * *

"WAL—TER!"

"Yes, dear," he said, wiping the sweat from his brow as he stepped into the living-room. Agatha looked at him sharply.

"Here I tell you about how I'm going to redecorate this place, and I turn around and you're off browsing somewhere. Fine thing, I must say..." She paused in mid-sentence.

"Did you hear something?"

Walter swallowed uneasily. "No, I—"

The sound was repeated. The faint tinkle of the doorbell.

Walter and Agatha stared at each other.

"Probably the doctor," sniffed Agatha, brushing back a lock of straggly brown hair. "Phoned the undertaker, probably, to take the body away."

Walter answered the door. He blinked nearsightedly and stepped back.

The stranger standing in the doorway bowed. He was tall, and impeccably clad in striped trousers and tails.

Walter stared entranced at his flourishing auburn beard.

"Good afternoon." Their visitor straightened and stepped into the room, smiling disarmingly at Agatha.

Agatha stifled a faint feeling of apprehension. "What do you want?"

"I?" The man smiled—oddly, it seemed to Walter. "I was wondering about Jonathan. Is he—"

"He's dead," said Agatha. "Passed away ten minutes ago."

"What a pity. Ten minutes, eh? I hardly expected him to last so long. Exceeded his time by a good three hours. Ah, well. Hardy fellow Jonathan. I—ah—decided I'd stop by and see what the delay was." One hand stroked his long beard absently.

Walter Simmons took a step backwards. There was a strange shine to this fellow's eyes he did not like, nor the way he kept looking about the big house, almost—reflectively.

"What's your name, anyway?"

"My name?" The man's eyes glowed. "Sat—never mind. Never mind. I managed Jonathan's—legal affairs for him."

"Legal affairs?"

"Certainly. It was largely through me, Madame, that Jonathan acquired all his money... this house." His eyes flicked around the room briefly, fixed themselves upon the crystal ring on Agatha's left index finger.

"Ah!"

"What's wrong?" inquired Agatha uncomfortably.

"That ring. Believe it or not, I gave that to Jonathan. It—helped him, a great deal."

"Oh," snapped Agatha. "You gave it to him. Well, it's mine now, see? He gave it to me."

"Gave it to you?" The stranger's shoulders shook silently, and he made a laughing face, though no sound came forth. "My, but that's good. Lively fellow, Jonathan. Always did have a sense of humor. Well, I always give warning..."

"Warning?"

"Yes. That ring. It's Jonathan's. It really should remain with him, you know."

"If you're trying to threaten me—"

"No indeed, I assure you." Again came that strange smile, and one hand stroked the brown flowing beard. "And this house was in the contract we made. It was to be taken too..."

Walter Simmons was not listening. He was staring, aghast, at the man's head. At the two little curls of hair jutting up just off his brow.

Like two horns.

And that shadow on the wall behind him. It had a very disconcerting shape, indeed.

Agatha had, however, regained her self-composure. "What do you want here?"

"Nothing—now." Their visitor smiled urbanely at them both and bowed. "I have it. Good day."

They both stood mute as he crossed to the front door. He opened it. He went out.

"Well!" said Agatha. "I never! Trying to scare me into getting rid of this ring. Walter. Go see which way he went."

Uncomfortably, Walter went to the window, looked out. The stranger was nowhere in sight.

"The lawn'll have to be changed," said Agatha.

Walter nodded, silently. He was wondering why the lawn outside the house was so parched and sere.

JAMES CAUSEY

Jonathan's funeral had been yesterday.

"As soon as possible," Agatha had told the undertaker. Well, thought Walter, the undertaker had certainly been obliging. He wished disconsolately for a cigar.

Agatha stared at the house possessively. "We'll go ahead to the bank tomorrow, and see what he had in his vaults," she mused.

"But—" Walter found himself saying desperately. "I—I don't think it would look good, Agatha. So soon after the funeral..."

"Don't be so childish. Of course it'll look all right. And I'm having the remodelers start in tomorrow."

Walter sighed and looked up at the old house, looming huge and gaunt in the gathering dusk. Like an old, empty skull, he thought. The windows like two dark eye-sockets, the door like—

He stopped thinking. He seized Agatha by the arm.

"Look!"

Agatha stared. Her mouth dropped open, and then she started screaming shrilly for firemen, police, anyone—to come and save her house. Her beautiful house.

The house was on fire.

It was no use. The firemen squirted streams of silver water against it, long into the night. Agatha bothered the firemen interminably, until finally a cop shoved her back into the crowd with the gruff admonition to, "Keep back, lady. We're doin' all we can."

Walter stood back in the crowd, watching the blaze. Great gouts of flame mounting crimson and splendid against the night sky. The screaming of sirens in the distance. The wild confusion...

Walter could not help smiling. He remembered what he had seen in that book on Jonathan Miles' desk.

Such a book as that should very well be destroyed. Walter thought of these things, and how he could not possibly live in this house now, and he was glad.

But afterwards, on the homeward drive, he did not feel so glad. Agatha kept wailing, and alternately blaming him, the firemen, and their strange visitor of three days ago.

"It's all your fault. You know it is. You dropped a cigarette or something on the rug and it caught fire—" She paused again for breath.

"But Agatha, I didn't—"

"Shut up!" Walter cowered back behind the wheel, and was silent.

"Or maybe," said Agatha ominously, "it was that fellow who said he was a lawyer. The one with the beard and the funny smile. I bet he did it. Just 'cause I wouldn't give him this ring."

Walter was silent. Their visitor had said something about Jonathan. Having his little joke. Giving the ring to Agatha. And that odd crystal set in it.

"Well, anyway," Agatha said with an air of apparent unconcern. "The bonds in his safe-deposit box at the bank are safe. Three quarters of a million worth, so the executors said.

"And besides, I got this—" She rubbed her ring reflectively. "Wonder how much it's worth? Sure shines pretty, doesn't it, Walter?"

"Yes, dear," he said mechanically.

He glanced sideways at the ring. He shivered as he saw the symbols carven in the sides. Strange twisting runes, like the ones he had seen on that little piece of paper back in Jonathan's study...

"Agatha," he ventured timidly. "Agatha, maybe you'd better sell that ring. I think—"

No answer.

He turned.

Agatha was staring into the crystal with a strained, rapt expression. Walter Simmons swallowed uncomfortably as he looked at the crystal.

In the darkness, it had a dim reddish tint, that seemed to be pulsing with a strange unsteady glow. It looked—eerie.

Walter bit his lip.

Yes, the crystal looked remarkably like some gleaming, baleful eye.

The next morning, they went to the bank. Agatha bustling ahead, buoyed up with a sense of her own importance; Walter trailing small and timid, just behind.

Agatha informed the bank clerk that they were the heirs of Jonathan Miles, and why they had come.

"Ah, yes," the clerk said. "Right this way, please."

They went down to the vault.

"Mr. Miles, you understand, always did business with us by mail," said the clerk, pausing uncertainly in front of them.

"Yes," Agatha said impatiently. "Of course. Let's see in the boxes."

The man drew out the two safe-deposit boxes slowly, opened them. "At last reports Mr. Miles told us he had two hundred thousand dollars' worth of negotiable securities in this one," he began abstractly. "And almost half a million in bonds in this—"

His voice choked off. He blinked.

Agatha stared, and Walter stared, and then Agatha's voice rose in a shrill, angry scream, demanding to know where the money was. Who was the thief, and why didn't the bank take care of what belonged to her, and was this the right deposit box after all?

Where was her money?

The bank clerk could not explain it.

The boxes were empty. That was plain.

And for a very brief moment, as Agatha stared around the vault, trembling, clenching and unclenching her fists on empty air, she seemed to hear the faint tinkle of distant laughter.

Jonathan's laughter.

The president of the bank could not explain it either. He looked quite grave, informed them there would be an investigation made, but Agatha refused to be consoled.

"We'll sue them, that's what we'll do!" she announced grimly to Walter afterwards. "First the house, now the money. You—you realize what this means?"

"Yes," said Walter a little wearily. "I suppose I'll have to get my job back."

"You certainly will! And furthermore—" And she was off on another tirade.

Walter did not say anything. He was thinking. Thinking about what the stranger had said.

"This house will have to be taken with the rest—"

The *rest*. The bank securities. The house. Everything. Remembering the way the stranger's shadow had looked, Walter Simmons was not surprised that the bank president had been unable to explain the disappearance of the bonds.

* * *

The remainder of the week dragged slowly. They managed to sell the lot the house had been on for a rather pitiful sum, but Agatha was at least half-satisfied.

"I can buy me that fur wrap from *Modent's* I've always wanted," she told him Friday night over the supper-table. "And maybe some new silver—"

Walter's forehead wrinkled. "But how about that pipe you promised me for Christmas, dear? The red briar—"

"Oh, shut up! Always thinking of yourself. Why can't I have a husband that thinks of his wife once in a while? Let's see... I'll wear it to church, Sunday. And will make them all jealous! Walter. Did you get your job back today?"

"Yes," he said slowly. "I got it back."

He neglected to tell her he was getting ten dollars a week less than formerly. If he had, she would only wither him with scorn and ask him, as she always did, why didn't he stand up for his rights? Why didn't he assert himself, instead of being a timid little mouse all his life? Why indeed?

"Pass the sugar." Her voice broke shrill, strident, across his thought.

Walter reached for the sugar bowl casually—and then paused, his arm in midair.

It was over by Agatha. He could have sworn it was next to his plate not ten seconds ago.

He could also have sworn that he had seen out of the corner of his eye, a dim red flash—across the table.

It was after supper. Walter was sitting in the front room, reading his paper and wishing he dared smoke a cigar.

"Walter!"

He looked up. Agatha was standing in the kitchen doorway. Her face was white.

He got up slowly, went into the kitchen. "Look, Walter."

He looked. The dishes were all washed and shining and stacked neatly into place.

"Very good, dear," said Walter vaguely, searching for some new compliment. "Very fast, too—"

"You fool! I didn't do these dishes!"

"Huh?"

"No. I was standing over by the icebox, putting food away, and wishing that I—well, I was wishing that I had a husband who was considerate enough of his wife to do the dishes for her. And I thought I saw something red."

"Red?"

"Yes. Behind me. A—a flash, sort of. I turned around, and there they were. Done!"

"Oh," said Walter weakly. Then he caught sight of the ring on Agatha's finger.

It was glowing like ruby fire.

About four o'clock the next morning, Walter Simmons was quite rudely awakened. Beside him, Agatha was screaming over and over in a shrill falsetto. Screaming, and still asleep.

Abruptly she woke, and clung, trembling, to him for a good five minutes before he managed to soothe her.

"Walt," she sobbed hysterically. "Oh, Walt! I had a bad dream."

She had not called him Walt for almost ten years now.

"I dreamt," she whispered, "that this ring had a funny little red man inside, and he was laughing at me and hiding. I wanted him to break the crystal, and let me see him, but he wouldn't.

"Then, all of a sudden, he did show me his face. Oh, it was… *awful.*" She sobbed shudderingly. Then she was silent.

She gazed dreamily into the ring.

Walter Simmons moistened his lips. He said, "Agatha.

"Agatha!"

She gave a little jump, and turned on him. "What?"

"Look, Agatha. Why don't you sell the ring?"

"Sell it?"

He gulped, took a firm hand on his courage. "Yes. After all, you said you were afraid."

Agatha looked at the ring. She was smiling strangely.

"I know. But I—I've changed my mind."

Walter Simmons left for the office next morning with a sickening apprehension gnawing at his insides. His fears were not relieved by the sight of Agatha, after breakfast, sitting on the sofa, staring at the winking bit of rosy crystal on her finger.

She did not even bid him good-bye.

That evening, Walter did not go home. He went instead to the library, and spent a good hour and a half browsing through the section marked "Demonology" before he found what he wanted.

FAMILIAR–he read. *A demon given to a sorcerer or witch as part of his compact with Satan. In the olden times they inhabited usually the body of a toad or black cat. Of late, however, it has been found more convenient to use for the dwelling-place of the familiar some more personal object–such as a bracelet, a necklace, or ring–*

"Ah," said Walter very softly. He read on.

...And if the owner of the familiar dies, or his compact with Satan runs out, then the imp should be buried with him. In the event another human comes into possession of the familiar, it owes him temporary allegiance–though it can, perforce, commit whatever mischievous pranks it will. Should the name of God be mentioned in the familiar's presence–

Walter Simmons gulped as he read the next few lines. He jumped up and went out of the library hurriedly, his short fat legs pumping, eyes wide.

He knew now who the impeccably dressed stranger had been.

He knew about the ring.

And–he had a very good idea what would happen should Agatha wear that ring to church tomorrow.

When he arrived home, Agatha was huddled over on the sofa, staring into the ring. She looked up as he came in, gave him a dreamy smile. "Oh, are you home already?"

Walter blinked.

"Look, Walt! Look at my coat."

He glanced briefly at the new fur wrap, and nodded. "Yes, dear. Very nice."

"Just wait 'till they see me tomorrow with it at church. And with this ring." She smiled in anticipation.

Walter blinked again. There was something odd about his wife's behavior.

"Agatha," he whispered numbly. "You've got to listen. That ring. You mustn't wear it tomorrow to church."

Agatha looked at him. "Why not?"

"Because. It's evil. Look, dear. Do me a favor, will you?"

She nodded, absently.

"Make a wish. Wish that, oh, that supper would be ready. Right now." Agatha's lips moved. For an instant the crystal on her finger sparkled with unearthly brilliance, and Walter thought he saw something red streaking toward the kitchen—and then back again.

"Now," he managed. "Come into the kitchen."

Walter had half-expected to see what he did, but the sight was still rather frightening.

The roast was done. The table was all set. The potatoes had been mashed and the salad was made. Everything ready to go on the table.

"There," he said weakly. "See that?"

Agatha was smiling. "Of course. It's the ring "

Walter fought down the black wave of panic that closed on his insides. "Then you'll get rid of it? Sell it, or—"

"Of course not. I rather like this ring now. Sort of... fascinating." She kept staring at it.

Walter argued and pleaded all through supper, but to no avail. Agatha liked the ring. She would wear it tomorrow morning to church and nothing Walter could say or do would change her mind.

That was that.

At church services next morning, all their neighborhood acquaintances were properly awed by Agatha's new coat. They oh'd and ah'd, as Agatha smirked, and displayed it to her heart's content.

A dull, fatalistic feeling had fallen upon Walter. He did not even respond to his wife's most barbed insults, paid no heed to her hisses of "Walter! Sit up straight. Everybody's looking at us!"

But as the service slowly dragged through the next hour, Agatha stopped prodding him. She was staring into the crystal on her finger, as if hypnotized. Walter closed his eyes very tightly as he remembered what he had read...

Somehow he couldn't stop trembling.

At the conclusion of the hymns, the pastor turned to the congregation and lifted his hands for the blessing.

This was it. Walter held his breath. The minister's voice thundered out.

"In God's name, may peace reign!"

As the pastor uttered the words, Walter felt Agatha stiffen beside him. Then she screamed. Horribly.

Everywhere there was commotion, a babble of excited voices, people shouting and demanding to know what had happened, ushers exclaiming and hurrying forward.

Very slowly, Walter Simmons turned. He looked at Agatha's face.

Her eyes were wide and staring, and at the expression in them, he felt the short hairs bristle at the nape of his neck.

He looked at the ring.

He was not surprised to see the dim red glow gone. Instead the crystal was white and lusterless, as if—whatever dwelt in it had fled forever.

Walter wondered briefly how the familiar had looked to Agatha, as it came out of the ring.

There were no complications. Heart failure, the coroner said.

At the funeral, many were the strange remarks at Walter Simmons' strange apathy.

"Don't look a bit sad," one of his friends whispered. "Well, that's not surprising either, if you knew how Agatha treated him. A regular shrew, she was."

The good neighbors of Walter Simmons might have been a great deal more concerned than they were, had they seen him the next night—seen him in the cemetery, digging furtively in a grave which could not have been over a week or two old. A grave with the name "Jonathan Miles" inscribed on the headstone.

They might have said much and wondered more, could they have seen the small crystal ring Walter left in the grave.

The ring which he was returning to its former owner.

THE WILL OF CLAUDE ASHUR

BY C. HALL THOMPSON

I

THEY HAVE LOCKED ME IN. A MOMENT SINCE, FOR WHAT WELL may have been the last time, I heard the clanking of the triple-bolts as they were shot into place. The door to this barren white chamber presents no extraordinary appearance, but it is plated with impenetrable steel. The executives of the Institution have gone to great pains to ensure the impossibility of escape. They know my record. They have listed me among those patients who are dangerous and "recurrently violent." I haven't contradicted them; it does no good to tell them that my violence is long since spent; that I have no longer the inclination nor the strength requisite to make yet another attempted break for freedom.

They cannot understand that my freedom meant something to me only so long as there was hope of saving Gratia Thane from the horror that returned from the flesh-rotting brink of the grave to reclaim her. Now, that hope is lost; there is nothing left but the welcome release of death.

I can die as well in an insane asylum as elsewhere.

Today, the examinations, both physical and mental, were quickly dispensed with. They were a formality; routine gone through "for the record." The doctor has left. He wasn't the man who usually examines me. I presume he is new at the Institution. He was a tiny man, fastidiously dressed, with a narrow, flushed face and a vulgar diamond stickpin. There were lines of distaste and fear about his mouth from the moment he looked into the loathsome mask that is my face. Doubtless one of the white-suited attendants warned him of the particular horror of my case. I didn't resent it when he came no nearer me than necessary. Rather, I pitied the poor devil for the awkwardness of his situation; I have known men of obviously stronger stomach to stumble away from the sight of me, retching with sick terror. My name, the unholy whisperings of my story, the remembrance of the decaying, breathing half-corpse that I am, are legendary in the winding gray halls of the asylum. I cannot blame them for being relieved by the knowledge that they will soon shed the burden I have been—that, before long, they will consign this unhuman mass of pulsating flesh to maggots and oblivion.

Before the doctor left, he wrote something in his notebook; there would be the name: Claude Ashur. Under today's date he has written only a few all-explanatory words. "Prognosis negative. Hopelessly insane. Disease in most advanced stage. Demise imminent."

Watching the slow, painful progress of his pen across the paper, I experienced one last temptation to speak. I was overwhelmed with a violent need to scream out my now-familiar protest to this new man, in the desperate hope that he might believe me. The blasphemous words welled for an instant in my throat, sending forth a thick nasal sob. Quickly, the doctor glanced up, and the apprehensive loathing of his gaze told me the truth. It would do no good to speak. He was like all the rest, with their soothing voices and unbelieving smiles. He would listen to the hideous nightmare that is the story of Gratia and my brother and myself, and, in the end, he would nod calmly, more convinced than ever that I was stark, raving mad. I remained silent. The last flame of hope guttered and died. I knew in that moment, that no one would ever believe that I am not Claude Ashur.

Claude Ashur is my brother.

Do not misunderstand me. This is no mundane instance of confused identity. It is something infinitely more evil. It is a horror conceived and realized by a warped brain bent upon revenge; a mind in league with the powers of darkness, attuned to the whimpering of lost, forbidden rites and incantations. No one ever could have mistaken me for Claude Ashur. To the contrary, from the earliest days of our childhood, people found it difficult to believe that we were brothers.

There could not have been two creatures more unlike than he and I. If you will imagine the average boy and man, the medium-built creature of normal weight and nondescript features, whose temperament is safely, if somewhat dully balanced—in short, the product of normalcy— you will have before you a portrait of myself. My brother, Claude, was the precise antithesis of all these things.

He was always extremely delicate of health, and given to strange moodiness. His head seemed too large for the fragility of his body, and his face was constantly shadowed by a pallor that worried my father dreadfully.

His nose was long and thin with supersensitive nostril-volutes, and his eyes, set well apart in deep sockets, held a sort of mirthless brilliance. From the outset, I was the stronger as well as the elder, and yet it was always Claude with his frail body and powerful will who ruled Inneswich Priory.

At a certain point in the road that fingers its way along the lifeless, Atlantic-clawed stretches of the northern New Jersey coast, the unsuspecting traveler may turn off into a bramble-clotted byway. There is (or was, at one time) a signpost pointing inland that proclaims: "INNESWICH-½ MILE." Not many take that path today. People who know that part of the country give wide berth to Inneswich and the legends that hang like a slimy caul over the ancient coastal village. They have heard infamous tales of the Priory that lies on the northernmost edge of Inneswich, and of late years, the town, the Priory, the few intrepid villagers who cling to their homes, have fallen into ill-repute. Things were different in the days before the coming of Claude Ashur.

My father, Edmund Ashur, was the pastor of the Inneswich Lutheran Church; he had come to the Priory a timid, middle-aged man with his young bride, two years before I was born. The night Claude Ashur was born Inneswich Priory became the house of death.

The night Claude was born. I have never really thought of it that way; to me, it has always been the night my mother died. Even I, child that I was, had been caught in the web of the pervading sense of doom that hung over Inneswich Priory all that day. A damp sea-breeze, smelling of rain, had swept westward, and perforce, I had spent the day indoors. The house had been uncannily quiet, with only the muffled footfalls of my father, pacing in the library, trying to smile when his gaze chanced to meet mine. I did not know, then, that the time for the accouchement was near. I knew only that, in the last weeks, my mother had been too pale, and the huge, cold rooms seemed lonely for her laughter. Toward nightfall, the village physician, a round apple-cheeked man named Ellerby, was summoned; he brought me taffy from the general store as he always did, and shortly after he disappeared up the wide staircase, I was packed off to bed. For what seemed like hours I lay in the dark, while a leaden bulwark of clouds rolled inland with the storm. Rain lashing against my casement, I fell to sleep at last, crying because my mother hadn't come to kiss me goodnight.

I thought it was the screaming that woke me. I know, now, that the pain-torn cries had died long-since with my mother's last shuddering breath. Perhaps some final plaintive echo had slithered along the blackened halls, finding my sleep-fogged child's brain at last. A cold, nameless terror numbed me as I crept down the winding carpeted stairs. At the newelpost, a soft, desperate, lost sound stopped me. And then, through the open library door, I saw them. My father was sunken in a leather armchair by the fireless grate; candlelight wavered on the hands that covered his face. Uncontrollable sobs wracked his bowed shoulders. After a moment, his face more solemn and pallid than I had ever seen it, Dr. Ellerby came from the shadow beyond my view. His thin, ineffectual hand touched Father's arm gently. His voice was thick.

"I... I know how little words help, Edmund... I just want you to know, I did all I could. Mrs. Ashur was..." He shrugged his plump shoulders in impotent rage at fate. "She just wasn't strong enough. It was odd; as if the baby were too much for her—too powerful—taking all the strength, the will from her. It was as if..."

His words withered into nothingness, and crawling abysmal darkness clawed me. I wanted to cry, but I couldn't. Fear and loneliness knotted in my chest. I could barely breathe. Years later, the completion of that last unfinished sentence of Ellerby's became more and more horribly clear to me. "It was as if he had killed her, so that he could live..."

They buried Mother in a shaded corner of the graveyard behind the church. The villagers came and stood in the needling downpour, their heads bowed in voiceless grief. And through all of it, irreverent and demanding, came the belligerent howling of the infant Claude; there was something blasphemous and terribly wrong about those dominant cries. It was as though, somehow, this dark-browed bawling child was an intimate of death and felt no need to grieve or be frightened in the face of it.

From that day forth, Inneswich Priory was Claude Ashur's private domain. It is true that the howling, open belligerence soon quieted, and even in his early boyhood, Claude's voice attained an unusually sibilant modulation. But, never did it become less dominant. On the contrary, the very calm softness of it seemed to lend it more strength, more power to influence the listener. It was Claude's will, not his voice, that ruled the Priory and everyone in it. The voice was merely an instrument of the will.

My father was Claude's slave. All the tender unpretentious love he had given my mother before her death was now lavished on Claude. I believe Father saw in him a final remembrance of the gentle creature whose grave was never bare of flowers. I was sorry for Father. For, from the outset, that brooding, frail creature seemed not to need love or help. All his life, Claude Ashur was coldly self-sufficient, and completely capable of getting anything he wanted.

Worry over the dubious condition of Claude's health led my father into further extravagances. Rather than send Claude to school, which would necessitate his leaving the gloomy protection of the Priory, Father brought in a series of tutors. The plan was never a success. Time and again, it started off well, and some bookish, middle-aged man or woman would think that he or she had a perfectly priceless berth at the Priory. The tutelage of one boy seemed like the easiest job in the world. But, invariably, the tutors eventually developed a violent dislike, hidden or overt, for Claude. They never remained at Inneswich Priory more than a fortnight. Often, when one of them had just gone, I would chance to look up from the garden to find Claude's pale, thin face framed in a window. The colorless lips were always haunted by a satisfied, malignant smile. And, once more, the brash intruder cast out, the furtive shadow of my brother's isolationism would settle, shroud-like, over the Priory.

II

IN THE EASTERN WING OF INNESWICH PRIORY, BEYOND A massive, baroque door, lay a chamber I had never seen. Unholy stories of that room have haunted the hamlet of Inneswich since one ghastly night late in the 18th Century. My father never spoke of the awesome legends that cluttered, murmuring obscenely, behind that carven portal. It was enough for him that, for more than a hundred years, the room had been sealed off and forgotten. But, Claude and I had heard others—the hired help who came by day from the village to the Priory—whisper the hideous details many times, seeming to relish the vicarious thrill they experienced while discussing past and hidden evil.

In the year 1793, one Jabez Driesen, then pastor of Inneswich Church, returned from a sabbatical spent in Europe. He brought with him the woman he had met and married on the Continent. There are written reports of her beauty in the archives of the library at Inneswich, but, for the most part, they are at cross-purposes and garbled. On one issue alone, every report is in accord. The wife of Jabez Driesen was a secret disciple of witchcraft; she had been born in some obscure Hungarian village of ill-repute, and it was whispered through the streets of Inneswich that this sorceress—this consort of the darkness—must die. The whispering grew to an open protest that reached Jabez Driesen's ears, and one night a frantic, witless crone who served the Driesens ran screaming from the Priory. Investigating the reason for her babbling hysteria, the villagers found the answer in that chamber in the East Wing. The charred remains of Jabez Driesen's bride were discovered, manacled to a stake in the tremendous, ancient fireplace, and, swinging noiselessly from one of the massive, hand-squared ceiling beams, was the corpse of the pastor of Inneswich Church. Next day, the bodies were removed and buried, and the room was sealed. When Claude Ashur was twelve years of age, he claimed that chamber for his own.

Father was more worried than ever; at last, he openly admitted that he was frightened of Claude's tendency to isolationism. With the acquisition of the room in the East Wing, Claude withdrew almost entirely from the outer world. There was something alarming and unhealthy in the way he spent whole days and nights alone in his inviolable sanctum. The heavy, exquisitely carved door was kept locked at all times. Occasionally, on clear, dry days, Claude would wander aimlessly for hours along the bleached desert of the beach; he always carried the key to that door with him. Prompted by my own curiosity and my father's concern, I tried often to find some basis of mutual interest that would draw me closer to Claude—that would put me in a position where I might learn the nature of the secrets he hid so jealously in his lonely, ghost-ridden room. Once or twice, I even made a move to join him in his solitary expeditions along the edge of the sea. His dark, resentful taciturnity soon made it obvious that I wasn't welcome. In the end, nagged by a vague sense of frustration, I gave it up. I should probably never have had the courage to defy Claude, and break into the forbidden chamber, had it not been for my Irish Setter, Tam.

Aware, as he was, of my affection for dogs, on the eve of my twenty-second birthday, Father presented me with Tam. Then little more than a year old, the dog was already well-trained; he had the keen intelligence, the gentle eyes, the shining russet hair that somehow set his breed in a special niche. In no time at all, Tam and I were inseparable companions. Wherever I went, Tam was at my heels. His coltish, often hilarious adventures, served to lighten somewhat the gloom that had coated Inneswich Priory like some loathsome, smothering scum that happiness and sunlight could not penetrate. And, from the moment he laid eyes on him, Claude resented Tam.

As though by some inborn instinct, the dog avoided my brother on every possible occasion. It was nothing new. Without exception, animals of every sort displayed an often vicious aversion to Claude. It was as if their antediluvian sensitiveness warned them against some buried evil of which the duller senses of humans were unaware. Generally, this open enmity caused nothing but a rather sardonic amusement on Claude's part. But, in the case of Tam, he seemed unusually irritated. Perhaps it was because, unwittingly, the dog was violating the domain so long controlled by Claude's will alone. In any event, in a manner that somehow roused uneasy suspicion in me, he made an unwonted effort to befriend Tam.

* * *

On that particular afternoon, Tam and I had been having our habitual romp in the ash-shaded quiet of the Priory garden. I remember laughing at the way Tam bounded off after an autumn-decayed twig of ash I had tossed in the direction of the flagstone terrace that lay just without the French casements of the library. Then, abruptly, before he had reached the twig, the setter stopped short. I saw his lean rusty body, dappled by late-afternoon sun, grow tense; his muzzle trembled, baring vicious canines. The frolicsome, gentle Tam of a moment before had turned into a terrified animal at bay.

I looked up and saw Claude standing over the ash-twig Tam had been chasing. He was smiling, his pale lips warped, showing small white teeth, but there was no humor in his eyes. Behind them lay the shadow of angry annoyance. I thought he winced at the snarl that sounded in Tam's throat. And then, before I could interfere, with a harsh furious laugh, Claude made a wild grab for the dog. I heard him say, "Come here, you little devil!" I heard Tam's hysterical yelp, and then, a sharp exclamation of pain.

"Tam!" I cried. "Down, Tam! Down!"

As suddenly as it had begun, the terrible furor quieted. A pregnant, awful stillness settled on the ash-grove. A single leaf quivered to the chilled stones at my feet. Tam whimpered plaintively as he slunk toward me, and cowered, shivering, against my leg. Claude didn't swear; he didn't even speak. He stood very still, staring down at the blood that oozed obscenely from the wicked gashes that scored the back of his white-skinned hand. When his eyes shifted to the shuddering beast at my side, they were seething with pent-up malevolence that whispered of satanic hatred older than man himself; a fury born of lost eons when such hatred ruled the world. After a long moment, Claude turned on his heel, and disappeared through the French windows into the murky dimness of the library. The hand with which I gave Tam a reassuring pat trembled. I told myself I was being foolish; there was no need to be afraid. But, the following evening, Tam disappeared.

At dusk, I had gone to the kennel to unleash Tam and take him for his nightly run into the village. I had found only the ragged end of the leash tethered to a metal ring by the kennel door. And standing there, in the gathering, mist-choked darkness, I had a sudden vision of the controlled rage in Claude's bloodless face, and that forbidding, truth-hiding door in the East Wing. I shuddered. I argued that I was letting my imagination run away with me. It was possible that Tam had gnawed his way to freedom, and dashed on to the village ahead of me. But, even before I walked the night road to Inneswich, before I made inquiries at the tavern, and questioned the children who played Lie-Low-Sheepy in the streets, I knew what the answers would be. No one had seen or heard of Tam since last night when he'd been to the village with me. A strange, frozen anger took possession of me as I returned to Inneswich Priory that night. I knew that I was going to violate Claude Ashur's sanctuary.

Before retiring, the housekeeper had left a tray in the library for me. There were sandwiches and scones and a pot of chocolate. I didn't touch any of it. Strangely wary, I crept through the catacombs of the lower hall, and in the sepulchral gloom of the pantry, found what I wanted. From a rusty, seldom-used tool-chest, I extracted a length of heavy wire; I bent one end of it into a neat hook, then, soundlessly, tensely, as before, I went back along the hall and climbed the wide, winding staircase. Somewhere in the house, a weary joist groaned eerie, century-old protest. From his room at the head of the stairs, came Father's heavy, reassuringly human snore. A little further on, the door to Claude's bedchamber was ajar. There was no light. I paused, not breathing, and stared into the Stygian blackness of the room. Slowly, cold watery moonlight picked out Claude's form sprawled across the great canopied bed. His breathing came slow and deep. With a painstaking furtiveness that somewhat surprised me, I closed his door and moved on through cloying shadows toward the chamber in the East Wing.

I was not sure I could do it. The twisted wire wavered in my unsteady fingers, rattling like hell-wrought ghost chains in the antiquated lock. I don't know how long I manipulated the wire before I was rewarded by the sullen, rasping click of reluctant tumblers. Under the pressure of my sweat-damp hand, the massive door swung inward. At first, there was nothing but a swimming, thickened darkness that seemed to suck me into the vortex of a black whirlpool. Then, I felt suddenly sick. A horrible, grave-smelling effluvium pressed in upon me from every quarter. It was the stench of lost ages, the noisome, ectoplasmic aura of carrion-flesh.

I lit a candle and by its luminance saw in a small cleared circle, surrounded by the baleful, winking-glass anachronism of test-tubes and retorts, a statuette that seemed to have been carved from damp, half-rotten wood. I took a step forward and stared down at a form of craftsmanship that was at once exquisite and indescribably evil; I had the feeling that the hands which chiseled this thing must have been directed by some unholy genius. No human art could have wrought so uncannily perfect an image of Tam. Sprawled on its side, the miniature animal gazed into the candle-glow with hideously blank eyes. There was an ugly gash in the full throat that ran from ear to ear, and from that carven wound pulsed the vile, greenish ichor that spread in a slow pool upon the scarred surface of the table!

I cannot say for certain how long I stood staring at that fetid, putrescent tableau of death. Disjointed, unbearable visions of the gentle animal that had come to mean so much to me infested the darkness about me. Physical illness returned, knotting my stomach, and I thought of Tam, alone somewhere, whimpering away the last of his brief life. At breakfast the next morning, the housekeeper bustled in to say that a fisherman from the village wanted urgently to speak with me. They had found Tam.

A dank mist fingered inland from the bleakness of the Atlantic. It swirled like seance-conjured ectoplasm among the dew-chilled fronds that spiked the crest of the dune. I knelt for a time beside the pitiful, limp form that lay half-covered with wind-blown sand. The rich rusty hair at Tam's throat was matted with a darker crimson stickiness. The horrid slit gaped redly, like the grotesque smile of a cretin. Tam had been dead for hours. I stood erect and the little fisherman wiped a furtive tear from the salt-burned seams of his face.

"Us at the village liked Tam, sir. He was so gentle-like with the children..." He snuffled and shook his head. "Musta been a awful big beast as could make such a tear in his gullet..."

I didn't say anything. I sent the little man for a spade and a length of tarpaulin. We wrapped Tam in the canvas and buried him there on the dune. The sand was damp and cold; icy mist settled in the shallow pit of the grave. When we had filled it in, I marked it with a single, bleached seashell. All the time we worked, I thought of the fisherman's words, and I knew that nothing natural, neither beast nor human, had destroyed Tam.

Father never knew the truth; I let him believe the story that circulated among the villagers—the tale of some wandering animal that had fought with Tam and killed him. I had no desire to aggravate my father's uneasiness in connection with Claude. He was getting on in years and had not been really well since Mother's death, and I wanted him to spend his declining days in peace.

When, shortly after dinner, I decided to retire, Claude climbed the long stairway at my side. He didn't speak but at my door he paused. Involuntarily, I looked at him. He was smiling, his pallid, mature visage an odd contrast against the boyishness of his clothes; I had seen that face before. It held the same triumphant, cruelly humorous smile that had been framed in the window the day the last tutor deserted Inneswich Priory. Once again, Claude Ashur's will had conquered the transgressor. After a long moment, softly, he said, "Goodnight," and walked off along the shade-clotted corridor that led to the room in the East Wing. I didn't see him again for nearly four years.

III

THE FOLLOWING MORNING, BEFORE CLAUDE WAS UP AND about, I bade goodbye to my father, and, as I'd been planning to do for some time, left for Princeton to study journalism. For several months the darkling memory of those last hours at the Priory hovered always at the rim of consciousness, but, gradually, forgetfulness pressed the horrible fate of Tam into a cobwebbed niche of the past. My life at the university became a comfortably mundane round that was far removed from the existence I had led under the shadow of my brother at Inneswich Priory. My sole material connection with Claude during those four happily crowded years was the correspondence I carried on with Father. With the passage of time his letters grew increasingly strained; try, as he obviously did, to seem cheerful and satisfied, he could never quite keep apprehensive references to Claude from slipping into them. Those scant phrases, hinting that Claude was becoming more and more secretive and unmanageable, invariably cast me backward through endless corridors of gloom, evoking a terrible picture of the loathsome, grinning face I wanted only to forget. Then, too, beyond the transient uneasiness caused by my father's restrained messages, there were moments when I felt certain that, even here, the fetid spectre of Claude's influence could touch me. To certain more conservative elements at the university, groups that numbered among them students indigenous to Inneswich or its surrounding country, I had become an object of rather distasteful curiosity. I was avoided as "that fellow from Inneswich Priory—Claude Ashur's brother..." When Father came down to Princeton for my commencement, Claude came with him. Looking back upon that last night in my sitting room, I realize, now, that, had we not been blinded by our wish to believe something good of Claude, Father and I should have guessed at the odious truth from the beginning. As things were, we were only too anxious to accept my brother's soft-voiced, trite lecture about having decided that he could best serve humanity through medicine. Happy for the first time in years, Father drank in every syllable of Claude's blasphemous lies. Before he retired, he told me confidentially that he would be grateful if I advised Claude on the choice of the most suitable university. It wasn't the sort of job one looked forward to; giving advice to my brother seemed like a rather pretentious idea. I was not at all sure he wouldn't laugh at me.

I returned to the sitting room to find Claude slouched in a battered leather armchair by the fireplace. Even in the roseate glow of a log-fire, his face seemed exceptionally pallid. I remember reflecting that it was as though he were suffering a blood-draining chill; a chill that went deeper than flesh to clutch the soul in icy fingers. His eyes came up quickly as I took the chair opposite him and lit my pipe. I fancied that the ancient, cryptic malevolence of the smile he turned on me was inexplicably tinged with anxiety. It gave me rather a start, when, while I was still searching for a proper approach to the subject, he said, softly:

"I've already decided on the college, you know..."

"Well... No... I didn't know..."

"Yes..." Quite suddenly the opaque cold eyes glinted with quiet cunning. In that moment I should have sensed the malefic import of Claude's choice. I confess I felt nothing but a vague uneasy puzzlement at his next words. "I've decided to go to Miskatonic University..."

He spoke the name with an unusually resonant clarity, and as he did, I saw again the unwonted hint of anxiety that seethed behind his reserved smiling mask. One would have said that Claude was afraid I might recognize that name; that it bore some corrupt connotation of which he hoped I was ignorant. Almost imperceptibly, when I asked where Miskatonic was located and what sort of reputation it had, he relaxed. In sibilant, strangely hypnotic tones, he drew a pleasant picture of a well-endowed college, abounding in charming tradition, nestled in the domed hills of Arkham, in northern New England. He did not speak, that night, of what obnoxious horrors lay hidden within the ivy-strangled walls of the Library of Miskatonic. He told his fetching lies with brilliant ease. And, despite the warning voice of danger that had nagged me from the outset, in the end I sanctioned Claude's choice. For, watching the frozen, grinning determination of his face, I knew I could never change his mind.

That first year at Miskatonic was a brilliant success; Claude's grades were so far above average as to exact an enthusiastic, complimentary letter from the Dean of Men. I remember how the pallor of doubt ebbed from Father's face as he read that message; there was a child-like pride in the way he handed it to me. I myself was inordinately pleased by this unqualified praise of Claude; the apprehension that had tortured me all that year began to melt away. Then, I read the list of subjects in which my brother had excelled, and the warm glow of the library hearth seemed to smother suddenly under an intangible, chill blanket of corruption. "Medieval Lore; Ancient Cults and Sects; History of Necromancy; Examination of Extant Literature on Witchcraft." The vile titles floated, smiling evilly, in the shadowed corners of the room. It was then that I realized the gross impudence, the monstrous significance of Claude's selection of Miskatonic University.

In his second year at Miskatonic, Claude came home for the Christmas holidays. He had been at the Priory only three days when Father suffered a sudden and irreparable relapse.

It was the argument that brought it on. I was passing the half-open library door when I heard Father's voice. I turned in at the threshold, my cold-stiffened face already wreathed in a holiday grin; then, I stopped. They had not heard me. Father sat slumped in a chair by his reading-table; in the lamplight his mouth looked twisted, his eyes anxious. A sickly pallor coated his parchment-dry skin. Claude, his back to me, stared silently at the raw orange corpse of a dying log in the fireplace.

"Claude..." My father spoke thickly, as though some insupportable burden crushed his chest. "You must try to understand..."

"I understand," Claude's voice was barely audible, yet brutally hard.

"No you don't..." Father waved an ineffectual, blue-veined hand. "You've got to see that I'm doing this for your own good. Yes; your mother left you some money in her will—she left equal amounts to you and your brother—but, it was put in trust, to be controlled by me, until you come of age, or... or, until I die... Claude, you must stay at Miskatonic. You..."

"I tell you I'm sick of college! I've learned all I can there. I've got to have the money! I want to travel. I want to see Tibet and China. I want to live in the Bayous and the Indies..." Abruptly, Claude spun to face Father. For the first time, I saw the feverish, seething hate, the uncontrollable rage in his eyes. I watched my father wilt before the power of an unhuman gaze. Claude's voice rose to a demented, grinding cry. He lurched toward the cowering form in the chair. "I tell you, I've got to have that money!"

"Claude!"

As I stumbled into the room, bundles spilled from my arms. Tree-decorations crashed to the floor, splintering into myriad scarlet and green slivers. Claude stood frozen, only a few feet from the easy-chair.

Terrified, prayerful relief flooded the wide eyes Father turned on me. He raised that hopeless, gentle hand as though he would speak, then suddenly sank back, death-pale and senseless, against the cushions of the chair. Choking with sick fury, I brushed past Claude, and knelt at my father's side. The pulse in his withered wrist was pitifully feeble.

"Why can't you let him be?" I said hoarsely. "Why can't you get the hell out of here, and let him alone?"

"One way or the other," he said softly, "I mean to have what I want."

Only the terrible urgency of Father's condition enabled me to struggle to sanity through the cold, throttling web of terror Claude's words had woven. Almost before the library door closed behind my brother, I had rung Dr. Ellerby's number on the desk-phone. He came at once. He had grown fatter and nearly bald with the passage of years, but that night, as he prescribed a sedative and several days in bed for my father, there was in his jowly, florid visage the same impotent puzzlement I had seen there the night Mother died. In a professional matter-of-fact tone, he advised that Father should have as little excitement as possible, and all the while I could feel him thinking that, here, in this ancient Priory, throve a malady that no worldly knowledge of medicine could cure.

Doctor Ellerby called every evening; after each mechanical, forcedly cheerful examination of his patient, he would come down to the library for a much-needed drink. I would watch the dejected slope of his shoulders, as he stood, before the casement, gazing at the winter-mauve shadows of the ash-grove. After a time, he would shake his head slowly and his voice would be heavy and beaten.

"It's so odd. I can't explain it. I've known your father ever since he came to Inneswich; he never had a blood condition. He has none now... And yet, it's as though... well, as though, somehow, the blood were being drained from his body..."

Sometimes his words varied; their hopeless, frustrated meaning was always the same. Ellerby's tones echoed softly in some hidden corner of my brain, warping into the cold, venomous cadences of another voice. Once more I heard the brittle snapping of splintered Christmas decorations under Claude's shifting feet. I listened as the pale spectre of him murmured that hideous warning again and again. "One way or the other, I mean to have what I want..."

It was on a sleet-chilled morning in mid-February that the letter arrived at Inneswich Priory. Addressed to Father, it was signed by one Jonathan Wilder, Dean of Men, Miskatonic University. The expensive bond paper rustled faintly in my trembling fingers. Apprehension rose in a gelatinous tide, clogging my lungs. It was a short letter; the sentences cryptic and strangely self-conscious. They said little and yet, they hinted strongly at some darkling fear that haunted the mind of the writer. Jonathan Wilder confessed that what he had to say was not meant to be committed to paper. He said he would be grateful if Father would visit him in his office on the campus at Miskatonic, so that they might discuss in private the strange circumstances which had brought about this unfortunate turn of events in the college career of his son, Claude.

Father never saw the letter. The next Saturday, I was aboard the late evening train bound for Arkham. I lay back wearily against the dusty green Pullman seat, and stared into the square of impenetrable light that was my window. I saw nothing of the spectral landscape through which the train rattled like some phosphorescent worm crawling endlessly in the subterranean darkness of a tomb. Before my burning, sleepless eyes, only the final sentence of Jonathan Wilder's message writhed in a depraved, hypnotic *danse macabre*. "Believe me, I am indeed sorry to have to inform you that, after long deliberation, the Board of Directors can see no other course. Claude Ashur has been expelled from Miskatonic University."

IV

JONATHAN WILDER WAS A TALL, CADAVEROUS MAN WHO TRIED to hide the sombre distaste in his eyes behind a blinking barrier of pince-nez. He made a bony steeple of his fingers, and, for a long time, gazed wordlessly at the barren expanses of the university campus beyond the window. His eyes studied the distant, gray coldness of the hills that hemmed in Arkham; they squinted against the icy glint of winter sun on the sluggish winding ribbon of the Miskatonic. Then, abruptly, decisively, Jonathan Wilder turned back to me. He cleared his throat.

"I do hope you'll appreciate our position in this matter, Mr. Ashur. The Board has bent over backward to be lenient with your brother; they know what a brilliant mind he has. But..." He shrugged faintly, wiping the pince-nez on the sleeve of his oxford-gray coat. "The fact is, from the very beginning Claude has shown a rather... shall we say, unwholesome?... yes... a decidedly unwholesome interest in subjects that are directly opposed to the concepts of medical science. He has spent virtually all his time in the University Library...

"You... ah... You haven't heard about the library here at Miskatonic, Mr. Ashur?... No. I see you haven't... Well, I might begin by saying that our library is reputed to contain the most extensive collection of forbidden and esoteric lore in existence today. Under lock-and-key, we have the only extant copies of such things as the *Unaussprechlichen*

Kulten of von Juntz, and the loathsome *Book of Eibon*... Yes, even the dreadful *Necronomicon.*" I fancied that I saw an irrepressible shudder pass through Jonathan Wilder as he said those damnable names; when he spoke again, his voice was scarcely more than a whisper.

"Your brother, Mr. Ashur, has been seen to copy whole pages of that horrible lore. Once, long after closing hours, one of our librarians—a wholly reliable girl, I assure you—found Claude Ashur crouched in a shadowy corner among the bookstacks, muttering some weird incantation. She swore his face was... not human..." The tall man drew a long shivering breath. "There are other stories, too. There have been whisperings of strange doings in your brother's lodgings in Pickham Square. People speak of foul odors and whimpering agonized voices... Of course..." He raised one hand palm-up. "Some of this may be conjecture; possibly it's been exaggerated. But, in any case, the tales about Claude Ashur are doing Miskatonic definite harm. Enrollment has fallen off. Students have left, midterm, without apparent reason, after a short period of friendliness with your brother. You see, the esoteric learning our library affords is all very well when assimilated by a normal mind... But, a mind like Claude Ashur's..." He broke off, self-consciously. "Well... I'm sure you see our point..."

"Yes," I said, slowly. "Yes... I see..."

A man opened the door of Claude's house, his unfriendly, age-scared face stiffened at mention of the name.

"Mr. Ashur's out," he said flatly.

"I see... Well, I'll wait in his rooms..." I took a step forward and the door all but slammed in my face. The jaundiced glow of a streetlamp winked in the old man's hard, wary eyes. I got out my wallet. "It's all right. I'm his brother..." He took the dollar bill without thanking me.

"Top floor." He opened the door to let me pass.

"Thanks..." I paused. "By the way, Mr. Ashur will be leaving here tonight... for good..."

I couldn't be certain, but in the dubious glare of a garish hall light, it seemed to me that the old man's face grew suddenly soft with unspoken relief. As I moved carefully upward through the Cimmerian darkness of the stairwell, I heard him mutter, "Yes, sir!" He said it with the fervor of one who was murmuring: "Thank God!"

From the moment I entered his room, I had been vaguely aware of an indefinable odor, at once sickly sweet and stinging in the nostrils, that seemed to permeate every corner of the room. Now, I knew I had been inhaling the pungent fumes of oily pigment mixed with turpentine. For the thing beneath the skylight was an artist's easel, and, propped on its cross-bar, hidden by a cotton veil, was what I took to be a canvas in progress. To the right of the easel stood an antique work-cabinet, its scarred top littered with paint-clogged brushes and a pallet. Mechanically, as though driven by some mystic compulsion, I went to the table. Not until I was standing directly over it did I see the open book that lay half-buried beneath the melange of brushes and paint.

A malicious gleam from one of the lamps slanted across the tissue-fine texture of the volume-pages. A stench of immeasurable age swirled upward to me as I bent to decipher the ancient hieroglyphs that crawled like obscene insects across the paper. The book before me was one of the earliest editions of Albertus Magnus; at the bottom of the right-hand page, a single passage had been underscored. Revulsion knotted my stomach as I read those accursed lines.

"...Three drops of blood I draw from thee. The first from thy heart, the other from thy liver, the third from thy vigorous life. By this I take all thy strength, and thou losest the strife..."

Beside this Medieval sorcerer's chant, on the wide, yellowed margin, Claude Ashur's spidery script confided: "There has been no news from the Priory, but I am certain the spell will work. The portrait is completed. Before long, I shall know victory; I shall have what I want..."

I cannot say for certain what wild conjectures seethed through my mind in that instant. I only know that some instinctive, fearful hatred warped my hand into the vicious claw that ripped the veil from the painting on the easel. A terrified cry snagged in my throat, and I staggered backward, staring sickly at the festering, noisome thing my brother had created. To this day, here in the white-walled sanctuary of my asylum cell, there are hideous moments in the night when I lay horrified, on the paralytic brink of sleep, while the loathsome creatures of that canvas of the damned writhe against the dark curtains of my eyelids. I pray God no other mortal eye shall ever be seared by any such horror as I beheld that night in Pickham Square.

In the slimy colors of some subterranean spectrum, Claude Ashur had wrought cancerous images of the slobbering, gelatinous beings that lurk on the threshold of outer night. Diabolically smiling, amoebic, gangrenous creatures seethed in the shadows of that hateful canvas, and slowly, as I watched, there emerged from its crawling depths, the portrait of what once had been a man. The visage that confronted me was barely covered with discolored, maggot-eaten skin. Its blue-tinted lips were twisted in agony, and in their corrupted sockets, the eyes held a pitiful, pleading expression. Not one feature of that ruined face was whole, and yet there was something terribly familiar about it. I took an unsteady step toward the picture, then stopped. Awful suspicion reeled madly in my head as I noticed for the first time the tiny scarlet globules that oozed from that decaying skin. It was as though every pore had exuded a dew of blood!

"You always were an incurable busybody, Richard..."

Echoing icily in the dim corners of that low-ceilinged room, the sibilant hardness of the voice seemed unreal. Only when I had turned to find Claude's angular, dark-suited figure framed in the doorway, was I certain that my confused brain wasn't playing tricks on me. There was no mistaking the malevolent reality of the half-smile that curled my brother's lips. Sunken in his pallid, immobile face, onyx eyes flashed with caustic humor.

"I'm afraid my little creation gave you rather a turn," he murmured. "You know, Richard, it's always best for sensitive souls to mind their own business."

The old, impotent rage blurred my vision; Claude's venomous smile faded and grew horribly clear again. When my voice came, it was thick and ill-controlled: "You'd better do your packing, now. I've made reservations on the midnight train for Inneswich..."

We reached Inneswich Priory at noon the following day. A winter storm had swept inland, and gray, needling rain made the ivy-choked walls glisten evilly. There was a fire on the library hearth; before it, Doctor Ellerby stood waiting for us. One look at his face, and the vile suspicion that had been spawned last night in that dark, narrow room, blazed into putrescent reality. In that instant, I knew who had been the subject of the hellish portrait in Pickham Square. I knew my father was dead.

Claude made no display of pretended grief. He made no secret of his eagerness to have the will settled. There was whispering in the village; the simple, superstitious people of Inneswich spoke of daemons and the consorts of hell who could laugh in the face of Death. My brother's terrible, inhuman cheerfulness became a festering legend muttered by witch-hunting nonagenarians. Only the brave, the few who had been closest to the Church and my father, attended the lonely burial service, and even they departed in haste, glancing apprehensively backward at the figure of Claude Ashur, black against the bleak and threatening sky. Two weeks after the interment, one week after the reading of the will, Claude cashed a check for the full amount of his monetary inheritance and disappeared.

V

YOU CAN MAKE A RELIGION OF ESCAPE. YOU CAN RUN AWAY from the memory of horror, and hide yourself in willful forgetfulness. You can fill your life with feverish activity that crowds out the shadows of diseased evil. I know. I did just that for nearly eight years. And, in a certain measure, I succeeded. Having acquired a modest, white-stuccoed cottage on the outskirts of a southern Jersey resort, I divided my time between it and the Priory. I made new friends. I forced myself to mingle with worldly society as I'd never done before. After a time, I was able to resume my neglected literary career. I told myself I had escaped. Actually, I was never able to pass that carven, padlocked door in the East Wing without having to suppress a nauseous chill. There were still moments when, alone in the dusk-dimmed library, I broke into a cold sweat and Claude Ashur's voice echoed demoniacally in the shadowed corners of the room. At worst, however, these terrible sensations were transient illnesses that could be cured by friendly laughter or concentrated creative work. Somewhere, I knew, the malign genius of my brother still existed, but I hoped and slowly grew to believe that he had passed out of my life forever. I never spoke his name. I knew and wanted to know nothing about him. Only once, in all those years, did I have any direct news of Claude.

By a lucky chance my first book excited friendly interest among certain groups, and I found myself on the invitation lists of the literati. I attended countless cocktail parties and dinners, and it was at one such soirée that I met Henry Boniface. He was a small man, almost effeminate, with a sandy top-knot and straggling beard to match. He shook my hand timidly, but I fancied a sudden brightness in his pale eyes as he repeated my name. I wanted to get away from him. Thinking of what my hostess had said of Henry Boniface as she guided me toward him through the crowd, I felt a sudden oppressive apprehension close in upon me. He was a surrealist painter who just returned from the West Indies, and, a few years back, he had taught at Miskatonic University.

"Ashur," his soft, persistent voice murmured. "But, of course! I knew I'd heard that name!" That odd, brilliant interest blinked in his eyes again. "You must be Claude Ashur's brother..."

For years no one had referred to me in that manner. The loathsome phrase whispered in my head maliciously. Claude Ashur's brother. The sound of it seemed to throw open some tremendous portal within me; all the ancient deliberately forgotten terror swelled in my chest like a rising, slimy tide. "Yes," I said thickly. "That's right..."

It seemed to me that Boniface's gaze narrowed, biting into my face. His tone was light, diffident, but mercilessly probing. "I suppose you haven't heard from Claude in some time? No. I daresay not. Well, in that case, I have a bit of news for you..."

I wanted to tell him to shut up, to quit opening old cancerous sores with his rotten chatter. I only stared at him.

"Yes... The fact is, I heard about Claude while I was in the Indies. Amazing. He was always a most amazing fellow. I knew him quite well while he was at Miskatonic. He was in one of my art classes. Said he wanted to learn to paint so that he could do some sort of portrait..."

Cold beads of perspiration coated my palms. The worm-eaten monstrosity of Pickham Square reeled evilly in my brain. Henry Boniface droned on.

"But, to get back to the Indies. The blacks there told me of a white man who was living in the back-country among their witch-doctors, studying voodoo. Seems he'd wormed his way into their confidence. He'd been admitted into the cult and took part in all those repulsive doings at the *humfortt.* They... ah... They said his name was Claude Ashur..." Boniface shook his tiny head slowly. "Amazing. Extraordinary fellow, indeed. What strikes me is how he can go on living there in immunity. He was never what you'd call robust, was he? And there are all sorts of horribly fatal diseases in the back-country... It's a miracle he's alive."

I felt a hard smile curl the stiffness of my lips. "Don't worry about Claude," I said bitterly. "He has a tremendous will to live. Nothing will kill him..."

The words fell flat and cold between us, and after a moment of awkward silence, I excused myself, leaving Henry Boniface to stare after me with those bird-bright, curious eyes. I never saw him again, but more than once in the horror-ridden years that followed, my mind reached back through limitless dark to the night I uttered that damnable prophecy. "Nothing will kill him." Had I realized then the corrupt truth of those words, I might have saved Gratia Thane—and myself. I might have destroyed Claude Ashur before he was beyond destruction.

Early in October, 1926, I returned once more to the monastic quiet of Inneswich Priory, intending to pass the winter there, and complete the last chapters of my second book. After so extended a period of freedom from my brother's influence, the Priory had to all intents and purposes reverted to kind. It had become again the sequestered, peaceful home I had known in early childhood. Settled down to work, living comfortably but simply, I was almost happy. My second novel was never finished. Less than a month after my arrival at the Priory, I received the letter:

My dear Richard:

I know that you hoped never to hear from me again. I'm indeed sorry to disappoint you. But, the fact is, the prodigal has grown weary of wandering, and is ready to come home. And, much as you might dislike the idea, you can't deny your devoted brother his right to live in the ancestral manse, can you? Be so good as to prepare one of the better bedchambers, Richard. The blue one in the West Wing would be ideal. For, you see, I'm not returning as I left—alone. I'm bringing home my bride.

In the week that followed the arrival of Claude's letter, the news had spread with awesome rapidity, and fear had flowered anew in the shadows of Inneswich, blooming like some malignant cancer whose growth had been hidden for a while, but never checked. Wild conjecture muttered from street to street. Who was this creature Claude Ashur had married? What could she be like? There were predictions that murmured of a woman of strange and evil beauty; there were hints at a reincarnation of the hell-spawned witch Jabez Dreisen had burned at the stake more than a century ago. Long before they had ever seen her, the people of Inneswich were haunted by an abject fear of my brother's wife. I too was growing strangely fearful of the nameless woman who was Claude's bride. I had finished the sixth brandy before I sprang to my feet at the sound of a car turning into the Priory drive.

Memories of that night have always returned to me in fitful, nightmarish segments, haunting impressions that flash brilliantly in some secret crevice of the brain then fade once more into the cloying yellow mist of remembered horror. I hear again the metallic summons of the wrought-iron knocker echoing through the darkened halls of the Priory. I recall a faint rustle of clothes and the housekeeper's awed murmur: "Mister Richard is in the library." I remember turning to face the door. Then, Claude Ashur stood on the threshold. He had changed. He seemed taller than when last I'd seen him. The aquiline face was paler and more emaciated, and yet it had taken on a certain regularity of feature that made it handsome in a striking, sardonic way. Claude, as I remembered him, had always been pointedly negligent of his attire. Now, his expensive, well-cut tweeds, soft-collared shirt and knitted tie were in the best of taste. He moved easily across the room toward me; his hand in mine was abnormally cold. He smiled.

"Richard, old man! It's been a long time!"

The casual heartiness of his tone gave me a start. In that moment, I decided that, if Claude had lived in the hideous back-country of the Indies, he had also spent some time in Europe. For that sibilantly powerful voice had taken on a very definite Continental cadence. He spoke with a faintly Germanic accent.

"Sorry we're so late. The trains, you know. They're always so..." He must have seen that I wasn't listening; my gaze had gone beyond him to the library doorway. His face vaguely puzzled, he turned, and then smiled again. "Ah... Gratia, my dear..."

I had never seen anyone like Gratia Thane. Her face was a softly squared oval framed by wind-blown auburn hair that emphasized the soft whiteness of her skin. A hesitant smile touched the corners of full, perfectly rouged lips, and as she came nearer, I saw that the rather wide-set eyes were sloe-black and strangely docile. The traveling tweeds she wore couldn't conceal the exquisite grace of her carriage. She stood only a few feet from me now. Her eyes had not left my face for a moment. As though from a great distance, I heard Claude's quiet laughter.

"Well, my dear? Aren't you going to say 'hello' to Richard?"

As the dark eyes swung slowly to meet Claude's, they underwent a remarkably subtle change. In the flickering amber glow of the fire, they seemed to grow suddenly warmer; they caressed Claude's face with a kind of hypnotic, voiceless adoration. Only when my brother had given her a barely perceptible nod of assent, did Gratia turn back to me. I took her extended hand in mine. When she spoke, her voice was throaty and beautifully modulated, but she said the words with the diffident air of a little girl who has learned her lesson well.

"I've been looking forward to meeting you, Richard..."

I cannot recall my mumbled reply. I know that the moment those warm, soft fingers touched mine an unwonted, boyish confusion swelled in my throat. For a time, I only stared at the loveliness of Gratia Thane, and then, suddenly realizing that I had held her hand too long, I let it go. I think I flushed. I was conscious of Claude's steady scrutiny of my face, and when I looked at him, I saw the tight, malicious curl of his lips. All the old, corrupt malevolence was in that smile. I knew, then, that despite his Continental manner, Claude Ashur hadn't really changed.

The dinner was not a success. I was frightened. It was strange, selfless fear that turned cold inside me, as I sat, pretending to eat, and studied Gratia Thane. Time and again, I saw that childlike devotion soften her lovely face; she never failed to smile when Claude chanced to look her way. It was a gentle, worshiping smile, and still, the longer I watched it, the more convinced I was that it was a mask—a mask that could not quite hide the mute, unutterable weariness that crept into her eyes in unguarded moments. I was no longer afraid of my brother's wife; I was afraid for her. I was haunted by the feeling that, somehow, the subtle, cancerous evil that had followed Claude Ashur since birth was reaching out its vile, slime-coated tentacles to claim this girl, to destroy her as it had destroyed everything it ever touched. And, quite suddenly, I knew I didn't want that to happen. I didn't want anything to happen to Gratia. She was the loveliest woman I had ever known.

After Claude and Gratia had climbed the wide staircase, disappearing into the gloom of the upper hallway, I didn't retire immediately. I went back to the cold hearth and poured myself a stiff drink from the decanter. The liquor didn't warm me. I felt tired and confused, but I knew that if I went to bed, I wouldn't sleep. I don't know how long I sat slumped in the chair by the lifeless grate. I lost count of the drinks I poured. I lost touch with everything but the pale, frightened image that floated before my closed eyes—the image of Gratia Thane.

The shadow-shrouded corners of the room closed in upon me, and through the French casements seething, icy fog swirled as though no earthy barrier could stop it. Terror clutched at my chest as slowly, out of the blinding, jaundiced mist there emerged two wavering figures. Horror warped Gratia's face, wrenching all beauty from it. Her lips parted as though she would scream, but no sound came. Madly she stumbled through the scum-coated labyrinths of outer darkness, and at her heels, its saturnine laughter shrieking in her ears, ran the swollen, slime-dripping thing that was Claude Ashur. The running feet thrummed rhythmically, like the sacrificial drums of some demon-worshiping tribe. Nearer, they beat. Nearer. Nearer.

I thought I was still dreaming. Cold sweat-beads crawled from the hair in my armpits along the sides of my body. My hands trembled. My eyes were open. Gradually, the familiar, shadowy objects of the library came into focus. But, the hellish throbbing of those ceremonial drums did not stop! For one horrible moment, I doubted my own sanity. Then, slowly, painfully, my numbed limbs obeyed the orders of my brain. I stumbled unsteadily to the darkened threshold of the library, and, clutching at the door for support, I knew that what I heard was no product of a diseased imagination. No one could deny the ghastly reality of the rhythmic sound that swelled like some obscene heartbeat in the blackness of the stairwell.

It came from the chamber in the East Wing. Even before my uncertain legs had carried me up the endless hill of the stair, I knew where I was going. With each step the demoniac thrumming grew louder, crashing madly against the walls of the high, narrow corridor that led to the East Wing. My lips were dry; breath made a rasping sound in my throat. For an incalculable moment, I stood staring at the rust-coated padlock that hung open on the latch of that hateful, carven portal. The doorknob was cold in my clammy grasp. The heathen tattoo of the drums exploded like thunder against my eardrums, as the door swung inward without a sound.

My brother, seated cross-legged on the floor with his back to the door, was swathed in the folds of a scarlet cloak. It was his bloodless hands, stretched outward, to the slimy skins of weirdly painted native tom-toms, that beat out that hypnotic rhythm of the damned. In an ancient sacrificial brazier which stood between him and Gratia, glowed the blue-white flame that was the only light in the room; with each turgid heart-throb of the drums, the tongue of fire hissed and flared to unholy brightness. And, in that eerie, pulsating luminescence, I saw the change that had come over Claude's bride.

The pallid face that seemed to float in a phosphorescent nimbus was no longer that of Gratia Thane. The soft oval had grown suddenly angular; wan, dry skin stretched tautly over high cheekbones. The eyes I remembered as wide and innocent had sunken into shadow-tinged sockets and turned oddly bright and crafty. Her mouth was a thin, bloodless gash that curled bitterly at the corners. It was a face that tainted the virginal loveliness of her white-gowned body. And, even as I watched, the horrible change grew more and more profound. At every thud of the tom-toms, wiser, subtler evil gleamed from those wary eyes.

Gradually, almost imperceptibly, while I stood horror-frozen in the doorway, the erotic thrumming had been muted. Now, above the distant rumbling, there rose a thin, godless wail that was more animal than human. Alien syllables, tumbling from Claude Ashur's parted lips, burst in the gloom like poisonous tropical flowers; the unholy tones of his incantation flowed through the stagnant air like pus that drained from a lanced abscess.

I saw the face that had been Gratia's grow tense. A caustic, horribly familiar grin warped the lips, and slowly, as a snake weaves to the mesmeric rhythm of the charmer's pipe, the firm white body swayed in time with the ghastly threnody Claude Ashur chanted. Then, abruptly, the shrill wild voice rose, and strangely accented but recognizable words trembled in the putrescent shadows of the room.

"Be gone, O will more frail than mine! Be gone, and leave me room! Gratia Thane is cast out, and this flesh belongs to me! Through these eyes shall I see; through these fingertips shall I feel. Through these lips I shall speak! Speak! Speak!"

The furious command whined coldly above the drums. The flame in the brazier snapped and leapt high. And, staring into its blue-white depths, Gratia was suddenly still. Only pale lips moved in the expressionless mask of her face. The voice that came was calm and sibilant; it was the soft voice of a man who spoke with just the hint of a Germanic accent!

"This body is mine. Henceforth, this flesh is the house of my spirit. Claude Ashur. I am Claude Ashur! I am! I..."

"Gratia!" Her name was an anguished cry in my fear-dried throat.

"Claude..." The bewildered murmur trembled on Gratia's lips. The hideous gauntness, the unhealthy eye-shadows had faded from her face, leaving it flushed and gentle. Her gaze moved slowly from Claude to me, and the frightened puzzlement behind her warm, dark eyes was that of a child awakened in a strange room. "Richard... Where are we? What's happened? I feel so weak, I..."

Her voice trailed off in a husky sigh; the tenseness drained from her body. The filmy white gown rustled faintly as she slid forward to the floor and lay still. I was the first to reach her. Her hand was icy in mine and coated with a clammy dew. I think I whispered her name and cradled her in my arms. Then, I became conscious of the shadow that was Claude Ashur looming over us.

"I'll take care of my wife, Richard." The familiar, stony calm had returned to his voice. I stared up into the colorless mask that was his face. In the glow of the guttering brazier-flame, it seemed to me that his pallid skin was spotted with faint, brownish blotches.

I said thickly, "We'd better get a doctor..."

"She'll be all right..."

"But..."

"She's only fainted," Claude said levelly. "She needs rest. I'll take her to her room..."

As she passed me, the cool whiteness of Gratia's gown whispered against my hand. I listened to the funereal murmur of his tread moving away down the corridor. Bewildered fear shuddered within me at each breath I drew. I wanted a drink. I stood staring into the phosphorescent glow of the brazier. A confused impulse to get to a telephone and call Dr. Ellerby swelled in me and died. I didn't move. Somewhere, in the seething tenebrosity of that chamber a hateful echo grew suddenly shrill and distinct. I heard again the sibilant, accented voice that had spoken with Gratia Thane's lips. "...This flesh is the house of my spirit. Claude Ashur. I am Claude Ashur."

I started violently at the sound of his laughter. Turning, I saw him standing once more on the threshold of that loathsome chamber. The tawny facial stains I had noted before were very pronounced, now; his face was scarcely more than a skull enshrouded by dry, unpigmented skin, and he seemed to breathe with difficulty. But, his rage had subsided into bland secrecy again. The old, cat-like smile had come back. The brilliant eyes laughed mirthlessly.

"Poor Richard. Really, you must learn not to intrude if you're going to continue being your old squeamish self..." There was an undercurrent of warning in the bantering tone. It stirred boiling coals of anger that seared across the chilled numbness of my terror. I had a fleeting vision of Gratia's weary, child-like face. Fury made my voice harsh.

"What are you doing to her, Claude?"

He didn't answer immediately. He sank into the chair Gratia had occupied, and, for a long moment, did nothing but stare into the white-hot heart of the dancing flame. I saw the smile rebend his lips; an obscene light flickered in the shadowed depths of his eye-sockets.

"She's really quite exquisite, isn't she?" he said softly.

I said: "She's decent. She's a fine person and you're doing something to her. I want to know what's behind all this rotten display..."

"Do you?" The searing gaze flashed up to meet mine. "Do you really, Richard? Are you sure you want to know? Are you sure it wouldn't offend your tender sensibilities?

"The lovely lady has inspired you, my dear Richard. She's made you a knight in shining armor." Abruptly, the lips drew into a taut line. "If I were you, I'd give up the notion of 'rescuing' the lady Gratia. You see, what you so vulgarly refer to as a 'rotten display' is really a scientific experiment. Gratia is my assistant. I've no intention of giving her up.

She's the perfect subject. Perhaps that's because she's so completely in love with me..."

Claude must have sensed the revulsion that shuddered through me at the foul suggestiveness of his tone. The taunting smile returned and he nodded slowly.

"Yes. My wife is quite devoted, Richard. That's why my experiments have been so successful. You see, I believe that, under proper conditions, a will that is powerful enough can take over the body of another person—transplanting its dominant personality in fresh soil, as it were—forcing the other person to exchange bodies with it. It requires only concentration and a suitable subject; one that is highly susceptible to the will of the experimenter..." Claude's eyes had grown maniacally bright as he spoke. Now, he breathed each word as though it were some heathen incantation. "I've found that subject..."

"You can't," I said dully. "You can't do this to Gratia. She's lovely. She..."

"That's just the point!" Claude's voice was a feverish whisper. "Lovely! She's the most beautiful creature I've ever seen. Think, Richard! Think what I could do with such loveliness. Think of a woman possessed of such beauty, and of my personality, my brain directing that beauty! A woman such as that could rule any man... a million men... an empire... a world!"

I struggled to keep my voice level. "I tell you, you can't do it. I won't let you. I know your 'experiments'. I know what they did to Father and Tam! Well, you're not going to hurt Gratia. Either you'll let her alone or I'll go to the police!"

"No, Richard," he said softly. "You won't go to the police. In a little while, you'll grow calm; you'll think. And, then, you'll realize the truth of what I told you about Gratia. She is entirely mine. She would never support any insane stories you might tell the authorities. On the contrary, if you should talk, she would readily agree with my testimony that you were quite mad."

He went out, closing the door soundlessly behind him.

VI

THERE WAS NOTHING I COULD DO. LIKE AN OUTSIDER, I STOOD by and watched while Claude Ashur's malignant genius slowly, inevitably reclaimed Inneswich Priory. By the end of the first week, I had grown to feel like some helpless intruder who has stumbled upon unspeakable horror and dares do nothing but turn his back. My nerves were like the strings of a sensitive instrument, keyed to the breaking point. Day by day I watched Gratia move through the gloom-infested hallways of the Priory; I saw the growing pallor of her gentle face; I saw the sickly fear that lurked behind the shallow mask of her eyes. Time and again, I set out upon walks that I meant to end in the local constabulary, but I could never escape the horrible rationality of Claude's warning.

In the night, I would start awake, trembling on the brink of mad rage, as the pulsing of drums thundered through the cavern of the house; always, after such nights, there was a marked improvement, a new vitality in my brother and Gratia seemed more wan, more silent than ever. I knew that the girl who drifted, wraithlike, from room to room, smiling obediently, adoringly at Claude, was not the real Gratia. I was convinced that she was controlled, that her voiceless devotion to Claude was a manifestation of some hideous form of mesmerism. But, I had no way of proving my theory. It is probable that I should never have known the real Gratia Thane, had it not been for the fever.

It came upon Claude quite suddenly toward the middle of the third week. The day had been overcast and unpleasantly cold; a sea-dampness had seeped into the massive Priory rooms, settling upon them a chill that no fire could dispel. Claude had spent the afternoon locked in his East Wing chamber, and when he appeared for dinner, it occurred to me that his wan face was tinted with an unwonted flush; his eyes were red-rimmed and oddly ill-at-ease when they chanced to meet mine. More than once during the oppressive silent course of the meal I saw Gratia's worried gaze seeking his. He didn't look at her. Directly after dinner, he retired.

It was well past midnight before I drifted into a fitful doze; for hours, I had puzzled over the strange silence of my brother. Since that first night of his return, the evil in Claude had grown into a bold, bantering thing that throve on barbed innuendo and secret, poisonous laughter. I wondered what had caused the change. The answer came in the form of a misty presence that floated at my bedside, like some troubled spirit. I think I must have cried out at the touch of a cool hand on my arm, for soft fingertips pressed warningly against my lips. Breathing heavily, I stared up into the moon-washed loveliness of Gratia Thane's face.

"Richard..." There was a timid urgency in her throaty whisper. "Richard, you must come... I'm afraid... I..." She fought to still the trembling of her lips. "It's Claude. I heard him moaning. It was horrible. He's in his bedroom... and he won't let me in... I'm afraid, Richard, he's ill... I feel it... We... we've got to do something for him..."

As I watched the wide darkness of Gratia's eyes, heard the mixture of anxiety and terror that throbbed in her voice, an odd thrill of hope shot through me. The girl who stood by my bed in that moment was no longer the will-less automaton I had come to know. For the first time since I'd met her, Gratia Thane was honestly, tremblingly alive. Her palm was moist against mine as we made our way through the Cimmerian blackness of the upper hall; I cannot say how long we stood before the door of Claude's bedchamber, listening, and scarcely breathing. I can only remember the sudden, terrified vise of her fingers on mine, when, from beyond the heavy oaken panels, there came a muted, agonized groan. I clutched the icy metal latch and twisted it sharply, throwing the ponderous door ajar.

The wild howl that rent the stillness then, was not one of pain; it was the vicious snarl of an outraged animal. For one terrible instant, I beheld, thrown into ghastly relief upon Claude's bedstead, the fever-bright eyes, the blotched skin, the raw scar of a mouth that had uttered that fury-torn cry. I heard Gratia gasp. Then, violently, Claude Ashur turned from us, twisting in the bed until we could see nothing but the frail mound of his body beneath the covers.

"Get out! Get out of this room and stay out!"

"Claude... you're ill...You've got to let us help you..." Gratia took a hesitant forward step.

"Stay away from me!" the voice commanded in a harsh whisper. "I told you not to come in here. I want to be left alone!"

I said levelly: "You'd better let me call Ellerby, Claude."

"No! I don't need a doctor! I don't need anyone! It's nothing, I tell you. Just a recurrence of a fever I had in the tropics. It'll pass. Just leave me alone! Alone!"

It was no different in the morning. Despite his wife's repeated entreaties, Claude stubbornly refused to let anyone enter his room. I stood by, silent, listening while Gratia begged him to be reasonable— to call in a doctor. He spoke only once in a quiet, desperate voice. He instructed her to have his food left on trays outside the door; he told her everything would be quite all right in a few days. After that, there was no answer to Gratia's anxious pleadings. There was only an occasional soft rustling beyond the bolted door, and the nauseous odor of putrefaction that seemed to grow more foul by the minute. As he always had, Claude Ashur won. We left him alone. The door to his hateful sanctuary remained closed for more than a week, and, as time passed, I began to entertain a strange hope that at once horrified and thrilled me. I began to wonder how it would be if that door never opened again.

That week was a jungle flower that blossomed with pitifully brief magnificence in the midst of a fungus-choked swamp of evil. It was the only beautiful thing born of those final hideous days at Inneswich Priory. It was a brilliant tender touch of normalcy caught in a cesspool of malignant madness. For, in those few hours, I came to know the true Gratia Thane. Set free of the vile will that lay prisoner in that upper chamber, she became the girl I'd always known she must be; a gentle creature, full of gay laughter, and quiet tenderness; a carefree child who loved to run along the white stretches of the beach with the salt air brushing her cheek, and ruffling the bronze softness of her hair; a Gratia who, despite the lingering shadow of Claude Ashur, soon endeared herself to those villagers she chanced to meet on the evening walks that became our habit. It was as though some dark curtain that had separated her from reality, that had let her see only Claude, had been lifted. And, watching the lovely aliveness of her face, listening to her warm laughter, feeling the excitement of her hand in mine, I knew that I was in love with my brother's wife.

The curtain fell again. As suddenly as I had found Gratia, I lost her. On the evening of the ninth day, Claude reclaimed his bride.

Gratia and I had been playing backgammon in the library window seat; I remember the way the dying amber rays of the sun glinted in her eyes when she laughed almost tenderly at my run of ill-luck. And, I remember how the laughter died, so abruptly, so completely. I looked up from the game and saw the blood drain from the warm mounds of her cheeks; the dark wells of her eyes grew suddenly shallow and secretive; her pallid lips moved, but no words came. A faint sibilant rustle made me start and turn my head. And, then, I saw it—standing in the gloom that shrouded the library threshold—the smiling, animated corpse that was Claude Ashur.

In that wasted visage, only the curled gash of the mouth and the pitted blazing eyes gave testimony to the corrupt flame of life that still burned within that fleshless body. The dry, achromatic skin of the massive forehead seemed swollen, and the hairline had receded markedly. The unwholesome brown splotches had disappeared, leaving the facial flesh seamed and sallow. A heavy, dark-colored scarf was muffled about his throat, and (oddest of all, I thought), pale, kidskin gloves covered his hands. From that day forward, I never saw Claude without them.

"Well!" The twisted lips scarcely moved, but his soft, insinuating voice held all the old malicious humor. "This is a most touching little domestic scene..." Shifting in their sockets, the seering pin-points of fire ate into the wan softness of Gratia's face. "I'm sure Richard has been a charming substitute, my dear, but really... Shouldn't you be just a bit more enthusiastic about your husband's recovery?"

With the hypnotic grace of a delicately wrought puppet, Gratia rose from the window-seat; her pale hand brushed against the game-board, and several scarlet backgammon pieces spilled to the carpet. She didn't notice them. Slowly, she crossed the dusk-dimmed room to where Claude stood. Her firm, bare arms went around his neck and, passionately, she kissed the ugly wound that was his mouth. For a long time, they stood embracing in the shadows, and all the while, over Gratia's shoulder, my brother's evil face smiled at me. That night, I heard the drums again.

I thought I'd had a nightmare. A moment before, the demoniac thrumming had been pounding against my eardrums, throbbing in the depths of the nighted Priory. But, when I started up from my sweaty pillow, peering into the dark that swarmed in upon me, abruptly, the sound was gone. I sat forward, taut and waiting. The silence was profound, limitless; the silence of the tomb. It was as though some titanic heart-beat had been suddenly stilled. I tried to relax. I passed a clammy hand over my forehead, and attempted a laugh. There was nothing but a dry rasping in my throat. Determinedly, I lay back; I told myself I was letting my nerves get the better of me.

It didn't work; the longer I lay there, forcing my icy hands to stillness, listening tensely to every silken, uncertain whisper of the night, the more conscious I became of the caul of impending danger that had spread its slimy veil over Inneswich Priory. The silence was unnatural; it was the seething quietness of the demented killer before he strikes. Cursing my nerves, I threw back the counterpane and struggled into robe and slippers. Clammy air swirled about my bare ankles as I opened the bedroom door and ventured warily into the Stygian gloom of the corridor. Instinctively, I turned in the direction of the East Wing. Through the single massive casement of the upper hall, moonlight fell, making a pale, shadow-latticed desert of the floor. It was as I passed through that livid pool of moonglow that I saw her.

"Gratia!"

She seemed not to hear; as she came toward me from the shadows, her white gown murmured. It was like the warning hiss of a poisonous snake. I stared at the hueless angularity of her wasted face. The deep-set eyes burned into mine and the narrow slit that was her mouth twisted in a sardonic smile. Her tongue, pink and strangely pointed, flicked out to moisten dry lips. The mouth worked.

"Kill!" it whispered in the accented, venomous voice that didn't belong to Gratia Thane. "I must kill... It's the only way... The sure way... He could cause trouble... It's best this way... Yes... He must be destroyed. Killed... Kill! Kill! Kill!"

I caught her waist as a knife slashed downward toward my chest; razor-edged steel grazed my left cheek; I felt blood trickle along my jaw. It wasn't easy to hold her; she struggled with a vicious strength that was out of keeping with the fragility of her body... with the power of a desperate madman. The colorless lips curled back from her teeth.

"You!" she hissed. "I must kill you! Kill! Destroy! Silence forever!"

"Gratia!" I shook her violently. "Stop it! You hear me? Cut it out!"

There was the flat, brutal slap of my hand across her hysteria-twisted face, and suddenly, she was still. Insane anger melted into bewilderment; her eyes widened and gained warmth and depth; the shadows faded. Gratia's lips, pink and moist, trembled. For an instant, she could only stare; her terrified gaze moved from the flesh-wound of my face to the glinting blade of the knife she still held. She gasped. I saw her fingers open convulsively; the knife thudded to the floor. Again, our eyes met, and then she was in my arms.

"Richard... Rick, I didn't mean to... I didn't know what I was doing... He made me... It was the drums... and his voice... Here... here in my head..."

The fresh perfume of her hair was in my nostrils; her cheek brushed mine. Gently, she was wiping the blood from my face with the sleeve of her gown.

"It's all right," I murmured. "It's all right, now..."

I held her close again; her body was trembling. She cried. It was the soft, bewildering cry of a little girl.

"I'm scared. Rick, I'm so scared! He's doing something to me... He's..." She shook her head frantically and clung to me. "Don't let him... Please... You won't let him! Promise you won't let him..."

"No." My voice sounded flat and hard in my own ears. "He won't hurt you... He won't hurt you ever again..."

"The triumph of true love!"

Bitter, weighted with sarcasm, the softly spoken words seemed to tear Gratia from my arms. Standing on the edge of the shadows, his eyes slitted in their blue-black wells, the desiccated flesh of his face more livid than ever in the moonlight, Claude Ashur laughed.

"You can't have her. You know that, don't you, Richard? I've tried to be patient with you; but, I'm afraid you've interfered once too often. You see, Gratia is more than a woman and wife to me. She's my very life; my one hope of survival. I'll never let you take that hope from me..."

He had begun to move slowly toward me through the moonlight; each stride had a fluid, evil grace that was almost feline. The brilliant gaze flashed to where Gratia stood, then back to me. Again, briefly, that loathsome smiled toyed with the corners of his mouth.

"You don't quite understand, do you, my dear brother? You're wondering how Gratia could be my sole hope of survival. No matter. It's better that you never know. We don't want to trouble your sensitive mind on your last night in this life. Indeed, no! We want you to be at peace. We want you to be ready—for death!"

What happened then I cannot clearly remember; the murderous violence of those few minutes returns only in disparate snatches. I recall the maniacal force of Claude's lunge, the cold, bony vise of his fingers closing on my windpipe. I think I heard Gratia scream. That pale, hateful face was horribly close to mine; his putrid breath hissed, hot against my skin. I remember crashing backward under the impact of his charge.

Darkness and moonlight spun in my head. I thought my lungs would burst. Then, by some desperate, instinctive twist of the body, I was free. Wind rasped in my chest. I had Claude crushed between me and the damp stone wall. My fingers clamped in his hair, jolting his head forward and back viciously. When his skull pounded against the stone for the third time, his frenzied grasp relaxed. He slid to the floor at my feet, twitched once, and was still.

He wasn't dead. With the brilliant eyes shuttered by blank, purplish lids, the pale waste of his face had every aspect of death, but, under my searching hand, his evil heart still pounded feebly. Mechanically, possessed of a strange, decisive calm, I bound him hand and foot with the heavy sash-cords of the window-drapes. I carried him to his room and laid him on the huge antique bedstead. I locked him in.

Gratia had stopped crying, but her hand was cold and trembling in mine as we descended through the chill darkness to the library. I talked, then; I told her gently that there was nothing more to be afraid of; I said it was all over now. I built a fire and poured drinks for both of us. And, the whole time, a single, inescapable thought coursed with harrowing persistence beneath my outward calm. I knew that, for the safety of everyone concerned, there was only one place for Claude Ashur: the State Asylum for the Criminally Insane. When I had finished my drink, I made two telephone calls. I asked Dr. Ellerby and the police to come to Inneswich Priory as quickly as possible.

VII

IT WAS ALL HANDLED VERY QUIETLY. NONE OF THE FACTS GOT
into the papers. The few reporters whose editors sent them to cover
the trial were refused admission. They returned, disgruntled, to their
respective phone booths and dictated brief, barren items that only
hinted at the abominable truth; these articles, if printed at all, were
mercifully swallowed by some obscure corner of an inner page. For
a while, the newspaper men tried another angle. They spent a good
deal of time in the Tavern at Inneswich; they asked questions. They
learned nothing. The people of the village, perhaps out of respect for
the memory of my father, met all inquiries with a cold stare and locked
lips. So, the loathsome secret of Inneswich Priory, the shame that had
scummed the name of Ashur, remained hidden beyond a barrier of
clement silence.

The only formal charge against Claude Ashur was one of assault
with intent to kill. I stood in the witness box and muttered the details
of his attempt on my life. That was all I had to do. The alienists did
the rest. It wasn't difficult. It was simply a matter of subjecting Claude
to countless cross-examinations; of recording the awed, reluctant
testimony of various villagers who knew of my brother's "oddity";
of questioning the timid, uneasy man who was Dean of Men at
Miskatonic University, and reading a letter from one Henry Boniface,
who had taught Claude Ashur to paint.

The strange, exalted manner in which Claude accepted Father's
death was brought to light, and, in the end, I admitted the story of
that odious portrait in Pickham Square, and the murder-incantation
of Albertus Magnus. In mid-September, 1925, the alienists reached a
decision. They declared my brother incurably insane.

On that last day of his examination, I went alone to the State Asylum;
alone, I felt the final, brutal impact of his hate-filled unblinking stare,
and glimpsed again the cold anger of the calculating mind that lay
hidden behind that emaciated mask. He showed no signs of hysteria
or violence. Between white-coated attendants, he walked quietly to
the doorway of the consultation room. Then he turned, and, for an
instant, his face gray in the gloom of a rainy afternoon, the features

somehow broadened and blurred, he was again the old, cynically smiling, indestructible Claude.

"You mustn't suppose that you've won, Richard," he said softly. "You mustn't delude yourself. They can lock me up. They can bolt doors and bar windows. But they can never imprison the real Claude Ashur. I'll be free again. Some day, some how, I'll reach out to you—to you and my devoted wife. Sooner or later, I'll have my revenge." His muted laughter whispered through tight lips. "You don't believe that, now. But you will. Wait, Richard... Just wait, and see..."

I tried to listen to the quiet reassurances of the doctors; I saw my brother disappear around a bend in the corridor; I heard a door open and close. The metallic grind of bolts drifted back to me through the dimness. I told myself that Claude had gone out of my life forever. But I didn't believe it. That last, soft-spoken warning echoed ceaselessly in my head; I had the terrible conviction that this was not the end of Claude Ashur.

The semblance of contentment which settled over Inneswich Priory was a thing born of our desperate need for peace of mind. The happiness wasn't real. It was as though our determination to shut out the hideous past had pushed back a musty drapery of gloom, letting in the feeble, timorous sunlight of normalcy. In the next months, I saw Gratia slowly reclaim the young, fresh vitality I'd first known to be a part of her during the week of Claude's illness. She laughed again; she walked with me along the winter-bleak strand of the beach; she planned little surprises in the way of food delicacies; and it was she who finally convinced me that I should go back to my writing.

Had anyone asked us, I know we should have said we were quite happy. It would have been a lie. I wrote; but the several literary articles I managed were somehow weak; they lacked spontaneity. The prose was stunted and overcast with a strange uneasiness. Gratia and I made plans. We talked of travel and marriage, but there was always a ghost of unrest that hovered between us—the knowledge that our plans could come to nothing. The realization that while that twisted, hateful creature in the asylum went on drawing the breath of life, Gratia would never be free. We were like lonely children, playing desperately at some pitiful game, trying to ignore the horror-infested night that closed slowly in on every side.

It is difficult to trace the stages by which the change overtook me. I think it began with an unwonted restlessness, that laid siege to my mind scant days after Claude had been committed to the asylum. I took to wandering, alone, along the most desolate, brine-eaten stretches of the coast; a seething uneasiness pounded mercilessly in my brain. There were horrible moments of blank detachment—moments when a wild exhilaration crawled along my spine, and I would prowl the nigh-dark labyrinths of the Priory, full of a sense of illimitable power. More than once I came to myself, damp with sweat, chilled, standing before that carven door in the East Wing; the door leading to the hellish tomb that housed everything that stood for the blasphemous evil of Claude Ashur.

Then, as suddenly as it had come, the moment would pass, and, shaken, bewildered, I would fall across my bed, sinking into a deep, restless sleep. I never mentioned those horrible nocturnal seizures to Gratia, and yet, there were times when her eyes met mine, and I saw the half-fearful question that lurked behind her gentle gaze. She sensed that something was wrong. Her unspoken suspicions became a hideous reality the night I played the piano.

As I crossed the room and sat down on the oval bench, I told myself music might have a soothing effect on my nerves. It was only a rationalization of the sudden, inordinately passionate desire to play that had overwhelmed me. The yellowing keys were cold and slimy to the touch; my fingers moved over them with a grace, a sense of ease I had never known before. The saccharine melancholy of a Chopin Nocturne billowed into the twilit room; thrumming bass notes pulsed darkly against my hypersensitive eardrums; then, abruptly, the music was no longer Chopin's. The pounding, demented chords that trembled under my feverish touch grew cruel and malignant. Through the drumming of the bass, treble notes blended wildly into the unholy wailing of myriad lost souls. Godless rhythm crashed against shadows that writhed obscenely, keeping time. Only once before had I heard such hellish music drawn from the whining bowels of a piano. The song that shrilled beneath my fingers, now, was the chant of the damned that Gratia had played for Claude Ashur.

I knew she was behind me. My nostrils quivered tautly; the scent of her hair and skin seemed to permeate the very air of the room. My fingers stiffened and were still; the final broken wail of the music lashed out, hung like some poisonous vapor in the stillness, and died. I turned slowly on the bench, and then rose. Her sports-dress was a vivid yellow blur in the dusk-shadowed doorway; her face, the soft fullness of her lips, the ripe body that was at once chaste and subtly sensual, wavered before my burning eyes. I was before her, now, and my hand touched the warm firmness of her arm. The smile that had trembled on her lips a moment before, shadowed away. Her eyes were suddenly bright with fear. I think I smiled; I felt my lips curl, slowly, stiffly. My tongue moved, and from some vast nothingness, a voice that wasn't mine spoke through my mouth.

"Gratia, my dear... my bride... my beloved!"

Sheer, hysterical terror twisted her face as I bent to kiss her; she tore free of my hand and cringed against the wall; the words tumbled, shrill and frantically pleading, from her colorless lips.

"No! Let me alone! No. Please! You have got to let me alone!"

Somewhere in an obscure corner of my brain there was a sharp snapping sound. The stinging blur of my eyes seemed to clear abruptly, and, for the first time, I actually saw the utter loathing and fear that warped Gratia's face. I felt weak; sweat trickled along my jaw and down my neck. Fear-fraught bewilderment did tricks with my stomach. I stared helplessly at the frail creature who cowered before me, her hands covering her face. My throat was terribly dry; it made words difficult.

"What is it?... Gratia, what have I done?... What..."

I stopped short; she had taken her hands from before her eyes. For a long moment she only stared, puzzled, terrified; then she was in my arms, crying gently. There was a strange note of relief in the sobs that quivered through her warm body. My dull puzzlement deepened.

"What is it?" I repeated softly. "What frightened you so..."

"Nothing..." She shook her head and a tinkle of brittle, half-hysterical laughter sounded in her throat. "Forgive me, darling... I had the oddest feeling just then... It must have been the music... his music... And... and, your face... It was so pale; the way you smiled at me... that crooked, rotten smile... I..." The laughter bubbled again and broke on a sob. "It's fantastic, I know... But for a minute... I thought you were Claude!"

VIII

I HAD NOT SLEPT. THE FIRE ON MY BEDROOM HEARTH HAD long since died to a few blood-red embers, and, well after midnight, the storm that had threatened all day had broken viciously over Inneswich.

I sat very still, strangely tense, listening, and the muttering of the sea echoed mockingly the tones of Gratia Thane: "...thought you were Claude, I thought you were Claude, Claude, Claude!" Chilled, trembling, I sprang to my feet and paced the floor aimlessly; lightning slit the blackness beyond my casement. I started and swore. My hand shook when I opened a fresh bottle of rye, and poured a stiff one. I sank into the chair again, trying to shut out the maddening chant of the surf. Time and again, in the last night-shadowed hours, I had done all these things. But I had not slept. I was not dreaming when I heard the drums.

And then, in some forgotten crevice of my consciousness, the unconquerable danger-signal flashed redly. No! the brain screamed, soundlessly. Don't. You can't give in! You can't let Claude win! Return! You must return... to yourself... to your own body! You must! I felt my numb lips twisting in an agonized last effort at speech.

"No!" my own voice roared hoarsely above the drums. "No! Go back! I must go back... must..."

With a tremendous effort I forced myself to stand. My legs were like jelly under me. I don't remember how I managed to stumble through the foul-smelling gloom! I remember only the door—the yawning, black rectangle of that final hope of escape—and that the hissing tongue of the flame seemed to leap higher in the brazier, stretching forth cruel, blazing fingers to hold me back. I had almost reached the threshold when it happened.

The dull, throbbing sound stabbed like a needle through my brain. The drums! I staggered and slammed into the doorjamb; leaden paralysis tangled my legs; I lurched crazily and slid to the floor. I tried to scream. It was no good. Voiceless, I careened downward through a bottomless pit of hate. And, out of the black, viscid whirlpool that swallowed me, Claude Ashur's voice wailed softly.

"Mine, Richard! I tell you, this flesh is mine! I have returned! I've come back to claim my freedom—freedom in the body that once was yours! You hear? I shall be free, and you shall be the entombed one! You, my dear brother! You!"

Babbling laughter echoed spitefully through the smothering night that welled up before my eyes; with a last frantic effort, I tried to gain my feet, then, gasping for breath, pitched forward, and lay there, utterly powerless...

Through all of it, as though from some tremendous distance, some other moment of time, Claude Ashur's muted cynical voice hissed in my ears.

"You see, Richard It wasn't hard. It wasn't hard at all. This body is mine, now. You hear? Mine! Directed by my brain, thinking my thoughts, speaking my words, doing the bidding of my will..."

The blasphemous words dribbled off into whining laughter that echoed mockingly, and died along the sterile stillness of endless corridors...

The first conscious sensation was one of gnawing pain that seemed to pervade every inch of my body, eating at my flesh like some needle-fanged cannibalistic monster. With an exhausting effort, I opened my eyes. The lids felt oddly swollen, and I saw only mistily through narrow slits. The whiteness wavered before me again; I made out a whitewashed ceiling and tall, colorless walls; pallid moonlight slanted through a window on my right. I blinked and tried to bring the ghostly rectangle of the casement into better focus. Then, the razor-edged knife of terror sliced into my brain. The moonlight that seeped into that barren chamber was cut into segments by shadowy stripes; the window was reinforced—with steel bars!

A dry scream tore through my stiff, swollen lips. No! These weren't my legs; these horrible bony stilts that stretched before me, the pale skin of them bloated and desiccated, covered with suppurating brown sores! Frantically, I tore at the nightshirt that cloaked me, and then, turned violently sick. The white flesh was raw and running, as though myriad maggots had fed upon it; a foul, noisome stench stung my nostrils. Madly whimpering, I rose and staggered to the barred casement. I think I prayed. I know I was crying. And then, reflected in a window-glass made opaque by outer darkness, I saw the moon-washed horror of the face.

The thing that stared at me from the viscid depths of the casement-pane was more bestial than human. Its tremendous white forehead was swollen beyond all proportion; the thickened nose, scarred by two gaping holes of nostrils, was like nothing but the snout of a leonine animal, and below it, quivered a slavering, decayed gash that was the mouth. Sunken in the blue-black sockets, twin pin-dots of demented flame flashed evilly. There were no eyebrows, and the sweat-damp, straggling patches of hair that studded a sore-covered scalp gave it the aspect of some monstrous Medusa risen from the bowels of the sea. And, even as I watched, strangled with loathing, those corrupt lips curled slowly in a malevolent grin, and I knew that the thing before me, wreathed in that vicious smile of insane triumph, was the face of Claude Ashur!

I think I screamed. Realization flooded in upon me like a rising, slimy tide. In that moment I saw and understood the unholy motive that had lain behind the rites I had witnessed in the East Wing of Inneswich Priory. I knew, now, why my brother had wanted the body of Gratia Thane; I knew that the added power he might have gained through her beauty was only incidental. Claude Ashur had needed a new body. For the flesh in which his spirit had been housed since birth was riddled with disease, tottering on the brink of the grave.

The normal, healthy body of his wife had been his only hope of survival. He had wanted it in exchange for the putrescent thing I saw, now, in the mirror of the window. And, when I had destroyed his hope of claiming Gratia's body, he had claimed mine, instead!

Reeling blindly to the steel-plated door, I pounded frantically at its heavy panels until the sickening pulp of those rotten hands bled. I felt these stiff lips working. I heard a voice that wasn't mine screaming from this diseased, alien throat. Words crashed wildly against the nighted stillness of the asylum.

"My brother! Claude! Find Claude! My body... I tell you, he's stolen my body! He's won! He's free! You've got to find him... He'll destroy Gratia... He'll claim her as he did me... Please! You've got to let me out! I've got to stop him! Please!"

They came. They came in their white tunics and shook their heads and talked in pitying undertones. They smiled kind, wise smiles that said: The poor devil is completely mad; humor him. They strapped me to the bed and went off a bit to whisper among themselves. After a while, the gray-haired one came over to me; he had the hypodermic in his right hand. I winced as the needle plunged into the crook of my arm. The gray-haired one spoke in a lulling voice.

"You must take things more calmly, Claude. Everything is all right, but you're ill, and you must let us make you well..." He smiled automatically. "You've been a very naughty boy for nearly a month now. That's why we must use the needle. I've told you many times; you must try to remember, Claude. Your brother, Richard, left the country nearly a week ago..."

I shook my head dully; my tongue worked in the foul-tasting hole that was my mouth.

"Gratia?" I gasped. "Where's Gratia?"

The gray-haired one looked away; the blurred white figures of the other doctors shifted on uneasy feet and mumbled sympathetically. The hypo was beginning to take effect; the voices were only a thick murmur in my brain now. The gray-haired doctor was trying to explain something to me in the same calm tones. The words didn't reach me. But I knew what he was saying. Soft, triumphant laughter gurgled bitterly in the white void, and I knew that, wherever my brother had gone, Gratia had gone with him. I knew that Claude Ashur had won.

There is no longer any fear in me. Fear died with the hope of saving Gratia. I know now that I could never have won out against the infernal evil of Claude Ashur. He was, and is, too strong. Too strong for all of us. I know that at this moment, somewhere, his foul mind lives on. Perhaps he has destroyed Gratia as he destroyed me. Often I wonder how many others have met the same monstrous fate. God only knows. But we, at least, are at rest; the destroyed have come to an end of horror. There is nothing left for us to do but give warning.

People will read this and scoff; they will call it the wild scrawling of a madman on the crumbling lip of the grave. They will laugh. But it will be a nervous, sickly laughter that doesn't ring true. For in the end, when they have correlated the things I have told with the accepted facts, they will know that I am right. Claude Ashur will go on. For, strangely enough, insane as he is, I think perhaps he has captured the vagrant dream of every man—the only true immortality; the immortality of the mind that will not be imprisoned in one fleshly tomb, but will find others, and, somehow, forever escape the ravages of disease, the oblivion of the grave.

It is ironic and cruel that such a man should have made the discovery. But it is more than just that. It is dangerous. Not to me; not to Gratia and the others who have fought with Claude and lost. Nothing can touch us now. But Claude Ashur can touch you. Perhaps, even now, he is near you; perhaps he speaks with the lips of a lover, or watches through the eyes of an old and trusted friend, smiling that ancient, enigmatic smile. Laugh, if you will, but remember:

The will of Claude Ashur is possessed of a strength that goes beyond flesh and blood. One by one, it has met and vanquished every obstacle in his path. Before it, even Death has bowed a humbled head. And what it could not conquer, it has destroyed. If you doubt such power, you have only to think of me. It was that unholy strength of will that usurped my clean, healthy body, and left me entombed in this swollen, putrescent mass of flesh that has been rotting these twenty years with leprosy.

THE FINAL WAR

BY DAVID H. KELLER, M.D.

THOMPSON SAT IN HIS LONELY LIBRARY READING A VERY OLD book. Written on vellum pages, it was bound with the tanned skin of a Chinaman killed by a magician in Gobi. The oriental liver had failed to unlock the past or give any information concerning the future. The skin, however, bound a book that was destined to save mankind.

The scholar had often read this very ancient tome, in what had been, so far, a useless effort to unravel its secret. Tonight, in the middle of the book he suddenly saw the solution to the mystery. He read on through the night with increasing fear grasping his soul in its icy clutches. At last he realized the terrific import of the message, hid so long in the old folio. The candle, fanned by the breath of impending doom, flickered over his shoulder. Death hung in hovering terror.

"The world and everything in it will be destroyed!" Thompson whispered. "I alone realize the danger. I am the only one who can save mankind. But I am only a dreamer. The scientists must help me. They only can win this final war."

That night Thompson read of Saturn, the distant, mysterious, threatening planet; a land of lofty mountains and of chasms so deep that falling rocks took years to reach their final resting place.

He read of caverns carved in the rock by millions of hopeless slaves who prayed for nothing but death to end their torment; of tunnels illumined by the cold light of gigantic glow worms, each chained to a pillar, who fed on mushrooms mixed with phosphorus; of cities inhabited by very ancient races.

The book described these beings, not men, but living things with shapes that could only be imagined by the opium eater. Foul and unclean monsters who loved and worshiped a God from the beyond.

This God, malign, powerful, mighty in wrath, terrible in intelligence, brooded through an eternity of time with only one desire: to conquer the earth, make slaves of the bodies of men and take their souls to a place of everlasting torment.

Thompson continued to read. Finally he wrote a transcript of one page; wrote with a hand that trembled. Even as he wrote, he doubted his translation of the ancient code.

"Ruling Saturn does not content Great Cthulhu. The beautiful people of Venus have perished; the men in the building of underground cities, the women in laboratories from horrible genetic experiments. The scientists from Mercury toil making new forms of destruction while the armies of Mars are prepared for conquest of other worlds.

"Cthulhu has many shapes but usually assumes that of a gigantic toad, with hypnotic eyes, poisoned claws and an intelligence which defies earthly mind to understand. The lesser Gods on Saturn are all controlled by this great God. At the appointed time he will visit the earth and make of it a desert. Let all who read beware! He will come with spaceships, mechanical armies, poisons and obscene weapons. If all these fail, he will, in the end, transform himself into a beautiful woman, and, thru her seductive beauty enslave and torture their souls."

The candle flickered.

"At least," Thompson muttered, "We have been warned."

The Earth-men accepted Thompson's warning. The United Nations erected a large experimental laboratory in the Arizona desert. With thick walls, it rose, an enormous cone, towards the threatening sky from out of which the invading forces would come. Astronomers kept a twenty-four-hour vigil searching for enemy spaceships. Scientists watched the spectrum for new elements from Saturn. Biologists perfected deadly cultures and prepared antiserums which would protect in germ warfare. Chemists found explosives more powerful than the atomic bomb. Air ships, rocket-propelled, were built.

But a final invention was perfected by Jenkins, based on a suggestion made by Thompson. This was so novel in its form, so subtle in its proposed use and so powerful, that the two men hoped, if all else failed, their invention would win the final war.

Various groups aided in the construction of this new weapon, but each made only a part. These parts were put together, vitalized, made into a perfect whole by Jenkins, watched and instructed by the dreamer, Thompson.

"It is the hand of Destiny," cried Jenkins, but Thompson replied, "I would call it the hand of God!"

Meantime, all was activity on Saturn. There the Great Cthulhu had brought to perfection his machine men. With metal bodies, electrified brains, those scientific workers could perform in their cavern laboratories tasks that would have been impossible to the greatest scientists on earth.

Back of them, controlling their every activity, directing their inventive genius, was the mysterious power of the Great God. Up to this time, he had made all his dreams come true. His history showed that a war begun was a war won. Only Earth remained to be conquered. Living from the beginning of time, confident that he would never die, he was impatient to conquer the last of the planets. Day after day, night after night, he drove the machine men who worked tirelessly toward their goal. Biological chemists perfected a new and terrible form of war.

"I will destroy their cities!" Cthulhu boasted to the lesser Gods. "I will make their earth a waste place. Finally, in their despair they will lose the power to resist and will seek only death, not realizing that I will take their souls and torture them in many obscene ways thru an eternity of years."

The machine men finally completed the space ship, which, hurtling thru the void of the skies, would finally land on earth and complete its mission of destruction. Skillfully made, rocket-propelled, every part of its journey had been carefully planned. Not a detail had been overlooked. The hypnotic, all-powerful intelligence of the Great God had so completely dominated the machine men that the final result, the death-carrying ship, was a masterpiece of devilish imagination.

It carried no crew. Once it was shot from the tube, it would go directly to the earth even as a splinter of iron flies thru the air and fastens to a giant magnet.

Cthulhu trusted no one to start it on its flight. At the appointed time he went to the tube which housed the ship and for the last time went over every detail of its construction. Once again he correctly charted its course so that it would land in the rich corn belt of the United States.

Finally he pushed the starting button and the beautiful cylinder started off.

"Those pitiful Earth-men will now have something to worry about," he cried to the lesser Gods.

"Great is Cthulhu!" they shouted.

The long cylindrical rocket ship approached the earth, encircled it, and then pausing over the upper Mississippi Valley, disintegrated, showering its cargo upon the black earth. Borne by the wind, the small seeds scattered over a large area, fell on the ground, germinated at once and in a day were full grown. The male plants, rootless, crawled into the female plants and impregnated them. In another day the ripened ovaries exploded, scattering seed for another generation.

Those plants were not only flesheaters, but exuded a vapor which killed all who breathed it and a juice that burned and rotted the flesh of all that contacted them. By the millions they spread from the country to the cities, bringing death so rapidly that it could not be avoided. Only the dry, lifeless desert was immune. There the airships, prepared for any eventuality, had been placed. Now they went into action with their flame jets. Patiently, methodically, the deadly plants were cremated.

Finally all were destroyed. The God Cthulhu had failed in his first assault. The cities were destroyed, but the best of humanity lived on to fight.

Cthulhu prepared for an assault which he felt would be the final step to victory. He was sure that he knew the souls of men, their secret desires, their fatal weakness. This time he would use, not a modern instrument of war, but the oldest known to all life on every planet. He was so confident of success that he decided to go by himself, unattended by even his most favored lesser God—go to Earth and, singlehanded, use his magical power in such a way that no mere Earth-man could resist him.

He had his machine men make a globular ship with a single opening. When the circular door was open, a much smaller globe could descend to earth on a guiding beam of light.

In this globe, the Great God sped earthward on what he was certain would be a journey ending in victory.

The Giant Toad hopped out of the small globe near the ruins of a Utah city. With giant leaps he rushed to Arizona. There in a desert of volcanic rocks and dead cedars, he underwent a metamorphosis revealing his primitive bivalency. Now the toad was gone, being replaced by a male and female such as man in his wildest dreams had never seen; or once seeing would have died of pure horror.

Male and female, they lived for the appointed time in the desert. The female, with one eye, a long tail, human hands ending in long claws, would, when alone, shake her mule ears and call loudly for her mate. He had the calves of a man, the thighs of a bear, the torso of a bull and the head of a devil. Hearing his mate call, he would gallop to her, roaring his impassioned love song. In every way he was the kind of a male that this kind of female appreciated.

They were in love!

Thus they lived in a garden of Eden. They satisfied each other but when the female realized her delicate condition, the male knew the honeymoon was over and hid his head in a rock hole and died. His soul, the half of the God from the Beyond, simply passed into the new life that the female was bringing into the world. She gave birth to a baby and then she too died. Now the God was once again united in this deadly menace to the world, a beautiful woman.

Standing there alone in the desert she realized her power. What man could resist her charms? Once in her power she could make him a slave. Thus women have always treated men, and now Cthulhu, as the Super-Woman, would show men that they were simply little animals to be twisted around her delicate fingers, sucked dry of blood and their souls sent to Hell.

Thompson had anticipated the Woman. The final pages of the old book had prepared him. With Jenkins' help he had made a trap. There was only one question. Would it work?

The Woman glided over the desert. Her beautiful face glowed with the expectation of victory. Her lovely fingers twitched in anticipation of tearing the bodies of all men. Within her, the Great God glowed with satisfaction as he thought of all the ways in which he would mutilate their souls. He did not realize that the beautiful body he had made to dwell in had, in one little convolution of her brain, curiosity and a desire for love.

Suddenly the Woman saw a gigantic hand rearing out of the sandy desert. It was a very masculine hand with short, stubby, powerful fingers. The back was covered with hair; the palm was soft.

"What a beautiful hand!" exclaimed the Woman. "I could rest in that hand while the fingertips caress my lovely body." She crawled into the hand and cuddled on the soft palm.

"Love me, you wonderful masculine hand," she commanded.

The fingers and thumb closed on her, slowly crushing her to death.

Cthulhu screamed. Now on earth he had no place to live. His failure was complete. There was nothing for him to do but return to Saturn.

Man had won the war. Humanity was safe. A finer civilization rose on the ruins.

THE DUNSTABLE HORROR

BY ARTHUR PENDRAGON

A PALEOGRAPHER CANNOT BE THOUGHT A MADMAN. TO AVOID such a charge I have suppressed until my retirement the story which I now add to this book of memoirs. Do not doubt the accuracy of the tale. My memory has not failed me in probing the skin of this earth; it could not betray me now, for I bear like an old unclosed wound the remembrance of that horror in the forest north of Dunstable.

I had come from the British Museum to Dunstable in northern New England during the rainy March of 1920 in order to find and study the long-buried records of the Massaquoit tribe of red Indians. They were an isolate and obscure nation, a sea-marsh people who perished shortly after the foundation of the Massachusetts Bay Colony. My grips and gear were thrown from the creaking passenger train at the Boston & Maine depot on the outskirts of the town. From the platform of the small Victorian building the landscape was singularly depressing. The continual drizzle of winter's end reduced all to a monochrome grey of muddy flats and dripping scrub-topped hills. I would have been stranded were it not for the New England type lounging with the stationmaster in the telegraph office. As I entered the warmth of the waiting room he casually surveyed my dripping waterproof and the cut of my clothes, remarking drily, "Looks like the tourist season has begun."

I took an instant dislike to the man which went beyond the sneer in his remark. However, since his was the only team outside I forced myself to be polite, to suffer his arrogance for the sake of a ride to town and a warm billet. After a few minutes of conversation he rose to his feet and grudgingly offered to drive me into Dunstable if I would help him load the wagon.

We wrestled several boxes of parts for his lumber mill, apparently the only industry in this area of rocky farms, into the back of the wagon, and added my gear. As the team plodded through the cold mist I found him more talkative than the traditionally taciturn New Englander. He commented, in a fragmentary fashion, on his mill, his position of authority in the town, and his affluence. From the very beginning his family, the Varnums, had inhabited the town, and he was the culmination of the line. Although unmarried at forty, he had decided to take a wife when time allowed in order to perpetuate the Varnum house.

The wagon swung onto a paved and wider thoroughfare posted as the Black North Road. Varnum finished his monologue and eyed me suspiciously, asking why I had come all the way up the coast to Dunstable. I decided to put an end to his egoistic spouting by exploiting the awe for learning shared by the middle classes, and so replied, "I am Thomas Grail of the British Museum, and I have come to find Pauquatoag." To my utter astonishment he recognized the name of the great sorcerer of the Massaquoits, the evil Merlin of the New England tribes.

Varnum saw the surprise on my face. "Oh, yes. The family had a certain—ah—contact with Pauquatoag when they first landed." He smiled darkly and alluded to several diaries he had inherited with his father's estate. I would not learn the peculiar nature of that contact, and its terrible result, until later.

We rolled onto the covered bridge over the Penaubsket River. On the far bank lay Dunstable, its lights wanly glowing against the foggy dusk. "I suppose this means you'll be going up north into the forest," Varnum said. "You'll have a hard time getting anyone to go with you." I told him that I could offer good wages, and that the work would not be difficult, merely a bit of digging. "You've got three things working against you," he replied. "Number one—the frost is coming out of the ground and the farmers'll be putting in the seed pretty soon. Number two—the ice broke on the Penaubsket and the Kennebago last week, so the mill will be running at top speed in a few days." He cracked the reins as we left the bridge for the main road. "And number three—everyone's been sort of reluctant to go farther north than the logging camps since the animals came floating down river."

He pointed out a mill pond at the side of a small dam. The oily water circled and foamed in endless eddies. "That pond has been almost full of dead animals two or three times since the thaw began. Came floating downstream from beyond the last logging camp. Squirrels, foxes, even a deer or two. Never saw anything like it."

I asked how they had died. "As far as we could tell, by drowning. As if something had driven them into the river. When the snow melts in the uplands the current gets vicious. You'll see it at its worst in about a week. Ever since then, nobody has gone beyond the camps. Superstitious peasants." He laughed wryly. "And some of my men who've been past the camps laying out cutting stakes even say they saw a glow in the forest after dark, near the marshes. I just couldn't convince them that they had seen an ordinary will o' the wisp."

I recognized the popular name for ignis fatuus, a light seen at night moving across bogs, thought to be caused by the slow oxidation of gases from rotting vegetation. "But surely," I said, "they must see that sort of thing often around here, judging from the number of fens I passed on the train."

Varnum snorted. "They all said this light was different—steady, not flickering, and moving from the marshes into the forest. They're just trying to get out of camp duty. Lazy oxes. I have to keep after them all the time."

We reined up before the Dunstable Inn, which looked as though it had received its last repair in colonial times. "Well, that's what you're up against, Mr. Grail-of-the-British-Museum." Varnum dropped my bags into the muddy street. "If you're going to come all this way to dig up a three-hundred-year-old Indian, you've got to expect little problems like this. If you ask me, you grave-robbers are all a little bit off." He laughed and reined on the team, spattering me with mud as the wagon was enveloped in the steady drizzle. Chilled and disgusted, I collected my gear and entered the inn.

Varnum was correct in his prediction about the difficulty of obtaining guide service. The following morning, after a restive night in a battered four-poster, I began to make the rounds. At the feed and general store

I was met with the reticence and suspicion of the highland New Englanders. The booted farmers and hands fell silent when I entered, awed by my accent. When I told them of my purpose they shifted their bodies uneasily. I promised a good week's wages, and in some I could see raging the battle between the desire for money and some strange dread. But they all hung back, muttering lame excuses, saying, "You're sure to get someone at the mill."

The millpond was already filling with rafts of logs ridden downstream by the pikemen. The rasp of a giant saw somewhere in the bowels of the mill trembled across the damp air. At the hiring office I was informed that the mill was laying on a second shift that night, and that no one would be available for a week's leave. Furthermore, the foreman doubted that I would be able to get a single townsman to accompany me because the news of the dead animals and the light in the forest had made the residents fearful of traveling beyond the logging camps on the two rivers.

When I left the office a small crowd of workers had gathered on the bank of a short canal which ran from the millpond into large dark orifices beneath the brick building, in which the rushing water turned underground wheels to power the saw. A line of wooden floats connected by a heavy chain closed the mouth of the canal against any influx of debris which might jam the wheels. Bobbing against this guardline were the bodies of numerous small animals. I walked into the knots of loitering millhands for a closer look at the animals—grey squirrels, chipmunks, and several large hares, forest dwellers which generally avoid the water. The squirrel which I examined bore no marks of disease or violence; it had apparently drowned, since the chest cavity was heavy with water. I remember that Varnum had spoken of similar occurrences during the past weeks, and a curious fear touched me for an instant. Had these animals actually sought out a water death, like the lemmings which I had seen literally choking the Trondheim Fjord in Norway the previous year? Or had something driven them before it, something so repugnant to even their coarse animal mentality that they preferred the water they abhorred to its presence?

I returned to the inn that afternoon puzzled both by the sight of the animals at the mill and by the fear of the townspeople at the mere mention of going north beyond the lumber camps. If necessary, I could go it alone—the previous autumn I had sighted from the air what I believed to be the remains of the chief Massaquoit campsite. But the location was thirty-five miles north of Dunstable, through an alien forest, and the going would not be easy.

I had not long been at the inn when a servant called with the message that Mr. Varnum would be pleased to entertain me at dinner that evening. Any company would have been preferable to the loneliness of the town after dark, so I accompanied the man in a wagon to the Varnum house, mystified at the sudden largesse of a person who seemed to resent my presence as one whom he could not awe with his authority.

My host met me at the door of his manse-like stone house. As he conducted me to his drawing room he smiled knowingly. "I hear you weren't too successful at the feed store and mill today."

"No," I said, "all the men I asked seemed too busy for the project. Or perhaps they were a bit afraid at the prospect of going beyond the camps."

"Craven, superstitious bumpkins, the lot of them! Since those animals began showing up at the mill, they've been acting like old women." Varnum dismissed the subject with a contemptuous wave of the hand. He poured me what he called "a hearty old colonial drink," aptly named The Dog's Noses: a bumper of warm ale to which he added a jigger of gin. The taste was wretched, but I stomached it in deference to his attempt at hospitality.

"By the way—you saw the millpond today?" he asked.

"Yes, the animals have begun to appear again," I said. "Forest creatures, which seldom go near the water. Puzzling, and a bit eerie."

"Why, Mr. Grail-of-the-British-Museum," said Varnum in mock surprise, "are you becoming a little unsure about the trip to find your sorcerer? Don't tell me that a few waterlogged animals are giving a man of science cold feet!"

"My dear Varnum," I replied, considerably nettled, "let me assure you that I have seen things far more eerie than a few squirrels bobbing in a millpond. Whatever the phenomenon, sir, it is all grist for the mill of science, and we will find it out."

Varnum grunted and motioned me to the dining room where dinner was laid out by his decrepit house-keeper. The menu was a boiled

New England dinner, more bland than the tasteless food which gluts Britannia. While eating I remarked on the gallery of portraits, mostly in American Primitive style, which covered the walls of the room. Varnum bore a striking resemblance to the first portrait, although the family features appeared in all of them—small, heavily lidded eyes, insipidity of the brow, large nose, and the surprise of a markedly narrow and thin-lipped mouth set between heavy and sensual jowls.

"You've noticed the resemblance between Prester and myself," Varnum said, pausing in ravenous devoural of the steaming food. He shook his fork at the portrait. "A real rake—for one of the old guard he was a high-stepper. You should read his diaries. By Nick, I'll show them to you, after supper." He flicked a fragment of cabbage off his vest. "The folks used to tell me that I was the reincarnation of Prester. But it must go only skin deep—I have no time for women. Too much to be done—the mill, the town council, and now this damned business beyond the camps to be settled."

I was amazed at his lack of interest in the subject of the ladies, myself having been without an amour since the pretty but petulant botanist at Harvard who had been a most charming companion until I became completely unnerved by the continual presence of beef-eating plants in her flat. Varnum's sangfroid, I decided, was simply another aspect of the consuming ambition which drove the man to his displays of arrogance.

We rose from the wreckage of the dinner and re-entered the drawing room for cigars and a look at the diaries of Prester Varnum. My host excused himself to go and fetch them, indicating the liquor cabinet to me before he left. I surveyed the dismal array of American firewater, fit for no civilized gullet, my spirit sagging, until I saw a tenth of Cointreau forgotten in the corner. The sugary crystals on the bottle's neck formed an unbroken seal—Varnum was obviously not an enthusiast of the delightful liqueur. I wrenched the cap off and poured myself a finger as he returned with several calf-bound octavos.

Varnum at first persisted in showing me the sections chronicling the romantic peccadilloes of his ancestor. These were of little interest, merely egomaniacal neighings of no great literary or historical merit. Far more to my use was the matter concerning the extinction of the Massaquoit tribe, of whose annihilation Prester was the root cause.

The cramped and miniscule script coldbloodedly narrated the tragedy of this race.

In the spring of 1657 Prester Varnum, accompanied by his Mohegan guide, Mamtunc, had passed from the hamlet of Dunstable Northward along the Penaubsket seeking the extent of the pine resources in that area. During the journey they had surprised a woman of the Massaquoits. Putting aside his stern Calvinism for the nonce, Prester had enjoyed her despite Mamtunc's warning about reprisals against Dunstable by her tribe. The woman later escaped and fled in shame back to her people.

Not long after, Prester had fallen ill with a fever in the forest, and was brought back to the settlement in a travois by the Mohegan. When they arrived the town was in the grip of the second outbreak of plague since its foundation nine years before. Worse, a friendly savage had informed the inhabitants that because a colonist had molested a wife of Pauquatoag, the Massaquoit shaman, the tribe was preparing for war.

During that black summer Dunstable buried its dead and readied itself for the Massaquoit onslaught. Smallpox claimed over a third of the villagers, including Mamtunc. But Prester Varnum recovered and was strong again by the time it was discovered that the Massaquoits had perished to a man, infected by the unknown white plague through the wife of Pauquatoag. The courier who brought the news also spoke of the curse which the sorcerer had levied upon the defiler of his wife—that the line of descent which produced such a man would end most horribly and in the same manner as the extinction of the Massaquoits. However, Prester discounted this a superstition and, indeed, came to a peaceful death in his sleep at seventy-two, leaving many children to mourn him both in Dunstable and the nearby Indian camps.

I closed the diaries of Prester Varnum and exhaled slowly. The narration of the needless extinction of the Massaquoits had depressed me considerably. But the flare of a match as my host lit his cold cigar, and then mine, brought me back among the living.

Varnum cleared his throat importantly. He had become increasingly impatient as I lost myself in the pages of his ancestor.

"You've probably been wondering all evening why I invited you," he said. "This—this phenomenon as you call it is beginning to be troublesome to me. There are some fine stands of pine beyond the last camp, between the Penaubsket and the marshes. I'll have that lumber at any price."

"If you can get your crews to go into the area," I said. "They seem to have little stomach for it."

Varnum took a deep draught of bourbon. "Exactly. As long as these animals that keep floating downriver are unexplained, my boys'll be jumpier than a bull at fly time about getting into that timber. We know the animals drowned. The vet examined a few, and found nothing from disease, no marks or broken skin, no singed fur from a brush fire—nothing except water in the lungs. The question is, why in Hell did they jump into the Penaubsket in the first place?"

"Perhaps they were *driven*," I hazarded.

"By what?"

"The Headless Horseman," I answered, sipping my Cointreau.

Varnum failed to detect the note of humor in my voice. "You're not superstitious too, are you?"

"It was merely a drollery," I assured him.

"Oh. Well, whatever the reason my friend, I won't have my men harassed by a will of the wisp and a few sopping animals. I'm going along with you. When do you leave?"

I was inwardly seething at being *told* that I would be accompanied, but allowed little sign of this emotion to betray itself on my face. It would be, at least, better than going it alone. "I plan to leave day after tomorrow," I replied. "Tomorrow I'll hire the horses at the livery stable."

"Good, I'll see you then," said Varnum, rising from his seat. Apparently the evening was over, although it was only ten o'clock.

At the door there were no amenities, simply a curt "Good night" by Varnum, as though dismissing an inferior. As I rode in the wagon back to the inn I found myself boiling over my host's bad manners. For the sake of a guide to my project site I would suffer the man's company, although it probably would not be the most pleasant two weeks I would spend at a site. I consoled myself by fondling the tenth of Cointreau which I had surreptitiously tucked into the inside pocket of my black greatcoat upon leaving. "Why waste it on a boor with no palate," I thought, and laughed aloud. The first frogs answered from the marshes where the faint blue will o' the wisp hung over last winter's cattails like an augury.

* * *

By the time of our meeting two days later I had hired four horses, two as mounts and two for portage. It had taken me almost a full day to prepare the gear we would transport to the burial site of the Massaquoits—the probing bars, shovels, picks, brooms, and padded hardwood boxes which would protect whatever fragile birchbark rolls had survived. This baggage, plus rations, camping equipment, firearms, and a copy of Pope's *Essay on Man*, composed the burdens of our two pack horses.

We left Dunstable as the sun rose on a clear day, a rarity in the New England spring. When I gave Varnum my compass readings and landmark notes on the site, he found that we would be able to use the most northerly of the logging camps as a jumping-off point for the burial ground. Thus, we were able to keep to logging roads and tracks for a good part of the trek.

On entering the great New England forest I experienced an almost religious awe which was never duplicated in any other jungle, veldt, canebrake, or tundra of this earth. A brooding stillness invested all. The light filtered greenly through the solemn pines and hemlocks so that even the air we breathed seemed the color of the vegetation which pressed in around us. The sound of hooves was muffled by the thick carpet of dry reddish needles, the organic sediment of the centuries. When a bird called, the echo amid the quiet was startling—one felt that a blasphemer had defiled a dark and sacred place. And the small towns and hamlets of the forest seemed to share my awe, huddled as they were along the seamarshes as if they preferred the known dangers of the sullen North Atlantic to the silent encroachments of the dark woods; their names stark, staunch, reflecting the cold indefatigability of the Yankee settlers—Sabbathday, Icepond, Landsem Depot, Wind Flume, and Bell Shoals.

Varnum was immune to such feelings, riding before me with his head sunk into a great woolen muffler, lost in thoughts of cutting schedules, board feet, and distances along the Penaubsket to the mill at Dunstable. He also seemed unmoved by the unshakeably ominous foreboding which had beset me since leaving the town. I found my mind turning back inexorably to the sight of the animals revolving lifelessly in the black eddies of the millpond, and to the thought of the blue nimbus, so much like the will o' the wisp, but feared by the lumbermen more than the Penaubsket at flood. I tried to concentrate on the work which lay ahead—finding the site, the excavations, the discovery, identification, and packing of the Massaquoit pictographs. But there in the greenish light and stillness north of Dunstable the emotion was irrepressible.

On the morning of the third day, after a night's halt at the most northerly of the logging camps, we arrived at the site. The reader may wonder at the ease with which we located the tribal ground of the Massaquoits. But in addition to compass fixes and landmark notes I had another factor working for me—the almost eternal sterility of land used for many years as a camping place. Because of constant foot traffic, cooking and smelting fires, and the disposal of alkaline solutions used in primitive tanning, the land is so leached and eroded that it can support only the hardiest of weeds.

I recognized the site immediately upon breaking out of the scrub pine into the roughly circular fifteen acre clearing. There were no middens, or refuse mounds, for these had long ago vanished under the winds of the summer hurricane and incursions of scavenger animals. There were, however, rows of blackish depressions in the earth which once held the lodge-poles supporting the Massaquoit dwellings. Except for these the ground was clean of any trace of a civilization; if anything were to be found here, it would be an occasional discarded arrowhead, or shard of pottery, or other artifact of the tribe. The birchbark picture records would be in the burial ground, distributed among the graves of the chiefs and first warriors. Unlike many of their neighbors, the tribe of Pauquatoag cremated their dead and interred the remains; the corpse was not lashed to a scaffold or tree limb to tatter in the wind.

We made camp at the center of the clearing, pitching the two one-man tents about twenty yards apart on either side of the fire. I was eager to find the burial ground, and Varnum wished to ride through the area both to inspect the stands of timber and to search for any trace of the mystery which had been worrying his men. Accordingly, we agreed to meet back at camp before sundown.

Through the long afternoon I made shallow preliminary excavations at the burial ground, about a mile north-west of our camp. It was not long before I found the first of the pictographs, interred with the remains of one who had been a major warrior. The primitive stick figures might have come from the hand of a child, so simple were they, carefully drawn in berry dyes on sheets of birchbark packed in a matrix of alkaline ash which preserved them from fungus and bacteria through the centuries. But while the analytical faculties of my mind feasted on the details of the records, my emotions were disturbed with the same sense of foreboding which had dogged me on the passage from Dunstable. Perhaps it was the starkness of the area, or the solemnity of walking in the footpaths of a vanished race. Whatever the cause, I was relieved to find Varnum waiting at the camp on my return.

He had lit the campfire although it was not yet sundown, and glanced up as he gingerly inserted a dry log into the blaze.

"Did you find your Indian comic books?" he asked.

"Yes—the records are buried with the remains, just as I thought they would be. I took only a sampling today, but the pictographs seem remarkably well preserved. But, a rather curious thing—I didn't see the grave of Pauquatoag, although that should be the most clearly indicated of them all, with at least a rock cairn atop it."

Varnum looked into the fire with an expression of absolute disinterest.

"Perhaps the old faker was assumed into the Indian heaven. He was supposed to be a witch doctor or something, wasn't he?"

"Well, perhaps I overlooked the grave. But it should be large and easy to find, what with the immense number of trappings they buried their shaman with." I poured myself a cup of coffee. "How did your day go? Any sign of—anything?"

Varnum laughed shortly. "Not a thing. Those old women who call themselves lumbermen are afraid of a will o' the wisp, just as I said. No tracks, nothing unusual for miles around. A moving blue light—nonsense!"

"But what of the animals in the millpond?" I asked.

"How should I know? Maybe they take some sort of a fit that makes them leap into the water. It could be anything like that." He was complete in his confidence, but his self-assuredness did not relieve me of that foreboding which was now almost a part of my mind.

We finished supper shortly after total darkness enveloped the forest. Varnum rose in the circle of firelight, stretched, and rubbed his unshaven jowls.

"Are you going digging tomorrow"" he asked.

"Yes, I'll try to find the grave of Pauquatoag. And you?"

"I'll ride north-west about eight miles. There's a stand of pine that looks good from here." He scratched his sides and, without a further word, entered his tent and drew down the doorflap.

Since the night chill had come up, I banked the fire and retired to my tent, bringing the few birch rolls with me. By the light of the kerosene lantern I sat for an hour deciphering those of the records which were easily legible.

Although fragmentary, they spoke of the last days of the tribe during the smallpox epidemic, which they believed was a curse levied upon them because of the illicit congress between Pauquatoag's wife and the colonist. One roll mentioned that at the first sign of smallpox tokens on her body the woman was slaughtered most cruelly and her carcass literally thrown to the dogs. But this gesture of appeasement to the gods was ineffectual—each succeeding roll was covered with drawings of dismembered bodies, the Massaquoit method of depicting death from disease. The living perished even as they keened the dirges for the dead in their birch lodges.

When I found myself drowsing over the records I snuffed the lantern, bedded down, and was immediately asleep. But it was not long after midnight when I suddenly awoke to the feel of Varnum shaking me. In the glare of his battery lantern I could see his rifle glinting in his hand.

"Get up," he said. "Something's wrong outside."

I drew on my leggings and seized my own rifle. In the darkness of the campsite the ashes of the banked fire glowed hotly.

"To the northeast," Varnum whispered. "Animal noises."

I listened carefully, straining to hear over the roiling of the Penaubsket, which had risen during the night. When I had retired the only sounds were the metrical chirruping of the crickets and the eerie call of a night-roving whippoorwill. I could still hear only these sounds, and the river. I looked at Varnum and shrugged.

"Wait till the wind swings around," he said.

The breeze, which had been at our backs, began to turn with excruciating slowness until it cooled our faces as we stared off into the black wood. As its direction shifted, the wind brought with it at first the merest suspicion of a sound on the very edge of audibility, which gradually burgeoned into a high murmur. With a thrill of fear I recognized the sound as a frantic chorus of animal voices.

"Coming this way," Varnum said. He snapped off the safety on his rifle.

"What's driving them?" I asked.

"I don't know—never saw anything like this."

Even as he spoke the murmur became a steady wail of individual yipping ululations. From the edge of the camp came the noise of bodies thudding through the thickets of scrub pine. We dropped to our knees by the tents, rifles at the ready, just as a wave of small dark shapes burst into the lantern-lit clearing filling the night with a mad chattering as they swept over the ground. Some of the larger animals could not check their momentum and plunged through the fire, sending a plume of sparks through the tops of the pines and hemlocks. Missing their grips on the dark branches above, squirrels dropped into the light, then scurried in confusion back into the total darkness. Under the press of bodies the two tents collapsed. Loose gear was thrown about the camp and into the thickets on the edge of the clear ground. All at once a full-grown buck exploded into the clearing and made for us blindly, his great rack of antlers lowered. We fire simultaneously, and the shock of the slugs lifted the spray from his sides as he leapt high in the air, then thudded dead to the earth. All the animals headed unerringly for the Penaubsket, as if they were being herded to their destruction. Behind us we heard splashings as the first of the wave skittered down the steep banks into the flood. But the noise did not subside—a horrible collective moan, made in the extremities of terror.

Then, as quickly as it had begun, the stampede ended. The night was still again, save for the river, the crickets, and the lone whippoorwill. We waited without a word for fifteen minutes, each on one knee, safeties still off and torches out, peering into the forest. Although the air was chill Varnum mopped his brow.

"Did you see anything?" I asked.

"I—I don't know." Varnum rose hesitantly and began building up the fire. "For a time I thought I saw something—something blue, like a glow, through the trees. But it was so faint I'm not sure."

I was baffled. "What could have caused such a flight? There was no fire, no sound except that of the animals. Yet they were running for their lives."

In the glow of the fire Varnum's face was haggard.

"Do you really think I look like Prester?" he asked.

"Why—yes. The resemblance is a bit startling. Why do you ask?" There was a macabre oddity about his question in these circumstances.

"Never mind—just a thought." He laughed, but it was a dry, whickering sound, rooted not in humor but in fear.

For the remainder of the night we sat by the fire, dozing on our rifles, never daring to fall asleep completely. The first timorous glow of dawn through the ground mist rising from the marshes was a welcome sight. With the coming of day we repegged our tents and retired for a few hours' rest.

By nine o'clock the fat sun had dispelled the forest chill. Varnum approached me as I tightened the harness about the pack horse in preparation for the short trek to the burial ground.

"Say, how much longer do you want to stay here?" His manner lacked the arrogance which had grated on me at other times. As he spoke, his tone was almost supplicating.

"After last night, I'm not sure," I replied. I had planned to stay at least a week, but now it seems there is something wrong in this forest. The warden should be notified about the animals."

"But how much longer?" he asked.

"If I can find the grave of Pauquatoag today, we can leave in three days at the very latest."

"Then I'll give you a hand," Varnum said. Apparently his desire to see the timber resources in the area had vanished.

We rode to the burial ground, each sunk in his own thoughts. Varnum was undoubtedly troubled by the wave of animals which had come to a watery end in the Penaubsket. As for myself, I was frankly puzzled and not a little disturbed. As far as I knew, there was nothing in the natural order that could cause such a phenomenon except fire— and in the fungused, dripping underbrush that night there had been no fire, save for the eerie but harmless glows over the fens adjoining the river. Disease organisms could cause such madness, but I knew of none that affected such a large number of species simultaneously. Had I been a zoologist, perhaps I would have exulted over the chance of discovering new information about the behavior of forest dwellers. As a student of ancient records, versed only incidentally in animal lore, I could only stand in awe and bewilderment.

All that second day we worked at the burial ground. I had abandoned my plan of collecting as many of the subsidiary rolls as possible, and instead aimed at locating the grave of Pauquatoag immediately. Varnum and I hammered our iron sounding bars into the flinty soil innumerable times, locating the individual graves by the softness of their contents as contrasted to the density of the surrounding soil. As we probed I noticed that Varnum's hand trembled as he guided the bar. He swallowed often, and although the day was cool his face and neck were covered with a web of perspiration. The man had a look of doom about him.

It was late afternoon when our probes found an area of soft soil which, because of its size, could only be the grave of an important member of the tribe. As we dug through the layers of decaying pine needles and sterile earth, my conviction grew that this was indeed the grave of Pauquatoag. We removed cache after cache of wampumpeag, the cowrie shell money which paid the spirit's passage to the next world. Our trowels and shovels uncovered fire-blackened cooking utensils, fine weapons, and the remains of what had been rich ceremonial vestments three hundred years before. But the richest treasure would be the records which chronicled the life of the shaman, his feats, his genealogy, and his death.

With each succeeding foot that we penetrated into the grave Varnum's tension grew, and was transmitted in part to me. He did not speak, but I could read his anxiety in his jerky motions as he wielded the shovel and in the serious cast of his features. Although I had opened many graves in my researches, I resonated with his emotion. A strange unreasoning pall of fear settled over the burial ground.

We struck the level of ashes in which would be buried the pictographs. The body, or bones, would be just below this. Gently, with a small whisk broom and an old lobster pick, I separated the fragile rolls from their protective crust of ash and handed them to Varnum as he knelt on the lip of the grave. He dropped one and apologized for his clumsiness, saying that he was not himself. And I, kneeling in the mold above the resting place of the greatest of the northeastern tribal sorcerers, was not completely composed myself.

When the rolls were cleaned and packed in their padded boxes I walked to where Varnum was sitting like a dumb man.

"Shall we have a look?"

He nodded and rose with an air of resignation. We re-entered the excavation and with trowels cut into the hardened ash, which the Massaquoits believed would preserve the skeleton for eternity, for any injury to the remains would affect the spirit in the next world. We scraped and sifted through at least a half-yard of the grey ash. Then Varnum's trowel rang against a granite ledge.

"Oh God," he whispered to himself, "the bottom."

I continued digging in my corner of the excavation, trying to uncover some part of the remains. But not a fragment of bone was at the bottom.

"Nothing," I said quietly. We stared at each other. The layer of ash had been unbroken, the funereal gifts in perfect arrangement, the grave undisturbed for three centuries—and yet, no remains.

Beads of perspiration broke out on Varnum's brow. The forest at dusk, which had been tranquil, became ominous because of our discovery.

"But bodies just can't vanish, can they?" asked Varnum, almost pleading.

"There is always a trace," I said. "Sometimes, if the soil is abnormally acid and water continually leaches down, the bones, the clothing, even metal objects will disintegrate. But the hair always remains. Yards of it, in the case of a woman, since it continues growing for a time after death."

"There's no water seepage here," Varnum said. "The grave bottom's on a granite shelf, and there's no hair at all. Almost as though there never were a body."

"Ridiculous—these Indians did not make mock graves. This one is genuine, but, inexplicably, something has happened to the remains. I've never encountered such a thing before."

We rose in the ashen light. "We've done all we can here," I said. "During the next two days I'll clean the rolls further and pack them in preservative for the trip back. Then we'll fill the grave and leave Pauquatoag for the paleontologists. We must get back to Dunstable and notify the authorities about that stampede last night."

Varnum helped me to strap the record containers securely to the back of the pack horse. We rode back to the tents, arriving a few minutes before universal darkness settled over the wood. Against the possibility of another stampede we decided to stand watches through the remainder of the nights we would be on the camping ground.

During the next two days I was continually busy preparing the records for transport back to Dunstable and, eventually, the British Museum. Every particle of ash which might abrade the delicately figured surface of each roll had to be teased away. A coating of paraffin was applied to protect the dry birchbark from the atmosphere. This would suffice until a more durable preservative could be used.

Despite my preoccupation with the rolls, I could not overlook a progressive deterioration in Varnum's morale. On the evening of our discovery at the grave he had suffered nightmares all through his sleep. Sitting on watch, I could hear him moaning and speaking unintelligibly to some unknown adversary. When he came on watch he was obviously unrested and bore a harried expression about his eyes which only first light would dispel.

On the second evening his discomfort was worse. I decided to wake him, since the sounds which issued from his throat were scarcely human.

"It's—it's the same as last night," he gasped, blinking in the light from my lantern. "I can see myself asleep in the tent, and you sitting on watch—but there's something else there beyond the clearing, something which is slowly moving in towards the tents. And you can't see it, but it's there, coming for—for me!"

The man was almost hysterical. In view of his condition I decided to stand his watch for him, and so administered a sedative from the medical kit which I hoped would at least quiet the terrible sounds and cries he had been making. When he fell back to sleep I took a turn around the fringe of the clearing, then returned to my seat by the fire.

For a time, wrapped in my blanket, I contemplated to try at deciphering the records of Pauquatoag, but the light from the embers was feeble. In retrospect I doubt that I could have long concentrated on the pictographs, given the situation. My mind was occupied with thoughts of the unnatural fear which hung over Dunstable and this forest—the unspoken fear of the townsmen at the mere mention of penetrating north of the lumbering camps; the bizarre sight of animal bodies circling aimlessly in the eddies of the millpond; the insane, chattering flight of the animal horde through the forest and into the Penaubsket. And now, our failure to find a trace of the shaman in his virgin, untouched grave.

With an effort of will I forced my mind away from these thoughts since there in the ruddy glow of the dying fire I found myself becoming mortally afraid. I was a grown man, only a few years away from the slaughter of Belleau Wood. I had been afraid there yet had never betrayed the emotion since I was among my fellows. With the romanticism of a nobler age we thought we were all marked for death, and so resigned ourselves. But there in that black forest where each breath brought the taste of mold, there was no flashing cannonade or shrapnel warbling into trenches or bullets thudding through the olive drill of uniforms—only the steady dripping of the leaves, the smell of unknown centuries of decay and dissolution, and the unbearable silence. Although I trust no human group above the size of a British Infantry platoon, that night I longed for the babble of a crowd.

To compose myself I reached inside my pack and drew out the dog-eared copy of the works of Alexander Pope, my beloved Pope, whose graceful verse had solaced me on many such a watch. I hunched in my blanket against the fire, rifle at my knee, and almost pushed the sense of foreboding from my mind. It was two hours before dawn, and I had just finished "Windsor Forest", when the pain began.

Without warning I was in the extremities of agony. Every joint, nerve, and organ writhed under a pain so intense it was exquisite. I bit my tongue and tasted blood as the volume slipped from my fingers. Entirely paralyzed I began to fall forward, afire in a frenzy of pain and fear but unable to scream and hardly to breathe. The brief interval of my fall seemed a day; although my mind was numbed a small, cold faculty dispassionately and at great speed reviewed the possible causes of my agony—a cerebral hemorrhage? An injury to the spinal cord, grievously damaging the major nerve bundles? A crushing blow to the cerebellum? With damp moss against my cheek I lay facing Varnum's tent across the fire, almost mad with the spasms which tettered up and down my limbs. "My God," I thought, "is this the end?"

And then, on the periphery of my vision, sliding in across the fringe of the clearing, soundlessly, inexorably, came the damned Thing. A cold blue glow, a lurid phosphorescence which gave no warmth to the night which enveloped it. It crossed the open space, my pain increasing with its approach. But no merciful unconsciousness came. The nimbus passed through the fire while not an ember stirred, not a spark rode the column of warm air. Ignoring me, it made for Varnum's tent, from which came the sounds of a sleeper in the throes of a horrid dream, the mumbled cries of a mind battling a hideous foe.

As I listened, lying mute like a felled animal, the cries changed in timbre and Varnum was awake. The glow hovered over, then invested the entire tent, its unearthly light playing over the canvas and ropes like St. Elmo's Fire in the rigging of a ship. The door flap burst open and Varnum bolted out, naked to the waist, clawing his flesh and the air as the radiance settled around him. On his chest and arms the muscle bundles were twitching and cramping spasmodically. From his frantic screams I knew he shared the agony in which I lay. Frenziedly he ran through the fire, setting his leggings ablaze in a vain attempt to outrun his tormentor.

"Grail, for the love of God, help me!" he cried. He wore the glow like a cloak; his limbs pulsated with an unholy light and thrashed about like those of a madman.

With a sudden shock that rose even above my numbing pain I realized that Varnum was headed toward the river. He passed out of my field of vision as his agonized screams were joined by the crackling of underbrush. I tried to move my arms, to grasp my rifle, to seize a brand from the fire—anything to relieve my terror through action. But I was paralyzed as surely as if my spinal cord were severed. I could only lie sobbing as the wails grew more distant, finally vanishing under the roar of the flooding Penaubsket. With the knowledge that Varnum now shared the fate of the stampeding animals, blessed unconsciousness came.

I revived shortly before dawn, groggy at first, then wide awake. The paralysis and pain had left me; now I experienced a wild desire to run, to leave the damned campsite. I loped to the brush near the river and lay amid the wet leaves expecting the reappearance of the awful Thing at any moment. Thoughts of Prester Varnum, the curse of Pauquatoag on the Varnum house, and the empty grave seethed through my mind, dominated by the image of that inexorable blue nimbus moving across the clearing and through the fire like a mad surrealist's rendering of the Angel of Death.

With the coming of dawn I returned to the campsite and hurriedly packed the more important gear and the precious rolls, leaving the tents and utensils to rot away. I paused briefly at the burial ground to pack the few cases of unprocessed rolls I had left there. Then I rode headlong through the forest, toward Dunstable, as fast as the pack horses and Varnum's riderless mount would permit.

A cloying fear hung over the town where I arrived after a two-day journey. Work had halted at the mill. The inhabitants gathered in tight knots along the main street. At the police office the Sheriff of Sussex County was talking with the district coroner. Varnum's body had been found that morning in the millpond, borne like the animal corpses on the flood of the Penaubsket.

Given the circumstances of his death, I chose to edit my statement— the events of that night seemed too fantastic to be believed. Accordingly, I reported that I had heard Varnum screaming in the underbrush as he ran toward the river, and that he had apparently tumbled down the bank in his frenzy and drowned.

The officials received my statement with no sign of disbelief. We walked to the local undertaking parlor to view the corpse. Although in the water for only thirty-six hours, the body was badly mangled from snagging on obstacles in the Penaubsket. However, it was unmistakeably Varnum, but with the remains of his face twisted into an uncannily ironic smile, a true *risus sardonicus*. The areas of unscratched flesh were covered with numerous reddish weals and puckers.

The coroner saw me stiffen at the sight of the marks. He tapped the cold flesh with his pencil. "Bee stings," he said. "He must have tramped down on a bee nest, and run from them down the bank into the river." His tone was that of a man disbelieving his own diagnosis. I nodded my head in false agreement, for I had seen such marks once in Alexandria. They were unmistakeably the first tokens of smallpox.

On the following morning I ended my stay in Dunstable, not wishing to remain for the funeral of a man who had perished in such a loathsome manner before my eyes. As I sat in the passenger coach lurching southward toward Boston and civilization, I mused over the events at the burial ground as if they were dreams remembered from the delirium of an illness. But they were real enough, as real as the pictographs in the baggage car, recording the extinction of the tribe and the curse on the Varnum house. Thinking of this I wondered who would believe me if I ever let it be known that on the morning after Varnum's death, while collecting the rolls at the burial ground, I saw at the very bottom of the open grave a faint area of bone-colored powder outlining the form of a man, and knew that after three centuries, Pauquatoag of the Massaquoits had come to rest.

THE CRIB OF HELL

BY ARTHUR PENDRAGON

What dark secret had driven Laurence Cullum to the edge of nervous hysteria? What unutterable obligation had forced him to cry out for succor like an agonized madman? These and other questions relevant to the desperate condition of the master of Cullum House perplexed Doctor Nathan Buttrick as he clucked his team homeward through Penaubsket Bridge on the fringe of Sabbathday in northern New England. In other circumstances, he might have been dozing, lulled by the cries of the nighthawks aloft and the peace of an upland twilight. But now, although his body craved sleep, his mind was vitally awake.

Doctor Buttrick was baffled by the peculiar malady which made each day a living horror for Cullum. All of the sedatives of the 1924 pharmacopeia had failed to quell the anxiety which gnawed at the mind of his patient. In his frustration at the failure of the tablets and injections, the physician had even resorted to folk remedies whispered by black-gummed grandmothers in the hills back from the sea. Infusions of tea and henbane, petals of amaryllis held under the tongue—he had tried all the high-country nostrums which once he held in professional scorn. They were as futile in calming Cullum as the most advanced drugs the age could offer.

As the feeble lights of Sabbathday came into view around the granite mass of Gallowglass Hill, Buttrick reviewed once again the particulars of the case. Laurence Cullum, age 47. Afflicted with a cerebral aneurism, a soft patch in a brain artery which might burst tomorrow, in five years, or never. He was the last of the Cullum line, a prominent family begun by Draper Cullum, the leader of the 1706 expedition which struck northward from Dunstable to find, on an August Sunday, the protected harbor on the North Atlantic around which would grow the seacoast town of Sabbathday.

The Cullums had always been influential in the town, yet oddly retiring. Laurence was the most hermitic of the lot. Since the death of his sister Emma and the diagnosis of his aneurism, he had shut himself up in the gray New England Gothic mansion at the end of Windham Road. His controlling hand was still felt on many of the town's business affairs, but this was merely the ghost of the man. His physical presence was sequestered behind the grotesque archway of Cullum House—two enormous jawbones of a sperm whale, erected during the tenancy of the last patriarch, Captain Hugh.

These facts and the few pleasantries that Buttrick had exchanged with Cullum during the man's infrequent visits to town were all that the doctor knew of the Cullum heir before treatments for the aneurism began. Except for the grim scene on the night of Emma's death two years before. The physician had been in attendance, accompanied by Cullum and most of the household staff. Buttrick would never forget the last words of Emma, spoken as she clutched her brother's arm in a white-knuckled hand.

"Laurence, you will keep—the guardianship?"

"I—I shall, my dear," Cullum replied as a mad, trapped look appeared in his eyes. Then the life of the frail spinster eked out its last heartbeat, and Buttrick's usefulness had ended.

The doctor heard nothing of Laurence Cullum for a year and a half after his sister's demise. Then came the midnight telephone call. Buttrick rolled groggily from his bed, expecting a summons to the side of any one of three wives who were awaiting childbirth. Instead, he was shocked into full awareness by an almost hysterical voice begging him to administer relief. Although years of medical practice had somewhat jaded his sensibility to human pain, Buttrick heard a voice so filled with a frantic tension that the listener himself became afraid in an unconscious resonance with the pleading tones. He whipped his team across the surly Penaubsket River and along Windham Road, guided only by the chill light of a three-quarter moon. At the end of the headlong ride he found Cullum in a state of extreme anxiety within the mouldering drawing room of the mansion. The earpiece of the telephone was still off its hook as the man cowered in a great wing chair, whimpering like an injured child in shocking contrast to the manliness of his six-foot frame.

Although he was wrapped in a dressing gown, Cullum's trouser cuffs bore traces of drying mud.

Buttrick quickly administered the standard dosage of a sedative. It had no effect. A second injection calmed Cullum, or rather removed the physical manifestations of his hysteria. But even as the drug subdued his trembling, Cullum retained a spark of horror in his eyes.

Repeatedly Buttrick questioned the sufferer about the cause of his alarming discomposure. And each time the gaunt-faced Cullum had burrowed deeper into the plush of the wing chair, mumbling under the sedation, "Can't say—mustn't say. No one must ever know. The guardianship!" Despite himself the physician felt a growing fear at the recurrence of that ominous term first uttered in his hearing by the dying lips of Emma Cullum.

At last the opiate calmed the man's chaotic nerves. With the aid of Amadee, an aged Acadian man-servant, the doctor wrestled the drugged weight onto a settee near the fire. He left a vial of tablets with the servant, and the assurance that he would visit his master on the next day. Then Buttrick returned to town exhausted physically but unable to quell the incessant questioning of his curiosity. What event or obsession could explain the mental disintegration of Cullum? What arcane significance had that curious term muttered by Laurence even in his narcotic stupor?

During the months of treatment which followed the first nighttime summons, the doctor had learned little else about the trouble at Cullum House. He had diagnosed the aneurism, but was certain that his patient's extreme nervousness and loss of weight were by no means related to his physical affliction. Rather there was some obligation, burden, perhaps something in the house itself, under whose presence the mind of the Cullum heir was slowly crumbling.

Besides the strange term spoken by both Emma and Laurence, there was one other fact which increased the peculiarity of the case. Buttrick had noticed that Cullum always avoided approaching a large tapestry hanging in the drawing room, another remnant of the patriarchy of Captain Hugh. The subject and rendition were unsettling at first glance—a highly realistic depiction of a Witches' Sabbath. The naked bodies of cabalistic women were ruddy in the glow from a fire which also illumined a bleeding victim. After a few visits, Buttrick had inured himself to the grisly scene. But Cullum would never pass within five feet of the cloth. Sometimes the doctor had the uncomfortable conviction that his patient was *listening* to the tapestry, as though hearing the whickering laughter of the coven.

Gradually Buttrick resigned himself to the frustration of trying to quell a malady of the spirit by chemical means. A difficult task, at best. With such a secretive, uncooperative patient, it was almost an impossibility.

Such were the reflections of the toil-worn leech of Sabbathday as he reined his team before the weathered frame bungalow from which his father had practiced before him. After stabling the horses he ate a light supper, then willingly gave himself to his mattress with a sighed hope that no major illnesses or accidents would befall the populace of the village that night. His last conscious thought was not a prayer to his Creator, but a mindless repetition of the eldritch phrase so full of puzzlement and, in Emma's tones, a taint of evil: "The guardianship."

In late afternoon of the following day Buttrick stood beneath the whale-jaw archway of Cullum House, marvelling at the curving bone monoliths of this striking manifestation of the family's eccentricity. It was one of the two days of the week on which Cullum was treated both for his aneurism and for the frenzy attacking his nerves. Amadee was waiting behind the door. He ushered the doctor into the dank coolness of the mansion. Once inside the entry-way, the aged Acadian drew close to Buttrick and seized his elbow in a surprisingly strong grip, a liberty he had never before taken.

"*M'sieur le docteur*," he said hoarsely, "do not be surprise' if the master, he tell to you some strange thing' today." There was a smile on the seamed lips, but the coldness of Amadee's eyes removed all traces of amiability from his manner. "It is some time now that the master, he has been saying strange thing' that you should not believe. *C'est la maladie*—it is the sickness, nothing more."

Buttrick was repelled by the servant's familiarity. During his visits to the house he had found Amadee a strange figure, given to eavesdropping impassively as Cullum made pitiful attempts at conversation with his physician. For some inexplicable reason, the presence of the Acadian always put Buttrick on his guard as though the stooped valet carried with him a hint of evil. Certainly the man added to the foreboding gloom of Cullum House.

Buttrick pried his arm out of Amadee's grip and strode quickly into the drawing room. As was his habit, Cullum was seated as far away from the tapestry as was physically possible. He rose unsteadily as the doctor entered the room.

"So—so good of you to come, Nathan," he said. Although his mind was on the verge of splintering into a thousand shards of madness, automatically the heir preserved the vestiges of a courtesy reserved for calmer spirits.

Buttrick placed his bag on a richly damasked ottoman, inspecting his patient's appearance with a quick, professional glance. He was appalled by Cullum's decline since the last visit. The man was wrapped in a crimson sitting-robe that seemed made for a larger frame, so grievously had his body wasted under the bearing of his mental burden. The eyes were preternaturally bright, staring from dark sockets. Cullum nervously plucked at the cord of the gown with a hand which shocked Buttrick by its resemblance to Emma's—blanched, and with yellowed nails. The doctor had seen patients harboring within them vile malignancies fall into such decay. But Cullum's dissolution was the result of a *mental* cancer which threatened to destroy both mind and body. It was moot which—soul or flesh—would perish first.

Now the man seemed inflamed by a strange eagerness. He motioned Buttrick to close his bag, and cleared his throat nervously.

"I fear, Nathan, that I have not been the best of patients. All your medications, all your attentions—useless." He dismissed them with a wave of his blue-veined hand. "Nothing will relieve me. Nothing can ease the weight of this hideous charge I labor under..." Cullum stopped briefly and seemed to listen to the tapestry. Recovering his train of thought, he continued. "Unless—unless I somehow ease my mind of this *guardianship!*" He spat the word out in mingled tones of fear and loathing.

"Unless I tell the secret I shall die, and the secret shall die with me. And if I tell the secret, the secret shall die, and I shall die with it. Almost a conundrum, eh Buttrick? A true gnomic riddle, eh my friend?"

The physician rose to steady Cullum, for his speech was assuming the peculiar cadence of madness. The man rallied, mumbling, "Not yet—not yet." In a moment his face took on a grave cast as he spoke in cooler, more ominous tones.

"You must have suspected, Nathan, that the cause of my agony was exceedingly strange. The aneurism," he tapped his temple, "it is nothing. We Cullums have suffered more unusual maladies than that. My trouble lies deeper than the fragile flesh." The heir paused reflectively, then continued. "I—I have stood it as long as I could, endured under this hideous burden longer than I thought possible. I am not as strong as Emma was. Not so much of a Cullum, perhaps. She was like my father, Captain Hugh, amazingly strong-willed. The secret of our family horror—I know no other name for it—was safe with her while she lived. But I—two years, man! Two years of ceaseless anxiety. And the last few months have been a waking terror!"

Buttrick had been engrossed by Cullum's narration. But suddenly he started. A sound, a muffled moan or cry, had issued from the direction of the cabalistic tapestry. Cullum saw the doctor's apprehensive glance.

"Not yet, my friend. Later you shall know all. For now, Nathan, hear me out." He flicked his hand at Amadee, who was loitering in the door of the drawing-room. "That will be all, Amadee. Go to your duties." The Acadian shuffled reluctantly into the bowels of the house. When his footsteps no longer sounded off the flaking walls of the passage, Cullum resumed his monologue.

"It is now time, Nathan, that you knew the well-kept secret of this house, for I shall tell you or die in the attempt. Only by sharing this intolerable weight have I any chance of keeping my sanity." His lips trembled as he fought to maintain calmness. "It is n-not easy to disburden oneself of such knowledge, but I must, despite the warning, or I shall most surely go mad. Be patient, Nathan, and let me tell it in my own way."

Buttrick settled uneasily into a sofa. For a moment he felt a sudden impulse to deny Cullum the opportunity to tell his tale. Why should he, Nathan Buttrick, participate in this secret? His precinct was the body, not the diseased mind. With its austere inhabitants and wild setting between the forest wastes and the sullen North Atlantic,

Sabbathday was eerie enough without compounding it by a knowledge of the secret of Cullum House.

But gradually Buttrick's professional instincts exerted themselves. If Cullum did not gain some mental relief, either the torments he underwent would render him mad, or his aneurism would burst under the strain. The doctor settled back and accepted a dark sherry from his patient's trembling hand.

"Nathan," said Cullum, "have you ever heard the name—*Ligea?*"

"Ligea was the... second wife, I believe, of your father, Captain Hugh," answered Buttrick.

"Yes, if she can be called—a wife!"

Immediately Buttrick knew the reason for Cullum's bitter statement. The doctor had been only a child when Ligea came to Sabbathday, yet the bizarre tales the townspeople told about her were preserved in his memory. After the death of his first wife, the mother of Laurence and Emma, Captain Hugh Cullum had consigned his children to the care of a relative. He then embarked on his last voyage as master of the steamer *Ogunquit* to the Baltic port of Riga. When he returned to Sabbathday almost two years later, he brought with him the numerous spoils of Yankee trading and a mistress for Cullum House, the dark Ligea.

Grotesque rumors about this woman soon sprang up amidst the villagers. Perhaps some originated in the mouths of goodwives who envied her exotic charms. For Ligea was oddly beautiful—a tall woman, with a luminous Eastern complexion, sinuous in her movements, heavily accented in her speech. Ligea's most distinctive feature was her long raven hair of a black deeper than the northern forest night.

Whatever their origin, the stories about Ligea soon were the common coin of conversation around the hearths of Sabbathday. It was said that she had brought the nighthawks to Cullum House. Before her coming, these nocturnal flyers had soared only over the backlands far from town. Now they roosted in the trees of the estate, trembling the night air with the beat of wings.

More serious, some reported that Ligea had been seen on Walpurgis Night wantoning naked through the woods at the fringe of town. One individual who had been abroad at that hour swore that a glowing cloud had passed in from the sea over Sabbathday, and that voices could be heard mumbling in strange tongues from within the floating mass. An ancient dame who dwelt alone near Gallowglass Hill averred that Ligea had spent many afternoons with the few Indian sachems still alive, the degenerate remainder of the Pequot tribe. This nearly extinct race, it was said, held powers over air and sea.

The more intelligent of the townsfolk dismissed these tales as fantasies. Yet all knew that Ligea exerted a strange hold on Captain Hugh. The gruff skipper was quite deferential to her in public, a far cry from his callous treatment of his first wife. There were some who even noticed more than a touch of fear in his attitude toward the tall woman whom he bore on his arm.

However, in her public behavior the woman was impeccable— haughty of mien, knowledgeable in the social graces, distant yet polite. During the couples' visits to town she comported herself as befitted the wife of a monied landowner. Only a few noted that occasionally she exchanged knowing glances with the most depraved of the town's moral outcasts.

A year after her arrival in Sabbathday, Ligea was big with child. At this time Hugh Cullum ceased his frequent visits to town and seemed to enter retirement at the end of Windham Road. The village believed that he had secluded himself in deference to his wife's condition. Not a soul understood that behind the captain's bluff facade lay a spirit sorely harried by some knowledge which he could impart to no other person.

Several days after her confinement was due to end the news reached Sabbathday that both Ligea and her babe had perished in childbirth. The father of Nathan Buttrick had been in attendance. In answer to the many queries he replied that there was nothing he could have done, and divulged no other details of the tragedy. Nathan recalled that his father had been unusually silent for days after the event, as though meditating on some incomprehensible problem. Once he had told his son that if he aspired to be a physician, there was something about the Cullums that he should know in the future. But then the normal course of town life was resumed. The remains of Ligea were cremated and transported to her native land as she had wished. The small casket of the child took its place among the Cullum ancestors in the family crypt. And Nathan Buttrick never heard the Cullum secret from the lips of his father, for the man died of a heart seizure a few months later.

"She was a *witch*, damn her eyes!" cried Cullum. The heir had become noticeably less calm toward the end of Buttrick's narration of the few facts he knew of Ligea. Now a torrent of suppressed emotion broke forth. "And *it* is not dead, do you hear? *Not dead!*"

Buttrick leapt to restrain Cullum, who seemed ready to run from the room. At the same moment a hideous clamor issued from the direction of the tapestry, a scarcely human screeching accompanied by thudding impacts as though a body were hurling itself at the wall.

"It heard—it heard!" raved Cullum. He swung around and faced the cloth. "You cannot hold me in bondage any longer. The guardianship is at an end! At last, an end..." His final words choked off in a sob. Cullum pitched into a faint on the settee.

The vicious sounds from the tapestry grew in intensity until the cloth and the wall behind it trembled. Amadee entered the room on the run, his features contorted with rage. Apparently he had overheard the entire scene.

"The weak pig," he snarled, "he has doom' us all—we are dead men, M'sieur, dead men!" He vanished down the hall, his footsteps giving way to the grind of a heavy door being swung on its hinges. In a few moments Buttrick heard the crack of a bullwhip over the horrid ululations. A note of pain entered the screams. They tapered off into piteous whimpers, until silence returned to Cullum House.

Buttrick knelt beside the heir, struggling to revive him. For a moment he feared the aneurism had burst. But the eyelids trembled, and slowly the man regained his senses.

"Ah, the relief, Nathan," Cullum sighed. "No longer a prisoner in my own house. No longer keeper of the vile heritage Emma passed on to me."

"Great God, Laurence," cried Buttrick, "what have you hidden behind that wall?"

"I could not describe it," he answered. "Walk to the tapestry. You shall see it for yourself."

Buttrick moved unsteadily toward the rich cloth, his breathing suspended in anticipation of whatever was to occur.

"Open the tapestry with the cord by your hand," directed Cullum.

The doctor grasped the weighted end of the cord. He closed his eyes for a moment, opened them, then tugged at the cord. The tapestry slid back smoothly across the wall. Beneath it, the wall was discolored but blank, except for a small glassed orifice at eye level. Buttrick hesitated. He glanced at Laurence, who feebly motioned to him from the settee, then fixed his eye to the peephole. A low moan escaped the physician's lips as his hand came up to clutch his throat.

The orifice gave a view through the thick wall into a smaller chamber behind the drawing room. Immediately opposite was a heavy steel door, with a similar peephole and a sturdy grating at the bottom through which a man might crawl, were it open. Gnawed bones and a basin of water lay before the grill, which was apparently an opening for inserting food into the chamber. A grayish light emanated from tiny clerestory windows along two sides beneath the ceiling. Knots of thread-like filaments—black, brown, and yellow—littered the floor.

Crouched in the far corner was the tenant of this chamber, a spectre so inhuman that Buttrick's vision momentarily blurred from the shock. It hulked panting on its hands, a living human torso, if such a distortion of man's form can be designated thusly. Raven hair fell in hanks and tangles from a misshapen skull. Bright, feverish eyes glared out from beneath the shaggy brows. From the face projected only a rudimentary nose, its nostrils dilating as an animal would breathe. The lips were tensed in a snarl, revealing discolored teeth more like the fangs of a carnivore.

The thing was naked save for a ragged breechclout tied about its middle. The torso showed superhuman muscular development—arms as thick as fenceposts, a barrel chest partly covered by a pelt. The lower extremities were piteously withered, dragging behind the upper body. Yet that monstrous form carried itself to and fro in the chamber with remarkable agility, supporting its weight on the arms and talon-like hands. As it lunged from one corner to the other, the creature sounded an ominous murmur from deep within its dark breast.

"Oh my dear God," whispered Buttrick, unbelieving before the grisly sight. He had seen men mangled by awful accidents in the logging camps, and even the pitiable distortions of infant bodies in stillbirths. But never had the physician's entire consciousness writhed before such a gross malformation of the human body. He slumped weakly against the wall beside the peephole.

"What is it, Laurence?" he asked. "Where—where did it come from?"

"Now you realize the desperate burden I have carried these months, Nathan," replied Cullum. "That thing has been in our charge since the death of my father's second wife. It is—Ligea's *Hell-Child!*"

As he watched Buttrick's reaction to the spectacle behind the tapestry, a transformation overcame Cullum. He seemed more in control of himself, as though the sharing of the secret with another not in the bloodline had relieved a great pressure within his spirit. Seeing Buttrick's revulsion, Cullum had the presence of mind to fill another glass from the squat ship's decanter and offer the stimulant to the doctor, who had moved slowly away from the wall like a sleepwalker.

"Sit down, Nathan, and calm yourself," ordered the heir. "I'm sure you must have many questions about our—bad seed."

When Buttrick had composed himself, Cullum spoke volubly about the origin of the chamber-dweller. The doctor listened as his host told him of Ligea's dying threat to the house of Cullum. Unless they maintained her infant in secrecy until its maturity, they would perish. *The Guardianship*, as she called it, must be passed from member to member. Only death could release a guardian, who was responsible for the care and nourishment of the creature. They would know, Ligea said, when the child no longer needed their protection.

Captain Hugh Cullum had always scoffed at superstitions and curses. But suddenly the occult had come under his own eaves in the presence of that incredible child, surrounded by a brooding evil even then in its infancy. He knew that he had not fathered such a monster. Gradually the conviction grew within his mind that Ligea had consorted with a spirit of darkness, and that the babe was the token of their devilish love.

Captain Hugh would allow the child no baptism. It was placed in the strong-room behind the main parlor, a chamber which the guardians came to call, sardonically, the Crib. From that time forward, the tenant of that dark room behind the tapestry was known as the Hell-Child.

"And so, Nathan, if Ligea's words were true, then you are listening to a dead man. The guardian who betrays the secret must die, you know."

"Superstitious nonsense!" cried Buttrick, who had recovered from his initial shock. "Why, look at you, man. You're more relaxed than I've seen you in months. Now, Laurence, I can't yet explain that thing in there, or why it's survived so long despite its grave malformation.

But it must have a natural explanation. I admit that at first I was shocked. It's a hideous thing. Yet I can see nothing that you should fear in it. Perhaps we can arrange for an institution to take over its care, relieving you of the burden. As to its being a Hell-Child—really, Laurence, I'd expect this type of thinking more of an upland farmer than the Cullum heir!"

"That is because you do not fully understand the terrible threat of the creature!" cried Cullum. "It must be destroyed, Nathan, before it can commit more of its evil. It's just begun, I tell you!"

Buttrick put out his hand to steady Cullum, who was becoming agitated again. "What evil? What are you talking about, Laurence?"

"Do you remember that first night I called you—how frantic I was?" The doctor nodded. "And do you remember Rupel Oldham?"

Buttrick involuntarily winced. Oldham had been found lying in a foot of stagnant water near a fire-road through Mohegan Swamp. Buttrick had signed the death-certificate of the aged muskrat trapper. The body had been badly mutilated, and a look of utter horror was indelibly stamped on its face.

"You don't mean—that?" asked Buttrick, pointing toward the wall.

Cullum nodded. "It broke out," he said helplessly. "We had underestimated its strength, and it burst through the wooden door which the steel door you saw later replaced. Amadee and I followed it as quickly as we could. It was dark. The spring rains had muddied the ground." Cullum's voice became dreamy as he relived the gruesome event.

"At first Amadee and I didn't know where to look. We stood in the drive, he with the bullwhip and myself carrying the lantern. It could have gone off in any direction. But then—then we heard the nighthawks crying over Mohegan Swamp in the valley behind the estate. A terrible, fierce sound, Nathan. They were swarming as though mad.

"We ran through the forest on the fire-road. The sound of the birds got louder, more shrill, until we could see against the gray sky the place over which they were swarming. I remember wishing that I had had the presence of mind to bring a pistol. But then the light from the lantern showed us its form ahead. Oh Nathan, Oldham had come down to check his traps, and it caught him there in the mud and scummy water. When we ran up it was—*feeding*!

"Amadee lashed it with the whip, and it drew back. I saw that we could do nothing for Oldham. The expression on his face—terrible. Between the two of us we drove the creature back to the house and into the Crib. It was more docile then, feared the bite of the whip more than now." Cullum paused and wet his lips with the sherry. "But the atrocity so unsettled me that I had to call you for relief, or I would have lost my mind.

"We should have recognized this murderous act as an unmistakable sign that it was approaching its maturity, Nathan. But we thought the killing of Oldham was an accident, a chance encounter. No more than a month later, Arnold, my groundskeeper, passed away. He was the last of the servants, save Amadee. At night the beast broke out again. I was awakened by the nighthawks massing over the house. The coffin lay within the parlor. That thing had overturned it, and was tearing, slashing..." Cullum clenched his fists in agony. "Do you understand what I've been living with, Nathan? Do you wonder that my nerves are gone?"

Buttrick stirred uncomfortably. He was being drawn into the macabre web of Cullum's narration. The doctor began to feel unsafe sitting only a few yards away from the tapestry. How may times had he entered the decaying drawing-room to treat the master of Cullum House, oblivious to the existence of a horror separated from him by only a few inches of plaster and lath?

"We then knew," continued Cullum, "that its ghastly appetite had been whetted. We realized that these events were not mere chance. The evil thing mothered by my father's second wife—I cannot call her my stepmother—had reached its maturity. For a week after we interred Arnold it screamed. I shall hear its cries until my ears are stopped by death. Ravenous, ferocious howls which sounded even beyond the walls of the house. Amadee and his bullwhip could not control it. I stuffed my ears with cotton, took laudanum, drank myself into unconsciousness—everything failed. That hideous keening could not be suppressed. It was then, at the end of my wits, that I made the decision for which, if ever a man were damned, I shall be. I had to stop the screaming, Nathan, do you understand that?"

Buttrick shook his head slowly, scarce daring to consider what awful revelation he would hear next.

"I ordered Amadee—ah, even now I cannot bring myself to pronounce the words!" Cullum fought visibly to control his rising emotion. He sprang from the settee and paced the room. "Amadee, in addition to being my only servant, is also," he blurted the words out, "custodian of the Sabbathday Burial Ground. Do you understand my meaning?"

"Then the bones in the chamber, and those fibers—hanks of hair?" Buttrick asked incredulously.

"How many evenings have I slumped in that very chair, listening to that beast at its unholy supper! How often have I considered suicide, anything to free me of this vile guardianship. Even Amadee has become infected by it—I truly believe he enjoys tending the creature and disciplining it with his bullwhip. He derives a sense of power from those duties. The old man thinks me weak and scorns me because my nerves cannot stand the strain. But what a burden—God help me, I am the protector of a *ghoul!*"

A long silence followed the impassioned confession. The room had become oppressively thick-atmosphered. Buttrick opened the French doors which led to a terrace and thence the drive. The sky was yet aglow, and only the drone of frogs at Mohegan Swamp heralded the approach of night. The birds roosting in the trees about the house had not yet begun their darkling flights.

The doctor turned and addressed Cullum. "Is there any danger that it will break out again, Laurence?"

"The steel door has thus far resisted its attempts," he replied. "Occasionally it hurls itself at the door for an hour at a time. Its ferocity is appalling. But the door and its frame remain fast." The heir sighed deeply. "Yet a mere steel door cannot be sufficient to hold such a malignant evil. It must be destroyed, Nathan, and quickly. I can no longer protect the town from its appetite. And now that I have discovered the Cullum secret to you, I feel that if we do not act soon the thing will be at large, with no one to stop it. For it heard me betray it, I am sure, and craves my death."

Buttrick was convinced. Now his mind no longer operated in accord with the civilized virtues of reason and mercy. His own experience that day at Cullum House, and his host's desperate words, had brought to life within him the savage's fear of the unknown. He agreed to assist in the extermination of the creature, and swore that no word of the proceedings would ever pass his lips.

Since Cullum assured him that he could spend another night in the house with the Hell-Child, Buttrick decided to return to Sabbathday. On the morrow he would return to the estate to plan the destruction and interment of the beast, for they would need daylight to dig its unholy resting place.

On the portico of the mansion beneath the arched jawbones, Cullum seized Buttrick's hand in a firm grip. "I only wish my father had taken this course in the beginning," he said. "Then perhaps he, Emma, and myself would have been spared the blight which has sapped our lives." He ran his hand along the cool ivory of the curving white monoliths. "I know that wherever he is, my father approves the action we must take."

Buttrick nodded in silent agreement. He bade the heir a good night, and turned his team onto the darkness of Windham Road. As he left the grounds of the estate, the nighthawks were beginning their evening clamor. Their rasping cries banished the peace of the autumn evening. After his return to the bungalow the doctor lay sleepless, distracted by vivid mental phantasms of what he had heard and witnessed that evening. Each time he closed his eyes the scene in the Crib flashed across the screen of his conscious mind in all its loathsome detail. He could not erase from his memory the glowering countenance of the Hell-Child, a face so evil it seemed impossible that flesh and bone could be tortured into receiving the stamp of such malignancy. Buttrick could well understand why Captain Hugh had disclaimed parentage of the child.

And now Buttrick himself had been drawn into the Cullum horror. He had sworn to aid in the destruction of the thing which might still bear within it a spark of humanity, despite Cullum's heated denials and the mystery of its parentage. Vicious, instinctively homicidal, yes; but was this enough, he asked himself, enough cause to betray a greater oath—that one which bound Nathan Buttrick to use his skills only for the preservation of life? It was a quandary, and the man writhed under the weight of his contradictory obligations.

The doctor had thus lain staring at the slowly rising patch of moonlight on his wall for three hours, when the telephone beside his bed rang. With a sudden clairvoyance Buttrick knew that this was no ordinary call summoning him to the sickbed of a villager. He swung out of the bed and snatched the earpiece from the hook. The voice of Laurence Cullum dinned in his ear.

"Nathan, come quickly, man. We can't hold it. It's breaking out of the Crib!"

Over Cullum's voice came the sound of splintering wood and a ravening ululation such as never sprang from human throat. The telephone crashed to the floor as Buttrick leapt to struggle into his clothes. He vaulted across the yard to the barn, scarce feeling the bite of the early hoarfrost. With frantic speed he harnessed the team and urged them out of their warm quarters into the chill darkness of the road where the moon hardly penetrated the roof of overhanging trees.

Five minutes after the call, the wild-eyed horses lunged through the shadows of Penaubsket Bridge onto the gravel of Windham Road. Although the doctor was a good master to his animals, now he whipped them cruelly. He called the two mares by name, hurling imprecations foreign to his lips in an effort to gain more speed. Black masses of maple and oak lashed by, their sharp twig-ends striking blood from Buttrick's face when the surrey veered too close to the road's edge. Twice it seemed that all—horses, surrey, and driver—must surely fall to perdition, so headlong was their flight in rounding curves where granite outcroppings changed the road's direction. If a goodman of the town had been abroad at that hour, he would have crossed himself in utter terror at the approach of the flying team and whipman.

It seemed an age to Buttrick, but at last the lights of Cullum House glimmered through the thickets ahead. At the stone pillars which marked the entrance to the estate the horses shied, nearly throwing the doctor from his seat. The whip cracked once, twice, but they would not enter. The team stood ready to bolt in the face of a terror which their senses could detect even at that far remove.

Cursing, Buttrick leapt down from the surrey and made for the house afoot. The rains of early autumn had washed innumerable gullies into the clay of the drive. Several times he stumbled, almost twisting an ankle beneath him. Over the sound of his labored breathing came a confusion of high-pitched cries. The nighthawks were swarming above the house in a dense cloud. Their mass eclipsed the light of the moon as they climbed to an apogee, plummeted suicidally toward the ground, then arced upwards. All about him the doctor heard the beat of their wings.

Nearing the great house Buttrick saw that the French doors which he had opened in another world, it seemed, were still ajar. The parlor within was lighted. Sobbing from his exertions he lurched onto the terrace and leaned against the door frame. "Laurence," he cried. "Laurence, where are you?"

The doctor's gaze slowly swept the room. The ottoman on which he had set his bag that afternoon lay on its side, the stuffing exposed through a long rent in the fabric. On the far wall the tapestry hung in folds from one of its corners. Beneath, the discolored area of the wall framed a gaping hole partially obstructed with shards of plaster and fang-like laths. By main force, the captive behind that wall had clawed and butted its way out of the Crib.

Buttrick stepped into the room, aghast at the wreckage of the once-sumptuous chamber. From behind an overturned sofa a moan broke the stillness, more like a sigh than an expression of pain. Cullum lay crumpled against the wall, hurled there by the inhuman force of the thing as it rushed from its confinement.

"Laurence! Are you all right, man?" cried the physician. There was a deep gash on Cullum's brow.

"See—see to Amadee. In the hall. I—I'm afraid it caught him, Nathan."

Buttrick found the Acadian halfway down the hallway which led to the steel door of the Crib. The Hell-Child had seized him at his middle, and dashed him fatally against the floor. Beside the dead servant lay the bullwhip, a puny weapon against a force of such unutterable malevolence.

The doctor returned quickly to attend Cullum. The shock of the events could prove dangerous to the aneurism. The weak spot of the brain artery might rupture from the slightest stress. But the heir indicated dazedly that he was unharmed except for the head wound.

"It went outside," whispered Cullum. "I could hear it scrabbling about on the portico before you came. Thank God it's stopped screaming. I could not bear that sound another minute."

"Are there any firearms in the house?" asked Buttrick.

"Only an ancient pistol which failed me." Cullum pointed to an old handgun lying at the middle of the floor. "I tried to fire at it as it came through the wall, but the mechanism was rusty from age. The beast flicked me off like a doll and went for Amadee, perhaps because he took so much pleasure in whipping it. But it will return to finish me, Nathan, because it has now matured, and needs its guardian no longer." Cullum smiled weakly as a wistful expression fixed itself upon his pallid face. "If death is the price of freedom from that child of the Pit, then I shall pay it gladly," he said.

Buttrick suddenly stiffened. Somewhere beyond the open doors of the entry-way he heard the sound of deep, animal respirations. A growl loosed itself from a savage throat.

"I must close and bar those doors," the doctor muttered to himself, for Cullum had lapsed into an almost trance-like state. He grasped a heavy poker and walked carefully through the hall. "If it comes at me," he thought, "I must slash at the eyes. The eyes."

The main doors of the house stood thrown open to the night. Although it now rode the treetops, the moon illumined the steps up which Buttrick would have raced had he not entered through the French doors. The cries of the ominous birds had ceased. They roosted in the elms and oaks, as though awaiting a climactic event.

The doctor peered out onto the lawn, keeping well within the shadows of the entry-way. Nothing stirred. He stepped into the doorframe and quickly scanned right and left. Again there was only the wash of moonlight on the lawn and long-deserted walks. No sound was audible except an occasional chirrup from the trees.

Buttrick exhaled slowly. It seemed that the thing had run off, perhaps to Mohegan Swamp where it had claimed its first victim. This was work for a search party in the morning, not for a middle-aged physician unarmed except for a poker.

Wiping his brow against his sleeve, Buttrick stepped onto the portico beneath the massive jawbones. The moon caught the whiteness of the eccentric archway. He ran his palm along the ivory smoothness, grateful for a touch of cool solidity. Standing there for a moment, the man seemed to gain strength from the contact of his hand with the curving pillars of bone. On the steps of the mansion he took a final surveying glance over the grounds, unwilling to stray farther from the light. All was quiet. "We will run the beast to earth in the bogs come sunup," he thought. "Surely it cannot escape us there."

Suddenly the trees at the edge of the estate swayed at their tops as the nighthawks again winged aloft. The doctor's calmness left him. He started up the steps to regain the relative security of the house. But as he mounted the last step his eyes caught a dark mass hulking at the very top of the arch where the whalebones intersected. At the same moment a guttural cry which seemed to tremble the entire portico pealed down at him. Buttrick's head snapped up. On the peak of the arch, balanced on its claw-like hands, crouched the Hell-Child! Its long, snarled hair cascaded down over the joint where the tops of the bones were clamped together. The fantastically developed shoulder and arm muscles knotted as the creature prepared to hurl itself downward upon Buttrick.

In the split-second it took his arm to bring the poker up, he realized that the thing had expected him to enter through the main door when he arrived in answer to Cullum's call for help. It had climbed to the top of the arch, hidden there by the shadow of the eaves, in order to fall upon him as he entered the house. Then all thought ceased for Nathan Buttrick as he saw the macabre figure let go the top of the arch and launch itself at him with a bellow.

The poker flashed sideways in a vicious arc, aimed at the point in space where the eyes should have been at that moment. But it smote the empty air. For as Buttrick began his stroke the long, raven hair of the beast caught in the ironwork which braced the top of Hugh Cullum's arch. The momentum of its lunge carried the Hell-Child clear of the ivory columns. It plummeted downward for the merest fraction of a heartbeat—then a terrible jerk ceased its plunge. It swung between the columns like a grotesque marionette, hanging by its own matted hair.

The doctor could not breathe as he gaped at the frantic contortions of the creature. The cruel arms flailed and beat the air as it struggled to haul itself back to the top of the arch. From that brutish throat came a scream of incredible fury. The face grimaced from pain and rage. Flecks of foam spotted the snarling lips. For a moment it seemed that the hair surely must part, unable to support such a weight. But then a report like a muffled gunshot stilled the writhing of that hideous form. Its neck broken, the Hell-Child hung limply above the steps of the house it had terrorized through the long decades.

Unstrung by the terrible self-execution he had witnessed, Buttrick fell to his knees on the floor of the portico. For minutes he sagged there, his fingers still gripping the haft of the useless poker. The trembling which shook his entire frame gradually subsided. Suddenly remembering the wounded heir who lay inside, he roused himself and entered the house.

Cullum was sitting as before, propped against the wall. His face was ashen, but his eyes glimmered with surprise as Buttrick knelt beside him. "You—you are alive, Nathan!" he whispered. "Does the beast still live?"

The doctor quickly related the grisly death of the Hell-Child. It was apparent to him that his friend was falling into a decline from which he would never recover. The aneurism had been fatally disturbed by the night's events.

"Then I am free!" cried Cullum. "At long last free of that terrible presence. Ah, liberty. Blessed, blessed liberty..." The voice of the heir trailed off in a final sob. Buttrick gently placed a pillow beneath the still head, and closed the eyes. The master of Cullum House, the last guardian of the Hell-Child, was dead.

For a long time the physician stood in the shambles of the parlor, trying to fathom some meaning in what he had experienced. Two corpses lay in that silent mansion. Beneath the whalejaw archway hung the carcass of the family's child of darkness, claimed by this architectural whim of its first guardian. The grim sequence of events was too unsettling to comprehend.

But now it was time for action. Impelled by some allegiance which endured even the death of the last Cullum, the doctor resolved never to divulge the horror in which he had participated. Crawling into the Crib through the broken wall, he cleaned the chamber of all traces of the Hell-Child's occupancy. On the portico he cut down the monstrous body and loaded it onto the surrey.

Buttrick inched the surrey down the dark fire-road to Mohegan Swamp. In a desolate reach of the bog he interred the remains of the vicious life which had brought Cullum House to ruin. Only then did he call the Sabbathday constable.

The account which that officer received was deliberately intended to excite no undue curiosity. As Buttrick told it, he had received a nighttime call from the heir requesting medication for his condition. Near the end of their conversation the line abruptly went dead. Upon his arrival at the house he found that apparently a burglar of considerable strength had slain Amadee. Cullum had been struck once, as the single gash on his brow testified. The blow had fatally aggravated his aneurism. Foiled by the steel door of the strongroom behind the parlor, the thief and murderer had broken through the wall into the chamber. But he found no treasure, for the room had not been used for years.

No person in Sabbathday, not even the investigating constable, questioned the veracity of the doctor's explanation. Nathan Buttrick hid within himself the memory of that ghastly night at Cullum House until death eased him of the woeful burden.

Now, residents of the village rarely speak of the Cullum tragedy. Since there were no heirs, the great house reverted to Windham County and was razed for its timbers. In the town cemetery the Cullum family crypt is sealed forever and the Sabbathday Burial Ground is a place of peace, embraced on all sides by the northern forest.

But in Mohegan Swamp, the nighthawks disturb the twilight calm. They have inhabited the lowlands since the pulling down of Cullum House. At sundown, while the main flock wheels and cries over the brackish water, a few night-fliers roost atop a curious mound near the shoulder of a fire-road through the swamp. Each year the mound grows somewhat higher.

The forest warden who first noticed the growth believed it to be merely a subterranean tangle of living willow roots sent out by the trees which overhang the bog. Yet the birds who frequent the hillock utter strange, fervid cries as if urging on the evolution of something within the peculiar pile. It is unlikely that the mound will stir the curiosity of the townsfolk. Whatever phenomenon is at work will reach completion undisturbed.

THE LAST WORK OF PIETRO DE OPONO

BY STEFFAN B. ALETTI

I ARRIVED LAST SPRING, FULL OF HOPE FOR THE EARLY AND triumphant completion of my doctorate in Italian Renaissance studies. Padua, Perugia, Ravenna, Firenze! All names that practically shivered me with delight. Here I was, in the very seat of the Renaissance, that bright green and gold arousing of mankind from his long, shaggy medieval sleep. It was through these sumptuous hills that Petrarch wandered, singing of Laura, and Dante of Beatrice. It was here that Landini lent his name to that cadence that would color music until the baroque, and it was under these bright Tuscan trees and skies that Leonardo and Michelangelo both strove to make men into angels.

But my quarry was more elusive than these giants; I was seeking a man who had been swallowed up in one of those tragic, dark pockets that even the Renaissance contained. Pietro, or Peter, of Apono had been born in 1250 in, logically, Apono, a little hamlet not far from Padua. He had been a great man; a philosopher, writer, poet, mathematician, and astrologer. Following the practice of his time, he turned these various skills over to the study of medicine, and his fame as a physician was renowned even as far as the great walled city of Paris, where his cures had been nothing short of miraculous. When he returned to Italy a famous man, he got into a silly squabble with a neighbor, over the use of a spring on the man's property. The man, apparently an ill-tempered lout, finally forbad Pietro to use the spring, and within a few days, the well mysteriously dried up. It was then rumored about the neighborhood that old Pietro was a sorcerer, and that it was he who, out of spite, caused the well to dry.

From this germ of nonsense, a great host of stories and accusations spread and fell upon Pietro's head; he was finally brought to the attention of the Inquisition.

The inquisitors took hold of the kindly old man and burned his flesh, broke his bones, and stretched him out of shape; still, Pietro would not admit to being driven by demons, or in consort with the devil himself. But his body was not as strong as his will, and the old man died painfully, yet free in spirit.

Of course the inquisitors were furious at being cheated out of an execution, so, only a few days after the luckless Pietro had been buried, a group of pious priests were sent to exhume his body and burn it in the public square. To their horror, the body had disappeared—risen it was assumed—and the inquisitors fled back to Padua with a tale that soon dissolved into legend.

Needless to say, the explanation was much less cosmic than that. One of Pietro's friends and benefactors, one Girolamo da Padova, had the body exhumed and re-interred in his own crypt, to save his old friend's spirit from the indignities that the Inquisition had intended. I alone of living men knew this, for I had found a collection of old letters, including one that Girolamo had sent a trusted friend to explain the "resurrection." In the letter Girolamo states that he took all of Pietro's books for himself, except the one that he had been translating at the time of his arrest. He adds:

It was in Maestro Pietro's province to bring all things to light, no matter how loathsome. He believed that the light of reason would make everything beautiful and holy, but I tell thee, my good Ludovico, this book from Paris is the devil's work. Cursed from remotest antiquity, this parchment hath caused the ruin of all who deal with it, and, as thou seest, Pietro himself was the last of their line. He tried, as was his wont, to turn the cursed thing to good, to use its blasphemies for healing and helping, but its grotesque blood rites and hymns to desecration shocked even good Pietro. He had decided that the work was too blasphemous and too degrading to ever be turned towards good, and he was resolved to destroy it and his own partial translation. But the Holy Inquisition caught him before he could accomplish this.

Fortunately, he had hidden both behind one of the books in his cabinet before the inquisition came through the door. I have taken both; his translation is now buried with him in my own family's crypt in the Church of San Giueseppe, and the parchment itself, unfit for holy ground, hath been buried outside the city walls. I pray that my own handling of it hath not endangered mine own soul.

So I, a lowly student, was about to find the bones and last work of the legendary Pietro of Apono.

II

THE BUSINESS OF THE BOOK HAD EXCITED ME. WHAT HAD IT been? Could it have been one of the early Latin translations of the *Necronomicon?* Or possibly the now-fabled Delancre translation of the horrid *Mnemabic Fragments?* Or was it some heretofore uncovered masterpiece of ancient or gothic imagination? I immediately envisioned my doctoral thesis as an edition of this newly discovered work; its first edition in 700 years.

Girolamo's family had died out in the plague that sent Boccaccio fleeing to the hills of Florence to give us the *Decameron.* Therefore, the crypt in the cellar of the San Giueseppe church was untended, and of only minor archaeological interest. My request, consequently, to spend the night studying the badly worn monuments and inscriptions was granted by the monks without undue trouble.

Alone, finally, and not a little nervous at being surrounded by the long dead, I began to poke my way about the ruins of the vaults. The cement binding the slabs to the coffins themselves had long since crumbled, so lifting off the covers was simply a matter of judicious use of a crowbar and a strong back.

Relative after relative, I studied—Antonello, Giorgio, Tonio, Lucia, etc. All I encountered in these beautifully decorated marble coffins was moulded skulls and various bones; mostly the bones no longer adhered to each other, so that all semblance of a body or human form was lost. They were just piles of bones and mounds of shredded, wormy velvet and silk. For some reason, I'm glad to say, it had not occurred to me that I was desecrating the dead. Scholars are well known to get carried away by their work, and so with me that night. I am not a particularly brave man, and I would not even walk alone through a graveyard at night without qualms; but that fearful night I was alone, because I did not want to have to share my discovery with anyone. There I was, marauding through a crypt at night, rummaging through bones and cloth, without any thought other than honest, if selfish, scholarship.

It must have been that black hour prior to dawn, that I opened the tomb next to Girolamo's. In it lay a surprisingly well preserved body, but it lay horribly twisted and broken, and on its legs and arms were the remnants of linen bandages. The skull lay at an odd angle from the body, and its lipless and crag-toothed mouth was open wide in what still, after 700 years, looked like a howl of pain. My fortitude was gone, in an instant. Here, unquestionably, was Pietro, still bearing traces of the horror of the Inquisition. I sickened and began to gasp for air as the foetid odor leapt at me from the long-shut tomb. I fled to the stairway and sped up it in an instant.

The church itself now seemed populated by millions of rustling, whispering things that were lent shape by my now rampant imagination. I imagined it to be visited by the shade of every lost man, woman and child who had ever sat within its walls. Terrified, I fell to my knees at the thought and, before I lost consciousness, I thought I saw coming up the dreadfully dark nave, a procession of decayed clergy, grinning, and swinging incense which smoked red and gave off the same horrid odor that met me when I lifted the slab of Pietro's tomb. I collapsed against a pew; at the same time my hand came to rest upon a cross carved in relief on its side.

Dawn had already begun to spread its silver to the inside of the church when I awoke to its vast, empty hall.

III

STILL BATHED IN SWEAT, I STOOD UP FROM THE POSITION INTO which I had crumbled a few hours earlier. I walked to the back of the church and climbed back down the stairs, each step presenting me an opportunity to exert every ounce of will power I contained.

Once in the crypt, I was faced with the choice of either replacing the slab and leaving the job to bolder men, or thoroughly searching the sarcophagus for the scroll. To my everlasting damnation, I girded up my loins and chose the latter course.

I brought the lamp close to the corpse, and looked at it. It had not changed in any aspect from the previous night; I was happy and relieved to see that. It rather convinced me that the only thing that had chased me up the stairs and down the nave was my own fevered and overwrought mind. And I was overcome with pity for poor Pietro. While I was thus sentimentally occupied, I noticed a still bright red ribbon lying by the crushed right hand.

My heart stopped; the ribbon encircled a scroll of parchment. I grabbed it, and, with effort—I found that I was considerably weaker than I had been the previous night—replaced the slab. I quickly gathered up my tools and lights and left the church.

Even the musty odor that hung about my hands and shirt did not drive away the incomparable smell of an Italian early summer morning. Everything was as bright as gold and glory, and, by the time I had reached my lodging, my night's terror had dissolved under the mantel of drowsiness. I slept, undreaming, until I awakened of my own accord, at dusk.

With the darkness, I was wide awake, and once more a bit jittery. I dressed and took the scroll. It was almost a foot long and rather thick with folds—apparently Pietro had done quite a bit of translating before his fate had overtaken him.

I unrolled it, and it still seemed surprisingly pliant and firm after such a very long time. It was a treasure! Not only did it contain translations, but what amounted to editorial comments in the vernacular by Pietro. I do not know from what language the original had been translated, but it was now in Latin, and its title stood out in disconcerting relief—*Gloriae Cruoris*; in English, roughly, the glories of blood or bloodshed. And the author's name was Serpencis—whether the author's true name or a latinization, I do not know. Pietro's opening comments are cautious and circumspect—the agony of a man trying to make something of value out of a blasphemous thing.

"Let us analyze," he writes, "the properties of blood as the learned Serpencis relates them. First, blood is the liquid of life, as the body is the vessel of life."

He then quotes Serpencis as saying that blood is the primal life force; that without it man will die, and with it, *no matter whose*, man can extend his life beyond its normal bounds. Serpencis concludes that:

> After one has committed the necessary desecrations, and has immured himself to the smell and touch of the dead, he can commune with them, liberating their souls and putting them to his own use and service. Man's power is measured by the number of souls he commands, and a great number can be attained by the twin sanctities of murder and the drinking of blood.

I sat there aghast, as Pietro must have done so many centuries ago.

"Gloriae" was the work of a vampire and necrophile who, at some remote time, either medieval or ancient, must have terrorized his neighborhood and possibly had been the leader of some foul and monstrous cult. This was not going to be easy to turn into the kind of benign and dignified research with which one gains a doctor's degree.

Still, I read on. I was too bound up in modern life to turn away from the book in fear, the way Pietro had done; as I read its gruesome pages I was battling nausea and disgust rather than terror. The margin of the manuscript contained Pietro's notes on how he combated the evil spells he felt influencing him; he used various incantations and equally efficacious spells of white magic to dispel the aura of evil. I, of course, did not; I merely read on through the jumble of medieval Latin and Italian, and descended, spiritually, to a depth of degradation and inhumanity which I had never imagined possible. Serpencis had been a master ghoul who would have made the monstrous and infamous Gilles de Retz look like an effeminate weakling.

At length I was near the end of the scroll. The last section contained what was apparently the first of a series of spells performed so that one can give one's self over to the demons who presided over vampiric activity. More a fool than ever, I decided to perform the rite.

Once the pentagram was chalked on the floor, I lit two candles and began to chant aloud from the manuscript. I was quite thrilled at reproducing a sound that had been unheard for centuries; it was in this spirit of re-enacting a play, that I first became aware of subtle changes within the room itself.

The darkness had closed in more around the candles, so that their glow spread only about six inches or so, leaving nearly the entire room and me in total darkness. Heretofore, the walls and bookcases had been dimly present, but they were now gone, and the candle closest to me illuminated the manuscript, my hand, and no more. And with this spreading blackness came now a stench that seemed to be some frightful amalgam of the twin odors of the sewer and the grave, an odor terribly similar to that in the church less than twenty-four hours earlier.

At this point I was all for stopping, for I realized that I had indeed succeeded in crossing that delicate line between the real and unreal, between the natural and the supernatural. And I was terribly frightened. But I also realized now that I was no longer in complete control over what was happening. I couldn't stop; cursing myself, I continued the daemonic chanting.

Suddenly there was a blast of foul wind, and the room glowed with a kind of ruby-red light that spread evenly from corner to corner without any seeming point of origin. There now appeared to be something forming right next to me, within the pentagram. It whirled together, like a motion picture of something flying apart that is run backwards on the projector. And as I stood there, within arm's length of it, it began to assume a horrifying, humanoid shape. I say humanoid, because, when it was formed, its dimensions were roughly human, but not close enough to be mistaken for anything other than what it was—a blasphemy from the malignant depths of hell, and the darkest corners of the human soul. Its quivering red face was turned toward me, and I could see, as I stared into it, not merely that sweating, featureless red jelly, but I could see, somehow, a vast complex of forests, rivers, mountains, a primordial land that suggested to me the vast land of Gaul when Paris was an undiscovered island, a land that would have to wait aeons for Caesar to be born to conquer it.

My terror was now too strong for whatever possessed me; I shrieked and dropped the manuscript into the whirling darkness. As the red melted quickly into a huge blackness, I saw the creature reach towards me. I felt faint, and my last memory was of being encircled in a slightly luminous and damp fog, which though itself impalpable, carried within it a solid network of bones, which I could feel around my waist.

I do not think that I remained unconscious for more than a few minutes; when I awoke I could tell, without opening my eyes, that the room was still dark. Too frightened to move or even open my eyes, I remained sprawled in the position in which I fell, until I was sure that sunlight had filled the room.

IV

THIS TIME THE DAWN DID NOT BRING WITH IT THE JOY OF LIFE, that strength that allowed me to renew my efforts at the church. I got up and searched the room, making sure that it was empty. It was, but it was also a mess. That whirling wind had torn everything loose; papers, books, utensils, even dishes, were scattered, ripped and broken. I had feverishly hoped that I would, on waking, be able to attribute the whole thing to an overactive imagination. No, I had not dreamed.

Before I hid Pietro's monstrous work, I read his last comments on the rite I had almost completed:

> This thing is too strong for me! I cannot fight its magic—it has at its command the legions of hell, its servants, human and not human. Despite my knowledge of magic and alchemy, I barely escaped the last rite with my soul still mine and God's. I will not go on with this work and imperil my soul and salvation. God save thee, O reader, from the knowledge this book contains. Unless thou art stronger than I, attempt not even those things that are written here. Certainly seek not the book in its entirety. In the name of God, I mean to see that my copy of *Gloriae Cruoris* is destroyed...

Here the manuscript breaks off, in mid-sentence. It was here, I suppose, that Pietro hurriedly hid the parchment and the manuscript, and was taken off to his doom at the hands of the Inquisition.

And I had attempted to materialize the blasphemy without the slightest knowledge of magic, white or black.

V

IT HAS NOW BEEN NEARLY A WEEK SINCE THAT HORRIBLE night; I have neither worked nor slept. When I close my eyes my senses are instantly bombarded with images of red corpses and ever-present pools and fountains of blood. I have thoroughly lost my appetite, but the thought of blood makes me swell with a sensation that is closer to hunger than anything else that I can think of. When I pass a butcher shop, I gaze at the various animals hung upside down, their throats slit and dripping blood; my own throat grows thick and my mind begins to haze with anticipation. I have to keep myself from running into the shop to do God knows what horrible and loathsome thing.

Whatever has my soul does not have it all; I can still feel, think, and function normally, but I feel myself growing less and less coherent, and the need for blood now and again fills me to the exclusion of every other thought or sensation. I cannot even seek help, as there are no longer men who are versed in the practice of white magic and magical curing; and any doctor would attribute the whole thing to some sort of fabulous psychosis, and put me in a madhouse.

Thank God there is enough of my soul and mind left at my own command so that I was able to burn the last work of Pietro of Apono. I hope that the place in which Girolamo chose to bury the original parchment will forever remain undiscovered.

Though I had unwittingly committed the first required acts of desecration, and had unwittingly undergone a sort of indecent communion with the dead spirits that apparently abound in San Giueseppe church, I had not completed the first rite. My only hope now is to die while the good in me can still overpower the steadily growing evil influence that is corrupting my mind and body like a leprosy. I have lost all that I was and all that I could have been; but my will to good is greater than my will to evil, and thus I hope to salvage my soul while I still can.

To any readers that this may have, I ask that they pray for my soul, and not exhibit curiosity of unwholesome things. Civilized man has lost the knowledge and ability necessary to combat this kind of evil. If some unwitting fool like me should find the entire *Gloriae Cruoris*, listen to me, the latest man to be destroyed by it; do not experiment with it, do not even read it. Burn it, or God help you and humanity.

I shall now take poison, and go out into the Italian sunshine and look once more at the lovely poplar trees, which I shall miss dearly.

THE EYE OF HORUS

BY STEFFAN B. ALETTI

THIS MANUSCRIPT IS HERE PRESENTED BY ME IN ITS ORIGINAL form, as handed to me on an incredibly hot June day by George Warren, an amateur Egyptologist from New York. My name is Michael Kearton; I am an importer of dyes and was staying in a town named Wadi Hadalfa for business purposes. It is the last stop before the train tracks cross through the terrible Nubian desert to Abu Hamed.

Warren had just returned from an expedition to a spot several miles outside of Akasha, a smaller town about seventy-five miles away. He was in a state of shock and fever, and was badly cut and bruised; but in the week and a half left to him, he typed the following report and gave me the carbon for safekeeping. It is well he did so, as the original unaccountably disappeared with his death. As I barely knew the man, I will not make any statements as to my opinion of his mental condition at the time directly before his death; all I will say is that whatever had happened in the heat of the Nubian desert had been terrible, for his physical condition was very bad. Yet, to me, he seemed lucid. At any rate, the reader must form his own conclusions from the manuscript.

M.K.

"I have risen, I have risen like the mighty hawk (of gold) that cometh forth from his egg; I fly and I alight like the hawk which hath a back of four cubits width, and the wings which are like unto the mother-of-emerald of the South."

So begins the chapter of performing the transformation into a Hawk of Gold, from the great Egyptian *Book of the Dead.*

"O grant thou (speaking to Osiris) that I may be feared, and make thou me to be a terror."

These words—I first read them when I was a boy—have now taken on a new and immensely terrifying dimension, a dimension that stretches back in time and touches the most archaic fear of men—the fear of death, and their resulting need for gods. Man still dies, but his gods live on endlessly—I know that now. Some day we will discover Isis and Osiris, Ptah and Anubis, Ishtar, Chemosh, and even Zeus and Jupiter. They are all waiting.

I don't know precisely where to begin this narrative, but should it turn out to be the only record of this whole affair, I shall start at the beginning.

Suffice it to say that I arrived in Cairo five years ago, an amateur Egyptologist who, by fortune or fate, had come into an immense sum of money by the age of thirty.

By offering money, I immediately became attached to the Cairo Museum expedition to the lower portion of Nubia. There it became obvious that the only reason I was along was that I financed the business, and therefore had a right to go along—but only as an observer. Though I became a friend of Mustafa, the native foreman of the diggers, the staff was no more than coldly polite to me, and my prying into their affairs was regarded with scorn.

Nevertheless I stayed with the museum expeditions and staff for three digging seasons, and got none of the credit for having been in on the discoveries of numerous early and predynastic grave sites.

Sick of being the silent partner with the money, I withdrew my support and went to Nubia on my own, accompanied by Mustafa, who was now too old for the museum's liking.

Thus we arrived at Aswan. Once there, I found that my fame (that is, my reputation for having a lot of money) preceded me, and shortly I became acquainted with William Kirk and Andriju Kalatis.

Kirk is a British Egyptologist, now a very old man, and generally rather drunk. Among his papers and papyri he found several bills of sale dealing with shipments of grain for the priests to the Temple of Horus, the Falcon God. One papyrus also gives explicit directions on the whereabouts of the temple, and, to my surprise, it was close to a city of which a few ruins still remain, about ten miles outside of a town called Akasha, not far from Aswan.

Kalatis, a young Greek soldier of fortune, proposed to accompany me on an expedition, financed by me, to find the temple.

After checking on Kirk's background and reputation and, after seeing the papyrus (it was undeniably authentic), I decided to give the business a try. Success would bring me worldwide fame and recognition as an Egyptologist. I did not particularly trust Kalatis, but I can take care of myself, and Mustafa would be along as foreman of the diggings. At any rate, I did not anticipate trouble from Kalatis unless we found something valuable enough to steal rather than give to the Egyptian government.

The first digging season was spent partly in research and partly in the digging of long rows of trenches in the chosen area. Kirk was too old to come, but Kalatis, much to my surprise, proved an admirable companion and a good worker despite his disappointment at finding no great treasure.

The second season went essentially the same way until one day early this month, when Mustafa came running to our tent to announce that he had found the top of what seemed to be a flight of steps. By that afternoon we had uncovered seven stone steps, and a small, narrow door.

II

THE SEAL WAS UNBROKEN! KALATIS AND I LOOKED AT EACH other in astonishment. An unopened tomb meant for me an unparalleled archaeological find, and for Kalatis it could mean the wealth that he so continually dreamed of.

I look the chisel, and, there, in the midday heat of Nubia, in a few moments I broke a seal that had remained perfectly intact since its placement there thousands of years earlier.

Curiously enough, once inside the foetid darkness, there was only an empty chamber less than five feet long, and only about three feet wide. At the end of the room was another very narrow stone stairway.

Our porters and diggers, of course, were too superstitious to enter with us, so, leaving Mustafa to keep an eye on them (these were not the trained museum expedition diggers), Kalatis and I had no recourse but to climb down alone. We were both slightly unnerved, being amateurs, and not a little worried about the condition in which the tomb might be after so many centuries. Also, as the tomb was unopened, there might still be some unsprung grave-robber trap awaiting us.

We began down the stairs slowly and cautiously, training both our lights directly ahead of us. The air was terribly hot and dusty, so much so that we had to hold our handkerchiefs over our mouths to keep from gagging.

Descending in this manner, we reached the bottom after about fifteen minutes. The heat was now so stifling that we both had to lie down and relax, at the same time mopping ourselves off, for we had been perspiring heavily.

The room we were now in was a large chamber with boxes piled up to a height of seven feet or so along the walls. As soon as this was noted, Kalatis went over to inspect them. I told him to be careful, since the boxes were sure to rot away at his touch, but his inspection proved them not to be of wooden gilt as I had imagined, but of gold! Here were perhaps a hundred large boxes, all of gold inlaid with lapis-lazuli and coral, done in an astonishingly sophisticated manner. Kalatis grabbed a box off the top of one of the piles and placed it, with much difficulty, on the floor. We bent over it, and, while I was looking for a seal or lock to open, Kalatis in his haste simply chiseled it open. I was rather angry at him, because archaeology is never served by people who go about breaking things in order to save a few moments.

Once open, the box revealed an exquisitely carved effigy of Horus, the Falcon God, the Avenger, Son of Isis and Osiris. It was about a foot and a half long, and, at its widest part about the shoulders, it was seven inches or so wide. Its grace, fluidity of line, and, if I may say, degenerate quality, dated it at being late in Egyptian history, possibly even as late as the Roman occupation. The figure was hollow, and, I imagine, contained the mummified body of a falcon, the sacred bird of Horus.

Kalatis, of course, was overwhelmed by the incredible amount of treasure that we had before us; from a monetary point of view it was the greatest archaeological find in history. He began to leap about, dancing, and shouting in Greek of his good fortune. For some reason, exactly what I cannot say, his gamboling about the place frightened me. I still had seen no evidence of it being a tomb—it could easily have been a storeroom or treasure room for the great temple—and yet, unaccountably, I felt the presence of something, something very remote in time, and bizarre beyond imagination, something very close to us, watching.

Then, in the beam of my flashlight, I caught a vague movement; there was something stirring on top of one of the piles of chests. I shouted this intelligence to Kalatis, who instantly sobered up and set his own beam atop the same pile. For a moment we saw nothing, then, over the rim of the box, as we drew closer, we saw a form and two positively blazing red dots staring at us. It was a bird—not a bat—a bird, and a large one from its silhouette!

When we got within about five feet, the thing took off and, with a terrible squawking, began to bang itself about the walls and boxes in the manner of birds who are trying to escape from an enclosure. Presently, with a flapping of its wings, it settled back on top of another pile of boxes and rested, glaring at us.

By this time, I was so unnerved that I was all for climbing back up the stairway and out into the fresh air. We were covered with dust, dirt and plaster dislodged by the bird's wild flight. Actually, a trained archaeologist would have immediately gone above to get cataloguing equipment, wires for stringing electric lights, brushes, and cloths for the handling and cleaning of the ancient trove. How much I wish I had done this straightaway.

In spite of my protests, Kalatis wanted to inspect the entire room before going back. It was, rather, a long corridor of sorts, since it stretched on for what must have been about fifty feet, narrowing visibly at its terminus. There, cut into the stone, was a small entrance. So, with the great treasure gleaming dully in the dim light behind us, we entered the third chamber. The room was again large and narrow, and, in the beam of the flashlight we saw the standing figure of a man with a hawk's head. There was something about the figure that startled us; it was certainly not unusual for statuary to be placed in tombs or sanctuaries, but there was a feeling pervading the entire chamber, a feeling that there was something alive, and that was the statue.

I don't know whether Kalatis felt this or not; if he did, it certainly was an immense act of bravery to walk up to the figure. I personally feel that he was ignorant of the entire aura of terror that the place had about it. Perhaps, because my mind is attuned to Egyptology and his was not, he sensed nothing.

At any rate, whether Kalatis was aware of it or not, he went right up to the figure. As he drew closer, his light illuminated every detail of it. It was a representation of Horus, divine son of Isis and Osiris, the Avenger of his father's murder, and whose great eye lights the world by day and calms it by night. The figure stood erect, in the typical Egyptian pose of walking, with one foot slightly ahead of the other. The fists were clenched, and under the great double crown of Egypt, the large round eyes were closed.

At this time I still had no direct evidence that my fears were anything more than imagined, but suddenly, to my unspeakable horror, the figure snapped open its eyes and fixed them on Kalatis! I screamed, for in that fatal gloom, those bird eyes shone with such malevolent red brightness, that I knew we would never take the treasure out into the light.

Kalatis stopped instantly, drew his pistol, and raised it. For what seemed like hours, the two stood glaring at each other. Then, slowly, the figure of Horus began to move, the dust of centuries flaking off and falling to its feet in gray-white clouds. Kalatis remained still for a few moments, then cocked his pistol and fired it. The first shot slammed audibly into the figure's body, but aside from throwing up a huge volume of dust, there was no visible effect on the thing. Then, in very rapid sequence, Kalatis emptied the gun, each shot answered by a thump and more dust.

By this time, the creature was less than a yard away from us. Neither Kalatis nor I could move; we were absolutely paralyzed. Then, with a sudden lunge, the hawk leapt to where Kalatis was standing, and grabbed him. Kalatis' resulting scream was quite sufficient to snap me out of my stupor, and allow me to once again move my legs. I pulled out my gun and, manoeuvering to the side of the thing, put a well-aimed bullet directly into the side of its head. There was more dust, and some feathers this time, and the creature relaxed its grip on Kalatis—who by now was either dead or fainting, for he dropped to the floor—and looked fiercely at me. I immediately turned and ran down the long corridor piled high with the boxes of treasure.

To my immense terror, I was now pursued by birds—the whole corridor was full of them, large birds with great burning eyes and sharp beaks, tearing at my clothes and flesh. These birds were falcons.

In spite of their hindrance, I made it through the corridor, and up the treacherously narrow stairway. I am forever astonished by the ability of the human body to cope with, shall we say, unique and taxing situations. My mind, frozen with horror, was now almost dormant, and my body alone and without mental command, carried me on. Fortunately, the stairway was too narrow to admit many birds and me at the same time, so they became less of a threat to my life now, and, by this time, I was so numb with pain and terror, that I could barely feel their clawing anyway. Every so often I would trip and fall on my knees and elbows—the stairs were irregularly hewn—and the pecking of the birds served to prod me to my feet again.

I don't know how long it took me to get up the stairway; I couldn't even make a guess.

When I got to the antechamber described earlier, I fell to the ground and, it being such a small chamber, crawled the rest of the way into the weakening sunlight. As I crawled over onto the sand, I realized that I had absolutely no strength left. I expected to be pecked to pieces, but the birds behind me flew out of the tomb and perched on its lintel. They sat and watched me, but flew at me no more.

The diggers had taken fright and could not be restrained from leaving, so Mustafa was all that was left of our company. He ran up to me, much alarmed at my appearance—when later given a mirror, I too was shocked; my face was (and is, still) a complete mess of bruises and long jagged rips from the birds' beaks. It was a miracle that my eyes were not touched. The rest of my body was also in terrible shape, and my clothes had just about been ripped off by those fiendish claws.

I collapsed, and, had it not been for the constant ministrations of Mustafa, I should surely have perished on the trip back.

Once we arrived at Wadi Hadalfa by Nile boat, it was an easy operation to get the train back to our base at Aswan.

It is now less than two weeks after that terrible day twenty miles out of Akasha, and now even this short time has begun to cloud my memory of the affair. Mustafa believes me, but he is little more than a superstitious old Bedouin who has been brought up on legends and tales of horror. Kirk and several Englishmen staying here think that I am lying or raving. I have no means of proving the story other than going back—which I will not, except that Kalatis is gone, and I am still recovering from my wounds.

I wired my agent in New York to stand by with ready funds; by this evening I shall be on the train to Cairo, and to the museum (to which I should have gone in the first place). Once there I shall convince them of the truth of the whole affair, and of the importance of my discovery. In the *Book of the Dead* there is the means of placating the Great Hawk through spells—you can fight the supernatural only with the supernatural. And when Horus is at rest, we can go back, and my find will be catalogued and published, and my name shall go to the head of the list of great Egyptologists.

Should something happen to me, I have made a carbon of this, and am giving it to one of the English businessmen here; I am giving it to Kearton because he is the least interested in the affair, and the least likely to have formed any theories of his own about it.

George Warren

The carbon is signed by George Warren. It was indeed a good thing that he gave me the above testimony. He never got to the train, and the original report was never found.

Just when the train was to have left, his body was discovered in his room. No cause of death could be found; he was just lying face down on his bed, with his hands, curiously enough, clasped at the back of his neck. The room—which was a mess—was literally covered with feathers.

Michael Kearton

THE CELLAR ROOM

BY STEFFAN B. ALETTI

I AM WRITING THIS IN AN EFFORT TO THROW SOME LIGHT ON the recent chain of appalling murders. I have no real evidence to offer, nothing more than prior knowledge of the existence of a dangerous creature loose in London, and a reluctant familiarity with its habits.

There have been to date seven murders. Four victims were women, two of them elderly, two fairly young; of the other three, one was a nondescript businessman, the second a tradesman, the third an officer investigating the screams of one of these victims. All of these crimes occurred in early evening or at night, in particularly dark places such as blind alleys, closes or residential courts off the streets; and all were within a short distance of 12 Cannington Lane, Chelsea.

These crimes do not seem to have sexual overtones; they are unique and traceable to a single source purely because of the appalling ferocity. In each case the victim was ripped apart, though absence of toothmarks would seem to suggest that the monster is a human one. I say humanoid. It is no madman ranging the streets at night, acting out his sexual fantasies as was the celebrated ripper of a generation ago. I feel sure that it is a species of creature that lies just beyond the measure of human existence and knowledge. The police will not give me the hearing that I desire; after the "multiple murders" of Sir Harold Wolverton and his manservant, they would rather not hear from me. Had that affair received the press coverage it deserved, I feel that a number of perceptive people would have drawn the same conclusions that I offer you now, but owing to the victim's importance and the affluence of his heirs, as well as the recent conclusion of the Boer War, journalists completely ignored it.

I had become reasonably famous; I was by no means Britain's best known or most influential psychical researcher—"ghost hunter" in common parlance—but I had done a good deal of work for the Society for Psychical Research, the College of Psychical Sciences, and the Marylebone Spiritual Society. I had published several monographs, written a book on Spiritualism, and produced a number of pamphlets describing my stays in various so-called haunted houses.

Sir Harold Wolverton had once been the president of the Royal College; at that time he was the most respected of the gentlemen engaging in the pursuit of that not-so-respectable science. His papers were widely held to be the most sane and scientifically accurate to come out of the ranks of the Spiritualists. Indeed, at that time Sir Harold was the only one of the brotherhood well enough thought of to appear in public without being heckled by closed minds unfortunately harnessed to big mouths.

It was about 1885 that a very mysterious tragedy occurred. Sir Harold, then not yet knighted, had been about to marry a young lady of good birth, by name Jessica Turner—a relative, as a matter of fact, of the artist. She died under most mysterious circumstances, and Sir Harold disbanded his group, the Chelsea Spiritualist Society, and retired from public life. As that was a very exciting time of Empire, the news did not long dwell on the affair, and, in time, all was forgotten.

Last week, however, I received, to my great surprise, a letter from Sir Harold inviting me to his residence at Cannington Lane. I lost no time in answering, and found myself a short time later in a carriage threading its way through the winding streets of Chelsea.

I was shocked to see Sir Harold. Naturally, we are all familiar with the photographs of him in his prime: heavy-chested, his great shock of red hair flowing over his ears and joining his bristly mustache, and puffing majestically on a massive *Oom Paul*. He looked the very essence of the British gentleman. I was perfectly aware, of course, that these photographs had been taken about twenty years earlier, but I did not expect the course of time to have exacted so many ravages. His face was bare, and his head had a sparse tonsure of wispy white. He sat in a wheelchair, a shawl wrapped around his knees. His thick hands, obviously once very powerful, shook with palsy; and his eyes, in his youth and middle age his most commanding feature, were vacant and rheumy. He was forty years old at the time of his fiancée's tragic death; he could now be no more than in his late fifties. He looked like a man of eighty.

"I have decided," he said, watching his servant back out of the room, closing the partition doors behind him, "to publish my diaries for the years 1884 and 1885. They end the night Jessica, my fiancée died. Will you handle the arrangements for me?"

"Of course, Sir Harold," I replied, "but surely there are others who arrange such things professionally; they would be more clever in these matters than I. I myself work through a literary agent."

"I have chosen you," he interrupted, "for several reasons." He wheeled himself feebly over to the bookcase, impatiently gesturing me down when I stood to offer my help. He took two handsomely bound books from a shelf, and wheeled back to the table, throwing them down. They sent up an impressive quantity of dust, arguing their antiquity.

"First," he continued, "you are presumably a researcher. As a scientist, you must see that these are published as records of scientific experiments. They must not be thought of as fiction or romance. They are serious and not to be taken lightly. Second, I presume that you are a gentleman. There are obviously, as in any diary, allusions to certain private matters that are to be deleted before publication. You will, I trust, see to it?"

"You may be sure," I replied; "but why, if I may ask, have you delayed the release of these diaries for so many years if they contain valuable scientific matter?"

Sir Harold remained silent for a few moments. At length, when the silence had begun to be painful, he spoke. "You are getting too close. You fellows think that what you are doing is new and exciting, but let me assure you that we here at the Chelsea Society had done it all fifteen years ago. We, too, were scientists; and like you, we toyed with things we were not properly equipped to handle. And you people are about to make the same mistakes that we did."

"Mistakes!" I protested. "I beg to differ. We are indeed on the verge of bridging the gap between the living and the dead, of piercing the veil." I could hear my voice mounting with excitement. "But be sure,

Sir Harold, we are doing so with the most modern scientific methods and all possible precautions."

"Balderdash!" he shouted with a ferocity I wouldn't have expected from such a fragile-looking old man. "Don't prattle to me about your 'scientific methods'. If you go to the Pole to explore, you take along an overcoat and a bottle of brandy. *That's* scientific! If you go digging about in Egypt, you take along a fan and a bottle of gin. *That's* scientific! But what, sir, what possible precautions can you take against the unseen and the totally unknown? Don't you realize the tremendous power and raw forces of evil you can invoke by accident? What precautions do you take against these, sir? A raincoat? A gun? Or a cross? Believe me, sir, if there is a God, He waits until you are dead before he enters the picture. The devil is not so polite!"

I had stood during that tirade, for no man can speak to me in that manner. It was no longer the Nineteenth Century! He spoke again as I picked up my cane.

"Please sit down, sir; I'm sorry to have shouted." He once again appeared to be a docile, harmless old man. It was a complete physical change.

"Very well," I returned, assuming an air of wounded dignity. "But you'll have to explain the entire business before I continue. I feel that our experiments have proven that we have nothing to fear from the darkness beyond the grave save our own superstitions and physical limitations. What I have learned through mediums is that the spirits beyond us want to help us, to teach us that we need not fear death, but should consider it as the parting of a curtain that has obscured our eyes during our earthly life." I sat down, pleased with my pretty speech, and rested my walking stick between my knees. The light was now waning, as it was mid-winter, and with the oncoming dark came a palpable chill.

"Very well," said Sir Harold. He wheeled himself to the liquor cabinet and withdrew two sherry glasses. After pouring a rather large measure of the amber liquid into each of them, he offered me the larger portion. I took it and began to sip it, observing a connoisseur's silence, a respectful pause before commenting on the wine.

"Excellent sherry," I said, falling short of poetry, anxious for Sir Harold to begin his story.

"Yes," he answered, staring at his glass absentmindedly. "It's old." He turned it around in his hand for a few moments, watching the light catch its color.

"In December, 1884," he began quietly, "the Chelsea Spiritualist Society was formed. It consisted of Jessica, my fiancée; Thomas Walters, a novelist; Dr. Edmund Vaughan, a fellow of the Royal College of Surgeons, and myself. At first we simply tracked down local Spiritualists and bade them come to my house; we had the cellar arranged with a large table and five chairs. The mediums, famous for remarkable feats within their own houses, provided very little of interest when taken away from their rigs, pulleys, and secret compartments. No ghosts, no spirits, no disembodied trumpets floating about in the air. But some of these so-called Spiritualists *did* seem to possess a certain kind of... sensitivity, shall we call it? They seemed to feel something in the cellar— and what is more remarkable, most of them expressed it in the same way: They felt a malignancy, a dark, angry thing that lived, or perhaps I should say, *existed* in the cellar.

"At first we felt nothing, simply darkness. But as we conducted these seances, most of us—Walters being the sole exception—began to feel a physical oppression that could not be attributed to simple fear of the dark or, for that matter, the power of suggestion.

"Once, just before we lost Jessica, Vaughan and I were trying automatic writing when the lamp suddenly went out. There had been no wind; the door is heavy oak, bolted shut, so there could have been no draft moving through the room. Afterward, we found the lamp easily three-quarters full, and the wick in perfect condition. But the lamp went out, and we sat in that total blackness before the eye accustoms itself to the shadows. I felt almost immediately a sense of overwhelming blackness—not darkness, mind you, but blackness, and worse, a sense of hate. There was something in the room that was projecting a furious driving hate, aimed possibly at me or Vaughan or both of us, but I felt at humanity—the living in general.

"I was overwhelmed, suffocated by this malignancy—now coupled with a mounting terror in myself. I tried to move, but found it wholly impossible and in desperation, trying to sound perfectly normal, I told Vaughan to light the lamp. He whispered, or I should rather say that he gasped that he could not. It was at this point that we both realized that we were in danger—just what kind of danger we were not sure then. And we just sat there all night, the two of us huddled together, shivering from terror and the cold. At length, as dawn began to penetrate the opaque glass of the cellar windows, we both found the strength to stir; as the sun began to warm the air outside, we burst out of the room, red-eyed and thoroughly frightened.

"Vaughan and I made our trembling way upstairs, and he resigned from the Society over a stiff glass of brandy.

"I think it was then that I first realized that I had some sort of mediumistic talent in me—or that Vaughan or I or both of us possessed such ability.

"Despite the fright it gave me, I continued my work, and the Chelsea Society's work. We investigated, held seances, table taps and whatnot, with a moderate amount of success, but never with anything like the results that night with Vaughan. Then I held my last seance.

"We had decided to hold a seance just before Christmas. It was an icy cold night, and I distinctly remember that the icicles hanging in front of the cellar windows cast irregular striped shadows that looked like prison bars on the floor and table. It was late, perhaps 11:30 or 12:00, and all was deathly still—complete silence, broken now and then by a horse's trot or a tinkling sleigh bell.

"There were five of us that night: Jessica, whom I was to marry just after the new year, Walters, and two of our new members, one a student—Cambridge, I think—named Wilson, who was home for the holiday, and a young scientist of sorts named Tice. Something to do with hydraulics, I believe. Just before the seance began, we all had a drink to toast the new year, since this was expected to be the last time we would see each other for several weeks. It was, I believe, the last happy moment I have had in my life. I remember especially Jessica, sitting directly across the table from me. Her blonde hair was done up in a bun, and she wore a topaz choker I had just given her as an early Christmas present. She was so beautiful... "Sir Harold paused as he seemed to gaze directly into the past. "Then young Wilson blew out the light and we began.

"Almost immediately, the room began to take on a stuffy feeling, as if it were getting somehow smaller and closer. I experienced a kind of dizzy sensation, and I began to think that I had had perhaps a swallow too many of the sherry we used for the toast. But I quickly realized that it wasn't a simple inebriate dizziness, because my senses were all fully acute. I let my head fall back, and allowed my neck to rest on the back of the chair while I began to perspire. After a few minutes I heard a few gasps and I opened my eyes. To my indescribable horror I saw that I was partially illuminated by a bright substance which seemed to be smeared over my face. My first thought, of course, was to wipe it away, but I found myself once again powerless to move. I simply sat there while this substance—presumably ectoplasm—dripped all over me, flowing, I was told later, out of my mouth. It felt sticky, and with each moment I felt weaker.

"The room was, of course, getting brighter as the glow of this infernal material got stronger; eventually the stuff began to float in the air, slowly, I fancied, assuming a shape. At first it was indistinct, just a round mass; then it gradually began to—how shall I describe it—fall together, brighter and darker areas falling together to create a face—a large, round face. It hung in the air for what seemed like several minutes—probably not much more than a couple of seconds, really—until it had become perfectly clear. It was round and hairless, with great closed eyes. It seemed like a corpse laid out on view, pale and serene, yet there was something about the structure of the face that suggested something less than human. Its nose was flat with wide nostrils, and its lips—if it had any—were drawn back to reveal great, craggy teeth, wholly unpleasant to see.

"As we watched it hover above us, the gelatinous white substance began to form something of a body—long, gaunt, yet somehow suggestive of great power. Then, slowly, the lids began to raise, revealing, God help me, great green eyes, pupiless, malevolent and terrifying. We could not be sure that it saw anything, whether it looked upon us or not, but I—and I was later to find out, the rest of them as well—felt that it did indeed behold us. Then, all at once, the horrible mouth opened and the room was filled with a great whispering sound like a distant waterfall. Gradually the sound grew, until its intensity was deafening. It was at that point that I fainted.

"I was revived later by Tice. I was lying on the cellar steps, my clothes torn. Tice was bloody and bruised, and Walters had gone to get an ambulance. Jessica and young Wilson were dead.

"Later, in hospital, I was told by Walters that the thing had begun to move—awkwardly at first, with sort of a swaying motion—then with agility and finally speed. First it simply ranged about the room—Tice described it as looking as if it were trying to get out—then, as the roaring increased, a great wind began to whirl about, knocking over the ash trays and unlit lamp on the table. By this time, everyone was up out of his seat and trying to get out of the room, though Tice said that Jessica tried to reach me through the maelstrom. The last that both Tice and Walters remembered was that creature actually grabbing at them. They managed to get the door open, and, with what must have been superb bravery, repeatedly went back to pull the rest of us out. They both concurred that after dragging me out, they could not find Wilson, and Jessica was obviously beyond help.

"Wilson was later found, crushed under the marble table which had been literally flipped across the room to land legs up in the opposite corner from which it had stood. Jessica was crushed beyond recognition. I obtained leave from hospital to attend her funeral; after the service, I prevailed upon the undertaker to open the closed casket for one more look at my lovely Jessica. There hasn't been one moment since then that I haven't regretted that request; she was smashed to a pulp—nothing but a mass of bruises and lacerations; all semblance of facial bone structure had entirely disappeared. The sight so shocked me that I fainted, and was taken to hospital again, this time for a stay of several months."

The old man finished his drink with a gulp, and stared down at his lap. "The Chelsea Society was disbanded, of course; and the cellar room shut. I never really regained my health. Some part of me, some vitality had been drained; and for all I know, that vital force may still be down there in the cellar room, waiting for release."

Sir Harold sat back in his wheelchair, apparently exhausted with the effort of dredging up such horrible memories and relating them, perhaps for the first time, to another human being. I moved in my seat sluggishly; it was completely dark outside now, and the room was quite chilly.

"My dear Sir Harold," I murmured, trying to console the old gentleman, "that is a frightful tale." I did not really believe the story, yet I did not doubt his sincerity; I believed that *he* believed it. I began to question tactfully.

"Perhaps a good deal of this was a... subjective occurrence—that is a hallucination of sorts rather than a literal, physical event?"

Sir Harold jolted upright in his seat, eyeing me with a hot ferocity again out of character with his physical weakness. "You doubt my story?"

"Oh, not at all," I hastened to assure him. "But you yourself admit that you were unconscious during most of the physical activity. Possibly Tice and Walters..."

"Tice and Walters were gentlemen," he interrupted. "I do not doubt their testimony. It was sworn later at a private inquest. Tice is now dead, and Walters left for South America about a decade ago, and is out of touch." He looked directly at me in an unmistakable challenge. "Is it proof you want?"

I cleared my throat. "Well, I should like to be positive that the material that I'm to release to the public is valid. I imagine that a man of your reputation would be of the same mind. Look at it from a point of law; the evidence you present is really no more than hearsay." I warmed to my argument. "Without Walters or Tice to corroborate your story, critics both within and without the Spiritualist camp would make a laughingstock of you." I stopped, afraid I'd gone a bit too far. The old man's temper was still healthy.

"What do you want as proof at this rather late date?" he asked.

"A seance," I replied. "We must prove to the world that there is a daemonic force in the cellar. Let me get a group of Spiritualists from the Marylebone Society here. We'll hold a controlled seance, and the results will either prove or disprove..."

"No. No groups," he said calmly. "You want the proof, and I can furnish it. There need be no more than the two of us. I want no repetition of the last debacle. Two deaths per seance is enough."

"But I did not mean to suggest that you conduct it, Sir Harold," I said, astonished that the old man would be willing to relive that experience. "You must consider your age and health."

"Neither is important to me. Besides, I am the agent of the creature; I think that it needs me to manifest itself. It got half of me last time; this time it can have the rest, or give me back that part that it has. Either way, I'll be satisfied."

I don't know why I agreed to it; curiosity, for the most part, though, not to my credit, I must admit that the thought of the impending notoriety—whatever the outcome—excited me. I really did believe that little or nothing would happen, and that the great neurotic burden with which Sir Harold had lived might be lifted when he realized that it had all been his imagination or the fancy of Tice and Walters. I forgot to consider the deaths of Jessica and the student. At any rate, we decided to hold the seance that night.

Sir Harold lit another lamp and beckoned me to begin pushing. Slowly and laboriously, for it is not an easy thing to let a man in a wheelchair gently down a flight of stairs, we began to make our way, the lamp throwing a dancing light down the mahogany paneling of the walls. The immense silence was broken by the dissonance of the large, hard rubber wheels of the clumsy chair.

At length we arrived at the bottom of the steps. The first part of Wolverton's story was clearly true. There had been no one down these steps for a very long time, for, glancing back, I could clearly see my footprints and the wheelchair's odd, snaking lines in the dust.

I took the lamp from Sir Harold and held it at the cellar door. It was bolted and nailed shut with large boards crossed over it, the way they bar access to condemned buildings. The wood of the door had split where the nails had entered, so it was no difficult matter to pull the boards off and pull open the bolt.

Once inside the cellar room, I wheeled Sir Harold to the far end of the table. It was, indeed, a large heavy table; it and the room were laden with dust. Clearly no one had been in that room for a long time. Other than the accumulated dust, the room had a perfectly normal appearance, though two chairs were lying on their sides by the windows. Without speaking, Sir Harold placed the lamp on the table and leaned back, signaling for me to begin. I made myself as comfortable as possible, after using my handkerchief to wipe away the dust on the seat and arms of my chair. I sat back and asked once more whether he was sure that we should go ahead.

"Positive," he said.

I blew out the light. In the resulting darkness I saw nothing, though after a few minutes I could barely make out the bent figure across the table. Sir Harold let his head fall back, his neck resting against the wicker back of the wheelchair. His mouth slowly sagged open, exposing a set of teeth complete but misshapen and tobacco-stained; his eyes remained open, but with a chillingly sightless aspect. I sat facing him for what must have been close to forty-five minutes until I noticed that his breathing had apparently stopped. I immediately feared for the old man's life; the terrible memories—real to him—might have given him a heart seizure. Then, in the dim cellar light, he began to exude an odd pale yellow glow. I looked behind me to see opaque windows; the glow was not coming from them. I began to feel an overwhelming fear. I had sat through numberless seances given by the most reputable mediums in the world, yet I never got so much as a tingle of fear. Now I was streaming with perspiration, my eyes nailed to the strange, bent form in front of me.

As I looked at him, I perceived a milky-white, viscous substance formlessly building up like mucous in his nostrils and mouth. Fascinated, I watched as it began to flow noiselessly out of his nose and mouth and down his lips and chin. It gave off its own glow, a rhythmically pulsating light, the quality of which was similar to lights seen from a great distance underwater. As the ectoplasmic substance glowed, I noticed that rather than lighting the room, it seemed to have darkened it. Whereas certain objects, especially the broken chairs under the window, had been quite clear, even bright, they now darkened to the point where the only visible things in the room were Sir Harold's face and shoulders, neck and shirt front, and a few inches of the table.

By now I fully regretted the entire affair. Whereas in the light, with sherry in hand, stories of great green monsters are absolutely ridiculous, they begin to get less and less amusing as the light wanes. I have seen many a seance break down with the turning out of the light; but I am a professional and, presumably, used to such things.

Yet I had never felt a room to be so laden with evil, and with the tension of something terrible imminent. It must be very similar to the feeling experienced by a soldier awaiting a bombardment he knows is to come momentarily.

The darkness now lay on me palpably, a damp blanket that caused the windows, chilled with the cold night air, to run with moisture. Sir Harold remained the only visible thing in the room. His eyes were still open, sightless it would seem. Though he appeared unconscious, I could see his hands wringing furiously in his lap. He was undoubtedly awake, and terrified at reliving that experience that had resulted in several deaths and his retirement from public life.

The viscous substance exuding from his nostrils and mouth was now joining and producing a mass of sizeable bulk that lay directly between the two of us; and as I watched it, very unpleasantly thrilled, it began to form a roughly spheroid shape, a shape that I was fervently hoping would not become a head. As, however, it began to do so, I began to marshal my efforts to shake off the fascination that bound me to my seat. I realized now that Sir Harold's story was true, and that I had best do all in my power to prevent a full repetition of the affair.

Perhaps you have had dreams in which you were in danger, a danger usually not specified, but somehow assumed by you to be mortal; yet you find movement is impossible. Often this same physical paralysis attends psychic phenomena—and so it did with me, and, I assume, Sir Harold. We were bound by some agent either within or outside us, to sit and watch as that creature slowly flowed out of Sir Harold's body, or perhaps his mind, and begin to take form.

In any case, the head was now forming; it was large, about twice the size of a human head, I should say, while very melon-shaped. It was supported by a column of pulsating ectoplasm, under which was beginning to appear the rudiments of a body—a long tubular shape with what seemed to be long, thin arms and legs. In all, the form was humanoid, but quite definitely not human, not in shape, and not in intent.

The face was now forming. It was perfectly smooth, unstamped by any of the expression lines that mark creatures of thought or feeling. It was clearly not a ghost in the conventional sense; it was indeed a spirit—that is a creature that exists on a plane other than our own—but in this case a spirit that never was human; it was an elemental, a spirit that perhaps populated Earth before humanity, and that resents us as usurpers.

With a tremendous effort I succeeded in pushing my chair back slightly from the table. It squeaked over the dirty floor, and the sound enabled me to shake off some of the stupor that unnerved me.

"Sir Harold," I managed to whisper, "Sir Harold, you must move."

He made a visible effort to move—I could see his hands rise to the table and feebly push against it, without effect. He then made a sort of shrugging movement with his shoulders and shook his hands in a gesture of futility.

Dripping with sweat, I began to lean across the table in an effort to get at the lamp and light it. It was too far away, and, as leaning forward brought me closer to the thing hovering now almost fully formed above the table, I shrank back in my seat. It would only be a matter of moments before it would break away from Sir Harold with a malevolent life of its own. I knew that we needed light. I reached into my vest pocket and withdrew my matchbox. Fumbling, I dropped one or two matches before I succeeded in lighting one. I held it up as it flared, bringing the room briefly into view. The creature seemed to dissipate, and the features that had been strongly apparent began to melt back into the mass of ectoplasm. As the match began to flicker the creature once more began to fill out. I realized then that the matches did not throw enough light to destroy it, merely to stave off its complete formation. And I could not have had more than five or so matches left. As the match went out, I immediately lit another, with the same effect. I was only putting off the inevitable. In a desperate gamble, I decided to light all at once inside the box; during the longer brighter flame, I would try to get to the door.

Lighting the match in my hand, I put it inside the box, letting it rest against its corner. As the box itself began to burn, I pushed it carefully under the writhing mid-air figure, which knew now, if it commanded any intelligence at all, that there were agents working for its destruction.

As the matches remaining in the box flared, I found my legs and bolted for the door, unlocked it, and flew upstairs. At the landing I shouted for the old servant, who came running out of the back in a dressing gown.

"Good Heavens, what is it, sir?" he asked, no doubt shocked at my appearance and the desperate manner in which I had called him.

"Light a lamp quickly, man, and come with me!" He did so, admirably quickly, I must say, for a man his age.

We both ran downstairs, I at the quicker pace. As I reached the bottom, the light carried by the servant was already spilling into the darkened room. I could not resist peering in—it was quite dark, though I could make out Sir Harold, still seated at the head of the table, in the same position I had left him. There was no ectoplasm to be seen. I breathed with relief; we had beaten it!

At length the old servant ambled up to me with the lamp. We both entered the room, I first, setting the lamp on the table.

I shall never forget the sight of Sir Harold. Despite the subsequent controversy, I never doubted that it was other than Sir Harold; at first the police believed me only because of the total lack of anything else that could be Sir Harold.

What sat before me was barely more than a skeleton. Its skin was stretched tightly to the bones, and its eyes were shrunken out of sight into their sockets. Sir Harold's clothes hung loosely on his frame, and the hands that I had seen writhing in that lap only minutes before, were now inert, bony extremities that would belong under normal circumstances only to the long dead.

I involuntarily stepped back in horror, bumping into the servant who was muttering. "It can't be, it can't be," he whispered, largely to himself.

I realized now that the demon *had* been able to materialize, but only at Sir Harold's expense, and that it took sustenance not only from his mind and spirit, but from his body as well; every drop of ectoplasm that flowed from Sir Harold was a drop of his own life's substance flowing out from him. That would explain why he was a shattered man after the first materialization, though his wounds were not so great as to account for such physical deterioration. But now, facing Sir Harold's skeletal remains, I realized that his death could mean only one thing: the creature's life!

I began to shake again, in the realization that the horrid thing must now be alive in that room. I grabbed the lamp and held it high, peering gingerly into the shadows of the far corners of the room.

The servant apparently gathered what I was about, and made quickly for the door.

"Don't open it," I shouted. "You'll let it out." I was wrong.

The creature was standing in the hall, just beyond the lip of light cast by the lamp I was holding. It was a sort of mottled yellow colour, perhaps cream—it's hard to tell in the glow of a lamp—punctuated by blotches of a darker colour. It stood about eight or nine feet in height, and had a perfectly round head with no ears, long spindly arms that looked as if they might be jointed in two or three places, and huge, bony hands a good foot across. But its most arresting features were its eyes—great holes on either side of a dark spot that I assume could be a nose. And, as Sir Harold had said, they did indeed glow green, a dull, angry green mist that suggested a primordial fury that no man could hope to contain.

Before I could shout for the old man to come back into the circle of light, the creature snatched at him with one of those long, spiderly arms, catching him about the middle with a huge hand. The old man gasped once, and then, with an unspeakable crackling sound, the creature literally twisted him apart and then threw his crushed body back into the room at my feet. He lay there, a widening pool of blood issuing from the crumpled and torn body.

The creature eyed me malevolently and began to move closer. I held the lamp in front of me, realizing with a sinking heart that it was only about half full, with only enough oil to last a few hours. And I knew that when the lamp would begin to dim, the creature would move closer and closer until it could reach me and snap me in two with those loathsome arms.

Closer and closer it moved, as the time passed glacially and the light flickered. Occasionally it would reach in and flail at me, withdrawing quickly, as if the light caused it pain. I sat on the edge of the table, eyeing with horror the lamp's dwindling oil reserve, my ears ringing with the preternatural silence and my head reeling from the terror of what I had been through and the fear of the outcome of my current trial. And the creature stood in the hallway, staring at me, its mouth leering in a wide, craggy grin. But at last, no doubt a matter of minutes before the light was to flicker its last, the dawn began to break, and light began to filter through the cellar room's windows.

The creature began to move back into the hall, leaving me alone with my two ghastly companions. Knowing that the hall would remain dark throughout the day, I shook off my terror and fatigue and, possessed of the excess energy that we are sometimes blessed with at times of trial, I picked up a chair and hurled it through the windows. Clambering onto the table, I cleared the broken glass from the sill, and hoisted myself over it onto the cold ground.

London never looked so wonderful, and its air has never smelled so sweet. The sun had not yet brought warmth, but even at that early hour, I could see men making their way to work, wrapped in mufflers, their breaths rhythmically condensing into clouds of steam. Despite my light dress and my dampness from perspiration, I ran down the street shouting for help. When it finally arrived, I collapsed.

The police certainly expressed reservations about my story, though my shaken state and the unspeakable condition of the two corpses found in that God-forsaken room argued eloquently in favour of the truth of my story. The coroner stoutly insisted that Sir Harold had been dead many months, but had to admit that identification of rings and physical features as noted by Sir Harold's physician, proved beyond a doubt that the body was his, and he had been seen as recently as a week earlier by Sir Clive Mathews, Bart., who had stopped by to discuss the sale of some property near Brighton. Moreover, I had in my possession Sir Harold's letter, dated only a few days before the tragic night.

Furthermore, the old servant, whose name was Tom, was torn brutally limb from limb, and neither the coroner nor the chief of police could imagine what agency would have the power or ferocity to crumple a human being in that savage manner.

So the police reluctantly reported that "Person or persons unknown attacked and murdered Sir Harold Wolverton and his manservant Thomas Cooper for cause unknown." And there's an end on it.

But the creature, that living part of Sir Harold, whose full "birth" left that ghastly shell staring at the ceiling of the cellar room, has the run of London, and I am positive that the current wave of murders and maimings can be attributed to it.

I would expect that its quarters are the now empty Wolverton House. It was apparently a simple matter for it to have eluded the police search after the murders; it could have made its way to the attic, or into the wainscoting, or perhaps even underground. Who knows what its powers, capabilities and intelligence are?

Wolverton House is a desirable property in an excellent neighbourhood, but rumours persist about it, and I expect that it shall stand vacant for a long time to come.

MYTHOS

BY JOHN GLASBY

"Well," said Mitchell, sucking on his pipe and staring intently across the desk, "what do you make of it? You think it could be a true record of what happened, or is it just another hoax?"

Nordhurst looked bored. He flung the manuscript onto the desk, then straightened in his chair, lit a cigarette, and stared out of the window as he blew smoke through his nostrils. "I was thinking of having a talk with you some time ago about this, Mitchell," he said quietly. "I know you've applied for permission and finances, to fit out an expedition to this place. Personally, I think I ought to warn you that I'm against the entire project. I know you hold very firm, and fixed, views on this subject. You've spent the past two or three years delving into the records we have in the library here. I haven't tried to stop you because you seemed to be doing no harm and it was always possible that you might, conceivably, turn up something new. But this—"

He indicated the manuscript on top of the desk with a sudden sharp jerk of his hand. "Really, Mitchell, I thought better of you."

"But surely, sir," protested the other mildly, raising a brow, "you aren't going to dismiss it like that. There ought, at least, to be some attempt made to look into it. After all, the legends of Easter Island have been known, in part, for a very long time now, ever since the island was discovered—or rediscovered, if you like—by Roggeveen on Easter Day, 1772. But as far as I know, no one has solved the mysteries of the ancient cult or religion which built those tremendous stone statues on the island."

"Doctor Mitchell," interrupted Nordhurst acidly. "As head of the Archaeological Department, I can assure you that I know something of Easter Island."

"I fully acknowledge that fact, Professor," said the other smoothly. He had the impression that he was getting nowhere fast with this man. "Your personal knowledge and integrity are not being challenged. All I ask is that we fit out a small expedition to check on the facts mentioned in this document. I believe that these notes made by Don Felipe Gonzales may help us to clear up some of the mystery which shrouds the place."

"Nonsense." Nordhurst shook his head vehemently. "Don't you realise that if we fitted out an expedition based on such flimsy, not to say ridiculous evidence as this, we might be the laughing stock of the entire University?" He got to his feet and walked to the window, standing with his back to the other. He went quickly, without turning his head: "Try to look at this objectively, Mitchell. I realise that may be difficult for you, because perhaps without even knowing, you're somewhat prejudiced in your outlook on the matter, but what have we got to go on? Nothing more than a note in the diary of the Spanish Captain who was the second person to land on Easter Island after the Dutch had left.

"Apparently they remained on the island for some time, claiming it in the name of the King of Spain. During that time, seven of their crew disappeared without trace and were never seen again. They certainly never returned to the ships. That much we can be sure of. But they could have remained on the island. It seems quite certain there are many places there where they could hide and not be found by any of their fellow crew members who went out hunting for them. On the other hand, I consider it far more plausible that they were murdered by the islanders and their bodies hidden."

"I see." Mitchell tapped out his pipe into the tray and leaned back in his chair. "Does this mean that no approval will be given to this expedition?"

"Not necessarily. I'm merely the Professor here. The question will have to be put to the committee of which I'm merely the Chairman. They will have the last say in the matter. If their decision goes against you, and you're sufficiently determined, I suppose you could obtain some form of private backing for this idea of yours, always assuming you could find anyone sufficiently interested in your ideas."

"And you yourself would not be interested in coming along, sir?"

Nordhurst read the expression in the other's face and a note of authority crept into his voice: "I appreciate your feelings in this case, Doctor Mitchell, and I detect a little sarcasm in your tone. But even though I do not believe in your theories, after all, I'm still an archaeologist first and foremost, and if it is at all possible to get away from my duties here at the University, I shall be only too glad to accompany you, if only to be present when you are proved wrong."

"And if I'm proved to be right, sir?" The other rose slowly to his feet and stood facing the Professor across the desk. He picked up the manuscript and held it tightly in his hands.

"Then this will be a case, not for an archaeologist, but for an expert on witchcraft and similar related topics, if you can find one."

Mitchell felt sullen, but tried not to show it. He had expected this, even before he had come to see Nordhurst. The other had no imagination, he told himself fiercely, could see nothing beyond the stones and pottery he found in his excavations. He knew for a fact that Nordhurst had done nothing along similar lines to the problem he had in mind. Mesopotamia and the Tigris Valley were about as far as he got.

He shrugged inwardly. The civilization he was seeking was certainly on a par with those ancient cultures with which Nordhurst was familiar, even though divided from them by thousands of miles of open sea. It would be relatively easy for the other to rig that committee meeting so that they voted to throw out his application and he knew that he would not get a second personal hearing after they had once made their decision.

"You think I've merely got a good imagination, don't you, Professor?"

The other went back to the desk and lowered himself into his chair, stubbing out the cigarette. "You've got to admit yourself that it's a pretty wild theory with nothing to support it."

He called Mitchell back once before he got to the door. He was seated easily in his chair, completely master of himself, confident that his decision, already made, was the right one and that nothing would ever alter it.

"You know, I think you ought to have a talk with Walton before you go any further with this. He might be able to straighten you out.

If not, at least you seem to be thinking along similar lines." His smile broadened, almost viciously, as he delivered this final, parting shot.

Mitchell eased out of the door and closed it quietly behind him. He didn't hate the other for what he had said and for what he would undoubtedly do when the committee met; he couldn't hate him. He was just another of the staff who saw only what they wanted to see in the old legends of the ancient civilizations.

He lit his pipe again, flicked the spent match into the basket halfway along the corridor and started for the hallway.

Halfway along the hall, he stopped. Perhaps it wouldn't be such a bad idea to have a talk with Walton after all, he thought. Walton was a curious fellow who kept to himself. Not merely because he liked it that way, but because the things in which he was interested seemed to have little in common with what was expected of a University. Officially, he was head of the Mythology Department, if it could be called a department, considering that he was the head and solitary lecturer all rolled into one.

He had a curious feeling of disorientation as he made his way to the other's room. Checking his watch, he saw that it was a little after four o'clock. The other ought to be free at that time of the afternoon, with most of the lectures over. He knocked on the door, went inside.

Walton was seated in the wide-backed chair in front of the empty fireplace. It was far too hot for a fire and even in this room with the window open, it was far too cool.

"Why, Mitchell. Come inside. It isn't often I have the pleasure of your company. Sit down and tell me what's on your mind. I assume this isn't just a social call."

"Not exactly. I've been along to see Professor Nordhurst."

"About your proposed visit to Easter Island?" The other raised a quizzical eyebrow.

"How did you know?" Mitchell stared at him for a moment in surprise.

"Word gets around a place like this," said the other easily. "Besides, I must confess I'm quite interested in your ideas myself. I've been reading some of the papers you've written on these ancient myths. Couldn't have done better myself and I'm supposed to be the head of that particular department."

"I assure you I didn't mean to tread on anyone's corns when I wrote them," said the other defensively.

"Think nothing of it. There's too little interest, real interest, shown in these old legends at the present time. I only hope that you get permission and money to finance this expedition of yours. If you do, I sincerely hope you'll ask me along. Not only for the ride, but so that I might take a look at some of these things at first-hand."

Mitchell felt suddenly a little more confident. Walton, of course, would have some say on the committee and he felt that here he had a staunch supporter.

"I'd very much like to have you along." Mitchell nodded. "But at the moment, things don't look too bright for me. Nordhurst is dead against the idea and he had plenty of influence with the committee. If they turn this down, I don't know where to start."

"Leave that particular bridge until you come to it," advised the other. "I may be able to swing things in your favour, although I don't want you to go building your hopes on that. It's going to take several thousand dollars to finance an expedition such as that, and in addition, you'll have to get the permission of the Chilean Government for any exploratory work. You shouldn't have too much difficulty there, however; they're usually quite willing to allow genuine archaeological expeditions to work there, provided they don't try to interfere with the ways of the people."

Mitchell leaned forward in his chair. "And you think there might be something in this idea of mine, that some of the old religion is still being practiced on the island, and that if we can only find out something about that, something which may have been handed down from before the dawn of history, we may find out more about those statues?"

"It's an intriguing thought," said the other slowly. He ran his fingers through his hair. "And I've no doubt that there's still plenty of mystery there for us to clear up."

"I wish I could think of something which would convince Nordhurst and those others who're bound to be on the committee. You know what they like, the way they think. Anything as dry as dust and they're all for it. They'll spend money like water, just to dig up a few old relics that have been buried for a couple of thousand years in Mesopotamia, but give them something like this, something that could turn out to be really big, and they look on it as so blasphemous, so beyond their limited imagination, that they clamp down on it immediately."

"Steady, Mitchell, steady," said the other, watching his face carefully. "We may pull this thing out of the fire yet. Tell me about your theory."

Ralph Mitchell leaned forward in his chair, a sparse young man in his thirties. He was the tweed-and-pipe man, who never went down well with the real intellectuals at the University. They tolerated him, but he suspected that none of them, especially the older, more dignified ones ever really liked him. Walton was possibly different in that he was only four or five years senior to himself, and his pet subject required far more imagination and intuitive instinct than any other in the entire Faculty.

"These vast stone statues that are present on Easter Island. I believe that they were put there by an advanced civilization many centuries before the present inhabitants, or their ancestors, visited the place. It's miles from anywhere and way off the main sea routes, although I'm prepared to accept the current theory that ocean currents are such that anyone leaving the coast of South America would be carried there by the currents and the prevailing winds.

"That, perhaps, could tell us how the ancestors of the present islanders arrived there several centuries ago, but I doubt whether we can look to the same explanation for this earlier civilization."

"Which is still only one of your postulates," put in the other gravely.

"Yes, that's perfectly true," replied the other solemnly, "but I think I have some concrete evidence for it."

"And what might that be?" The other raised an interrogatory eyebrow and studied him calmly from the depths of the easy chair.

Ralph Mitchell shrugged. "The strange ichthyic figures which have been discovered on the bases of some of these statues and more important still, small statues of birdlike creatures, having human bodies, which are present in the hidden caves on the island."

"I see." The other nodded. "You've been extremely busy discovering all of this. And from these scattered shreds of evidence, what have you deduced?"

"That there was a civilization on Easter Island many thousands of years ago, an extremely advanced civilization. I don't know, at the moment, whether or not it was a good or an evil one. Somehow, I think it was evil."

Walton looked at him sharply. "Why do you say that?"

"From those statues and from the inscriptions which have been carved on them. They all seem to speak of an earlier time, far beyond that of recorded history, possibly before that of the early Egyptian dynasties, when there were strange cultures on Earth. Almost all of them have now been destroyed, and only fragmentary evidence remains. That—and quite a lot of legend and folklore. The difficulty with the latter is, trying to shift the grain of truth from the tremendous mass of exaggeration and fiction which has grown up about it. Remember, these stories which are told in the legends of countless races, all over the world, have been passed down by word of mouth for centuries. It's only natural that they should have been embellished on the way. And the older they are, the more closely the truth is hidden."

"And you want to get at that grain of truth which existed in the very beginning. Is that it?" smiled the other.

"Yes." Mitchell nodded his head slowly. "I'm convinced that the answer, or one of the answers, is there on Easter Island. I've spoken to several men who've been there and they all say, without exception, that no one can stand and gaze upon those tremendous statues and not feel a sense of terror that lurks still in hidden places. I want to see these things for myself, question the people there with regard to their ancient legends, find out if any of their religion still exists and examine the figures and inscriptions on these monstrous creations for myself."

"Don't you think that others must have had the same idea in the past, ever since those stone figures were discovered? If what you say is true, why hasn't some of it come out into the open by now?"

"I don't know. I think it may be that some people have discovered the truth for themselves and they've either died because of it, or they were made to stay there, out of sight, until the ships had left. I think that was what happened to those sailors mentioned by the Spaniards who visited the island in 1770."

The other said eagerly, "Now this is the kind of thing I like, Ralph. I'm glad you came to see me. I hadn't realized you were so serious, nor that you had learned so much. Most of what you've told me, I've known for some time. The legends of Easter Island have long been one of my favorite topics of research, only I think it only fair to mention now, that I haven't got very far with them. There's not only an air of utter secrecy about them, but the natives there simply refuse to discuss them with strangers."

He gazed at Mitchell without smiling, his eyes very still and hard, with a speculative expression in them. "You are hoping to link these researches of yours with anything in particular?"

"Easter Island could be an outcrop of a larger, submerged land area. Possibly one of the legendary continents which are mentioned in the old books."

"Mu?" said the other in a whisper. He leaned forward resting his elbows on his knees. "Now you're getting into the spirit of things. You may be on the track of something important. I don't think we can persuade Professor Nordhurst of this. He's far too wrapped up in his own dry-as-dust discoveries. But we may be able to bring it to the notice of the other members of the committee. I'll certainly do my best."

"Nordhurst mentioned that if the funds were granted for an expedition, he'd like to come along."

"Simply for the chance to gloat over us if we found nothing and it all turned out to be a wild goose chase, no doubt."

"I'm certain those were his only motives," agreed Mitchell. There was a touch of bitterness in his voice. "Whichever way the decision of the committee goes, he's determined to be on the winning side."

Walton nodded. "Whatever happens, until we know their decision, try not to rub him the wrong way. In the meantime, I'll get in touch with the other committee members and sound them out. There are bound to be a few of them on our side and others I think I might be able to win over. It would be quite ethical for me to do this, whereas you might be reluctant to associate yourself with talking them around, seeing that you're the proposer of this scheme."

"Do you think we stand a chance at all?"

The other pursed his lips. "I'll know the answer to that one once I've had a talk with some of the others."

Mitchell had expected little to come of Walton's promises. He was, therefore, all the more surprised when Professor Nordhurst called him to his room one afternoon three weeks later.

"Sit down, please, Doctor Mitchell," he said gravely, indicating the chair in front of his desk. "I'd like to have a talk with you."

Mitchell sat quite still, wondering what was coming next. Obviously it was something to do with the committee meeting which had been held earlier that day. Probably wondering how he can break the refusal gently, he thought bitterly, without making it obvious that he was the one who had stopped the grant.

"As you know, the committee met this morning to discuss your application for a grant to finance an expedition to Easter Island. I made it quite clear the last time we discussed this question, that I was not in sympathy with such an undertaking, that it did not merit the expenditure of so much money from the University funds.

"However, a majority of the committee members were of the opinion that something useful might come from such an expedition and consequently it has been decided to finance this trip of yours. I hope for your sake, and that of the University as a whole, that something will be discovered which is of concrete, scientific interest."

He twisted his lips into a dry smile. "I would also like to remind you that I would like to be included in the group to go on this trip."

"But of course, Professor." Mitchell felt a sensation of sudden exultation and excitement rising within him. This was far more than he had ever dared hope. Most of it, he owed to Walton, he reflected. The other had certainly been busy during the past three weeks.

"Then that's settled. All that remains now is to settle on a date. I realize that it will take some time to make the preliminary arrangement, but I'd certainly appreciate it if you'd keep in close touch with me."

Mitchell nodded in silent agreement. Now that everything had turned out in his favour, he could forget the way in which Nordhurst had reacted when they had first talked this idea over.

"I'll begin the necessary arrangements right away," he said quickly, getting to his feet. There was a sudden sense of urgency in him now that the first obstacle had been cleared. He had the strange feeling that time was somehow running against them. It was a peculiar sensation, one which he could not even begin to explain. Somewhere out there in the heart of the Pacific, he thought tensely, lay the secret to most of the ancient legends, he felt certain of that. If only he could find it, prise it loose from whatever it was, from whoever held it.

Mitchell stirred restlessly under the sheets, then swung his legs to the floor of the cabin and sat on the edge of the bunk. The ship was rolling slightly in the swell and it was still dark outside. He tried to make out details through the porthole close to his head, but could see nothing through the thick glass. The previous evening, the Skipper had estimated that they were little more than seventy miles from Easter Island and that they ought to reach it some time the following evening.

There was no light in the cabin, and he was content to sit in the darkness, smoking. During the past weeks when progress had seemed slow and at times non-existent, the urgency within him had risen to the point where he could scarcely stand it any longer. Even now, when they were almost within hailing distance of their objective, he still felt tense and tight inside, as if something were bottled up inside him, waiting for release.

They had easily picked up a crew for the converted fishing vessel which they had succeeded in fitting out, and the journey so far had proved uneventful. The ship had proved to be extremely seaworthy and had been sufficiently large to carry all of their equipment. The necessary permission had been received from the Chilean Government to land on Easter Island and carry out their investigations.

He stubbed out his cigarette and lit another almost immediately. If only he could rid himself of this feverish tension which seemed to be riding him incessantly, never leaving him. Was it because he was inwardly afraid of what he might find here? That there might be something in the tales of horror which the other men he had talked with had spoken of? Or was it because, deep down inside, he was afraid of being proved wrong by Nordhurst?

Deliberately, he considered the various alternatives and immediately dismissed the last one. Simply because he was wrong would not bring this subtle fear in its train. There might be a little ridicule, and an I-told-you-so attitude on the part of Professor Nordhurst, but that was about all.

On the other hand, if there was anything in his belief in an older, tremendously ancient civilization on Easter Island, and vestiges of it still remained there, it might conceivably be dangerous to probe too deeply. He tried to dismiss the idea, to put it out of his mind altogether. Whatever his reasons for coming here, he was still a scientist, first and foremost. And as such, he had trained his mind to examine everything minutely and carefully and reject anything which had no scientific reasons for its existence.

Well, to hell with it, he thought savagely, drawing deeply on the cigarette, watching the tip glow redly in the darkness. Very soon, he would be in a position to find out things for himself. Not that he expected to make much headway at first. The natives would undoubtedly be reluctant to talk with total strangers, especially about their ancient beliefs, and even when they did, he would still have to sift the truth from the mass of spurious data with which it would be embellished.

He sat there for a long time, so sunk in thought that he scarcely noticed the darkness fading beyond the porthole, and the sun climbing up out of the sea. He dressed after a while and went up on deck. There was a stiff breeze that caught hold of his shirt and flapped it around his waist.

Walton was already there, leaning over the rail, peering into the sun-hazed distance. He turned as the other approached.

"Not much further now, Ralph," he said genially. "Beginning to get excited, I suppose."

"A little," admitted the other quietly. He fell silent and stared down at the water which ran in a stream of white foam past the hull of the ship.

"Something wrong?" inquired the other concernedly. "You don't look so good."

"Just that I didn't sleep much during the night, got too much on my mind, I guess."

"Well, whatever happens, don't let it get you down. There's one hell of a lot to be discovered here, I can feel it in my bones. You may be on to the discovery of the century before very long."

"I only hope you're right." Mitchell's laugh was oddly brittle and hollow, with little mirth to it. "I'd hate to have to go back to the University and live with Nordhurst telling me all the time how wrong I had been and that he had advised against this expedition in the first place. Superior knowledge and all that, you know."

Walton grinned and nodded in sympathy. "I know how you feel. But somehow, I don't think you ought to let that worry you. I've been thinking about this place myself and the more I consider the possibilities here, the more convinced I am that you're on to something, something big. Only don't take that as anything definite, it's only a hunch at present, although I must admit, I'm very seldom wrong about anything like this. Some kind of instinct I've developed over the past years, I reckon."

He clapped Mitchell on the back. "How about getting something to eat? I'm starving. It'll help to pass the time until we sight Easter Island. After spending all of this time on the ship, I'll be glad to set my feet on dry land again."

They went below where the others were already at their morning meal. Nordhurst looked up from his half-empty plate. "Still confident that there's something here worthy of all the money we've spent, Doctor Mitchell?" he asked. His voice was toneless.

"I think so." Ralph forced evenness into his tone. "We will soon know now."

The other shook his head slowly, dubiously. "I've spent almost twenty-five years hunting through the ruins of the Tigris and Euphrates valley and I've found no indications of any older civilizations than those whose existence we've been able to prove. In my opinion, the Sumerian is the oldest of all proven cultures."

"Aren't you forgetting Atlantis and Mu?" asked Walton innocently.

Nordhurst grimaced. "I said proven cultures, Doctor Walton," he murmured acidly. "There's no evidence whatever for the existence of Atlantis or Mu."

"What about all of the old manuscripts? The *Popul Vuh* of the Mayas and the Hindu *Vedas*? Don't they speak of a far more ancient civilization on Earth which predated that of even the Sumerians by several thousand years?"

"I'm afraid I possess an utterly scientific outlook when it comes to records such as those you have just mentioned," went on the other calmly, regarding Walton closely. "These old records have all been shown to be fiction. Certainly it is fiction of a highly skilled order, but none the less, there isn't a grain of truth in any of them."

"Oh, come now, Professor," grinned the other easily. "You can't possibly dismiss everything as easily or as simply as that. Life would be extremely easily and well-ordered for people such as myself, if we looked at things that way. And there's no doubt it would remove some of the fascination out of life."

"It would also relegate these works to where they belong," snapped the other sharply. "To the realms of fiction."

"I'm sorry you think that way, Professor," said the other, still retaining his equanimity. "But I've a feeling that, skeptic as you are, even your faith in the scientific approach to these problems will be severely shaken when we get to Easter Island."

"That remains to be seen," said the other in a tone which ended the conversation on that particular topic.

It was almost dark that evening before they came within sight of Easter Island. It rose up out of the sea like a great smudge on the horizon, taking shape as they bore down upon it through the surging swell. Mitchell stood on the deck and watched it through narrowed eyes. Even from that distance, he could sense the strange air of mystery which lay like an invisible pall over it.

Small wonder, he reflected, that the people who had been living here when the Dutch had first arrived, had known more about the sun and moon and stars than about any other land on the face of the earth. They were so far removed from the nearest land, from the nearest place of human habitation, that their language had been filled with references to the celestial bodies which were visible all the time in the clear sky above their heads, rather than to other islands, which were so far away that they had almost sunk to the status of myth.

They sailed closer and dropped anchor in a small bay which sheltered them from the current. Mitchell could feel the breeze on his body, a breeze which blew off the island, bringing with it a feeling of mystery, and a little touch of terror also as he thought of those carved stone images which dotted the grassy slopes. What race of creatures had posed for those vast statues? he wondered inwardly. A race of men long dead who had left behind these relics of civilization at which it was only possible to guess?

When he finally went below, a riot of thoughts ran through his spinning mind. In the morning, they would go ashore and their work would begin. Above all, he wanted to see these weird inscriptions on the stone statues and to talk with the people, try to dig back into their past, not to the legends of their own race, but those, if any, of the race which had inhabited this place possibly thousands of years ago.

He slept little that night and his uneasy dozing seemed troubled by strange dreams, more real and frightening than any he could remember before. Mostly, they consisted of a jumbled series of kaleidoscopic scenes or vivid glimpses of vast, hideous creatures walking a landscape which seemed totally unfamiliar to him, but which he felt he had seen before. He seemed, in his dreams, to hear a weird and awful chant that seemed never-ending and he worked with it ringing in his ears, the sweat starting out on his body and a shivering fit which seized him in spite of all he could do to fight it off.

He sat up in the bunk and looked about him, trying to force calmness into his mind. What had brought about that nightmare? he wondered as his heart slowly thumped into a more normal, slower beat. It was now almost dawn and there was a faint grey light showing through the porthole. He got up and stood on the cold floor of the cabin in his bare feet, staring out at the island less than a quarter of a mile away.

It looked bare and deserted, an undulating place with rocky, rising hummocks of land here and there and a few of the enigmatic statues just visible on the slopes. The sight of them stirred something inside his mind, and for a moment, he felt his breath catch at the back of his throat.

The air over the island seemed laden with mystery. He wondered whether Nordhurst was awake yet and if so, what emotions were running through his mind as he gazed out at the curious, almost awe-inspiring landscape which had opened before them. Possibly, he too, would be a little apprehensive, wondering what they might find out there. And Walton. He would be excited now, he felt sure of that. A fellow-spirit, he reflected, among the disbelievers.

Breakfast was a meal of silence, quickly over. Everyone, including Nordhurst, seemed anxious to get ashore, if only to get away from the monotonous swaying and pitching of the vessel. Even though they were at anchor here, there was still a swell running from the ocean.

Mitchell went in the first boatload, along with Walton and the Professor.

By now, the grey of the dawn had turned to roseate light edged with gold and suddenly, above the rim of the sea, the sun came up, leaping into the cloudless heavens. The boat touched down on the rock-strewn beach and Walton clambered out, giving a hand to Professor Nordhurst. Mitchell stepped out after them and stood looking about him in awed wonder for several moments. It seemed scarcely credible that he was here at last, that the mystery of which he had dreamed for so many years was actually there, all about him, spread out on all sides.

Stretching in both directions, the grey lava beach curved away around the rocky headland, cut here and there with precipices and loose blocks of stone, but these had obviously been carved by time and not by man.

"God, what a place," breathed Walton hoarsely. His eyes were wide in his head. "If there are ghosts of ancient civilizations anywhere in the world, surely they must be here."

Nordhurst snorted derisively. "I'll believe that when I see it," he said thinly. "I suppose we'd better find a suitable place to set up camp first of all and then start exploring the area. I noticed several of those huge stone figures on that slope over there about a half a mile away. It ought not to be difficult to locate them."

"It also looks as though we have company," said the Skipper, pointing.

Mitchell glanced up in the direction of the other's finger. A crowd of natives had gathered at the top of a narrow, winding lava path which ran up the steep side of the slope in front of them, meandering between grotesquely etched boulders, like a naturally formed stairway.

"I wonder how many of them speak English?" muttered Mitchell.

Before anyone could answer, Walton had stepped forward. He cupped his hands to his mouth and yelled at the top of his voice:

"*Ia-o-rana kurua!*"

"*Ia-o-rana kurua!*" Yelled from a score of voices, the sound came rushing down the cliff wall, bouncing from boulder to boulder like a crushing wave. They came down, following the vast shout.

Mitchell stood to one side as Walton spoke quickly to the natives who crowded around them. Several of them spoke English, he discovered, and almost all of them spoke some form of Spanish. It was not going to be difficult to converse with them, he decided, but how difficult it would be to get anything worthwhile out of them was another matter altogether.

After setting up camp, under the inquisitive eyes of the natives, bringing most of their supplies ashore, they left two of the ship's crew on guard, the natives of Easter Island being well-known for their thievery. It seemed almost a fetish with them and was certainly not looked upon as a crime on the island.

Mitchell set off with Professor Nordhurst and Walton, accompanied by a score of the crew members and many natives. Half an hour later, after stumbling over uneven, treacherous ground, they reached the place which Nordhurst had spotted from the ship, where the great stone statues stared out across the island with their backs to the sea.

All of them, thought Mitchell, with a faint sense of curiosity, facing away from the sea.

A coarse type of grass, yellowed by the sun, grew around the bases of the statues which towered above them, to a height of twenty feet or more. Mitchell shivered a little as he stared at that strange, frightening, inscrutable gaze. There was something here which he could not understand. But what it was, he didn't quite know.

He turned, looked around at Nordhurst. The other stood several yards away, issuing a few orders to the ship's crew as they lowered their spades and picks from their shoulders and stood ready to begin excavations. How far they would have to dig before they came upon anything important was something no one knew at that time. Mitchell could only guess that they would have to dig at least as far as the feet of these statues, if they had any feet, and judging from the side of the heads, which was all that stood out above the ground, they would have to go down at least forty feet; and if they hit solid rock on the way, then it would undoubtedly slow up their progress in that direction to an unguessable extent.

"What do you think of it, Professor?" he asked, going over to the other.

"I'm not sure, Doctor Mitchell. We may find something of archaeological importance here, but I'm not banking on anything. Certainly, I'm convinced there's nothing here to support your theory, that of an ancient, almost prehistoric civilization."

"Not even forty feet down at the base of these statues?"

"Not even there." The other shook his head and there was a gleam in his eyes which Mitchell had never seen there before. Goddamnit, he thought savagely, the other was actually enjoying himself now, playing like a cat with a mouse, waiting for the expedition to turn up nothing more important than a few earthenware pots, relics of the recent civilization. Then he would really be on top of his form.

The men started digging in the hot sunlight. Sweat boiled off their brown bodies as they worked. The earth was reasonably soft on top, easily loosened by the picks. Within three hours, the earth had been cleared away to a depth of almost seven feet. As Mitchell had guessed, the statues had been buried in the earth and the bodies, brought to light for the first time in God knew how many years, were made of exactly the same kind of stone as the inscrutable heads which gazed out across the land towards the center of the island.

That night, as he lay in his blankets, inside the white tent which had been thrown up along with several others, on a smooth plateau, Mitchell felt strangely contented. There was still a feeling of tension in his body, a tightness which had not yet gone away, would probably not go away until he knew for certain what lay under the ground around those graven images. The moon had risen and was gleaming vividly over the great stone faces, some of which he could see through the half open flap of the tent. For some reason, he felt a trifle afraid as he lay there on his side, his head pillowed in his arm, eyes running through his mind; a hundred burning questions to which he had, as yet, no answers, but which he knew he would have to answer before he left Easter Island.

What strange race of people had hewn and erected these great images and how long ago? Five hundred—a thousand years? Or beyond the dawn of recorded history as they knew it? During the daytime, he had questioned one or two of the natives as to the origin of the statues and had learned that they had been dug by the Old Ones, the Long Ears, from a quarry inside the extinct volcano of Rano Raraku.

So far, he had seen no reason to doubt this statement. There had to be somewhere on the island where these vast colossi had been hewn from the solid rock. It was totally inconceivable that they could have been brought there from any other islands so many miles away.

Yet somehow, he had the strange and unshakable impression that there was something more about the island than they had seen. It was true that they had only been there for a day and, quite naturally, there was a lot they had yet to see. But he had the feeling that there was something hidden—but where? Possibly inside the crater of Rano Raraku. Possibly even somewhere underground. In the morning, he would question the natives still further. Any who were unable to speak English or Spanish, he would bring along to Walton and allow him to act as interpreter. It had been a stroke of unexpected luck to find that the other was able to speak the native language sufficiently to make himself understood.

All in all, he mused, Walton was proving himself to be something of a mystery. There were many things about him which he was only beginning to realise. The strange way in which he was able to find his way around the island. The way in which he could converse fluently with these people.

None of this had been apparent while they had been at the University. The man's talents were entirely unexpected.

In the moonlight darkness, before he finally fell asleep, fragments of half-forgotten demoniac lore flashed through his mind, things he could just remember reading in his student days. He shivered. There was a strangeness about this island, set so far from any other inhabited place, holding its mystery hidden from prying eyes. And what had happened to those seven men from the Spanish ship which had anchored offshore as their own vessel was at that very moment? Where had they vanished to, in the darkness of the abysmal night?

It was just possible, he reflected, that even if he discovered the secret, he might not live to tell it. The natives seemed friendly enough at the moment, willing to help in the excavations provided they were well paid, but they might change completely if he started probing too deeply into the past, into things which they might consider did not concern him. Holding this view, he fell asleep and when he woke, the yellow moonlight was gone and the greyness of dawn was giving way to the full light of day.

In spite of his thoughts the previous night, he ate a hearty meal and then went off with the others to the excavation site. Work was progressing a little more slowly now that they were digging deeper into the ground. Here the earth was far harder than before and on many occasions, the picks struck sparks from hidden rocks under the soil and large boulders had to be heaved manually out of their age-old resting place.

A few of the natives had gathered to watch once more and he walked over to them, motioning to Walton to accompany him.

"Are you going to question them, Ralph?" asked the other, and there seemed to be a touch of uneasiness in his deep voice.

"That's the general idea. Apart from what we manage to find down there, I think there's a lot more we can learn by questioning the natives. They must have some legend, some myths."

"It's quite likely, but whether or not they'll talk about them is a different matter," warned the other. "We can only try to worm something out of them, but something tells me they'll be very reticent."

They approached the small knot of natives. Mitchell eyed them curiously. Olive-skinned, they seemed to bear no resemblance whatsoever to the images which dotted the plain. It was quite obvious that the human, or subhuman likenesses which had been the models for those stone faces, had long since left the island, had vanished in mystery somewhere in the far mists of time.

One of the men, a tall, stern-faced man in his fifties as near as Mitchell could judge, spoke reasonably good English.

"Those statues over there," began Mitchell, waving an arm which embraced the plateau where the rest of the crew were toiling in the glaring sunlight. "Do any of you know when they were made, and who carved them?"

The man regarded him closely for a long moment, so long that Mitchell had half despaired of an answer. Then he said slowly: "They have been here since the beginning of time. They came from the inside of Rano Raraku. If you go there you can see many more which have not been taken to their final resting place. They are waiting there now."

Almost foolishly, Mitchell went on: "And do you believe that they will ever go to their final resting place? Or will they remain there forever?"

"That we do not know. If they wish to go, then they will go."

"And yet you have no stories about them—no legends as to why they were carved?"

"There are stories, but they cannot be told, not to strangers."

"Why not?" pressed Mitchell sharply. "Are you afraid to tell us?"

He had noticed the brief expression which had flickered over the man's face, and there seemed to have been a fragmentary glance in Walton's direction. Mitchell felt puzzled. He could understand a reticence on the other's part if he was trying to hide something until the price had been made right for any information, but this was something he did not understand. That the other seemed afraid was obvious. But afraid of what? Of some reaction on the part of the other natives if he should talk of sacred things, or reveal any of the carefully guarded secrets of the island?

It seemed feasible, but the other must have known that none of his companions spoke a word of English and therefore could not understand anything he said.

"These are things so old that no one can talk about them. They have been guarded from the beginning of time."

So that was that, thought Mitchell angrily. Once again, he had come up against this stone wall of impenetrable silence. It was almost as if this was killing knowledge, as if possession of it could be dangerous. But now, more than ever before, he felt certain that it had been handed down by word of mouth from one generation to another on the island, that the old knowledge was still there, but whispered around the fires in the night, or perhaps incorporated in the weird chants he had heard the previous night, the eerie sound wailing over the silent plateau.

He brushed aside the other's sudden silence and said harshly: "If you won't talk to me about these things, then at least tell me someone who will, someone who isn't afraid like a child."

If he had expected the insult to sting the other into some unguarded retort, he was sadly disappointed. The other merely pursed his lips, then shook his head, turned on his heels and stalked off with his head held stiffly in the air. After a moment's pause, the other natives followed him.

Mitchell turned impulsively, exasperated, to Walton. "How in God's name do you get stubborn people like that to talk?"

"I warned you that it wouldn't be easy," said the other evenly. He took out his pipe, filled it slowly, methodically, and lit it carefully, blowing the smoke into the air through pursed lips. "But there may be a way. I think we may have our friend Professor Nordhurst to thank for it, too."

"How do you mean?" countered Mitchell.

"He's been spreading it around that he doesn't believe in the old legends, whatever they are. Sooner or later, I have the idea that someone is going to show him how wrong he is. We only have to wait until then to find out some of the answers."

Mitchell gazed at him without smiling. "You seem to know a lot more about these people than I ever gave you credit for," he said eventually. "Just where do you fit into this deal? First I discover that you can speak their language, speak it fluently, too. Secondly, you seem to know how their minds work."

"Let's say I've made quite a study of them, especially on the voyage here. I've had plenty of time to read up on most of what there is to know about them."

Mitchell would have liked to have questioned the other further, but at that moment there was a sudden shout from the valley a little below them and he turned to see. Nordhurst was waving his arms excitedly. They hurried down the grassy slope.

"What is it?" he asked breathlessly.

The Professor pointed. Mitchell stared down at the body of the great stone statue where it had been uncovered by the sweating men. He leaned forward, realising as he did so, that Walton was peering intently over his shoulder. He heard the other's sharp intake of breath.

The designs etched into the solid stone sent little shivers running up and down his spine. They were unlike anything he had ever seen before, carvings of unmistakable significance, of brooding terror, of creatures which were neither man nor bird, but something inexplicably between the two, all speaking mutely of a way of life, strange and terrible, led by inhabitants which were perhaps half-beast, half-man, possibly gigantic, although there was nothing there to give any indication of their true size.

"You're thinking of those strange images carved on the walls of the caves in New Guinea," said Walton quietly.

"Yes—and in a few other places of the world," Mitchell nodded. "Those in Peru are extremely similar to these, although there are some differences which may be significant."

"Hasn't it already been established that the people of Easter Island must have originally come from South America?" suggested Nordhurst.

"That's true," agreed Mitchell, straightening his back. "But those carvings weren't quite like these. There's something—well, terrible—about these, something you can almost feel."

"Nonsense! It's merely because these have just been exposed after centuries. I've seen those ancient Aztec and Mayan inscriptions for myself first-hand." The other spoke with a certain amount of pomposity. "At least give me some credit for knowing what I'm talking about."

"My apologies," said Mitchell thinly. He kept his temper with a supreme effort of will. "I didn't mean to question your authority to speak on that point. I gather that we differ only on one point, Professor. I firmly believe these drawings had once a living model, you don't."

"Certainly not," Nordhurst stared at him as though doubting his sanity. "Surely you aren't going to suggest that at some time, on this island, there was a race of creatures like that. But it's utterly preposterous, completely ridiculous."

"Professor Nordhurst," muttered Mitchell hoarsely, keeping his temper tightly under control. "I not only believe that at one time such a race existed here on Easter Island, but that another race co-existed with them, namely the race of giants who built and erected these images. And furthermore, I'm equally convinced that we shall find sufficient evidence here to convince you."

He half expected the other to make some form of protest, but Nordhurst merely smiled knowingly and bent to examine the carvings more closely. As the work went on, more and more carvings were found on the trunk of the stone giant which lay half-uncovered now. All in all, Mitchell judged its length to be close on sixty feet and its weight many tons. How it had been brought down from the interior of Rano Rardaku without machinery of any kind, seemed an insoluble problem.

Three weeks later, the excavations had reached a stage where a few questions had been answered to Mitchell's satisfaction; but a hundred more had been posed. To them, there seemed no possible answer. The natives still refused to speak in spite of everything that Walton had been able to do to make them talk. None of the presents which had been offered to them, to their headman, or the religious head, had made the slightest effect on their refusal to talk.

On any other subject, they would converse for hours in an extremely friendly manner, but once he tried to turn the conversation towards the old times before their race had come to the island, to what they had discovered when they arrived there, the talk had abruptly dried up and they had politely refused to be drawn into any further conversation.

He was beginning to despair of ever finding out anything of importance with which to counter the sarcasm of Professor Nordhurst which was daily becoming less veiled and more direct in its manner. Then, one evening, shortly after dark, Walton came into his tent and sat down on the stool with his back to the flap.

For a long moment, he remained silent, then he said very softly: "I've been talking with one of the old men on the island. I think I've finally talked him around to telling you something. How important it will be, I don't know. But it seems that he's heard what the Professor has been saying and it must hurt his pride because he seems ready to talk."

"Did he ask you to come and fetch me?" asked Mitchell carefully. So many times in the past, he had gone out to meet these natives, only to be disappointed when he arrived. Either they had suddenly shut up like a clam or they had talked endlessly about nothing important, merely telling him several things which he already knew.

"Yes," Walton nodded. "I think we may be on to something this time. I think he's a little scared, but he'll talk. And what's more to the point, I really believe that he knows something. Not the lies they've tried to give us in the past whenever they've claimed to tell us the old secrets, but something worth knowing."

"Very well, I'll come," said Mitchell wearily, as he got to his feet. "But if this is just another false trial, then—" He left the rest of his sentence unsaid and followed the other out into the darkness. The moon was half full, lying out over the smooth water, throwing weird, grotesque shadows across the lava track which they followed around the shoulder of the hill.

Mitchell shivered as the night wind blew about him. There was sweat on his forehead and across the small of his back and it made his thin clothing stick uncomfortably to his flesh. Time seemed to pass with abnormal slowness that was oddly disconcerting and he had the feeling of eyes watching him every step of the way, unfriendly eyes, not those of the natives, but of something else which crouched in the black, moon-thrown shadows.

His ears seemed at times to catch faint sounds along the track, sounds which could not quite be identified with anything which seemed to inhabit the island normally. He wished that his senses were not so preternaturally keen in the darkness. But something in the solitude and the stillness seemed to have sharpened them above their normal pitch.

He thought of vague, irrelevant things as he stumbled close behind the other, of the strange things he had seen in other places, how they fitted in with what was here, and of the unknown, inaccessible, alien things which must have existed at the very beginning of time and which could, conceivably, still exist in such an out-of-the-way place as this, where civilization had barely touched the people, where they could still believe in the old things. This could be one of the last outposts of these alien things on earth, he reflected. He often liked to speculate about these things, but never had they seemed so vivid as at that particular moment.

Whether it was the surroundings or the utter stillness which had brought such ideas to his mind, he did not know. But in spite of everything he did, it was impossible to rid his mind of them. The deadness and the silence were virtually complete. After a while, he found himself deliberately shuffling his feet on the smooth rocks to make some kind of noise, to still the nerves which jumped and twitched spasmodically in his body.

Around him there was the suggestion of odd stirrings. Of things, half-hidden at the edge of his vision, which moved over that strange and alien landscape, lurching forward with a cumbersome manner out of the black shadows. It seemed abnormally cold, too; a coldness which could not be completely explained by the fact that they were some distance above sea level and the wind was blowing directly off the water. Nothing was so definite he could put his finger on anything wrong, and yet he felt that the swirling air about him was not uniformly quiet, that there were strange variations in pressure which made themselves felt, but which he couldn't even begin to understand.

They made their way down the narrow, twisting path as they came over the top of the hill. In front of him, he could make out nothing but blackness, then he saw the small cluster of native huts. Walton walked directly towards one of them, climbed the narrow, swaying ladder and went inside, motioning Mitchell to follow.

For some odd reason, his heart was bumping madly inside his chest as he followed on the other's heels. He hardly knew what to expect inside. There was a little candle flickering on a small table and behind it sat an old, wizened figure, skinny hands pressed firmly on top of the table.

Mitchell judged the other to be almost ninety, but from his features, it was impossible to be sure. He could have been far older than that, with only the black swiftly darting eyes alive in the skeletal face.

"Does he speak English?" asked Mitchell, seating himself in front of the other.

Walton shook his head. "No. But he knows some Spanish. I think you ought to be able to converse in that language."

Mitchell nodded, tried to force his heart into a slower, more normal beat. After all, he tried to tell himself, there was nothing to fear from the other. Merely an old man who thought he knew some of the ancient secrets, who was possibly the only one on the island who did. But would he talk? And if he did, would he be telling the truth, or were there more lies to come?

"My friend tells me that you have something you wish to speak to me about," he said slowly, loudly, speaking in Spanish.

The other's lips moved and his voice, like a dry whisper said, "You come here asking questions about the stone faces of the island. Who made them and who carried them here?"

"That's right. Do you know anything of this?"

The other nodded his head almost imperceptibly. "I would not have agreed to tell you these things had I not thought that you might believe," whispered the other thinly. He sat very still, watching Mitchell unwinkingly with black, empty eyes. "But your friend has assured me that you are not like the others, that you might believe."

"Yes, yes. Go on." Once again, Mitchell felt that curious twinge of doubt about Walton, but let it pass in the sudden surge of excitement. At last, he thought with a savage exultation, he might discover something which would show Nordhurst who had been right from the very beginning.

"If I told you that the great statues moved themselves down from Rano Raraku to where you now find them—would you believe that?" There was a beat of sarcastic humor in the dry voice.

For a moment, Mitchell felt his hands tighten on the table in front of him, then he forced himself to relax. Somehow, at the back of his mind, he had always subconsciously known that it might have been something like this, incredible as it was.

"Go on," he said tightly. "I'm not going to deny what you say."

"That is good." The other nodded his head slightly once more. "We have been here on Easter Island for many centuries, but as you will have guessed, we were not the first to come. Long before we arrived, there were others. They were not like us. Compared to them, we are as pygmies. They were the long ears whose stone faces you can see outside. Now they ring the island, watching for any who may try to escape to the sea."

"And those others. The bird-men!"

"Yes. They were here, too. The struggle between those two mighty forces was long indeed. This was the primal struggle of good and evil between the Old Ones and the Gods."

Ralph Mitchell nodded. Everything seemed to fit into place. The carvings and the manner in which those huge figures had been brought many miles from that quarry in the heart of Rano Raraku.

"So good finally triumphed," he said finally. "At least Nordhurst will have to believe me now."

He grew aware that the other was shaking his head and there was a curious smile on his lips.

"No," said the reedy voice. "That is not so. The good were not triumphant."

Mitchell stared at him, scarcely able to frame his thoughts and put them into words. He remembered the feeling which had all but overpowered him on the way there in the darkness. Suddenly, he knew what the other meant, but he wanted to hear him say it.

"No?" He forced his voice to remain steady.

"No. It was the forces of evil which triumphed over those of good. The Gods were defeated and that evil still exists here to this day. The struggle continues and will do so until the end of time."

Mitchell turned his head to glance at Walton. The other, he saw, was not looking at him, but was staring straight ahead, his lips pursed into a hard, thin line, his face fixed into a strange expression.

"Do you believe what he's saying?" he asked, switching to English. "It seems utterly fantastic."

"I warned you it might be difficult to believe," said the other quietly. "But I see no reason to disbelieve him. After all, why on earth should he lie to us? He isn't making anything out of it; and he was the one who approached us with this story."

"It's possible," admitted the other. "But somehow, I don't think that's the answer. I'm inclined to believe that he's telling us the truth."

"Do you realize what you're saying? That there still exists on the island, if not actual remains of that lost race, people who can perpetrate this evil he speaks of?"

"I know. I find it incredible, difficult to believe, but I've studied enough of these people to get to know when they're lying and when they're telling the truth."

Mitchell turned back to the old man. While they had been speaking, he had been staring into space, taking no interest in what they were saying. He scarcely seemed aware of their presence there.

Mitchell swallowed hard and forced down the sudden inexplicable rising of fear in his throat. The dark, empty eyes stared impassively into his and for a moment, the feeling was there that a black, intensely malignant aura lay around the other like some odd cocoon, spreading out from him in an evil wave. He blinked his eyes rapidly several times and forced himself to look away. It was more than likely that such men had mastered the art of some form of hypnotism, he thought tightly.

Finally, he forced himself to speak quietly. "There are writings of my people which tell of men who landed here from a ship many, many years ago. They were never seen again and the ship had to leave without them. Do you know what happened to them?"

The eyelids never flickered. "The Old Ones must have taken them," was the simple reply.

"The Old Ones?" persisted Mitchell, "and are they still here?"

"They are all here. Those that the Old Ones take to themselves have immortality. They cannot die."

Mitchell shrugged. What the other was saying was impossible, of course. This didn't make sense at all. He had the feeling that this conversation was about two different things, that neither of them was on common ground. But he was damned if he was going to let this superstitious old fool beat him. He had come here for information and he intended to get it at any cost. These natives had fobbed him off once too often. He glanced out of the corner of his eye at Walton, but the other had fallen strangely silent and seemed reluctant to take any further part in the proceedings.

"This immortality you speak of," he went on, "just what does that mean? That they still live here, as you or I, and that they'll go on living for all time?"

For the first time, the other smiled; a toothless grin that sent an involuntary shiver through him.

"They are here with the others and here they will remain," was all that he could get out of the old fellow. Finally, in exasperation, he climbed sharply to his feet, and stood looking down at the other, his face angry.

"This is what I expected, of course," he said tightly, deliberately speaking in Spanish so that the old man could understand every word. "A pack of lies and half forgotten superstitions which anyone could have told me. I don't know why I listened to you, Walton. I thought I might learn something here which would be important. More and more, I'm getting the impression that perhaps, although I don't like to admit it, Professor Nordhurst had been right all along the line. There is nothing here to bear out my ideas and theories. This expedition was nothing more than a complete waste of time. I'm going and this is the last time I agree to come and meet any of these—fools!" He spat the words out as he turned on his heel and moved towards the door. He had almost reached it when the old man called him back. There was a sharp, biting quality in his voice now, a note of warning.

"Just before you go, señor, there's one thing I want to tell you. Don't make the mistake of thinking as your friend thinks. He came here disbelieving everything and swears that nothing will change his mind. He is a very foolish man, because there are things here far beyond anything he can comprehend. I know them for what they are, the power of darkness and evil that were spawned thousands of years ago, between good and evil on this lonely island.

"Things which were born then and have not died over the centuries. They can never die so long as the island is alive. They're out there now, in the darkness. Perhaps you felt their presence on your way here tonight. But your friend will soon discover these things for himself and when that happens, be sure that you are not of the same mind as he is. Be guided by your friend here," he inclined his head slowly in Walton's direction. "He can see these things, he has the mind of one who believes."

"Is that a threat?" asked Mitchell thinly.

"Not a threat, but a warning. Believe me when I tell you that it is not a good thing to gain immortality—this way."

Ralph Mitchell glared at him in silence for a long moment, then pushed aside the straw over the entrance of the hut, clambered swiftly down the shaking ladder to the ground and stood in the cold darkness.

Above him, he could hear Walton saying something to the old man in his own tongue. Waiting for him to come, Mitchell smiled grimly. Probably the other was apologizing for what had happened. If so, he could save his words. His patience was finally almost exhausted.

From now on, he would look for these hidden things himself and take little notice of what was told him by the natives. If there was anything hidden here which they did not want him to find, then by God, he would never rest until he did find it. Until he had brought it out into the light of day and shown it proudly to the skeptics.

But in spite of all this and the seething rage inside him, he felt oddly disturbed by what the old man had said. This veiled threat against Professor Nordhurst. What exactly had that meant? Did they intend to murder him because of his beliefs—or to be more precise, his disbeliefs? On the face of it, it seemed hardly likely that anything such as that would happen at the present day, even here. Nevertheless, he wondered whether or not he ought to warn the Professor. He would probably only laugh in his face, call him a superstitious fool and tell him that all of this work was simply beginning to get on his nerves.

He decided against telling him anything of what had happened that night. Two minutes later, Walton came down the ladder, dropped to the ground beside him. Without saying a word, he led the way back along the path, towards the top of the lava ridge, on the other side of which lay their camp.

The wind had risen now and shrieked at them like a mad thing, whirling their clothing about them, hammering at their faces and yelling in their ears. Spray seemed to reach up from the depths and lash at their bodies until they were soaked to the skin. There was the sharp taste of salt on Mitchell's lips and he had to lean forward against the wind to make any headway.

The moon still shone, close to the sea now, where it was dipping towards the horizon. Gradually, however, the wind dropped until it became quite calm. Mitchell struggled forward, feet slipping on smooth lava underfoot. Walton seemed to have little difficulty in walking, holding himself stiffly upright, not having to look down at where he placed his feet. He seemed to know every inch of this way, although Mitchell could have sworn that the other had trod this path only twice since they had been on the island. The man's memory seemed fantastic, to be able to pick his way amid that jumble of rocks in almost pitch darkness.

At the top of the low, saddle-backed ridge, they paused and looked about them. Mitchell was breathing heavily by this time, his breath coming in great, gasping sobs which burst from his lips in the silence. Presently, however, as he stared about him, his eyes becoming more accustomed to the blackness, he had the peculiarly illusory impression that there were dark shapes which moved in the darkness on either side of them. He screwed up his eyes in order to see them better, knowing that in the night, averted vision was far more acute than looking straight at anything which moved.

The first movement was of tall, grotesque shadows, far taller than a man, but having human shape which seemed to glide down the side of Rano Raraku some distance to the east. Then, abruptly, they were no longer shadows, but solid things, most of them upright but some wriggling along the ground with a terrible sinuous motion. He opened his mouth to scream, but Walton, stepping forward to his side, clamped a hand over his mouth and muttered a hissed warning.

Not until the convulsive shivering in his body had died away, did the other remove his hand and release his restraining hold on Mitchell's arm. Then he could only stand there, dumbly, the muscles of his throat constricted so that no sound could possibly have been uttered even if he had wanted to shriek out loud with what he saw. Those vast colossi, those graven images which looked out forever across the rolling, undulating hills of Easter Island, were moving in utter silence through the darkness.

Oh God, his mind screamed at him, colossi like this had no right to be moving around at all, and certainly not in such utter silence. The sight caused every hair, even the tiny growths on the back of his hands, to rise with a vague fright beyond all description or classification. For a moment, he lost all power to draw a single breath. His lungs seemed crushed and paralyzed. His eyes were starting from his head.

Was this what the old man had meant when he had said that the Old Ones, the evil ones, were still on the island, that they had immortality?

Now, he saw it all clearly and the thought itself was what brought all of the horror to a head. Of course the Old Ones were immortal. There was nothing on the island which could outlive those vast stone images.

The terror seeped through him in a surging wave, leaving his body exhausted, his spirit spent. How long they stood there, watching that terrible sight, it was impossible to estimate. When he could finally think clearly again, when the breath came back into his body and the mad thumping of his heart had subsided, the moon had sunk out of sight below the western horizon and there was no further movement in the pitch blackness where only the bright, alien stars looked down on the scene.

It was a long time before he could pull himself together completely. Then he turned to look at Walton. If he had expected to see an expression of fear on the other's face, he was strangely disappointed. Instead, there was a look which he could not analyze.

"I think we had better go now," said Walton in a strange voice. "The others will be wondering where we've got to and I think you've seen enough."

"It must have been imagination," whispered Mitchell, more to himself than to the other. "Yes, yes, that's it. Nothing but imagination, something conjured up by that old fool's talk." He was babbling a little wildly now, but he did not realize it.

The other smiled, turned and led the way down the side of the ridge, back to camp. As they approached, Mitchell saw that there were torches burning among the tents and that most of the men were still awake and moving hurriedly around, fully dressed. Possibly they were making ready to come looking for Walton and himself, he thought, and wiped the sweat from his forehead. Nobody would believe their story, even if they told it to them. He licked his lips dryly and knew that he would have to remain silent, would have to keep it to himself unless he wanted them to lock him away in some asylum.

He could imagine what Nordhurst would say if he ever learned of it. The Skipper came rushing towards them as they came within the circle of torchlight. He seemed agitated.

"Where've you been at this time of night, Doctor Mitchell?" he asked harshly. "And is the Professor with you?"

"Professor Nordhurst—why no, he isn't with us." There was a sudden feeling of alarm in Mitchell's mind. That strange threat which the old native had made against Nordhurst. Had there been anything in it?

"He must have gone off somewhere," said the other throatily. "His bed seems to have been slept in, but judging from the ground around the hut and inside, there seems to have been some kind of struggle. We wondered whether any of the natives had come while we were asleep and the Professor had caught them at the usual game of stealing our equipment. Nobody seems to have heard anything, although Carlton here thought he heard a faint scream, but imagined that it had been one of the sea-birds. It wasn't until we decided to check with the lookout that we found he had gone. Then we discovered you and Doctor Walton were missing too."

"Doctor Walton and I have been over to the native village," said Mitchell, just a trifle too quickly. "But we saw nothing of the Professor. If he did decide to go anywhere, it must have been in the opposite direction. In the moonlight, we ought to have seen him if he had been anywhere in that direction."

"We'll make a thorough search in the morning, sir," said the Skipper tightly. "He may have gone over to have a word with the Governor, but I wouldn't have thought that would be likely at this hour of the night.

"Don't worry, though, we'll find him even if we have to take this whole island apart. There isn't going to be any repetition of what happened when the Spaniards came."

But though they searched all of the following day, and for several days afterwards, there was no sign of Professor Nordhurst. The Governor ordered all of the natives to make a search in any of the secret places known to them, but without avail. The only possible explanation was that the Professor had vanished off the face of the island as if he had never existed.

For six weeks, while the search continued, excavations were made at various points on the island. Some evidence to support Mitchell's theory was turned up, but with Nordhurst's mysterious disappearance, there was no sense of triumph in this. Now that the chief antagonist of his ideas had vanished, he lost all interest in the expedition. He was strangely glad when the time came for them to leave.

As the anchor rattled metallically up the sides of the ship, Mitchell stood on deck, leaning against the rail, staring at the dim greenness of Easter Island. Through the powerful binoculars, he could make out the various landmarks which he had grown to know so well. Halfway up the wide slope was the isolated figure of the statue they had dug out of the ground, exposing the entire body for its tremendous length of sixty feet. Around it were others, still standing there or lying on their faces. He moved the binoculars gently from side to side, studying the faces with a detached interest.

That there was some mystery, there was not any doubt but—

His thoughts gelled in his head. His hands shook so violently that he could scarcely hold the glasses steady as he stared at the vast stone face, the only one looking out to sea, the face of Nordhurst as he had seen him just before he had vanished.

THERE ARE MORE THINGS

BY JORGE LUIS BORGES

ON THE POINT OF TAKING MY LAST EXAMINATION AT THE
University of Texas, in Austin, I learned that my uncle Edwin Arnett had
died of an aneurysm at the far end of the South American continent.
I felt what we all feel when someone dies—remorse, now pointless, for
not having been kinder. We forget that we are all dead men conversing
with dead men. My course of study was philosophy. I remembered that
it was my uncle, at the Casa Colorada, his home near Lomas, on the
edge of Buenos Aires, who, without invoking a single proper name,
had first revealed to me philosophy's beautiful perplexities. One of
the after-dinner oranges was his aid in initiating me into Berkeley's
idealism; a chessboard was enough to illustrate the paradoxes of the
Eleatics. Years later, he was to lend me Hinton's treatises which attempt
to demonstrate the reality of four-dimensional space and which the
reader is meant to imagine by means of complicated exercises with
multicoloured cubes. I shall never forget the prisms and pyramids that
we erected on the floor of his study.

My uncle was an engineer. Before retiring from his job with the
railroad, he decided to build himself a house in Turdera, which offered
the advantages of almost country-like solitude and of proximity to the
city. Nothing was more predictable than that the architect should be
his close friend Alexander Muir. This uncompromising man followed
the uncompromising teachings of John Knox. My uncle, like almost all
the gentlemen of his day, had been a freethinker or, rather, an agnostic,
but he was interested in theology, just as he was interested in Hinton's

unreal cubes and in the well-constructed nightmares of the young H. G. Wells. He liked dogs, and he had a great sheepdog that he had named Samuel Johnson, in memory of Lichfield, his far-off birthplace.

The Casa Colorada stood on a height of land, bordered on the west by sun-blackened fields. Inside its fence, the araucarias did nothing to soften its air of gloom. Instead of a flat roof, there was a slate-tiled saddle roof and a square tower with a clock. These seemed to oppress the walls and the meager windows. As a boy, I used to accept all this ugliness, just as one accepts those incompatible things which, only because they coexist, are called the world.

I returned home in 1921. To avoid legal complications, the house had been auctioned off. It was bought by a foreigner, a Max Preetorius, who paid double what was offered by the highest bidder. No sooner was the deed signed than he arrived, late one afternoon, with two helpers and they carted off to a rubbish dump, not far from the old Drover's Road, all the furniture, all the books, and all the utensils of the house. (I sadly recalled the diagrams in the Hinton volumes and the great globe.) The next day, Preetorius went to Muir and proposed certain alterations that the architect indignantly rejected. In the end, a firm from Buenos Aires took charge of the work. The local carpenters refused to furnish the house again. Finally, a certain Mariani, from Glew, accepted the conditions laid down by Preetorius. For an entire fortnight he had to labour by night behind closed doors. It was also by night that the new owner of the Casa Colorada moved in. The windows no longer opened, but chinks of light could be made out in the dark. One morning, the milkman found the sheepdog dead on the walk, headless and mutilated. That winter they felled the araucarias. Nobody saw Preetorius again.

News of these events, as may be imagined, left me uneasy. I know that my most obvious trait is curiosity—that same curiosity that brought me together with a woman completely different from me only in order to find out who she was and what she was like, to take up (without appreciable results) the use of laudanum, to explore transfinite numbers, and to undertake the hideous adventure that I am about to tell. Ominously, I decided to look into the matter.

My first step was to see Alexander Muir. I remembered him as tall-standing and dark, with a wiry build that suggested strength. Now the years had stooped him and his black beard had gone grey. He received me at his Temperley house, which, foreseeably, was like my uncle's, since both houses followed the solid standards of the good poet and bad builder William Morris.

Conversation was sparse—Scotland's symbol, after all, is the thistle. I had the feeling, nonetheless, that the strong Ceylon tea and the equally generous plate of scones (which my host broke in two and buttered for me as if I were still a boy) were, in fact, a frugal Calvinistic feast offered to the nephew of his friend. His theological differences with my uncle had been a long game of chess, demanding of each player the collaboration of his opponent.

Time passed and I was no nearer my business. There was an uncomfortable silence and Muir spoke. "Young man," he said, "you have not come all this way to talk about Edwin or the United States, a country that I have little interest in. What's troubling you is the sale of the Casa Colorada and its odd buyer. They do me, too. Frankly, the story displeases me, but I'll tell you what I can. It will not be much."

After a while he went on, unhurriedly. "Before Edwin died, the mayor called me into his office. He was with the parish priest. They asked me to draw the plans for a Catholic chapel. My work would be well paid. On the spot, I answered no. I am a servant of God and I cannot commit the abomination of erecting altars to idols." Here he stopped.

"Is that all?" I finally dared to ask.

"No. This whelp of a Jew Preetorius wanted me to destroy my work and in its place get up a monstrous thing. Abomination comes in many shapes." He pronounced these words gravely and got to his feet.

Outside, on turning the corner, I was approached by Daniel Iberra. We knew one another the way people in small towns do. He suggested that we accompany each other back to Turdera. I have never been keen on hoodlums, and I expected a sordid litany of violent and more or less apocryphal back-room stories, but I gave in and accepted his invitation. It was very nearly nightfall. On seeing the Casa Colorada come into view from a few blocks off, Iberra made a detour. I asked him why. His reply was not what I anticipated.

"I am don Felipe's right arm," he said. "Nobody has ever called me soft. That young Urgoiti who took the trouble to come looking for me all the way from Merlo—you probably remember what happened to him. Look. A few nights ago, I was returning from a party. A hundred yards or so from that house I saw something. My horse reared up, and if I hadn't had a good grip on him and made him turn down an alley, maybe I wouldn't be telling this story now. What I saw justified the horse's fright." Angrily, Iberra added a swear word.

That night I did not sleep. Around dawn, I dreamed about an engraving that I had never seen before or that I had seen and forgotten; it was in the style of Piranesi, and it had a labyrinth in it. It was a stone amphitheatre ringed by cypresses, above whose tops it reached. There were neither doors nor windows; rather, it displayed an endless row of narrow vertical slits. With a magnifying glass, I tried to see the Minotaur inside. At last, I made it out. It was a monster of a monster, more bison than bull, and, its human body stretched out on the ground, it seemed to be asleep and dreaming. Dreaming of what or of whom?

That evening, I passed by the Casa Colorada. The iron gate was shut and some of its bars were bent. What once was garden was now overgrown with weeds. To the right, there was a shallow ditch and its outer edges were trampled.

There was only one move left, but for days I kept putting it off—not because I felt it to be altogether a waste, but because it would drag me to the inevitable, to the last.

Without much hope, I went to Glew. Mariani, the carpenter, was a stout, pink-faced Italian, common and cordial and now somewhat advanced in years. A glance at him was enough for me to dismiss the stratagems I had contrived the night before. I handed him my card, which he pompously spelled out aloud with a certain reverential stumbling when he reached the "Ph.D." I told him I was interested in the furniture made by him for the house in Turdera that had been my uncle's. The man spoke on and on. I shall not try to transcribe his torrent of words and gestures, but he told me that his motto was to satisfy his customer's every demand, no matter how outlandish it was, and that he had carried out his work to the letter. After rummaging in various drawers he showed me some papers that I could make neither head nor tail of; they were signed by the elusive Preetorius. (Doubtless, Mariani mistook me for a lawyer.) On saying goodbye, he confided to me that even for all the world's gold he would never again set foot in Turdera, let alone that house. He added that the customer is sacred, but that in his humble opinion Mr. Preetorius was crazy. Then he grew quiet, obviously repentant. I was unable to worm anything more out of him.

I had allowed for this failure, but it is one thing to allow for something and quite another to see it happen. Time and again, I said to myself that the solution of this enigma did not concern me and that the one true enigma was time, that seamless chain of past, present, and future, of the ever and the never. Such reflections turned out to be useless, however; after whole afternoons devoted to the study of Schopenhauer or Royce, night after night I would walk the dirt roads ringing the Casa Colorada. Sometimes I caught a glimpse upstairs of a very white light; other times, I thought I heard a moaning. It went on this way until the nineteenth of January.

It was one of those Buenos Aires days when a man feels himself not only bullied and insulted by the summer but even debased by it. At around eleven o'clock at night the storm broke. First came the south wind, and then the water in torrents. I wandered about looking for a tree. In the sudden glare of a lightning flash I found myself a few steps from the fence. Whether out of fear or hope I don't know, but I tried the gate. Unexpectedly, it opened. I made my way, pushed along by the storm. Sky and earth threatened me. The door of the house was also open. A squall of rain lashed my face and I went in.

Inside, the floor tiles had been torn up and I stepped on matted grass. A sweet, sickening smell filled the house. Right or left, I'm not sure which, I tripped on a stone ramp. Quickly, I went up. Almost unawares, I turned on the light switch.

The dining room and the library of my memories were now, with the wall between them torn down, a single great bare room containing one or two pieces of furniture. I shall not try to describe them, since I am not altogether sure—in spite of the cruel white light—of having seen them. Let me explain myself. To see a thing one has to comprehend it. An armchair presupposes the human body, its joints and limbs; a pair of scissors, the act of cutting. What can be said of a lamp or a car? The savage cannot comprehend the missionary's Bible; the passenger does not see the same rigging as the sailors. If we really saw the world, maybe we would understand it.

None of the meaningless shapes that that night granted me corresponded to the human figure or, for that matter, to any conceivable use. I felt revulsion and terror. In one of the corners, I found a ladder which led to the upper floor. The spaces between the iron rungs, which were no more than ten, were wide and irregular. That ladder, implying hands and feet, was comprehensible, and in some way this relieved me. I put out the light and waited for some time in the dark. I did not hear the least sound, but the presence there of incomprehensible things disquieted me. In the end, I made up my mind.

Once upstairs, my fearful hand switched on the light a second time. The nightmare that had foreshadowed the lower floor came alive and flowered on the next. Here there were either many objects or a few linked together. I now recall a sort of long operating table, very high and in the shape of a U, with round hollows at each end. I thought that maybe it was the bed of the house's inhabitant, whose monstrous anatomy revealed itself in this way, implicitly, like an animal's or a god's by its shadow. From some page or other of Lucan there came to my lips the word "amphisbaena", which hinted at, but which certainly did not exhaust, what my eyes were later to see. I also remember a V of mirrors that became lost in the upper darkness.

What would the inhabitant be like? What could it be looking for on this planet, no less hideous to it than it to us? From what secret regions of astronomy or time, from what ancient and now incalculable dusk can it have reached this South American suburb and this particular night?

I felt an intruder in the chaos. Outside, the rain had stopped. I looked at my watch and saw with astonishment that it was almost two o'clock. I left the light on and carefully began climbing down. To get down the way I had come up was not impossible—to get down before the inhabitant returned. I guessed that it had not locked the doors because it did not know how.

My feet were touching the next to last rung of the ladder when I felt that something, slow and oppressive and two-fold, was coming up the ramp. Curiosity overcame my fear, and I did not shut my eyes.

THE HORROR OUT OF TIME

BY RANDALL GARRETT

IT HAS BEEN MORE THAN THIRTY YEARS NOW SINCE I SAW THAT terrifying thing in the crypt-like temple, but I remember it as clearly, and with all the horror, as if I had seen it but an hour ago.

In those days, twenty years before the turn of the century, the sailing ship still held sway over most of the world's waters; now, the steam-driven vessels cover in days distances that took months. All that no longer matters to me; I have not been abroad since I returned from that South Sea voyage, still weak from fever and delirium, over thirty years ago.

I think that before the end of this new century, scientific researchers will have proven as fact things which I already know to be true. What facts lie behind the mysteries of certain megalithic ruined cities found buried beneath the shifting sands on three separate continents? Are they merely the constructs of our prehistoric ancestors? Or are they much older than we know, the products of some primal race, perhaps from this planet, perhaps from another, far distant in space? The latter sounds wild, phantastick, perhaps even... mad, but I believe it to be true, and mayhap this narrative will be of some service to those researchers who already suspect the truth. Long before our ancestors discovered the use of fire, even before they had evolved beyond animal form and intellect, there were beings of vast power and malignant intelligence who ruled supreme over this planet.

I have always been a person of leisure, spending my time in historical research, in reading books on philosophy, both natural and metaphysical, and in writing what I believe to be scholarly articles for various learned journals. When I was younger, I was more adventurous; I traveled a great deal, not only to read and research in the great universities of the world, but to do original research in hidden places of the earth, where few learned folk have gone. I was fearless then; neither the rotten fetidness of tropic jungles, nor the arid heat of harsh deserts, nor the freezing cold of polar regions daunted me.

Until the summer of my twenty-sixth year.

I was aboard the *White Moon*, sailing homeward through the South Seas, after having spent some months exploring the ancient ruins on one of the larger islands. (Their age can be measured in mere centuries; they have nothing to do with the present narrative.)

During the time I had been aboard, I had become quite friendly with Captain Bork, the commander of the three-masted vessel. He was a heavy-set, bluff, hearty fellow, an excellent ship's officer, and well-read in many subjects far divergent from mere nautical lore. Although self-educated, his behavior was that of one gently born, far above that of the common sailor of the day. He was perhaps a dozen years older than I, but we spent many an hour during that tedious journey discussing various subjects, and I dare say I learned as much from him as he learned from me. We became, I think, good friends.

One evening, I recall, we sat up rather late in his cabin, discoursing on daemonology.

"I'm not a superstitious chap, myself, sir," said he, "but I will tell you that there are things that take place at sea that could never happen on land. Things I couldn't explain if I tried."

"And you attribute them to non-material spirits, Captain?" I asked. "Surely not."

In the dim light shed by the oil-lamp swinging gently overhead, his face took on a solemn expression. "Not spirits, perhaps, sir. No, not spirits exactly. Something... else."

I became interested. I knew the captain's sincerity, and I knew that, whatever he had to tell me, it would be told as he knew it to be.

"What, then, if not spirits?" I asked.

He looked broodingly out the porthole of his cabin. "I don't really know," he said slowly in his low, rumbling voice, staring out at the moonless sea-night. After a moment, he looked back at me, but there was no change in his expression. "I don't really know," he repeated. "It may be daemons or spirits or whatever, but it's not the feeling one gets in a graveyard, if you see what I mean. It's different, somehow. It's as if there were something down *there*—"

And he pointed straight downward, as though he were directing my attention down past the deck, past the hull, to the dreadful black sea-bottom so far beneath. I could say nothing.

"*Way* down there," he continued solemnly. "There is something *old* down there—something old, but living. It is far older than we can know. It goes far back beyond the dawn of time. But it is there and it... *waits*."

A feeling of revulsion came over me—not against the captain, but against the sea itself, and I realized that I, too, had felt that nameless fear without knowing it.

But of course I could not fall prey to that weird feeling.

"Come, Captain," said I, in what I hoped was a pleasant tone, "this is surely your imagination. What intelligence could live at the bottom of the sea?"

He looked at me for a long moment, then his countenance changed. There was a look of forced cheerfulness upon his broad face. "Aye, sir, you're right. A person gets broody at sea, that's all. I fear I've been at sea too long. Have to take a long rest ashore, I will. I've been planning a month in port, and it'll rid me of these silly notions. Will you have another drink, sir?"

I did, and by the time I was in my own cabin, I had almost forgotten the conversation. I lay in my bunk and went fast asleep.

I was awakened by the howling of the wind through the rigging. The ship was heaving from side to side, and I realized that heavy seas had overtaken her. From above, I heard the shouts of the captain and the first mate. I do not remember what they were, for I am not fully conversant with nautical terms, but I could hear the various members of the crew shouting in reply.

It was still dark, and, as it was summertime in the southern hemisphere, that meant that it was still early. I hadn't the faintest notion of time, but I knew I had not slept long.

I got out of my bunk and headed topside.

It is difficult, even now, for me to describe that storm. The sea was rolling like a thing alive, but the wind was almost mild. It shifted, now blowing one way, now another, but it came nowhere near heavy gale force. The *White Moon* swerved this way and that under its influence, as though we were caught in some monstrous whirlpool that changed its direction of swirl at varying intervals.

There were no clouds directly overhead. The stars shone as usual in every direction save to the west, where one huge black cloud seemed to blot the sky.

I heard the Captain shout: "Get below, sir! Get below! You're only a hindrance on deck! *Get below!*"

I was, after all, no sailor, and he was master of the ship, so I went back to my cabin to wait the storm out. I know not how long that dreadful storm lasted, for there was no dawn that day. The enveloping cloud from the west had spread like heavy smoke, almost blocking out the sun, and the sky was still a darkling grey when the sea subsided into gentle swells. Shortly after it had done so, there was a rap at my cabin door.

"The Captain would like to see you on deck, sir," said a sailor's rough voice from without.

I accompanied the sailor up the ladder to the weather deck, where Captain Bork was staring into the greyness abaft the starboard rail.

"What is it, Captain?" I inquired.

Without looking at me, he asked, "Do you smell that, sir?"

I had already perceived the stench which permeated the sea air about us. There was the nauseous aroma of rotting sea flesh combined with the acrid bitterness of burning sulphur. Before I could answer his question, the Captain continued. "I caught that smell once before many years ago." He turned to look at me. "Have you smelt it before, sir?"

"Once," I said. "Not exactly the same, Captain, but similar. It was near a volcano. But there was no smell of rotten fish."

Captain Bork nodded his massive head. "Aye, sir. That's the smell of it. Somewhere to the west—" He pointed toward the area where the black cloud was densest. "—there's been a volcanic explosion, the like of which we've not seen before. I knew it was no ordinary storm; this is not the season for typhoon."

"But what is that horrid miasma of decay?" I asked. "No volcano ever gave off a smell like that."

Before the Captain could answer, a call came from the top of the mizzenmast. "Land Ho-o-o-o!"

Captain Bork jerked his head around and squinted toward the north. He thrust an arm out, pointing. "Land it is, sir," he said to me, "and that's where your stench comes from. The seas are shallow in these parts, but there should be no islands about. Look."

In the dim, wan light I saw a low, bleak headland that loomed above the surging surface of the sea.

I knew then what had happened. The volcanic eruption, and the resulting seismic shock, had lifted a part of the sea bottom above the surface. There before us, in black basalt, was a portion of the seabed which had been inundated for untold millennia. It was from that newly risen plateau that the revolting odour came, wafted by the gusting sea-breeze.

The Captain began giving orders. There were certain repairs which had to be made, and he felt it would be better to have the ship at anchor for the work, so he directed that the ship be brought in close to the newly risen island. Not too close, of course; if another volcanic quake stirred the sea, he wanted leeway between the White Moon and those forbidding rocks.

He found water shallow enough to set the anchors, and the crew went to work with a will. The stench from the island, while mephitic enough, was not really strong, and we soon grew accustomed to it.

I was of no use whatever aboard, and might as well have gone to my cabin and stayed there while the crew worked, but there was something about that bleak, malodorous island that drew my attention powerfully. The ship was anchored roughly parallel to the beach, with the island to port, so I found a spot forward where I would be out of the way of the work and examined the island minutely with a spyglass I had borrowed from Captain Bork.

The island was tiny; one could have walked across it with no trouble at all, had it been level and even. But it would be much more difficult over that craggy, slippery black surface.

The close-up view through the spyglass only made the island look the more uninviting. Rivulets of sea water, still draining from the upper plateau, cut through sheets of ancient slime that oozed gelatinously down the precipitate slopes to the coral-encrusted beach below. Pools of nauseous-looking liquid formed in pockets of dark rock and bubbled slowly and obscenely. As I watched, I became obsessed with the feeling that I had seen all this before in some hideous nightmare.

Then something at the top of the cliff caught my eye. It was something farther inland, and I had to readjust the focus of my instrument to see it clearly. For a moment, I held my breath. *It appeared to be the broken top of an embattled tower!*

It could not be, of course. I told myself that it was merely some chance formation of rock. But I had to get a better view of it.

I went in search of the Captain and requested his permission to climb a little way up the rigging, so that my point of view would be above the top of the cliff. Busy as he was, he granted my request almost offhandedly. Up I went, and used the spyglass once again.

The tower was plainly visible now. It appeared to be one of two, the second broken off much lower than the first. Both rose from one end of a rectangular block that might have been a partly buried building, as if some great fortress, aeons old, still stood there.

Or was my over-fervid imagination making too much of what, after all, was more likely to be a natural formation? I have often watched cloud formations take on weird and phantastick shapes as the wind shifts them across the sky; could not this be the same or a similar phenomenon? I forced my mind to be more objective, to look at the vista before me as it actually was, not as I might imagine it to be.

The spyglass showed clearly that the surface of that ugly, looming structure was composed of coral-like cells and small shellfish like those which cling to the bottom of sea-going vessels when they have not been drydocked for too long a time. The edges of the building—if building it was—were rounded, and not angular. It could be merely happenstance, a natural formation of rock which had been covered, over the millennia, by limeshell creatures which had given that natural structure a vague, blurred outline resembling an ancient fortress. Still, would not a genuine artifact of that size and shape have looked the same if it were covered with the same encrustations? I could not decide. Even after the most minute examination through the spyglass, I could not decide. There was but one thing to do, so I approached the Captain with my request.

"Go ashore?" Captain Bork said in astonishment. "No, sir; I could not allow that! In the first place, it is far too dangerous. Those rocks are slippery and afford too precarious a foothold. And look to the west; that volcano is still active; a second quake might submerge that island again as easily as the first raised it. In the second place, I cannot, at this time, spare the men to row you ashore in a longboat."

I had to make a firm stand. "Captain," said I, "surely you realise the tremendous scientific importance of this discovery. If that structure is, as I surmise, an artifact rather than a natural configuration of stone, the failure to investigate it would be an incalculable loss to science."

It required some little time to convince the Captain, but after I had persuaded him to climb the rigging and look for himself, he conceded to my request, albeit grudgingly.

"Very well, sir, since you insist. Two of my crew will row you ashore. Since we are within easy hailing distance, they will return and work until you call. I cannot do more. I feel it is risky—no, more than that; it is downright foolhardy. But you are not a cub, sir; you have the right to do as you wish, no matter how dangerous." Then his stern countenance changed. "To be honest, sir, I would come with you if I could. But my duty lies with my ship."

"I understand, Captain," said I. Actually, I had no desire for him to come ashore with me. At that time, I wanted to make any discovery that might be made by myself. If any glory were to be earned in that exploration, I wanted to earn it myself. How bitterly was I to repent that feeling later!

The "beach"—if such it could be called—was merely a slope of sharp coral permeated with stinking slime. I had had the good sense to dress properly in heavy boots and water-resistant clothing, but, close up, the nauseating odour was almost unbearable. Still, I had asked for it, and I must bear it.

The "beach" ended abruptly with a cliff nearly twice my own height, and I had to circle round to find a declivity I could negotiate.

Up I went, but it was hard going over those slippery, jagged rocks to the more level portion of the island.

I cannot, even now, describe the encroaching dread that came over me as I topped that rise and beheld the structure that squatted obscenely before me. Had I had less foolish courage, I might have turned, even then, and called back the longboat that was moving away, back toward the *White Moon*. But there was the matter of youthful pride. Having committed myself, I must go on, lest I be thought a coward by the Captain and crew of that gallant ship.

I made my way carefully across that broken field of coral-covered basalt but, try as I might, I could not avoid slipping now and then. More than once my feet slid into malodorous pools of ichthyic ooze. I would not care to take that walk today, for I am more brittle and my muscles are not as strong as they were then; even my younger, stronger self was fortunate that he did not break something.

Suddenly the going became easier. The area around that looming structure, some ten or twelve paces from the base of the wall, was quite level and covered with pebbles and fine sand rather than coral. But even up close those dripping, encrusted walls gave no clue as to whether they were natural or artificial. Slowly, carefully, I walked along the wall toward the east and, after thirty paces, turned the corner and continued north, along the shorter side of the structure. That eastern wall was as blank and unyielding of any evidence as the previous one had been. At the next corner I turned west and walked along the northern wall. It, too, looked exactly the same as the southern one. It was not until I came to the fourth side that I saw the opening.

I approached the breach in the wall with equal dread and fascination. Here, at last, I might find an avenue through which to reach the answers I sought. I paused at its edge, reluctant somehow to look inside. The way was difficult here, for a great stone slab lay flat on the sand, a mire-filled trench marking where it must have been resting upright for millennia, until the recent volcanic disturbance unbalanced and toppled it, unsealing the doorway before me.

There was no question remaining in my mind that it was indeed a doorway; a single fearful glance revealed a smooth, dry stone floor. Even in the wan grey light of the smoke-clouded day, an astounding fact was evident to me; that the mysterious structure was indeed an artifact constructed by intelligent beings, and that until a few hours ago the stone slab at my feet had covered the doorway which surrounded me, sealing out the corrosive sea water.

The vapours which wafted from within were malodorous enough, but the stench was musty and dry. In spite of the strong sense of foreboding that was tugging at my heart and bowels, I could no longer contain my scientific curiosity. I slipped from my back the supply pack provided me by the Captain, and drew out the most bulky object, one of the ship's lamps. Beside the great slab of stone, I struggled with flint and steel to light the oily wick.

I recall clearly how I felt at that moment. The *White Moon* seemed aeons away, unreachable. I told myself that the excitement which made my body tremble was the incredible fortune of my find. That I should be at this place and time to avail myself of this unprecedented opportunity seemed miraculous. A different angle of course, a slightly stronger wind, the Captain refusing flatly to have me escorted to these forbidding shores; any of these might have deprived me of the knowledge I was about to gain.

So I told myself then. But looking back I know that I searched my mind for some rational reason for the lump of fear that seemed to choke me. For I am sure, now, that in my heart I already knew that what I had found would change my life in ways far different from the fortune and acclaim I tried so hard to believe I would receive.

The lamp finally caught, and its cheerful yellow light was most welcome. Braced up by its dancing glow, shielded within it from the baleful grey of the day, I walked into that ancient, long-hidden temple.

How did I know, immediately, that the large, shadow-shrouded room I entered had been a place of worship? I have tried, many times, to understand what I sensed when I stepped through that doorway. I can describe it only as a many-particular presence, a malignant energy which swelled and eddied around me. And that energy was not random or undirected. It was focused far across the floor, against the far wall. The area was completely hidden from the brave little light of my oil lamp—to inspect it I would have to cross the great room.

Gone, now, was the brief impulse of bravado inspired by the lighting of the lantern. I moved across that endless room in the grip of a terror so profound that my mind was virtually paralyzed. I walked not through my own volition, but out of a reluctance to resist the pressure of that force which surrounded me, drawing me inexorably to the hidden area where I knew I would find an answer which I was becoming ever more certain *I did not want to find!*

The lamp swayed with my every step, casting inadequate illumination on the pillars that lined my path, and causing fearsome shadows to billow out into the blankness beyond them. I could see symbols on the pillars; unintelligible, weird carvings which were somehow utterly repulsive, and from which I looked quickly away. Now and then the nether regions of the room would catch a ray of light and reveal drifts of dust, all that remained of wooden furniture or fabric wall-hangings. A part of me still stubbornly mourned the loss and surmised that the originals had been perfectly preserved until the advent of fresh air had accelerated their long-delayed decomposition. But that objective, scientific interest was almost totally submerged in a great relief that I was spared the scenes depicted in those ancient tapestries.

If those aspects of the huge room which I could see in the glow of my lantern contributed to a sense of apprehension, consider the effect of the vast areas which remained concealed. I began to fill the darkened corners with fancy. What lurked there, just beyond the light, watching me? Did I hear whispering in the gloom above me, or was it only the sea-breeze becoming reacquainted with these aged stones? Surely the latter was true, for I could smell afresh, with sharpened senses, the foetid odour of the "beach." Or was this scent original within the temple, caused by the same sudden decay of once-living flesh as had struck the objects which had been reduced to dust?

For the first time in my young life, I cursed the imagination which had always enriched physical experience for me. If I persisted in conjuring spectres to satisfy my straining senses...

I saw the altar.

It rested atop a long, shallow stairway which stretched the whole width of the aisle. From where I was, I could see three steps, a long platform, and another set of three steps. At the end of that second platform stood a massive block, only a rectangular shape at the end of the light.

I recognized that it functioned as an altar because I could now sense the exact focus of the energies which had drawn me across the room. On the wall above and behind the altar was an idol. Not even its vaguest outline was visible to me, yet I knew it was there, and that when I looked upon it, I would know the truth.

At the moment I looked back across the blackness at the patch of grey gloom that was the only doorway, the only way in... or out. I knew that I had reached the only remaining moment of choice. To mount the first step toward the altar was to commit myself unremittingly to viewing what waited beyond it. I could turn back now, escape this dark and horrid place, return to the honest sunlight, however obscure.

But with my goal in sight, the hard stone step at the toe of my boot, I was shamed by the memory of my terrifying phantasies. I could not quite scoff at them, standing as I was almost within reach of what I could think of only as a *sacrificial* altar. But I argued with valid logic that the truth, whatever it might be, would dispel forever the lingering trauma of that fancy-ridden trek. So, with a grand and foolish determination, I turned and stepped upward.

As the altar loomed into the circle of light I carried with me, I could not repress a shudder of horror. Here was not the indestructible grey stone I had seen throughout the temple, but a giant block of scabrous white marble. Once smooth and gleaming, it had been etched and scarred by the elements of the air confined for—how long?—within these walls. The pattern of the marbled surface was lost beneath scattered patches that reflected an unhealthy white, as though some thin, pallid fungus were feeding on the evil, glistening stone.

I looked down at last upon the entire altar, and try as I did to resist, I was swept up in another eddy of phantasy. For what blasphemous rituals had this hideous altar been used? I could not shake the impression that living sacrifice had been offered here. In my mind's eye I could see a razor-sharp spear blade hovering ever nearer a terrified victim whose outline was blurred and unclear. And who—or what— held that threatening blade? Was this really only phantasy, or was I seeing a scene so often repeated that its impression had remained these countless thousands of years?

I knew the moment had come. I lifted high my lantern and looked upon the thing to which the ancient sacrifice had been made.

The carven image on that wall was never meant for our eyes. I am the only person who has ever seen it, and time has not yet erased my sense of utter revulsion when the light of my lantern exposed it at last. Numbed by the horror of it, I stood as if paralyzed for what seemed an interminably long time; then, driven nearly mad by that ghastly visage, I threw the lamp at it with all my strength, as though I could destroy the sight of it. I must have screamed, but I can remember only the echoing of my boots as I ran back to the welcoming gloom of the still-dark day, fled for my soul's sake from that revolting and nauseous vision.

Past that, my memory is unclear. I retain an impression still of the total panic in my mind, as my body ran back across the sandy level to the noxious sea-scudded rocks. Some thankful instinct guided me toward the *White Moon*. The joy that surged through me when I saw her masts above the slimy crest that marked the edge of the "beach" is totally indescribable. Those masts represented safety, refuge, security. To my unbalanced mind they represented wholesomeness. All I need do, so my mind ran, was reach the *White Moon*—there I would find forgetfulness. It would be as though I had never set foot in that gruesome temple; it would never have happened at all. And how I longed to escape the memory of that place, of the indescribable horror that ruled over that dishonourable altar!

I ran for the *White Moon*'s masts, slipping and falling, heedless of the dangerous coral which cut repeatedly at my extremities. With a soulfelt sob of relief, I ran straight over the edge of the crest and plummeted to the breach below.

I do not remember the pain; all I remember is the shock of the blow that knocked the breath out of me. And then, gratefully, I gave myself up to the sweet oblivion of unconsciousness.

I was told later that I was unconscious for two days, and thus did not experience the second volcanic eruption and the resulting quake which allowed the merciful sea to flood over and cover again that horrid island and its tomb-like temple.

Some infection from the coral cuts must have invaded my body, for I was in a fevered delirium for the next five days.

But delirium or no, I did not imagine that carven figure above that gruesome altar. No living thing has that much imagination, even in delirium.

I can still see it clearly in my mind's eye, although I would far rather forget it. It tells too much about the horrible and blasphemous rites which must have been performed in that evil place, rites practiced by monstrous beings that ruled this planet a quarter of a million or more years ago.

The hideous thing was almost indescribable, and I cannot, *will not*, bring myself to draw it. It was thin and emaciated-looking, with two tiny, deep-sunken eyes and a small mouth surrounded by some kind of bristles or antennae. The muscles were clearly visible, as though its flesh were all on the outside. It had only two arms, and these were flung wide. The horrible, five-fingered hands and the five-toed feet *were nailed firmly to a great stone cross!*

THE RECURRING DOOM

BY S. T. JOSHI

NEVER IN THE HISTORY OF THE WORLD HAD CIVILIZATION SO closely escaped annihilation as in that period of time over two months ago wherein occurred those incidents in which my friend and colleague Jefferson Coler and I were involved; never in all the years of man's existence had such a shadow of death passed over all humanity, to be cast away only at the last moment; never in recorded history had chance and coincidence so conjoined as nearly to cause man's decimation. My own part in the affair was minor: I was but a pathetic and inconsequential acolyte to Coler, who, by piecing together the scattered notes and fragments he had accumulated, detected and foiled the efforts of those things who ever encroach upon us from outside and from within; and averted—for now—a monstrous and recurring doom which shall hang over men as long as men are.

Yet, as irony would have it, had Coler not saved the world, and had those things then slaughtered us all, it would have been the fault of Coler himself; it was his initial actions which set in motion the aeon-forgotten plots of those things who once ruled the earth but were then expelled, and who in cosmic revenge wish the devastation of the world. Coler is our saviour; but had he not been, he would have been our exterminator.

Jefferson Coler is now four days dead, through utter physical and mental exhaustion, an old man at forty-two. I can now write this document so as to show the world how close it came to unthinkable turmoil, and to show that Professor Coler was not, as he was deemed in life, a madman, or an eccentric, but one who, through his own genius, realized and then forfended an outcome of whose proportions it is not pleasant to think.

Mankind is safe—but only for a time.

Coler was an archaeologist whose rivals were few. In actual knowledge he was almost unsurpassed; yet it was his instinct which lifted him above all others, and which allowed him to make startling breakthroughs in many fields then adumbral with misunderstanding. One of his early works, a report on *Ancient Civilizations of Divers Polynesian Islands* (1925), had earned him both envy and scorn—envy for its scholarship and erudition, and scorn for the several dubious yet seemingly authenticated extrapolations made in it. His research on the volume also awakened an insatiable thirst for things diluvian and arcane; a thirst which in time developed into an obsession for procuring archaic and curious tomes, many times for inconceivably fabulous prices. Who would give such a sum, many asked themselves, for not even an original but a copy of something called *Necronomicon*, by, indeed, a mad Arab named Alhazred? Or again, a work called *De Vermis Mysteriis* of Ludvig Prinn, or Comte d'Erlette's *Cultes des Goules*, Laurent de Longnez's *L'Histoire des Planetes*, Jawangi Warangal's *Civtates Antiquae Fantasticae*? Coler's acquisition of these volumes did much to brand him as one whose talents, though prodigious, were being pathetically wasted on subjects bordering upon the lunatic; and his assiduous learning of ancient tongues and dialects which had evaded the memories of even the best of linguists further gained him a reputation for eccentricity. Fanaticism is rarely productive of good; but, as it turned out, Coler's fanaticism was the very thing that saved our lives.

His reclusiveness, another trait that earned the mockery of many, was thus not innate but gradually acquired through the ostracism resulting from his unique theories. While he was oftentimes the butt of transparent sarcasms by other archaeologists, he himself did not refrain from ridiculing those of his profession for what he called "their vile and pompous blindness at things which they can't explain or understand"; of particular note was the epistolary argument between Coler and Sir Charles Burton concerning the origin and use of those curious statues on Easter Island, published in the *British Archaeological Digest*. This constant bickering between him and his associates served only to sever more and more their respect for one another, so that in time each cast the gravest doubts as to the other's competency and ability. I, a lifelong friend of Coler's, eventually became the only archaeologist with whom he would consult, for the simple reason that I did not disclaim the views he expressed. I listened to him not simply to humor him, but because I knew that men had yet to gain all the answers to the world and the universe.

Yet above all, Coler was secretive: through what seemed an inherent lack of faith in men, Coler refused to reveal to anyone his thoughts, his involvements, his actions. It might have been that he, through past experience, feared ridicule; yet this cannot totally explain why, in his most recent affair, he deigned not to tell even me of what he was doing or what was to come; he kept almost everything to himself, intermittently throwing out to me vague hints and remarks which could leave me only with my mind's eye peering confusedly into his fog of ominous implications and portents. Coler did not explain everything to me until the very end: only then did I know how close we had come to death; only then did I understand Coler's previously inexplicable *manoeuvres*.

The events began for me in the summer of 1940. Coler had just returned from an expedition to Arabia, and had asked me to stop in at his manor in Severnford because he wished to show me "a little curiosity which I dug up in the Arabian desert." As I was myself not involved in anything of overwhelming exigency, I came immediately. Inviting me in, he then left to fetch his prize. He returned moments later.

It would be both trite and untrue to say that the thing was then at all significant of terror: it was anomalous only in that it was unfathomable. What it seemed to be was a roughly rectangular glass or crystal box, of a dull viridescent color. The one peculiarity was that the figure had no seam or opening in it; so that if it were indeed a box, then it was a box whose manner of use had yet to be discovered. That it was merely an object of decoration seemed improbable, for it was, by our standards, hardly attractive in any way. Seeing all of this I looked up to Coler, mutely expressing my apprehension.

"I'm as confused as you are," he said, "not only as to its function but as to its constituents. It does superficially resemble fluorite, and, if it were not so dull, one might think it pure dioptase; but my chemical tests prove that it is neither. It certainly is some sort of crystal, yet it is a crystal which seems to have few or no earthly elements."

"My dear fellow," I cried, "you must show it to the Archaeological Institute!" I was referring to the Royal Archaeological Institute of Great Britain and Ireland. "What a find!"

"No, Collins, no," he replied: "my reputation is too precarious. They will think it a hoax or some cleverly planned practical joke on my part. I've been in similar situations before: the result has always been the same." He spoke with a dreary acerbity from which one could glean his remembrance of the past.

"How did you find it, anyway?" I queried.

"That's another curious business! Our party was exploring some strange pillared ruins (possibly, though not certainly, Alhazred's 'fabulous Irem, City of Pillars'), and it happened that, while I was digging somewhere with a trowel, the ground beneath me suddenly gave way, and I plunged down what seemed to be a narrow pit. I fell down some twenty feet, landing finally on another sandy surface under the ground. Now my falling must have unearthed this crystal, for I then saw it lying next to me, still half-buried in the earth. Some of my men, who had seen me fall, threw me a rope, and I climbed out of the pit, bringing this thing up with me."

It was, as he said, curious, but not totally out of the ordinary. When I asked him what he planned to do with the object, he replied:

"I don't know, Collins, I don't know. At present, there is nothing I can do, save somehow to find out its constituents and its purpose."

"One moment, Coler," I suddenly burst out. I had only then remembered some of my own readings in the arcane, which, although not within Coler's level, were not inconsiderable. "Might this not be Blake's Shining Trapezohedron?"

"I thought of that, too, Collins, but I've now dismissed the idea. Remember what Blake says about the Shining Trapezohedron: it is a many-faceted crystal or 'glowing stone' inside an 'open box of yellowish metal.' Now, in addition to the fact that our discovery has no opening, what we have here is simply a crystal box itself, or perhaps a solid block of crystal. Whatever it is, it is not the Shining Trapezohedron."

Coler was staring at the thing as if hypnotized, and my gaze too became fixed on it. Its apparent functionlessness was what made it peculiar, not any inherent quality of the crystal itself. I am tempted to write that it even then gave off a miasma of otherworldly manufacture, and I cannot definitely adduce whether this view is actual or merely born of imperfect memory and subsequent explication. The thing was strange, but really nothing more; terror would come a little later.

Research and publishing of an historical-archaeological report on Roman ruins in Wales kept me almost constantly busy for an entire week after my visit with Coler. Indeed, it was exactly a week later that Coler called me again, saying that there had been a new development concerning his discovery. I had only concluded my work that morning, and was glad that Coler's summons had come at such an opportune time. Again, I must refrain from adding that any feeling of dread was then overcoming me; for the enigma of the crystal was as yet minute, and in the course of my own activities, I had all but forgotten it. It would be the most pathetic of platitudes to say that the importance and significance which I gave it was far short of the mark.

The "new development" of which Coler had spoken was not as radical as I had supposed: its shape and color were still the same, and the only change was that there could be detected in the center of the green object a small glowing, as if some sort of phosphorescent ball had been placed within it. That this had resulted of its own accord was obvious, what with the seamlessness of the thing; and, because we knew not what the purpose of the box itself was, we could hardly have any notion as to the function of this odd glowing. I asked Coler when the glowing had begun, and he replied:

"I first detected it this morning, though it could well have started any time last night. But it is not that which bothers me: it is what we are to make of it."

I could not but agree.

"What does it mean, man," he said, more to himself than to me, "what does it mean? I cannot even begin to hypothesize on it, so *outré* and senseless does it seem. I can't help feeling, however, that there is more here than meets the eye...

"The answer," he continued, "may well be in one of my books. I've begun looking myself—there's nothing in Prinn—but I still have dozens of volumes to go through."

There could be nothing clearer than that Coler wanted help in his task. Being free of my own activities, I proffered my services, and he assented with an eagerness which told of his relief at not having to ask me himself. In his experience-gained self-sufficiency he had grown loath both of asking favors and of doing them. My suggestion that we begin at once was quickly adopted, and we two retired to his library, where his priceless collection of tomes lay.

Coler had already been some two-thirds of the way through von Junzt's *Unaussprechlichen Kulten* when I called, and, taking up that book again, advised me to look through any of the other volumes I wished. I had never completely read Alhazred's *Necronomicon*, and considered that now would be as good a time as any to do so. I took down the handwritten copy which Coler had purchased from an old occultist in Massachusetts, and began its perusal, seating myself in one of the two occasional chairs in the room, in the other of which Coler himself was seated.

How many hours we were in that room reading I have been unable to determine; but the fact that the first time I looked up from Alhazred's volume, I saw through the window that night had fallen, and that the grandfather's clock in the library registered well past 9, proves that no inconsiderable time had elapsed in the course of our task. Coler's despair at discovering not even the vaguest reference to his find in von Junzt was matched by my own discouragement at the apparent uselessness of the *Necronomicon*. I had managed to get half through the tome, and there could not be discerned in even its allegorical whisperings any obscure allusions to Coler's crystalline receptacle. Alhazred's mentioning of a box which was a "window to space and time" could be nothing other than a citation of the Shining Trapezohedron, coinciding as it did exactly with the descriptions in both the Blake manuscript and in Prinn's *De Vermis Mysteriis*. That being the case, it could be of no use to us; although Alhazred's later noting something called "Nyarlathotep's weapon" could have meant anything from those "Druid" stones in Avebury to that mysterious round tower in Billington Woods near Arkham, Massachusetts. Coler, late in the afternoon, had finished the von Junzt and had begun

Warangal's *Civitates Antiquae Fantasticae*, though even that Indian philosopher's work seemed to be as ignorant of the green crystal as Prinn's and Alhazred's had been, so that our disheartenment at finding no clues soon turned to a dread that not a single volume in Coler's library would bring any facts to light. Our exhaustion was as great as our frustration, and Coler, gentleman to the last, told me, at close on 9:30, to stop our work and partake of a late supper. No suggestion could have been more apt.

The next day proved to be more productive, though in ways which we could not yet understand. The morning found me again in Coler's library recommencing my examination of the Alhazred volume, while Coler himself continued to tackle the Warangal tome. Some time afterwards, perhaps an hour before noon, I, resting my eyes from the crabbed and blurred writing, looked at that morning's paper, which was lying haphazardly on the floor next to me. In it was an article which, though small and of apparent inconsequence, proved later to be vastly significant. The article was this:

OCCULTISTS HOLD CLANDESTINE MEETING

Brichester: 2 *July 1940.* A band of some two dozen occult worshippers, ranging in age from eighteen to over seventy, were seen performing some dark ritual on the top of Sentinel Hill outside Brichester yesterday night, where there are located some primitive Druid megaliths. No sacrifices seem to have been made, but the leader of the flock, an old man of about sixty, who seemed to serve the function of a priest, was heard intoning weird chants which the "congregation" echoed. The whole incident seemed to be of little importance, for the ritual or ceremony lasted scarcely half an hour. This was the first of such meetings in over six months, and officials are fearing a recurrence of the disappearance of various young children which occurred the last time the gathering met, in late December 1939.

It cannot be said that, when I first read the article, I paid any great attention to it. In the quest for ascertaining the origin and function of

Coler's crystal, I was hardly about to give much notice to some absurd litany performed by a handful of degenerate, semi-crazed individuals. I remember remarking to myself that the *Brichester Herald* must truly be desperate for news, if it were lowered to including such trite and ludicrous affairs in its pages.

My subsequent finishing of the *Necronomicon* two hours later coincided almost exactly with Coler's completion of the huge Warangal tome; the result, of course, was as before: although both the *Necronomicon* and *Civitates Antiquae Fantasticae* contained detailed accounts of Irem, the City of Pillars, there was nothing in either volume which we could relate to the excavated crystal. Our minds were already weary with reading, and Coler's suggestion that we take some lunch was heartily accepted by me.

The phone call came immediately after we had finished. Coler was informed by the operator, when picking up the instrument, that he was receiving a call from Wolverhampton Airport from a man who was a resident, of all places, of Arkham, Massachusetts! Wilmarth, who had probably forgotten Coler's very name, surely could have nothing to do with us, and the reputation for eccentricity and, it must be admitted, rank enmity of his colleagues which was Coler's further created a mystery as to the identity of our transatlantic caller. The enigma was solved, however, immediately upon the utterance of the American's first words.

"Meredith!" Coler jovially exclaimed in reply. "It's been nearly fifteen years since I've heard your voice! Why in the world are you in Tewkesbury?... To see *me*? For what reason?... I understand... As a matter of fact, I am, but it has been so discouraging that I'd be glad to give it up and tackle something fresh... We will be there shortly. Good day."

Upon Coler's hanging up the phone, he related to me the gist of the conversation. It seemed that Joseph Meredith, now head of the Archaeology Department at Miskatonic, and one of Coler's few friends, had come here to give Coler an ancient and curious hieroglyphic tract which a Miskatonic expedition to Egypt had recently discovered. Meredith's staff, unable to decipher the evidently millennia-old fragment, had decided to put the thing in Coler's hands, knowing that he was one of the world's foremost authorities on elder tongues. The archaeologist had just arrived here, at Wolverhampton Airport in

Tewkesbury, and had asked that Coler come and fetch him and bring him back here so that work might be begun on the text; to which request Coler had agreed.

When we arrived at the airport, we saw Meredith with, not only suitcases, but another small black container which we knew was a special housing case for old parchments, a case which would protect the manuscript from the decimating effects of time and the elements. As we entered the car and drove back to Coler's manor, Meredith explained more about the find.

The trip to various ruins in Egypt had been made only that winter, and, aside from other minor archaeological artifacts, this parchment had been the only significant product. Its being unearthed in a ruin near the town of Kurkur had given it the name of the Kurkur Fragment. Linguists, archaeologists, and antiquarians alike had been baffled as to the language or dialect of its writing; that it was either a modern or archaic dialect of Egyptian had been almost at once ruled out, and, as it might easily have been transported to Egypt from as far a place as India, tests had been made as to whether the document was in either Arabic, Sanscrit, or the dozen modern and obsolete Indian dialects; but the results had all been equally negative, serving only to confirm that it was either penned in a language of unbelievable obscurity, or that it was inexplicably written in code. Meredith himself, remembering Lang's Voynich Manuscript, had put forth the theory that the work might be in a sort of hybrid language, i.e. Sanscrit letters (for this much was obvious from the text) perhaps forming Hittite or Assyrian words. The work on this hypothesis had only begun, for there seemed to be, considering the unknown origin, almost no end of permutations that could be had. Meredith had then thought of letting Coler scrutinize the tract so that the possibility of its being in some abstruse tongue, known only to Coler and other such specialists, might be explored. This was, then, the reason for Meredith's arrival.

Coler would not stand for Meredith's lodging in a hotel, and offered his own mansion—a multi-roomed stone edifice whose construction might have dated from the sixteenth century, and only a fraction of which was used—as a temporary residence and base of operations. The afternoon was progressing by the time we had returned to Severnford, and Coler's suggestion of an early dinner which would leave the entire evening free for studying the manuscript was accepted by both Meredith and myself.

That evening, however, was important not so much for our working on the Kurkur Fragment as for an incident which made us realize, perhaps for the first time, that we were involved in matters whose scope was far greater than we had originally supposed.

Putting forth the thoroughly justifiable plea of fatigue from his 4,000-mile trip, Meredith retired early that night. We did not fail, however, first to show him Coler's anomalous crystal; indeed, it was Meredith himself who had requested to see it, having heard of the find from one of Coler's party, a Miskatonic graduate student named Craig Phillips. Coler told his colleague all the facts about its discovery, its sudden commencing to glow, and our own inefficacious efforts at trying to enucleate its origin and use. Coler, too, explained that the glowing had definitely grown larger since the morning, the phosphorescent ball inside now approaching a diameter of two and a half inches. Meredith, not unnaturally involved in his own arcanum, seemed to pay Coler only enough attention as might just be within the bounds of courtesy, and then tried to steer Coler's mind back to the new mystery which he had dropped in his lap. This was not a difficult task to perform, considering our double irritation at the total absence of any clues as to the crystal's function and significance.

It must have been close on 11 o'clock when it occurred. Coler had initially given me a part of Meredith's manuscript and had me make certain arrangements of the curious and faded letters which would allow him to break the centuries-old cipher, but after a time stopped me, telling me that he had perhaps discovered the base and method of the text. I had recommenced finding the answer to our other enigma, picking up Laurent de Longnez's comparatively recent *L'Histoire des Planetes* (1792), to see if that contemporary of Sade and La Bretonne had any knowledge of the age-old green thing that had come from Arabia. De Longnez's French was filled with irritating punctuational and literary archaisms that made reading none too easy, so that after a time I found myself bent almost double over the book, perpetually squinting my eyes and following with my head each individual line. Several hours of this had hypnotized me to the book, so much that I all but forgot the presence of Coler at the desk across the room. Only until I heard a sudden shuffling movement close at hand did I merge from my reverie and, for the first time in hours, look up.

What I saw was another man in the room, not Meredith, nor Coler, but one whose slovenly attire and facial vacuity told that his origin could be nothing else but that squalid decadence called Lower Brichester.

How the man had gotten in the house became more an enigma than what his object was, for it was now obvious that his steps were leading in straight to the glowing crystal on Coler's desk, and now only yards separated him from his prize.

Coler, miraculously, was so entranced in his studies that he still had no inkling that this intruder was here at all, and only looked up, mutely baffled and disturbed, when I flung myself bodily at the man, half wrestling him to the ground. Either through my underestimation of the degenerate miscreant's strength or through my own unrealized enervation, I found myself soon with my back to the ground, looking up into a visage which now held the image of absolute terror. Seeming now to be possessed of an incontrollable lunacy, the thief suddenly raised himself to his feet and, disregarding both his bizarre quest and any concern for bodily injury, flung himself headlong through the window of Coler's library. Falling to the ground amidst a frightful shattering of glass, the man got up and ran off into the night.

Too awed at the whole spectacle to speak, I could only stand at the window and regard the curious *voleur*, who had now stopped running when he saw that he was unpursued. Coler, however, had not been idle: he suddenly came up behind me and, laying a hand on my shoulder, spoke the words:

"Quick, Collins! Follow him! See where he goes!"

"What?" I burst out. "What on earth for?"

"It would take too long to explain now: just follow him, man. It's vital! I've nearly solved the Kurkur Fragment, and Collins, it *deals with the very crystal I dug up!* Everything is fitting together, everything is making sense. I think I even know why that robber came here. But go now, Collins: follow him, and tell me where he went. Go now!"

Coler would not hear another word of protest nor any demand at explication, and I could do nothing but carry out his request.

Trailing our erstwhile criminal proved to be of no difficulty, as he had no intimation whatever that anyone would want to watch his movements. He was walking easily now, and the simplicity of my task allowed me to ponder on the several enigmas which had so suddenly formed minutes ago. Paramount was the almost ludicrous audacity which this fellow had demonstrated; what phenomenal idiocy or urgency had impelled him to attempt his criminous act in our very presence, where his chances of success were of such exiguity as to be explained only by resorting to the appellation of lunacy? Then there was the matter of Coler's fragmentary utterances concerning his success in decoding Meredith's ancient tract. What could Coler have meant when he said that everything was "fitting together"? And how could the Kurkur Fragment, the green crystal, and this unsuccessful try at larceny be in any way related? I think that it was about then that I first began to perceive vaguely that we were dealing with great and appalling matters beyond our ken, involving elder secrets of galactic menace inexplicably joined with incidents in our own midst, the end result of which seemed to form such a devastating implication of doom as might, when correlated and understood, cause the mind to totter on the outermost reaches of irremediable insanity.

I had been following the man with only half my mind, ruminating on the mysteries which seemed imminent of solution by Coler. But even now, as we approached the outskirts of Brichester, I saw that our bucolic brigand could have only one destination: Sentinel Hill, the site of that occult nocturnal ritual of yestereve.

When we reached the hill itself, I felt no surprise at the sight: the congregation that had met almost exactly twenty-four hours ago, for what was taken to be a suggestive if innocuous assembly, was there again, all clustering around the flat, table-like mass of stone that lay on the very summit of the hill, surrounded by a score of carven menhirs whose prodigious age was evident even in near pitch-darkness. Sheltered behind a clump of trees, I saw my shadow timorously approach the others and, when he had reached him who seemed to be the leader of the band, mumble, with head bent low in mortification, a handful of words, arms gesturing plaintively. Upon the man's concluding, the leader, a small, chunky man of sixty, was suddenly seized with a maniac rage, and slapped the erring subordinate in the face again and again, ceasing only when exhaustion overcame him. The brigand, who was almost twice the size of his punisher, seemed to have no notion whatever of retaliation: although he could easily have annihilated his violent castigator, he chose instead to endure the chastisement, seeming to regard the other with an ineffable respect that was as incredible as it was absurd. When finally the affair was concluded, the elderly *padrone* adjured all the members to depart, then himself left. I saw that the unfortunate young man who had been so severely reprimanded walked alone, the object of ridicule and outright hatred by the others.

When I returned to Coler's manor and reported the incident, he, still working on the Egyptian document, nodded slowly and thoughtfully, as if it had only confirmed his hypothesis on the matter. He refused to tell me anything regarding either the attempt at stealing the crystal or his deciphering of the Kurkur Fragment, saying only that he must be left alone so that he could finish its translation. But here I intervened: seeing Coler's haggard and dishevelled appearance, realizing that he was on the brink of utter physical and mental exhaustion, I refused to allow him to work any more that evening, and bade him get a good night's sleep; Coler was either too weak or too sensible to resist.

There was hardly any indication when I awoke the next morning that the very night would see the culmination and end of the horrific incidents in which we had so accidentally become involved. Realizing, since Coler had already broken the code of the Kurkur Fragment and that only the arduous work of transcribing had to be done, that my presence at his home would be more a hindrance than a help, I decided to pick up the threads of my own archaeological studies. Leafing through my small report, I found that it contained a number of unsubstantiated statements which could only be rectified by referring to contemporary manuscripts, and in the late morning I journeyed down to Oxford and looked through the Bodleian Library collection of ancient documents to find the necessary sources. When I concluded this work it was mid-afternoon, and, since my time was my own, I decided not to return home but to reacquaint myself with an Oxford which I had not seen for well-nigh a dozen years. My particular architectural predilections tend toward the High Gothic, and few places could satisfy my desires better than Oxford. I must have spent hours in examining the buildings and in roaming the countryside, and

I think I can be forgiven for so letting my fancy overcome me, though I often shudder at the thought that I came back to Severnford in what proved to be the very nick of time.

At about 7:00 I dined in a restaurant in Oxford, and, finally coming to the conclusion that I had wasted enough time in frivolity, made the return trip, reaching home at close on 8:30. Exhausted by my ramblings, I must have dropped off almost immediately afterwards, awaking some forty-five minutes later. For the first time in the day I thought of Coler, the crystal, and Meredith's Kurkur Fragment, and decided to give the man a call to see how far he had progressed.

Curiously, I received no reply, though I let the phone ring several times. Surely, I thought, Coler could not have retired so early; and even if he had, why did Meredith not answer? Had the two gone somewhere, as I had done, on an archaeological mission? Or had pleasure spurred their departure, Meredith wishing to catch a brief glimpse of England while he was here? The possibilities were endless, and it was useless of me to speculate haphazardly in this manner; the only way I could solve this absurdly minor enigma was to go personally to Coler's manor.

I cannot say that I was particularly surprised when no one answered either my vehement knocking at the door or my calling out loud of Coler's and Meredith's names. Indeed, I was about to come to the conclusion that the two must have gone somewhere, despite the late hour, when I saw something that, though it did not actually defy this hypothesis, did put a more curious and sinister significance upon the whole affair:

Coler's car was still in his garage.

It was certainly possible that they had gone on foot to wherever they were going, and their absence could well indicate that some accident had befallen either one or both. For a time I considered scouring the countryside in my car for them, but then I became aware of another odd circumstance that almost definitely precluded any innocuous explication of the matter:

Coler's front door was unlocked; and the reason that it was unlocked was that the lock was broken.

This was not Coler's work, nor Meredith's. There also came flooding back to my memory the unsuccessful criminous attempt of the night before, an incident to which Coler had attached a considerable and as yet an unaccountable importance. Something serious was involved, I knew, and I felt also that the consequences of whatever it was were not only overwhelming, but imminent of realization.

I burst through the door and began searching for Coler's presence. The first place I looked was of course the library, and there I found him—on the floor, unconscious, with blood oozing thickly from a head wound which seemed remarkably recent.

Although I was shocked at this abrupt discovery, I remember noticing that the room was, paradoxically, in relative order: no papers were scattered anywhere, no chairs overturned, no books disturbed save those which we had ourselves perused, and only Coler's prostrate form signified that any physical struggle had taken place here. I saw, too, that Meredith's Kurkur Fragment was still on Coler's desk.

My first task was to revive Coler, and this was accomplished with no great difficulty, for though Coler's head wound was ugly, it was not serious. Only a minute or two after I began my ministrations I heard Coler moan gruffly and shuffle about, trying to get to his feet. When he opened his eyes, he first expressed a startled horror which again reminded me of our bootless miscreant of the preceding night; then, upon recognizing me, he became tranquil, murmuring:

"Oh, it's only you, Collins. Thank God you've come—"

Breaking off suddenly, his face abruptly registered a wide-eyed dread which seemed to hint of the most awesome of horrors, and which allowed Coler to mutter only the words, "Oh, my God!" and then precipitously to arise from the floor and cast frenzied glances all about the room, *as if he were looking for something...*

Then I noticed that the crystal was gone.

"Collins, they've taken it! They've taken it! Come quickly, man, we must go immediately! If we are too late, Collins..."

Disregarding his injury, he first went to another room and seized a rifle, then urged me to come with him as he made his way out of the house. Trying to ignore what was so affecting Coler, I asked him what in the world had happened to Meredith, and Coler gave me this amazing reply:

"He has gone back to Arkham."

"What!" I cried. "But he arrived here only yesterday! What made him go back so suddenly?"

Flinging at me the day's newspaper, which was lying on an armchair in the living room, Coler snapped, while exiting through the front door: "The answer is there, Collins; read it on the way."

And read it I did. The article was almost on the last page of the issue, ironically tucked away in a corner, as if it were some sort of filler:

BIZARRE RIVER TRAGEDY

Arkham, Massachusetts, U.S.A.: 3 July 1940. The shores of Devil Reef near Innsmouth and the Miskatonic River were the sites of peculiar deaths yesterday night. A number of citizens of Arkham, including some young students of Miskatonic University, were found murdered while fishing or swimming: their bodies were torn apart as if by great claws, and a noxious fishy smell adhered to them, along with a curious green slime which was so foetid that the bodies could not be approached for several hours. Whether a human agency was involved could not be determined, but officials and various old inhabitants of Arkham and Dunwich have expressed the belief that this event is somehow tied with the hushed-up government intervention at Innsmouth in the winter of 1927-28 and to the terrible holocaust at Dunwich which took place some months afterwards. They also refer to the great floods that occurred in the hills of Vermont in late 1927, the subsequent disappearance of an old folklorist named Akeley, and the resultant madness of Miskatonic instructor of literature Albert N. Wilmarth. How those diverse incidents could have any relation to the recent tragedy was not explained, though it has been noticed that the townspeople of Innsmouth have been unduly restless in the past few days, and that there has been unprecedented activity in the depths of Devil Reef on several occasions. Some lunatics have gone so far as to mumble about the Salem witch trials, which occurred two and a half centuries ago, though it is to be noted that no one has cared to disavow any of these rumors.

Officials are still looking into the matter, while state and federal authorities have again been contacted...

This certainly explained Meredith's return home, although it hardly seemed to have any significance to our own affairs. Still running alongside Coler, with only the moonlight to guide us, I then saw another article which was of interest:

CURIOUS SEA INCIDENT

Papeete, Tahiti: 3 July 1940. Some twenty persons—many of them English and American tourists—were killed yesterday night by so-called "sea monsters," which were said to have come from the sea. Several of the bodies were mutilated beyond recognition, others with limbs amputated and partially eaten. A green trail of slime led from the bodies back to the sea, and the odor of dead fish also prevailed. It is believed that some ordinary sea animals came out of the sea and wreaked the havoc, the claim of "sea monsters" being passed off as the exaggerations of superstitious natives...

Here were two identical incidents, tens of thousands of miles apart. My own readings in the weird could allow of only one answer to those twin disasters, yet the mystery lay in why these things had chosen this especial time to attack. If these two events were unrelated, then it was the most fabulous coincidence ever to come within the scope of my knowledge.

Coler was still rapidly running, and I had trouble in keeping up with him. We had now reached the outskirts of Brichester, but long before this I knew that our eventual destination must be Sentinel Hill. The incredible determination of Coler was what most impressed me: although I knew something of great consequence was involved, I could hardly envision that it was so great as to impel the man into this maniac haste with, further, the deadly rifle at his side. Could the possession of a mere block of crystal, anomalous and supermundane though it may have been, be of such earth-shaking importance? What awful power and significance lay in its weirdly glowing interior? What implications of future devastation could it hold? That the answer was as titanic as it was complex seemed evident, and I can truthfully say that even the wildest arabesques of my imagination did not encompass what I eventually learned was the truth.

We finally reached Sentinel Hill, and, hiding behind a thick copse of trees, I saw again a sight which had to me become monstrously familiar: the infernal congregation was there again, and this time a few of them carried torches to give the whole scene an unhallowed illumination. They were gathered in a close circle around the flat stone at the top of the hill, those with torches standing while the others knelt. The elderly priest also stood, and walked, his back to us, slowly toward the stone. He then reached out his arms and put something on it.

The crystal now lay in the center of the stone.

We could see even from where we were that the glowing had only grown in size, seeming to be close to twice as large as when I had seen it last. There now fell over all a great and deathly silence, yet in the air there was such a tension and apprehension as might make one think that Nature was holding her breath in the expectation of some ineffably towering cataclysm.

The priest now raised both his hands to the sky in a supplicating gesture. Just as he was about to speak Coler fired his rifle.

The priest fell dead to the ground without uttering.

Silence died as quickly, as the other members of the band now began clamoring at the abrupt interruption of their ceremony and looked about to find its cause. They did not have to look far, for Coler now sprang from his place of concealment and ran toward the hill, gun in hand, urging me to follow.

We were madmen to throw ourselves in the midst of that depraved band of blasphemers, yet necessity of the most terrific sort drove us on. We were two against twenty, but we, too, seemed suddenly filled with a bestial madness that made us claw and tear our way through, Coler intermittently firing his rifle in someone's face or stomach. And when I grabbed the crystal and tucked it under my arm, there came over me an even greater rage at these grotesque perversions of all that is sane and normal, these handfuls of lunatic scoundrels whose desire of absolute decimation was born only of their failure to co-exist with a race who had so surpassed them in mental and spiritual progression that they no longer deserved the appellation of human but became a species apart in their odious and lurid decadence.

I kicked, I scratched, I maimed, and, using my head as a battering ram, thrust my body through the crowd, twisting and writhing away from them as they turned to wrestle the crystal away. I soon found myself in the open, Coler at my side, and we began sprinting away with a velocity we had never before known; and when we turned around to measure the extent of our escape from pursuit, we saw the score of fanatics now a considerable distance behind us, but still giving chase, leaping and tripping over one another, foaming at the mouth in multiple apexes of fury, arms outstretched as if itching not only to win back their other-worldly prize but to rend us apart for having so foiled the consummation of their ritual. But because we also possessed a thankful modicum of insanity, we pressed ourselves on almost beyond the farthest reaches of human capacity, racing through Brichester, Temphill, and finally to Severnford without allowing ourselves one minor yet irrevocably fatal pause.

But we were not finished yet. When we reached Coler's manor, we stepped not inside but into his car, and drove off to a destination which only he knew. Some minutes later, we pulled to the side of the road and approached what seemed to be an abandoned mine shaft to our right. Coler took the crystal from me and plunged it into the deepest and darkest pit he could find, emitting a heavy sigh of relief after doing so. I recall that though we stayed there for perhaps a full minute, we never heard the crystal reach the bottom.

We had just succeeded in saving mankind—for now.

I had to wait until the next morning to learn the answer. Our exhaustion had reached such lengths that almost immediately upon seating ourselves in some chairs in Coler's home, we dropped off into a heavy, dreamless, and undisturbed sleep, not waking until it was almost noon. The actions of the preceding night and the long rest had stimulated our appetites, and when our breakfast was prepared we abandoned any pretensions of dignity and attacked the meal like savages. It was some considerable time before we reached anything close to satiation, and when we did Coler led me back to the library, where finally he could reveal to me a truth which he had himself known for less than twenty-four hours.

He began by saying: "You know as well as I, Collins, how we got involved in this business: I accidentally dug up the crystal in Arabia, brought it back with me, tried unsuccessfully to ascertain its use and manufacture, and then noticed how it began glowing, first minutely, then with greater and greater strength. We began looking through my ancient texts to find some sort of reference to the thing, but came up with nothing. Then Meredith came with his Kurkur Fragment from Egypt, and asked me to try to solve it. I did exactly that. It was really very simple: Meredith had himself suggested the answer that it might be a mixture of two languages, which it was—Sanscrit letters forming words roughly akin to these in the *R'lyeh Text*.

"Now there came those strange meetings on top of Sentinel Hill by those occultists of Brichester. They were up to something, to be sure; but their doing nothing serious the first time seemed to suggest some curious *expectancy*, and it was of course proved by that incredible effort to rob the crystal two nights ago. It was obvious that they wanted the crystal, but what we could not understand was *why*.

"I found the answer, as I told you, in the Kurkur Fragment. But before I tell you that, let me show you something else."

He went to his desk and picked up a packet of about a dozen newspaper clippings, all from various London newspapers of the past few days.

He continued, as he handed them to me: "While you were at Oxford, Collins, I telephoned to London and asked to have recent issues of the *Times*, the *Guardian*, and the *Daily Telegraph* brought to me. (I was not fool enough to go myself and leave the crystal unguarded.) Read the articles: their significance is obvious enough."

And it was. I read of curious deaths and disappearances in the Australian desert, in the heights of the Himalayas, and in the frozen wastes of Antarctica. I read of an uprising of dolphins in California; I read of the recommencement of human sacrifices in Manitoba; I read of unheard-of excitement amongst primitive tribes in the depths of the African desert, in Panama, in south France, in the Yucatan peninsula, in southern Louisiana, in Polynesia; I read of ships sighting bizarre objects in the Pacific Ocean, in the north Atlantic, in the Gulf of Mexico. It was incredible, the worse because I sensed what was causing it.

"All across the world," Coler said, "these things have been

happening, the incidents in New England and Tahiti were but a part of it. And I could not help but ask myself: *why now?* What ineffable forces were spurring those things to attack now? Meredith's Kurkur Fragment told me."

Again going to his desk, he took hold of a sheet of paper which I could see was Coler's translation of part of the text. What I read was this:

...And the minions of Azathoth first moulded the Earth as a plaything of the gods, who might fashion upon it what they would—living travesties of the planet's scarce-cooled crust to serve as ultimate signs of the mistake that is Life. But Cthulhu and the Deep Ones came to wrest the earth away, so that they could serve as the gods of the hoary denizens that shambled before there were men; and this pleased not the minions of Azathoth, who by a supreme jest entrapped the feeble god within the waters. Thence did the prehuman worshippers of Cthulhu fashion the Crystal of Zamalashtra from elements spawned on Yuggoth, burying within it the fire from Nyarlathotep. And when the stars are right, the fire will glow; and may this serve as a sign to the worshippers of Cthulhu to deliver the Crystal of Zamalashtra to their entombed god, whereupon he shall break through his shackles and crush the plaything of the gods called Earth..."

"Need I say more, Collins? need I say more?

"You know that Yuggoth is nothing but that recently discovered planet called Pluto. And you know, too, that the orbit of 'Pluto' has been calculated as roughly 248 years. Once every 248 years Yuggoth lines up perfectly so that 'the stars are right'; now is it not obvious what has happened?

"*I dug up the crystal in that exact 248th year!*

"Think of what a phenomenal coincidence that was! What an unbelievable stroke of bad luck that I dug it up at the exact time when Cthulhu could be freed from his prison! The glowing confirmed it.

"But why, then, was Cthulhu not released aeons ago? Why has the earth not been crushed? What must have happened was that the crystal was lost before 'the stars were right,' and because of this Cthulhu and his minions could never completely escape their watery tombs! All they could do was to make random and ineffectual attacks on men, as the Johansen narrative and the Wilmarth manuscript prove. Without the crystal, it would all be futile...

"Yet the worshippers seem somehow to know when 'the stars are right,' and as a result their activities, and the activities of Cthulhu's spawn, suddenly increase. This most recent attempt proves it; yet this time, because they knew that the crystal had now been rediscovered, their anxiety was a thousandfold greater: for the first time in millennia, they had a chance finally to annihilate the world! Why else did one of the worshippers try to rob the crystal in our very presence? Why else, when that failed, did they resort to physical violence? Why else did they so madly try to get back the crystal when we had taken it from them? Why else did those incidents occur all over the planet?

"Then, too, Collins, think of this: this is 1940; we know that this is the period when 'the stars are right'; then 248 years ago, the stars must again have been right. And what is 248 years from this date? *Is it not 1692, the time of the Salem witch trials?* Is there any other explanation for the sudden activity of the witches? Then, as now, they knew it was time; but the crystal was lost, and they could do nothing about it. They had to be content at merely intensifying their rituals, to such an extent that they were caught and killed. But it was all useless: they could do nothing without the crystal.

"If it had not been for me, we would not have gone through what we have; yet think of our marvelous good fortune that Meredith dropped in our laps the very thing we needed to counteract all that had happened! There has never been a time when coincidence has been so devastating, when chance so entered into the composition of events, when sheer accident first threatened, then saved our lives.

"We need not worry about the Crystal of Zamalashtra for another 248 years: by now, the stars have surely moved their alignment, and the crystal has again become powerless. We shall both be dead before the proper time next comes: let us hope that no idiot stumbles upon the crystal as I did, or if someone does, that he has the sense to leave it in its place. I don't see how we can ever escape the recurring doom of this crystal; and I don't see how in time Cthulhu will not escape his prison. Uncontrolled curiosity has ever been our worst enemy."

Jefferson Coler died thirty-six days later, having saved the world yet having left a legacy of eternal dread that seems destined eventually to overcome mankind. The preservation of this document is vital to the preservation of our race: if men cast doubts as to its veracity, then they will pay the consequences of their folly.

Really, it would be the most priceless irony.

NECROTIC KNOWLEDGE

BY DIRK W. MOSIG

"MAY I HELP YOU, SIR?"—THE LITTLE OLD MAN WITH THE gray beard leaned solicitously over the counter.

Rashd hesitated momentarily, then walked past him without uttering a sound. Moving toward one of the many tall shelves filled with musty volumes, he stared at them for a few seconds, and then wandered down one of the poorly lit aisles of Ye Olde Occulte Book-shoppe. He silently scanned row after row of the brittle, brownish and grayish spines, occasionally touching one of the mouldy books. Removing a tome lacking any visible lettering on the spine, he replaced it after discovering that the silverfish had not been merciful.

The little man sporting the beard that gave him an uncanny resemblance to Sigmund Freud shrugged, accustomed to being ignored by some of the rather unconventional types that frequented the ill-kept dump. With a grunt he returned to the copy of *Anal Lovers* he had picked up a few minutes ago to combat the early afternoon boredom. The heat was sweltering, and the tall and wiry stranger with the aquiline nose was the only customer—or potential customer—he had seen in the past two hours.

"Kitb... you have kitb... book... kitb-ul... nekrut?"

"What?" The dealer lifted his graying eyebrows.

"The book. *Nekrut. Al-nekrutic. Nekrotico?* Sati' said you had *kith, kitb-ul-majnn...*"

The little man gasped, and his knuckles turned white as he grabbed the edge of the counter and leaned forward.

"Satih sent you? That bastard! *Ibn-Sharmtah!* Son of a bitch! You know..."

Rashd paled considerably, and his long fingers reached under his ill-fitting coat, his eyes narrowing into slits.

"No, no, I didn't mean you! Satih... *Sati'?*..."—the smallish man pronounced the '*ain*' sound only with great difficulty.

Rashd stared blankly for a moment, then insisted:

"Necrotic? *Kitb-ul-majnn... kitb-ul-necrotic-ul-majnn?*"

"All right, dammit!"—said the little Freud look-alike. "Wait a minute." He walked nervously around the counter to the door of the shabby shop, pulled down the shades, and quickly flipped over the OPEN sign, securely fastening the door. Turning around, he rapidly walked past Rashd, who had observed the proceedings with a curious lack of interest.

"Come with me."

The gaunt Arab followed him silently to the back of the shop.

"JACK DAVIS—PRIVATE—KEEP OUT" read the stained yellowish sign discernible on the padlocked door. The little man, apparently Jack Davis himself, reached inside his trouser pocket and produced an odd-looking key, while his customer pressed closer.

"Hold your horses"—he grunted while fumbling with the lock.

A gratifying "click" rewarded his efforts. Removing the padlock, he pushed the door open, reached for an invisible light switch inside the dark room beyond, and gestured to his unusual client to enter the smallish enclosure revealed by the single lightbulb.

As soon as Rashd penetrated the crowded room—all four walls were lined with ancient-looking books, and a large desk, covered with papers, occupied most of the remaining space—Jack Davis followed him, carefully closing the door and padlocking it from the inside.

A musty odor of rotting paper seemed to float thickly in the cramped quarters, mixed with other, more disturbing scents of decay, but Rashd didn't seem to notice, nor did he object to the almost unbearable heat in the poorly ventilated room. Davis, on the other hand, perspired profusely as he slipped around the desk to drop his body on the single chair behind it.

"*The Necrotic Book*, huh? Do you have any idea what you are getting into?" The diminutive dealer seemed genuinely concerned.

"*N'am*... yes, yes, of course"—uttered his interlocutor, impatiently—"and I have the price—you give me the book..."

"Let's see what you got, first." Davis's voice revealed a touch of irritation.

The tall cadaveric Arab quickly unbuttoned his shirt and reached inside, producing in rapid succession five elongated plastic bags, which he deposited carefully on the desk, facing the sweaty and now slightly agitated dealer.

"Here... hashish"—he said, matter-of-factly. "Pure... good quality... *khirun*... hashish of the best... *wal-lh!*"

Davis carefully opened each of the bags, touched with his index finger the darkish substance within, then the tip of his tongue.

"Yes, it seems to be all right—awfully good stuff—where the hell did you get it? Never mind. But are you really aware of what you are trying to buy with it? How about settling for some other book of equal value—look, I have here an original of the *Book of Eibon*, no less, and..."

Rashd snarled and his right hand darted out with incredible speed, fastening itself on Davis's windpipe. Jack Davis's mouth opened soundlessly, and for an instant he stared right into the cold eyes of death incarnated.

"Give me the *nekrutic* book!" The words of the Arab cut through the thick air like knives.

"O.K."—Davis choked, struggling to free himself from the painful hold. "All right. Let me go, dammit! There—let me warn you, although I'm tempted not to... that *Necrotic Book* is too dangerous! I saw what it did to the guy who had it before. Gawd, I can't even think about it without my stomach turning over. A fate I wouldn't wish on my worst enemy—and believe me, I have several! An end that was just not human—or perhaps all too human, but not like *that*... Damn, if the boss hadn't *insisted* that I keep the blasted thing again, I would've..."

"*Nekrutic KITB!* Where?!!" interrupted the Arab, his patience obviously exhausted.

"I don't think you realize..." Jack Davis made a last, desperate effort. "The accursed book, scroll, or parchment—I've been spared actually seeing the damned thing—really *has* necrotic powers! Do you know what *that* means?..."

For the first time a faint smile appeared in the olivaceous face of Rashd Abdul Wahb Al-'Iraqui.

"Yes, I know—we know. *Kitb of Thumarn Al-Miit-ui-Majnn* has the power not of other books, not even of *Kitb-ul-Azif*. My master knows, too—him great collector of forbidden—he knows—he *'lim-ul-kitb*! Yes, *Thumarn...* Tomeron?... found something other men and *djinni* have never found. Book necrotic can make flesh rot—rotting in life—like spider venom that my master study... *Loxosceles...* ah, *laeta...* necrotic toxin... must be careful when handling. We also very careful when dealing with necrotic *kitb* of *Thumarn*. See, we never touch, work from space away... ah, distance... very safe, see, and besides *al-duktr...* ah, al-master, master collector, he many other books—we protection of other books, no? We with many forbidden books, many powerful *kitb*, strong protection against... outside. Now, where is the book? Which is *kitb*?"

"You people are nuts! Stark-raving lunatics! I don't see how you think you can..."

"*KITB!*" Rashd's tone had changed again. A thin dagger appeared in his left hand. "Enough games, *kfir*! The book!" he demanded imperiously.

"O.K., crap, it's your life, and that of the nut who hired you! I tried to warn you... here... here..."

With quivering hands Davis removed four thick volumes from one of the musty shelves that covered the wall to his right, revealing a strangely sealed and decorated box behind. Pointing, he whispered:

"Here, take the damn box, take it... the book or whatever the damn hell it is, is in there..."

In an instant Rashd moved around the desk. His arms darted out and without hesitation greedily removed the closed box from its hidden niche, turning it around in the air while fingering the large wax seals and the thin greenish chain wrapped around it.

"Ah, seal of *Ar-Rajm*, as promised... but must open and check..."

Jack Davis jumped up, livid, and pointed a small bluish revolver that appeared to have materialized miraculously in his hand.

"The hell you are going to open that thing in here!"—he shrieked, his sweaty face contorted with a curious mixture of anger and fear. The gun pointed straight at Rashd's head, as he continued, practically out of breath. "I told you I saw what happened to the last idiot who fooled around with that crazy thing, and I'm not about to take any chances with you opening that damn box while I'm around—you touch one of those seals again, and I swear I'll blow your brains out—hell, I would be doing you a favor! Take the damn thing and get the hell out of here!"

Rashd's features contorted into a grin, and he seemed to be strangely amused.

"*Wal-lh!* No need to threaten me, *kfir!* I'm going... I'm going! I'm sure you realize that if you have betrayed us and the book of Tomeron is not in the box you will die a death worse than... than... a thousand hells...*wa la'nnat-ul-'alamn 'aleikum!*"

The Arab burst into insane laughter, then pointed at the padlocked door:

"Open it!"

The agitated dealer hastened to the door, keeping his gun pointed at his visitor. Removing the padlock, he threw the door open in an instant, getting out of the way to allow his client to march past him. Rashd walked out of the bookshop without glancing back.

Carlo Corelli looked up from the newspaper spread out on his ornate desk, as the diminutive man with the gray beard was ushered into the office by one of his bodyguards.

"Hi, Jack, *caro amico,* how are you? Here, sit down, make yourself comfortable. Hey, did you see the paper this morning? Quite a mess, no?... Awful, the things that happen in this town, tsk, tsk."

"Damn, Mr. Corelli, how can you take it all so calmly?" Davis seemed to be tied in knots.

"Oh, c'mon, Jack! You are not only getting old—you're getting soft! I think those kooks were actually funny! Imagine, all the trouble they took... They get *la cosa* from you and place the crazy thing under a glass bowl, and use remote control and mechanical arms to open the box from another room, for goodness sake, as if they expected the thing to go *boom!* Giuseppe got there later, posing as a reporter, and swears they had also drawn pentagrams, had a bunch of candles burning, and books on funny pedestals in front of their observation window. C'mon, Jack, loosen up! We have been together in this for quite some time..."

"Not in *that* kind of thing, Mr. Corelli. Junk is one thing, but this..."

"Aw, Jack, c'mon, can't you see the humor of this whole situation?"—

laughed the heavy-set man behind the luxurious desk, puffing at his cigar. "I can see the poor nuts... surrounded by all their occult garbage, reading from their useless books, that crazy Arab no doubt reciting the *Necronomicon* or some such crap! Ha! And no doubt encouraged because nothing happened when their instruments succeeded in opening the box, that lunatic collector, Dr. Carl Ericson, had the Iraqui creep read from the Arabic text of the *Necrotic Book* as soon as they got the thing open. Jeez, they even had three rats in cages around the book, as if the book could have affected *them*! The idiots never realized that the necrotic powers of the book composed by Tomeron, that renegade priest of the corpse-eating cult of Leng, do not act upon him who touches it, or on those around it! Hey, Jack, you look pale... I bet you yourself do not know *how* the thing acts!"

"Mr. Corelli, do *you* know what powers are behind that demon book? Do you understand what makes it work?"—the smaller man shuddered.

"No, Jack, not precisely—but then, I don't know exactly how this watch works"—Corelli pointed at his expensive digital wristwatch—"or what makes a jet fly, or how acid consumes a man's head. And I don't know how the H-bomb works, either—but let me assure you, old boy, I wouldn't hesitate using any of those things if necessary, available, and convenient... You don't have to be a mechanic to drive an automobile. It was fortunate that the old chink told us all we needed to know about that crazy book before he died—he must have really hated the guy that did him in. Those collectors are something else! No, Jack, I don't understand the damn book, and I'm no mechanic... but I know how to drive a car, and how that book must be used!"

"But this is different, this is not at all like a car, a flask of acid, or a bomb—there is something devilish about it, Mr. Corelli. I don't like it!" Davis shuddered visibly, and seemed to become even smaller for a moment.

"Aw, don't be a fool, old boy. I'll tell you what's the matter with you. You have too much imagination! Here, you can look at this article—I think you will be able to figure out for yourself exactly *how* and *when* and *where* our little toy took effect. Look..."

Carlo Corelli turned the newspaper around, and pointed at several paragraphs in the report of the strange deaths which had shocked the Boston community that morning. Davis read, feeling a deep chill inside, in spite of himself:

The condition of the two bodies was described by the janitor who discovered them as having suffered partial decomposition, "puss-like rotting," although the unusual condition was apparently localized in specific areas. Dr. Ericson's body exhibited the puzzling condition on the sides of the head—particularly the ears, which seemed to have melted away, along with adjacent areas of the skull and the brain—while his butler showed similar decomposition in the mouth area, as well as on the sides of his head.

According to Jim Martin, the janitor, the butler's mouth had completely rotted away, exposing parts of the jaw and mandible bones. The police have refused to comment on the Martin story, or to allow examination of the remains by members of the press. The officer in charge of the investigation also refused to indicate whether or not the autopsy reports would be made public.

Dr. Ericson owned a valuable collection of occult and rare books. The presence of gaps in the shelves of the room where the bodies were found has led some friends to speculate on theft as a possible motive, although the evidence for foul play is not clear, since the cause of death has not been determined, much less any possible weapon. The possibility of acid has been suggested, although Martin rejects this explanation, insisting that the heads of the victims looked as if they had burst from inside, which is patently absurd. He also admitted having had several drinks earlier that evening.

Jack Davis had paled considerably while reading the report, and now stood up, his face as gray as his unkempt beard, only to stagger and grab hold of the lamp-post decorating a corner of the room, for support.

"My God, Mr. Corelli, the same as with the other—there must be things that are truly unspeakable, horrors that cannot be tolerated by a human brain or heard by a human ear... this is sheer madness... this is more than madness... if I hadn't seen that other one with my own eyes... Gawd, Corelli, how can you be so calm? I don't... I don't want to have anything more to do with this kind of thing... no more!" Davis's eyes protruded slightly as he addressed the plump man sitting at the gold and onyx desk, peacefully puffing at his cigar.

"Aw, Jack, c'mon! Too much imagination, I tell you. And besides, surely you haven't forgotten your daughter, have you? Cynthia Davis is such a pretty girl, such a little innocent birdie... Now, we wouldn't like for anything like this to happen to little Cindy, would we, eh, Jack? Sit down, old boy, and calm down."

Davis remained standing for a moment, then collapsed on his chair as if all his strength had left him. He was a broken man, and a resigned look appeared on his face.

"Did... did... did the thing... come back?"—he asked with a tremulous voice.

"Yup, never fails!" laughed Corelli, and opened a large drawer in his desk. "Here, buddy-boy." His thick, bejeweled fingers removed a large black box, with an ornate design on the top. "Just like the old chink said—look!"

Jack Davis recoiled in horror as his boss removed from the inside of the black box the smaller box he knew so well, the hellish Pandora's box of the demented Tomeron the Decayed, with all its waxen seals intact.

"Here, Jack, take it..."

"Please, Mr. Corelli, I'm afraid, dammit, I'm scared, hell, aren't you human—doesn't this thing *bother* you? Such things should not be! Please, Mr. Corelli, couldn't someone else?..."

"Enough! *Basta!*" Corelli's fist slammed on the top of his desk. "Don't you be a fool, Davis! This has been a most profitable enterprise for both of us—you know I can't use anyone else. You have the connections and the reputation as a dealer in kook books. No one else would do. Here, take that crazy toy—c'mon, it won't bite you. And I know you can't read Arabic, so you are pretty safe, even if curiosity got the best of you—not that I think you'd ever open the little box! You'd rather open your own coffin, huh? Ha! Take it, and perhaps I won't have to give your little Cindy a personal visit, not yet, anyway!" He winked an eye and flashed a lascivious smile.

Visibly shaken, Jack Davis accepted the odd-looking box with the waxen seals with obvious repugnance, and immediately proceeded to wrap it with the newspaper pages on the desk, as if anxious to avoid further physical contact with the instrument of death and madness it contained.

Corelli laughed loudly. "My, Jack, old boy, one would think I had asked you to finger a snake! Well, you'll get over it, won't you? Yeah—

well, those crazy book freaks do get good stuff, you know? The quality of the latest batch was the best ever. The poor nuts will do anything to get the book they want. Well, to each his fetish, no, Jack? Gimme good ol' greenbacks any time, and I'll give you the world... how about you, Jack—what is your fetish?"

Davis did not reply, sullenly staring straight ahead.

"Oh, my, don't look so pissed! Think of the good side—your commission on the last one is ten per cent, as usual, and I'll add a grand to your account, to show my appreciation! By the way... you may soon be hearing from a wealthy occultist, a kook known by the name 'Stag' Dawoud, who gets really high on them crazy nut books. You know, he recently learned, quite by accident"—here Corelli grinned and winked at his silent interlocutor—"that a copy of the fabled and legendary book of Tomeron, the loathsome *Necrotic Book*, exists in this country... Should I add that he is extremely anxious to add it to his collection? I'm sure he has heard your name mentioned as a possible source of information, if not of the actual thing..."

Corelli started laughing hysterically. "The price has been doubled, of course. You know how those rare books increase in price, particularly the out of print ones, when there is a lot of demand... But I shouldn't be telling you this, should I, Jack? I understand this guy Dawoud has quite a few connections in the Orient, and has access to some of the best stuff, and in quantity—it should be a pleasurable transaction, don't you think? And there will be more—a great gold mine, my boy— who would have thought books could be that much fun? I don't think I've read any since my dear departed mother gave up on teaching me the Catechism! *Ciao, amigo*, and keep in touch, huh?"

Jack Davis whispered—"Forgive me, Cindy..."

He stood up, slowly, leaves of the newspaper falling at his feet.

"I have been reading, and I have learned many things, Mr. Corelli— even some *lghat-ul-'arabyah*, you bastard, *ibn-sharmtah*..."

Carlo Corelli stopped smiling.

"Hey, Jack, you gone nuts? Armando! Arturo! Hey, don't..."

It was too late—Jack Davis had opened the box, and the book within, and commenced reading in a deep voice...

* * *

There was stiff bidding at the auction disposing of some of the stuff the recently widowed *Signora* Maria Corelli decided to get rid of. Particularly noticeable was the extremely high bid a certain Stagnus Dawoud made for a queer oriental box. Maria Corelli felt strangely relieved to see it sold, although she could not explain why...

NIGHT BUS

BY DONALD R. BURLESON

I CAUGHT MY MIDNIGHT BUS FOR BRATTLEBORO IN A QUIET, nameless town in northern Vermont, at one of those typical little ramshackle bus stations that deepen one's sense of vague depression at traveling alone at night, with their dull-eyed and incommunicative ticket sellers, their dingy rows of well-thumbed magazines and tabloid newspapers beneath bare lightbulbs, their dirty floors, and their faint odours of perspiration and urine. The air was still and humid, and as I stood with my valise among nondescript people, I sighed at the seemingly frozen clockhands on the wall over the ticket counter. It was with some relief that I finally saw the bus pull up and stop in front of the station. I got in line, handed my ticket to the driver, and boarded the bus, which already carried a number of passengers; I was able, however, to find a seat all to myself on the right-hand side of the bus near the back, and no one sat next to me. I leaned back in the cushioned seat, knowing that I had never been able to sleep on a bus, but hoping to get some rest during my four-hour ride, which I knew would be interrupted by unwelcome stops at other colourless little terminals along the way. Soon the bus had pulled out of the station, and dark, low hills were slipping by in the night outside the window, slipping by like amorphous and evanescent thoughts.

I stretched and tried to relax. The bus had no sooner found its stride on the road, however, when the driver slowed suddenly and stopped to pick up a straggling passenger who had waited on the side of the road. I could see his form only dimly in silhouette while he fumbled for money to pay the driver and then picked his way back among the seats as the bus jolted into motion again. He paused a couple of times, but, to my displeasure, finally chose the seat next to me and dropped into it.

My sidelong glances in the near-dark gave me no favourable impressions of this new fellow-rider, nor was my olfactory assessment of him any more promising. He seemed to be a gaunt, elderly man, though I could not clearly see his face, and his clothes were tattered and musty. He exuded an odour which I found difficult to characterize, but decidedly unpleasant, and this impression grew in potency as the minutes wore on. I had the vague sense that he was ill with some obscure and detestable malady, and this feeling in me was not diminished when he cleared his throat with a sticky-fluid sound that made me shudder. When I reflected on the prospect of a long night's ride next to this repellent companion, my mood grew ineluctably sombre.

After a while I managed, staring out the window at the dark, domed hills gliding by, almost to lose him in the dreamy tangle of my thoughts, though his offensive odour was still such that I breathed shallowly and would have kept my face averted even if there had been no window to look out upon the night. But I was brought sharply back to awareness of him when, as I think I had unconsciously dreaded, he actually spoke to me.

"Gonna meet my wife jes' this side o' Akeleyville."

"Hm," I replied, with a slight nod, trying to convey a tone which neither seemed rude nor particularly invited further conversation. His voice had had a repulsively liquid quality almost like an articulated gargling. Turning my head to glance at the man, I received impressions in the dim, sporadic flashes of light, from passing autos, that were not reassuring at all. The man's face, only glimpsed momentarily, seemed to have an odd greyness about it, an unclean quality that heightened, or was heightened by, the ghoulish way in which his lips seemed drawn back from his stained teeth, and the way in which his eyes peered hollowly out at me from deep, tenebrous sockets. The face was not unlike a death-mask, and when a passenger two seats in front of me flicked on an overhead reading light, I was startled to see in the dim peripheral glow of the bulb that from the stranger's eyes there welled a trickle of some yellow, pus-like fluid. I shuddered anew; I felt, indeed, almost choked by the proximity of this loathsome wraith, and only a curious sort of dullness in my muscles kept me from rushing up to the driver and demanding to be let off the bus at once.

A seemingly endless stretch of time ensued, during which the man, I could see from the corner of my left eye, turned to look at me from time to time. As the minutes passed, the stench of the man grew well-nigh intolerable, and the thought crossed my mind that only the fact that the immediately adjacent passengers were asleep could have kept them from noticing it; I wondered that the man with the reading light, though two seats away, had not caught the odour, if indeed he had not. As I struggled to keep the smell from invading my nostrils, I could not help trying at the same time to place it; and it gradually dawned on me that it was very much like the odour of organic decay—like rotting meat neglected in a kitchen.

"Say."

The word came at me with a sibilant rush of foetid breath that very nearly made me retch. I turned with the greatest reluctance to glance at him as he spoke again.

"We're gettin' near Akeleyville. I'll be biddin' ye good night in a minute or two."

I smiled wanly and hoped that my sigh of relief was not noticeable. Then, just as he began to rise from his seat, he sent a thrill of ineffable horror straight to my bones with his next, last words to me.

"Ya *know* me, don't ye? Wal, it's true—I ain't like yew, young feller. Yew're still among th' livin'. But it ain't so bad—my wife is like me. Keeps a body from bein' too lonely."

Just as he turned to stand up in the aisle, a quick flash of pale light revealed him to be scratching his cheek with a scaly and malodorous hand, and I saw that pieces of flesh were coming off in a rubbery, sliding cascade as his fingers seemed to slip into his face. It took all the fortitude I had, then, to keep from vomiting, but I only moaned as he turned and was gone, picking his way back up the aisle to the front of the bus and gesticulating with the driver, apparently to be let off on the road.

As the bus disgorged this revolting creature, I caught sight of another figure waiting for him on the side of the road, illumined faintly by the lights of autos that had stopped behind the bus, evidently unable to get around because of traffic in the other lane. She was as tattered and loathsome of aspect as he, with a face that, like his, was a death-mask now burned dreadfully into my memory. They embraced loathsomely as the bus pulled away, and they were grinning cadaverously at each other as the night swallowed them up again. Would to heaven that I had taken my gaze from them a moment earlier—in the dark I might not have noticed. Oh God, I might not have noticed!

I might not have noticed that the woman, in all her charnel ghastliness, was obviously eight or nine months pregnant.

THE PEWTER RING

BY PETER CANNON

His coming to New York had probably been the smartest move of his life—though he had not begun to think so until, after months of monotonous job-hunting, he had settled on some stimulating and marginally profitable publishing work. Scion of an ancient French Huguenot family, Edmund Aymar had left suburban Westchester for the metropolis of his forefathers, who had been among the island's earlier and more prominent citizens. There he had anticipated making his mark on the world—not as a lawyer or banker or stockbroker, professions customarily pursued by Aymar men—but in one or another of the more Bohemian, less financially remunerative trades.

With the support of inherited money, wisely husbanded by the intervening generations since his great-great-grandfather, John Marshall Aymar, laid the foundation of the modern family fortune before the Civil War, Edmund Aymar was used to enjoying all the privileges of his class. (Educated privately, he had always been a dreamer who felt himself apart from the conventional classroom routine. Given his prep school record as an underachiever, he had failed like many of his background in these latter days to gain entrance to the Ivy League college traditionally attended by his people.) His independent income covered his basic needs: a one-bedroom, ground-floor rear West Side apartment; a wardrobe of Brooks Brothers clothes; and a freezer filled with Stouffer's dinners. Freed from the anxieties faced by most young men embarking upon careers in the city, Aymar could indulge in cultivating his already richly refined aesthetic sensibilities.

An avid amateur student of architecture, Aymar delighted in strolling past the quaint brownstones that lined the side streets of his neighborhood, picking out such pleasing details as an elegant cornice here or an exquisite balustrade there. On occasion he ventured farther afield, exploring the curved lanes and irregular by-ways of Greenwich Village and other antique districts of the city. At first the imposing Manhattan skyline served only to oppress his spirit, but in time he came to relish the rugged beauty of those concrete and glass monoliths that soared, especially at night, like so many *Arabian Nights* arabesques to the starless haze above.

He took a keen interest in the history of New York, in particular in the activities of his ancestor, John Marshall Aymar, who had figured so eminently in the city's business, political, and social life in the eighteen-forties and fifties. Spending much of his free time either at the New York Historical Society near him or else at the Museum of the City of New York (a brisk twenty-minute walk across Central Park), Aymar became increasingly fascinated with his great-great-grandfather the more he learned of him. The official accounts depicted the conscientious man of affairs, who had built a shipping empire, contributed generously to the Whig Party, and entertained lavishly at his Fifth Avenue mansion. Contemporary letters and diaries, however, gave hints of the inner man: a seeker after truth and beauty, sensitive and retiring, a poet, author of a slim volume of verse privately published in 1849. Portraits showed him to be slender, youthful, and fair, with the trace of an ethereal smile on delicate lips. (Oddly enough perhaps, Aymar looked nothing like his ancestor—but then everyone told him he strongly resembled his mother.) In no portrait did John Marshall Aymar betray the encroachment of age, for he had died in his forties of a queer, lingering disease that had baffled his physicians.

Immersed in his researches, Aymar learned as well of the past literary life of the city. He took particular satisfaction in knowing that in 1844 Edgar Allan Poe had lived in a farmhouse, where he had finished *The Raven*, at a site just two blocks away from him on Broadway. Old photographs showed a white wooden-framed home surrounded by shade trees on a hillside. By the end of the century the house had been razed, the trees cut, the hill leveled. Only a plaque affixed to the present-day Health Spa and Fitness Center reminds the passer-by that on this spot once dwelled America's most illustrious author. Aymar was among those who petitioned the mayor to rename a stretch of West 84th Street in Poe's honor; later he was one of those who wrote testy letters to the *Times* regarding the misspelling "Allen" for "Allan" on the street signs erected by the city.

During the first several years of his New York sojourn, Edmund Aymar took a quiet pride in residing in an almost forgotten, no longer fashionable neighborhood, inhabited at its core by a sizeable community of poor Hispanics. As the city as a whole recovered from a period of economic decline, however, prosperity like some insidious, viscous sea-creature began to spread its tentacles north from Lincoln Center along the broad, decayed avenues. In shockingly short time the mom-and-pop variety stores, the laundromats and shoe repairers, the ethnic bars and social clubs, and the plain, low-cost American eateries gave way to chic boutiques, trendy foreign restaurants, and slick singles joints catering to the BBQ crowd. Appalled, Aymar witnessed the pokey, two-story commercial buildings along Broadway succumb in a fever of real estate gluttony to hideous, high-rise apartment houses, whose tacky twin towers grotesquely aped the tasteful originals on Central Park West. Like a child who discovers too soon that instead of the stork leaving him under a cabbage leaf his parents had to engage in a gross physical act to bring about his existence, Aymar realized that the rapid, radical development of the city was not confined to some distant era in the history books, but was happening literally around the corner from him.

Disillusioned, Edmund Aymar retreated increasingly into those arcane studies that already had such a hold on his imagination. He withdrew to the billiards rooms and libraries of certain venerable clubs, where the old traditions were still esteemed among the genteel and bigoted members. His great-great-grandfather had helped to found the athletic club, where according to locker-room legend he had habitually escaped to avoid the demands and cares of business and family. The club library contained his volume of poetry, *Damon and Pythias and Ganymede*, tenuous verses celebrating the manly ideals of the classical world, which Aymar read and reread for inspiration.

A potent dreamer (in the usual sense of the word) from youth, Aymar often dreamed vividly of early New York: of bands of stoic

Red Men stalking meager game over marsh and meadow; of comical Dutchmen with broad-bore muskets strutting between stepped-gabled houses and a wooden wall that would in time become Wall Street; of Negro slaves rioting amidst fire and smoke; of redcoated soldiers, more grimly determined than their Dutch predecessors, seizing illicit arms and being quartered in private homes; of sailors jostling one another on wharves stacked high with barrels and boxes before a forest of ships' masts; of men parading in the street carrying torches and anti-draft placards; of a gloomy, long-bearded fellow inspecting a waterfront warehouse; of a slight, wispy-goateed gentleman supervising the construction of a gigantic pedestal on an island off the tip of Manhattan; and—most strikingly—of a blond, bland handsome figure with an enigmatic smile who seemed to be addressing him, teasing him with some maddening half-memory and the promise of titanic wonders just beyond the limit of ordinary human comprehension. This latter personage, he recognized with a thrill as soon as he woke up, was of course his own great-great-grandfather, John Marshall Aymar.

His ancestor became a larger and larger presence in his dreams, until one night Aymar could discern quite clearly his speech; indeed, his distinguished forebear instructed him to get up, get dressed, grab a flashlight, and go to a certain building site some ten blocks distant, where he would find in the rubble a ring—a pewter ring, to be exact. Not really knowing whether he still slept or was awake, Aymar obeyed and in a short while found himself prowling about in one of the many construction pits that made the West Side resemble Berlin circa 1945. Giving scant thought to the prospect of being picked up for trespassing, he felt as if he were being guided by some preternatural force and within a few minutes located a filth-encrusted object that he believed at first to be a pre-1965 quarter. Closer examination, coupled with an ecstatic shiver of the kind commonly experienced by those who are "born again," convinced him that this had to be what he was after.

Back at his apartment an assiduous application of Gorham silver polish brought forth a gleaming pewter ring, incised with primitive jungle motifs, and inscribed on the inside with what initially appeared to be an alien alphabet but when turned the other way around proved to be an ornate monogram—the initials J.M.A.! A confirmed skeptic of psychic phenomena, Aymar was overcome with confused emotions of horror and elation in the face of such an uncanny and startling discovery. He could not begin to guess at the colossal significance of the pewter ring, but dared to hope he would soon be enlightened. Sleep being out of the question, he passed the remainder of the dark hours fondling the ring, trying it on, ultimately deciding that it fit perfectly on the fourth finger of his left hand.

He wore the pewter ring to his office, an art gallery off Madison Avenue, where he had recently secured employment as an assistant. Still in a daze, he had scarcely noticed where he was on the bus ride across the park. At his desk, as he was on the verge of attending to some long overdue correspondence, Aymar saw the electric typewriter dissolve before his eyes, exposing not the woodlike surface of the desktop but genuine oak. The Bic ballpoint he customarily used had in turn, he realized upon seizing it, been transformed into a heavier, finer instrument—a fountain pen. An inkwell and sand stood on a blotter where none had stood before. Peering out the second-floor window, he beheld not a stream of fast, noisy motor vehicles but a thoroughfare alive with horse-drawn carriages of every description; men in beaver hats and swallowtail coats; vendors hawking their wares in heavy Irish accents. The weather suddenly was warm and foetid; the low hum of the air-conditioner was no longer audible.

As if propelled on some vital errand, Aymar rushed down into the street—a street paved with rough, square-cut stones—but he paid this marvel no more heed than the rest. He headed for Fifth Avenue, knowing that there he would find his destination. When he came up to the gate of the Palladian mansion he recognized it instantly as the home of his ancestor. The manservant who answered his rappings at the brass doorknocker seemed to be expecting him, and ushered him into a parlor decorated in the sumptuous Gothic Revival style of the mid-Victorian period. There against an oversize mantel leaned a gentleman in early middle-age, dressed in luxurious silks, whose bland, blond features seemed to glow with an otherworldly radiance.

"My dear young fellow, welcome," said John Marshall Aymar. "You cannot imagine with what delight I have anticipated this meeting." Finding himself at last face to face with the man of his dreams, Aymar was in too much awe to do any more than mutter his thanks. "Ah, you sport the pewter ring; but of course, how else are we united now? It is

owing to its agency that you have been able to transcend the barrier."
For a moment his ancestor gazed at the ring with singular intensity.

"I have a great deal to impart to you, Edmund, but we cannot tarry
here. Should my wife and children happen upon you, I would be sorely
tried to explain how I came to be entertaining an unknown relation,
a relation who has journeyed from so far away—in time." The servant
appeared in the doorway and announced that the hack awaited them.
"Come, we shall repair to premises where we can confer without fear
of interruption."

On the ride downtown his ancestor kept silent, smiling with the
serenity of one seemingly possessed of some vast, cosmic secret. From
the enclosed coach Aymar watched the confusion of a hot, dusty,
congested city, again accepting with equanimity his presence in a
bygone age as somehow part of the natural order of things.

At last they arrived at a quiet side street near the river—Weekawken
Street it may have been—and disembarked before a clapboard house
with the sign "Saloon" above the entrance. In the dim front room a
gang of dusky-skinned sailors huddled at the counter. The barkeeper
showed them to a backroom, and poured them a dark liquid out of a
labelless amber bottle.

John Marshall Aymar began his narrative by relating how he came to
acquire the pewter ring. As part of his charitable work among the poor
of the city, he had spent time visiting the Free Men who lived in the
shantytown far west of Fifth Avenue. There he had encountered some
Africans recently arrived in America via Haiti—"savages" who engaged in
occult practices. Impressing them with his eagerness to pierce the veil, he
had been granted the privilege of undergoing a physical rite of passage
that few dared to brave. He had proved worthy in the process of initiation
and had earned the pewter ring, though at a cost: he had contracted a
fatal illness, whose subtle course would bring him to an early grave. The
sacrifice was necessary, however, in order to attain "immortality."

"I have already had a glimpse of what lies in the Beyond," said
his ancestor, who could not repress a smug, condescending smile.
"Time is an illusion—all history is fixed in one omega-null continuum,
toroidal in shape. Gödel and Rucker of your own century, by the by,
are correct in their speculations on the ultimate nature of the space-
time synthesis."

He went on to explain that the ring had later been "reclaimed" by his African associates, with whom he had had a falling out. While his powers had been severely diminished, he still was able to exert some control over the "psychic energy" of the ring. Through the agency of dreams he could stretch across the decades and reach his first descendant to reside in the ring's vicinity over a substantial enough period of time. Once that descendant—he, Edmund Aymar—had found the ring (which had been lost again fortuitously after his "death"), then it was a relatively simple matter to summon him back into the past.

"I have worked hard, Edmund, for success in this world. I am an ambitious man." John Marshall Aymar grinned, relishing his triumphs. "I have enjoyed but a mere taste of the ring's glories, and no longer take an interest in the usual diversions of earthly existence. Circumstances have forced me to lead a double-life, but I shan't have to maintain appearances for long.

"You as well can achieve a similar transcendence—and I don't mean the sort of 'transcendental' experience extolled by those New England prigs, Emerson and Thoreau. It will require the surrender of your bodily shell; but the loss is small when you consider the gains to be had in return. What's another forty years of dilettantish dabbling, when if you choose the path of the pewter ring you can meet my late friend, the editor of the *Broadway Journal*, at the height of his powers? You can dwell in the New York of any era you wish. Millions of years from today, you may be piqued to know, volcanoes will dominate the horizon and once more New York will be a pastoral paradise, free of the teeming, uncouth hoi-polloi...

"I need your help, Edmund. You must give me back the pewter ring, for only then will I have the strength to aid you and secure your ultimate salvation. You shall follow, but first you must return to your own age. You cannot depart unless you release the ring to me... Here, lad, take a little more grog."

Dizzy with strong drink, Aymar had no desire to disappoint his ancestor and yet hesitated to give him the ring. But John Marshall Aymar would brook not the merest hint of opposition. Grinning maniacally, he lunged at Aymar's left hand. Instinctively recoiling from the assault, Edmund Aymar lurched clumsily to his feet, upsetting the table and glasses before them. More accustomed to heady beverages than his descendant, the older man regained his balance in a moment and seized him from behind. The two tumbled to the sawdust floor, where they rolled like beasts until their cries brought men rushing in from the outer room. Dark faces filled with cruel anticipation were the youth's final sight before he lost consciousness.

When Edmund Aymar woke up, bruised and sore, he found himself lying in the street, next to a homeless person also stretched out and disheveled, in front of a familiar house. Indeed, it was the same building he had entered perhaps hours before, but now it was covered with brown shingles where clapboard had been; too, electric street lamps illustrated the scene, not gas-lights. Aymar made his way to the Sheridan Square subway. That the pewter ring was missing from his finger he was too numb to notice.

In the months that followed Edmund Aymar wondered whether his coming to New York had been such a good idea after all. He obliquely discussed his "dream" experience with his therapist, sounding him out on the matter of free will versus determinism and the paradoxes inherent in time travel. Eventually he became fed up with the tiresome sessions and, like some Creationist repudiating evolution, dismissed his therapist, unshaken in his belief that heredity is more important than environment and that personality is largely innate. Resigned to whatever fate might bring, indifferent to his usual aesthetic pursuits, he gave up working altogether and scarcely stirred outside his cave-like apartment.

He also began to lose weight, to be prone to colds and the slightest infections.

The night before he was supposed to enter the hospital for tests, Edmund Aymar dreamed again of the old things. He was picking his way uncertainly along an unfamiliar path in what he thought was Riverside Park—though it was a wild, unlandscaped Riverside Park. Ahead of him, on an imposing outcropping of rock, he spied a cloaked figure, silhouetted against the setting sun. The man turned to meet his gaze, displaying a head of fine-webbed hair, wide brow, liquid eye, and silken moustache, then vanished into a copse beyond. Gaining the crest of the rock, Aymar beheld a great river, surely the Hudson, whose far shore was an unmarred stretch of cliff topped by an expanse of green rapidly darkening as night closed in. Then from behind he was accosted by the bland, blond form of his ancestor who, as he held out his hand to reveal a gleaming pewter ring, laughed with deep, sardonic pleasure.

The vision faded, and he realized that he was back in the New York of his own time, in the park at night—where three Hispanic youths were now demanding of him that he "hand it over, mister, or—" His protests that he no longer had the ring did not satisfy them, and in the ecstatic moment just after the fist struck his cheek and just before he lost consciousness Edmund Aymar felt renewed in his faith—faith in all the promises of his ancestor that he soon would be "having it all."

JOHN LEHMANN ALONE

BY DAVID KAUFMAN

JULY, 1993

I guess I should begin by saying that it's not the easiest thing in the world for me to tell a story. I don't really know much about that sort of business. I never went but to the fourth grade, and even then I didn't hardly care for reading. I did like arithmetic a lot, though. Arithmetic's not like other things. You've got something solid there. You always know what you have with an arithmetic problem.

It's a funny thing to me now, it really is, but I didn't want to do nothing but get out of school and go to work on my daddy's farm. And I was let out early for need.

In those days, you see, you could leave school to help out at home if you were needed bad enough. That was the law then. Well, I couldn't wait, and my daddy did need me, so I got to quit school very early in life and go to work with him. It was a happy day for me.

My mother was against it, she wanted me to go on at least to the eighth grade, but I insisted. I figured I knew better. So I finished the fourth grade, as I said, and then I quit.

The only reason I say all of this is because I went to school with John Lehmann. And we been friends for all these years since. That was nearly sixty years ago, so you can see that I knew him for a long time.

What happened to him and to his shouldn't of happened to anybody.

Well, his daddy's farm was right below my daddy's farm, down low in the valley south of Garlock's Bend, and so in time it turned out that his farm was right below mine, they both come down to us by rights. It was good bottom ground. And so wonderful for water because the Susquehanna cut right through it. It even flooded every dozen years or so, and that made the ground around there even better. There was a lot of water. That's important to remember.

I never got married. John, he did, to a wonderful girl from over to Skinner's Eddy, Caroline Jacobs, and they had kids, and time passed like it does for us all. The kids grew up and didn't want to stay around Garlock's Bend so they left and went down to Harrisburg to work. Carrie, his wife, she sort of just seemed to not quite care so much about things after that.

Now I always liked Carrie, don't get me wrong about her. I really did. A whole lot more than *liked*. A whole lot more. In my own way, of course. I guess that in the end that's important to remember, too.

Miller's Store, where all this sort of comes to a head, you'll have to understand about. It's kind of the place in Garlock's Bend where everybody goes. You can buy groceries there, and you can buy clothes there. And tools. And even light meals. You get so you don't have to leave town very often. It's an honest-to-goodness general store, in the middle of town right down along the river. I knowed it through four owners ever since the building was put up. And my daddy was one of the men who helped to do that. The current owner, Bill Miller, bought the store off of his second cousin, Henry, who decided to retire pretty nearly thirty years ago now, and he's run it ever since.

Generally it's open by eight, only hardly nobody would ever be in there that early but Bill, fussing around with boxes and cans on the shelves, keeping things all straightened up. Not hardly ever anyone else, though. Not much happens early in Garlock's Bend. It's a town used to slow starts. But the people of the town and the hills around, too, consider Miller's to be something of a meeting hall, so it is almost always open. Later in the mornings there's lots of them comes in. The talk is just plain satisfactory. You'll have that. And the coffee is special. So it's not at all unusual at ten or eleven in the morning to see a fistful of men stuffed into orange hunting jackets all clustered around the home-made wooden tables, elbows on red-checkered table cloths, sipping hot coffee rich with cream and sugar. Listening to young Dale Heberlein, the morning disk jockey from over at Towanda. Every one of them men laughing at Dale's humor. With maybe a bought doughnut or some eggs and home fries, all peppered up. Add the smell of that coffee, maybe even some hand cut bacon, and it's as good a way to start the day as there is.

Well, that's Miller's for you. That's where things started to go haywire.

Funny thing is, even though I lived so close to John Lehmann, I got to talk to him mostly there at Miller's. At home, right next to him, it was all farm business until the evenings. And then he had his family to attend to, with very little time at all to jawbone with me. I was alone, and like as not off doing things myself, chasing around, so mostly I saw and talked to him after growing seasons in the late mornings at Miller's, and I sometimes think he wouldn't of come there even then but for my sake, to befriend me and spend even just a little time with me. I always appreciated that.

I now and again think he knew, too, how very much I cared for Carrie down through the years. Maybe better than she did. But I never said a single word of it to either of them or to a person alive. I just would never have done that.

Over the seasons I sure liked the mornings I spent with him at Miller's, but I especially liked those last few times. We used to sit and talk and drink that coffee. God, how I remember that!

It makes the loss of him all the more painful.

Some things, I guess, you'd end up going mad if you tried to keep inside of you. Just completely mad. And so I guess the best thing is to just tell the story, no matter how painful, to say what happened, get it out in the open finally and maybe get a handle on it. I have to admit, though, that John Lehmann's story has me licked, and more than that—it's got me scared, too.

Well, there isn't a whole lot happening on a small farm in late October, except maybe finishing up your apples, and getting the ground ready for next year, that sort of thing, so for a couple of weeks this particular October I had been going just as regular as anything to Miller's for breakfast and for talk. Mostly it was just to pass time.

For the first of those weeks John and Carrie occasionally came in, too, and we had some good mornings together. All the usual stuff, bragging about farming and hunting, and me teasing Carrie and finagling an invitation for a supper from her soon.

Carrie Lehmann, I've got to tell you, was the gentlest, kindest, most friendly woman I ever knew. That's a certain thing. And it's not the most important thing in the world, but she had such beautiful light blue eyes. Those last times I saw her over there at Miller's are dear times to me yet. They seem now to me to be a kind of adding up of all the earlier times I was ever around her. Sort of like they were the real times and all the ones before were like dreams. I don't know. I guess I can't say it exactly like I mean it.

Then they began to not come to Miller's so often. Winter wasn't so very far off and we had a cold snap, and I guessed maybe it just was easier for them to stay home when that cold spell set in. There wasn't anything too unusual in that.

But then there was that last time I saw Carrie. It had rained hard more or less on and off for about a week. It was cold and damp and all the water had pushed up the Susquehanna until it was as high as it's ever been. I mean, it was *high*. And there we were in Miller's, just like always.

But this particular time there was something really different about Carrie. I could see that right away. She hardly touched her coffee at all, hardly touched it at all, and she wouldn't talk about any of the usual things no matter how we tried to get her to. And she fussed and she fretted.

"We've got to go back, John," she said. "It's time to go back home."

Well, they had just come. I didn't know quite what to think of that one, they had really just arrived not ten minutes before. And she seemed so nervous and so far away in her head when she talked. So I just stayed out of it.

"John, the water's getting so high," she pleaded. "I'm sure it's nearly high enough. We had better go back. It's not safe to be anywhere away from home when the water's this high." Her old blue eyes were glistening as she said quietly, "It'll be right up next to the house. It'll be high enough for it to..." She caught herself and looked down.

God, but she did seem scared of something.

John, he just sort of looked at her, like he didn't know quite what to say either. And then he looked away. He tried to keep a little conversation going on with me, but you could see how helpless and embarrassed he was.

Carrie, she got real quiet, and she just sort of kept looking at

John pleadingly. When she did finally talk again she just mumbled, and it was about the high water, how dangerous that was, and how easy it would be to break through. And they better get home to keep everything safe. How she was scared bad for the both of them. And crazy things like that. All in sort of low and broken sentences.

But I sure was feeling badly for John, and I was scared for Carrie. There was something wrong with her, all right. She wasn't acting normal, not for her nor for anyone else, talking like that. She seemed so scared because of the rain and the water rising in the river.

John, he ended up putting his arm around her and leading her quietly out of Miller's. And he bent over and kissed her head lightly once as he did. I was really touched by that display of love, him being so matter-of-fact and all. He never even looked back.

Well, John did come alone a few times more to Miller's, but he seemed distant somehow. He just sat there, quiet. He never brought up Carrie, and he wouldn't answer any questions about her when someone else did. And then he always just left, like he had decided it was a bad idea to come there in the first place. And he did that pretty nearly always right away.

We never did get to see Carrie no more. No sir, I never saw her alive after that day.

There was something strange in the air. I just had this funny feeling. You know how a person can get.

For instance, I used to sit out on the porch in the evenings, no matter how cool it got—I like the cold weather—and I could see over to John's farm. Towards the end I noticed that there was always only a kitchen light on, never one upstairs. Never. And once when I wasn't sleeping good I looked out my window at about three in the morning and that light was still on. Now no farmer stays up like that. It just is never done.

Then John stopped coming to the store.

Well, one thing led to another, and I got to thinking that something had gone sour over next door. I figured Carrie was real sick, or something like that. Hell, we were *all* old. And I decided to go over and see them and ask if I could help. Now, that may seem like the most normal thing in the world to most everybody, but you must understand this, around Garlock's Bend a piece of interference like that is very serious business, because we tend not to trouble each other, not even to visit without first being asked. We respect each other and let each other alone. It's just that we keep this feeling of distance, sort of.

Well, finally I couldn't help it. I couldn't have stayed away any longer even if I wanted to, and so I went over late one Saturday evening and knocked on John Lehmann's door. There was no answer. That didn't ring true to me, I knew better, and soon I was pounding hard on his door.

I was shocked when John finally opened it just a little. I could see into the room to his kitchen table. It was all cluttered with dirty dishes and spoiled food. There was more used dishes in the sink. And the whole kitchen just looked absolutely filthy. John, too, had a kind of wild, dirty look. His hair was going every which way, and he needed a shave. He looked like he was real confused.

He stood with the door opened only a little ways, kind of peeking out, like he was afraid I would try to come in. Right away then I knew something was wrong, because friends don't do that to each other. He was shaking his head back and forth slowly, and already starting to close the door, almost as if he didn't know me. "I'm forbidden to let anyone in," he said. His voice was weak and full of fear. "I'm just not allowed to."

"John," I said. "You got to let me in." Something was very wrong. "I'd like to talk to you, John," I said. "John? Let me in." I started to push on the door, but he got it closed before I could do anything. And then the kitchen light went out and the whole house was dark.

I just stood there for a minute or more, collecting myself. I was really scared. Well sir, the next thing I did, I went all around the house and peeked in every window that I could, only I couldn't see anything, because all the lights was out. I tried to pull up on every window, but they were all locked. And then I tried all three doors and the cellar door, too, but I got nowhere.

It was as if no one had lived in the house for years, it was shut up so tight. I stood there in the dark, with just the silence and a little night wind blowing ever so easy.

The river was really coming up, rising up the slope in back of the house. It made an eerie slurping sound in the dark, sliding along heavy like it did.

My stomach was rolling with pain, and I was sweating, no matter the cold. I was really scared that something terrible had happened to

Carrie and John. What it was I didn't even want to guess.

I didn't see any movement over at John's all the next day or that night either. I thought about it off and on all day and decided against saying anything to anyone else just yet. Actually, it really wasn't none of my business. And for all I knew, everything was like it always was with the both of them.

The next afternoon then I spied John out back going into his milk-house. He was carrying a box of something that looked real heavy. Well, to me that was as good a time as any. I figured to go on over and talk to him while he was still in the milkhouse, maybe even block his way and keep him in there until he told me what was going on.

When I got to the doorway I could see him taking quarts of peaches from the box and letting them down easy into the water to cool them. He looked up at me as I stood there, for I blocked the light from outside, you see. He did not smile at me.

"Carrie always liked her peaches," he said finally. He was cleaned up pretty good this time. He nodded. "And I do, too." He shook his head carefully. "Got lots of them." He reached me a quart. "You want to take one home?" Except he didn't seem too happy, it was almost as if it was the most normal day in the world to him. Just like nothing was unusual. I could hardly believe it.

"Look here," I said, and I was trying to hold down both my Dutch temper and all my fears. "Just what is going on, John? Just what the hell is going on with you?"

"There ain't nothing going on," he said slowly, eyeing me carefully. I felt really awkward. It was *his* farm and all. I didn't want him thinking I didn't trust him. If you don't trust a man, you got nothing good between you and him ever again. I didn't want that to happen.

But I waited just a moment and then I decided to take the chance. "Where's Carrie?" I asked.

He stood there quietly for a little bit, looking me over. And then I guess he decided I had the right. "In the house," he said. "She's been bad sick. Real bad." He put the last of the peaches into the trough. "Well," he said quietly, "you know how it is. Ain't none of us getting any younger." He tried a smile that didn't quite work. "Ain't that right?"

"Maybe somebody ought to come in," I said. "Give you a hand. Lots of us would be proud to."

"I don't need no hand," he said. "I don't want no one helping."

"Maybe Carrie needs a doctor," I tried.

"No doctor," he said. "Ain't no doctor can help Carrie now." Just as matter of fact as that.

"Well," I said, "I could do something." I said it as slowly and as clearly as I could. "Somebody should be helping you out."

He dropped the empty box onto the floor. "I don't want no help," he said. "I don't want nothing from nobody." He almost seemed angry or something.

I looked at him for a long time. But there was nothing to see in his face.

"Okay," I said, after what seemed like a couple of minutes of him staring at me and me at him. "If that's how you want it, John."

"That's how I want it."

"You know I consider you my friend."

"I know that," he said.

Well, there it is. That's the whole of our conversation that day. I shrugged my shoulders and left. I looked back once and saw him still standing tall in the doorway of the milkhouse, glaring out at me. And when he turned around I left and didn't look back no more.

Now when you go over all this you have to remember that we are an isolated and a rural people, as I said, and we have our ways. If he wanted to be all by himself to take care of Carrie until she died, if that was what was happening to her, who was I or who was anyone to stop him. May seem odd, but that's how people our way are. We take care of our own. We mind our own beeswax. And if we don't want no help, why, that is our concern entirely. I guess I understood that in him. I didn't like it, but I understood it.

The idea of Carrie being on her way to dying just almost destroyed me is all. The thought of never even getting to see her again. That was an awful thing to think about. It wasn't till a couple of days later, after going over and over it in my head, that I got the first feelings that maybe there was more still, maybe John was not telling me the full truth. Just all of a sudden I had that thought. And then I couldn't get it out of my mind.

But it was obvious to me that he was nervous and frightened and not acting like himself at all. So I concluded that maybe the idea of him holding back wasn't so far fetched.

Maybe Carrie wasn't just sick.

Maybe it was far worse than that. *Something* was making him act peculiar. And I sure did want to find out what that was.

I sat on my porch swing that evening, kicking myself easy and watching John's place. I felt sneaky and miserable doing it, like I was some kind of spy, but I just kept on staring over there. And as it started to get dark, only his kitchen light was on, just like always.

Sometimes when a thing's going wrong, a body gets to having a compulsion. It just takes hold of him, and he can't help but do the first thing that occurs to him. He's just got to.

Well, that was what happened to me. All of a sudden I couldn't sit still no more. I figured to go on over to John's house and get inside somehow and see what was going on. Whether he wanted me to or not. Trust or not. I had to see if Carrie was still alive, see if she was sick, see what was up. Anything would be better than sitting on that old swing and looking at his kitchen light and wondering.

I moved down off my porch and started towards his house. My stomach had begun to churn with fear, although to be truthful, I don't know even yet exactly what I was afraid of. Maybe just of what I was about to do. Handy to his house I began to slow up. My upper lip got to feeling cold and clammy. And the closer I came to the bright light of John's kitchen, the darker everything else around me seemed to be.

It was really strange and unusual that night. In spite of all the rain just earlier that evening and in the past weeks, the sky was so clear and so dark you could see stars right down to the horizon. There was some houses way off in the distance, with their lights on, and it was hard to tell what was lights from the houses and what was stars. You don't often get that.

I stopped just outside his gate, stood there for a couple of long minutes before I even dared to go into his yard. And I guess I never knew how much noise a creaky old wooden gate can make until that night.

I got to the edge of the house and then, bent over nearly double and moving slow as I could, I snuck on over to the window. I stood up carefully at the corner of it and peeked in.

It seemed so bright inside. John was sitting alone at the kitchen table. He was looking right at the window, but I was sure he didn't see me. He appeared to be in a daze. He nodded his head. He did it again, like he was listening? I couldn't see anybody else in the room. There was a look of unhappiness on his face that I'll never forget, and it appeared like he had been weeping. He was just painful to see, is all.

Well, sir, all of a sudden he starts to shake his head no, just a little and then a little more, and next harder and harder, like he had had enough. And then he sort of throws the chair backward and jerks himself up real quick, till he was standing. He let out this long, low moan that got louder and louder until it was a scream. And again he screamed.

Then he run out of the kitchen, wailing things all the while, but I couldn't make out what any of the words were.

Well, I was shocked so bad I could hardly move. But then I knew I had to do something, and so I circled the house slowly in the dark, trying for a look inside. There wasn't a light in any of the windows or anywhere else but the kitchen. I could hardly believe that. He had to be in there somewhere.

It was fully dark outside now, too, and I kicked a pail that I didn't see or it was some fool thing, and I was scared he would hear. Or maybe I was scared he wouldn't hear, I don't know. But when I stood quiet, everything was still only the silence.

Around the back of the house I was surprised that the river had got so close up the bank there that I had to be careful I did not slip into it as I circled. I could hear it moving by ever so slowly and ever so quietly. And it was a *lot* closer. Massive, is what the Susquehanna river was that night. Dark, and quiet, and massive. And somehow majestic. Big rivers are like that.

I guess maybe it had got to within three feet of the house. Real close anyways. And it was still rising. I could hear clumps of sod falling in, washing away. It was an awesome thing, being in all that dark and knowing that the river was hissing quietly by almost tight up against the house, like a giant, slowly coiling snake that had a life of its own. I could *feel* it going by as well as hear it.

So I carefully worked my way round back to the kitchen window again, and I looked in, pretty boldly this time. But there was nothing unusual in there, except for how filthy it was.

I waited for about five minutes. No signs of John returning. Everything was quiet.

I tell you, I felt about as strange as I want to, just standing there. The sky was almost completely dark now, and the stars were really shining. It could have been peaceful that night, except for what was going on in the house. Or what I feared was going on.

My stomach was really cramping up good by this time, and my hands were all cold, and my upper lip. It felt as if someone were sticking needles into the back of my neck.

I stood there for a few more minutes, trying to decide. And then just suddenly I knew what I had to do. Moving as quietly as was possible for me, I came round to the steps and eased up onto the porch. I stood in front of the door, hesitating.

My head was going this way and that. I wanted to run. But the Lehmanns were my friends, and I had to try to help, whatever the problem was.

I opened the door carefully. I moved inside, at first as quietly as I could, but then in consideration of John I decided to make as much noise as possible, so he wouldn't think I was sneaking around in his house.

"John?" I called.

There was no answer.

"Where are you, John?"

Again there was no answer of any kind.

Then I got to really be frightened for him. I figured to try upstairs first, and I climbed up the steps to the bedrooms just as quickly as my old legs would take me, looked in one after another of them, but neither John nor Carrie was anywhere. Each room was clean and neat and all made up. Next I got myself up the narrow steps to his attic, and I searched around everywhere, but all I saw was old cribs and picture frames and boxes tied with faded ribbons. It looked like no one had even been in the attic for years.

I stood up there shaking, and I expelled all the air that had been building up in my lungs. I forced myself to relax, and then I worked my way, slowly now, back down to the kitchen. I cannot tell you how depressed I had become. Their marriage, our friendship, the passing of the years, the joy of the last few weeks with them—all of it was a big whirl in my mind. I don't know what I expected to find up there, but I did expect to find *something*. Carrie was missing, that was for sure, and that was bad news. And John was not answering my calls.

Only the cellar was left.

I was tired enough by the time I got back into the kitchen that I had to sit down for a little. The table was cluttered with dirty dishes and empty quart jars. That depressed me even more, because it looked to me like John had been alone for a good while, eating peaches out of a jar like an old bachelor who no longer cared very much. Or maybe the peaches reminded him of Carrie, I don't know. Whatever it was, it was not a good sign either way.

God, my head was awhirl with all these strange thoughts!

I suppose I sat at that table for another five minutes, trying to calm myself. The only sound was the slow, even ticking of John's Ansonia, which Carrie brought him home from the Chicago's World's Fair.

But it was inevitable. I knew I had to go into the cellar. Wherever Carrie was, that was another story, but John, he couldn't be anyplace else but down there.

So I moved into the hallway, switched on the light, and stood in front of the cellar door. I know now what it means to be shaking like a leaf. I was so scared of what was ahead of me. I forced myself to wait for even a few more minutes till I got a better hold of my nerves.

Finally I was ready. I eased open the cellar door just wide enough to squeeze through, and then I stood at the little landing at the top. It was pitch dark down there, pitch dark, and I switched the landing light on and off, but the bulb was burnt out or loose or something, because no light would go on. I couldn't hear anything or anybody downstairs.

"John?" I called out. "John?"

It's strange to me now, but I remember I called his name gently, almost as a loud whisper. Reverently even, I don't know. Like I was afraid to be too loud. That's a remarkable thing.

There was no answer.

I pushed open the cellar door as wide as I could to let in some light. And until my eyes got used to the darkness I just sat down on the second step from the top and waited.

Still I heard nothing, but I could not get it out of my mind that John was down there somewhere, and he just was not answering my calls. Why, I could not say.

Then little by little I started to see shapes, and before long I could see most of the cellar. I could make out the furnace and the air ducts, a cluttered work table, the churn, things like that. Not good, but I could see them.

Nothing was moving. And I decided that I had guessed wrong when I figured John Lehmann was down there.

But I wanted to be sure, and so I slowly and quietly eased myself, still sitting, one step at a time lower till I was maybe a third of the way down and could see all around the cellar, both in front of the steps and behind them.

And then, God help me, I did see something. I was not in any way prepared for what was over on the far side, the side of the cellar along the river. I would never have guessed it in a million years.

Everything was still only in shades of gray, nothing had any color, but by this time I could see lots of details. Close to the river wall was an old brass bed, with rumpled bedclothes. I guessed soon enough that it was where John had been sleeping, it sure looked like it, down there in the cellar. Probably ever since Carrie had disappeared.

Then right away between the bed and the wall was a long mound, newly dug in the dirt floor. That took my breath away. I knew what it was, all right. That mound was just long enough, and slightly rounded, and I knew what it was.

Lots of feelings went rushing through my head then. Fear, and anger, and pity, and hurt. And the inevitable, "Why?"

Aw-w, God, that scene did pain me so.

I could not imagine what the mound was doing down in the cellar. And why in the world he had buried her down there. She had died, sure enough, my fears were right, but Carrie belonged in a proper grave. She did. But here she was, down in a hidden pit in a moldy cellar. With a bed right next, and with the dark and the mildew. It was such an awful place.

I do not think I can tell you just how sad and how alone I suddenly felt. With Carrie gone.

Then I was able to see John moving a little. I had missed him till that moment. He was kneeling at the head of the mound, with his hands clasped together. And he was trembling, I made that out. I didn't quite see his face, but he had to mean what he was doing, kneeling down like that. He was praying, is what.

I could hardly believe he did not hear the noises I was making, nor the shouting. But he paid no attention. It was as if I did not exist.

Well, he was right next to the wall. And the wall was right close to the river. And there was no way to tell what happened next but to say it right out.

All of a sudden I caught hold of a noise, low down and far off, a kind of vague rushing sound. Then it got to be like a grinding noise. It grew. And it kept on. It got louder and louder and closer and closer until I could tell it was coming from *outside*. And still it got louder. Soon it was a roar, a loud whirring roar that was deep in the river and coming towards the house and then, whatever it was, it crashed into the cellar wall and broke clear through and forced the water through the hole like a piston. And that water lifted John clear up and smashed him hard against the wall right in front of my eyes.

In just no time at all.

The water came thundering through the hole now, wailing through the hole, and it thrust every which way just violent, and I screamed and scrambled up the steps and out of the cellar just as the water pulled the steps away and filled the whole of the cellar. In only a few seconds. No more time than that.

And I run from the house as fast as I could just as the water swirled up out of the cellar and across the floor and out of the house.

I run till I couldn't go no farther, up a little hill just about a hundred yards from my house. I fell down on the ground and couldn't move, I was so tired. I lay there aching and heaving and panting, and I was crying and scared out of my wits.

Then I sat up finally and forced myself to look. And what I saw didn't even seem real to me. The water was spilling out of the house it looked like in slow motion now, out of the door and the first floor windows, with odd little gurgling sounds, slowly, slowly, as if it had almost found its level. But it surrounded the house as it came out, and the house became like an island in a sudden little lake that was connected to the river.

In nothing but the moonlight it was an eerie sight, let me tell you. The moon glistening easy on the water. And the house all black.

John was done for, that I knew. He was finished.

Well, the house started to creak and groan now, from the heavy tow of the river, and the pressure got to pulling at it and pulling at it until it started to come up and away. It began to break apart and splinter, with awesome tearing sounds, and it wasn't too long before there wasn't no house there at all. The house was gone, torn all to pieces.

And then all the pieces of it floated away, almost like each piece took its own turn, until there wasn't even nothing left to see. And the river smoothed down again, as if the house in the moonlight never existed.

There was one great deep swirl in the water right out in front of me. It lasted for only a few seconds and then it was gone too.

John and Carrie Lehmann and their farm had disappeared forever, just like that.

That's the story.

I know how crazy it sounds, but there was a live thing in the water, that I *know*. I don't know *what* it was, or where it came from, but something smashed a hole in John's cellar, right through from the river, and the high water that come in took away the house and everything in it and left only that silent inlet when everything was gone. Right in front of my eyes. And there was that great swirl. Something alive did that. So I *know* what I'm talking about.

But there are lots of things I don't know.

For instance, I know what happened to John. I know how he died. There is no question about that. But I don't think I or anyone will *ever* know what happened to Carrie.

I hope she died natural. I know deep in my heart it wasn't John that did it, I know him too well, but I just hope she died natural. I hope it wasn't nothing else. I mean, I hope it wasn't nothing *she* did, or caused to happen.

I'm sure as I'm gonna die myself one day that she was down there, though. And whatever happened to her, John just went crazy with grief. It had to be that.

I never told anyone what I saw. Right away when it happened there was talk about the bad flood in the valley below Garlock's Bend, about all the heavy rains, and about poor John and poor Carrie.

But I never told. I figured it was no one's business but mine. It was me that seen it, and I had to deal with it my own way.

Just about that time there was some trouble right up in Garlock's Bend, in the church, and I was there through the whole of that one, too, but I hid the fact that some of it seemed so much the same to me.

I don't know, I guess I thought that one problem at a time was enough. But partly I kept quiet on account of Carrie. She was scared about something, she said. And she wanted to get back home because of the high water. She said it wasn't safe because of the high water. And she used a line about the water being high enough for "...it to..." What the *it* was, and what it could do, those are good questions.

She had to know something, or she wouldn't have talked like that.

So, I guess to somehow not stir things up, I didn't tell. Maybe, considering everything, that was wrong.

Maybe.

But then come *all* the *maybes*.

Maybe Carrie was innocent of anything bad, and I am doing her a terrible injustice, thinking evil things that go through my mind so often. I hope so. I hope to God she was innocent. I hope to God she was.

But maybe, just maybe, she was involved in something or controlled by something or even just aware of something so wrong that I can't even comprehend it. She had predicted the trouble to come, so at the very least, she *knew* of this thing in the water. She had to know of it. How she knew, and why, no one will ever get a handle on that.

Some things, I guess, it's maybe even better not to understand. What good would it do anyway?

John now, I don't know. That time we talked and I wanted to come in to see him, he did say that he was forbidden to let anybody in, he was "...just not allowed to." Whatever that meant. He sounded so weak and frightened. Somehow, though, I get the feeling that he knew a whole lot less than Carrie did.

All of this sounds crazy, and just even impossible, but there it is. I know it happened because I went through it, and I'm telling the truth. The sad thing is, I'm sure in my heart of hearts that I'll never have the answers. That's the terrible thing for me, not knowing the truth about Carrie.

But one thing is certain—something alive was in the water. That much I know. I *know* that. Something alive that come from the river.

My guess is it's still there. Wherever it came from, it's still out there somewhere. Waiting, maybe?

You get these little hints at Miller's, like maybe a few other people have been through something, too, but they have decided to keep quiet.

There's a thought could make anyone afraid.

Carrie's been on my mind a lot lately. In my quiet times. Her and those ice-blue eyes and all the passing years. And what I thought was lifelong innocence. And always I'm left with the questions that keep coming back. What did she know? What did she do? And *why*?

And the question of questions—what took her?

Well, whatever came for them out of the river, whatever it was that happened to them both, John did love her, no matter the cost to him in the end. He hung on like a man, too, and you can't ask for more than that. Even if he died because of her, because of something she did, I believe he still loved her. I do.

And maybe, at the last, that's partly why I'm so troubled by the whole story myself, why I have so many questions, why I feel so much dread.

I loved her too, you see.

THE PURPLE DEATH

BY GUSTAV MEYRINK

THE TIBETAN FELL SILENT. THE EMACIATED FIGURE STOOD quietly for a while, erect and unmoving, then disappeared into the jungle.

Sir Roger Thornton stared into the fire: if the Tibetan had not been a *Sannyasin* and a penitent to boot, if he had not been making his pilgrimage to Benares, then not a single word would have been believable. But a *Sannyasin* neither lies nor can be lied to.

And yet, that horribly malicious expression that had flickered in the Asian's face! Or was it just a trick of the flickering firelight that reflects so strangely in Mongolian eyes? The Tibetans hate the Europeans and jealously guard their magical secrets, with which they hope one day to exterminate the haughty, pompous foreigners, one day, when the great day dawns.

He, Sir Hannibal Roger Thornton, himself one of these hated Europeans, must see with his own eyes whether supernatural powers really rested in the hands of these remarkable people. But he would need companions, brave men whose wills cannot be broken, even if they were pursued by the very screams of hell.

The Englishman assessed his companions: there, the Afghan, the only one who could be considered an Asian, fearless as a panther, but superstitious. That left only the European's servant. Sir Roger roused him with a nudge from his walking stick (Pompeius Jaburek had been completely deaf since the age of ten, yet he understood every spoken word, fantastic as it may seem, by reading lips).

Sir Roger explained, with frequent gestures, what he had learned from the Tibetan: About twenty days ride from here, near the Himavat, lay a very strange land, surrounded on three sides by sheer rock walls. The sole passage led through poisonous gas, which flowed out of the ground and would instantly kill any living thing which passed by. In the ravine itself, which was about fifty square English miles in extent, there lived a small tribe in the thick of the rankest vegetation. These people were of Tibetan stock, wore pointed red caps, and rendered worship to an evil, satanic being in the form of a peacock. This devilish entity had, over the course of centuries, instructed the inhabitants in the ways of Black Magic and imparted such secrets as could turn the whole earth upside down and kill even the strongest man in the blink of an eye.

Pompeius smiled mockingly.

Sir Roger explained that he planned to use diving helmets and aqualungs to pass through the poisonous plane to penetrate the mysterious ravine.

Pompeius Jaburek nodded in agreement and rubbed his dirty hands together gleefully.

The Tibetan, indeed, had not lied: there, below, in the midst of vibrant greens, lay the strange ravine, a gold-brown desert-like belt of weather-beaten earth. It was roughly an hour's walk in length, and then the entire area disappeared from the outside world.

The gas, spiraling up from the earth, was pure carbon dioxide.

Sir Roger Thornton, who had surveyed the width of this belt from the safety of a hilltop, decided that they would begin the descent on the following morning. The diving helmets, sent from Bombay, worked perfectly.

Pompeius carried both repeating rifles and various equipment which His Lordship had considered indispensable. The Afghan, on the other hand, had stubbornly and fearfully refused to join the expedition, explaining that he would sooner climb into a tiger's lair. He must, he objected, weigh the risks very carefully, since even his immortal soul might well hang in the balance. So, in the end, only the two Europeans dared the venture.

* * *

The diving helmets were functioning flawlessly. Their copper globes gleamed in the sun and threw fanciful shadows on the spongy ground, from which the lethal gas swirled up in tiny geysers. Sir Roger had chosen a fast pace so that the compressed air would last them long enough to pass through the entirety of the gas zone. He saw everything before him shift unstably, as if through a thin film of water. The sunlight rose in ghostly green and colored the distant glaciers, the "Roof of the World" with its gigantic profile, like an eerie dead landscape.

Soon we found that he and Pompeius had emerged onto a fresh grassy field, and he lit a match to test the atmospheric quality first. Then he doffed his helmet and unencumbered himself of his air tank.

Behind him lay the wall of vapor, shimmering like a living mass of water. The scent of amberia blossoms in the air was overwhelming. Shimmering butterflies, strangely marked and as large as a man's hand, rested like open magical tomes upon the unmoving blossoms.

The pair walked at a considerable distance from one another towards the west in the direction of the forest which obscured their field of vision. Sir Roger signaled his deaf servant; Pompeius cocked his rifle.

They walked along the forest edge, and before them lay a clearing. Barely a quarter of an English mile ahead of them, a group of men (clearly Tibetans, with red, pointed caps) formed a semi-circle. They had obviously been waiting for the intruders. Fearlessly Sir Roger advanced to meet the crowd, Pompeius only a few steps from his side.

Only the customary sheepskin costumes of the Tibetans seemed familiar. Otherwise, they scarcely even seemed human: expressions of hideous hate and supernatural, terrifying evil had distorted their countenances beyond recognition. At first they let the pair draw near. Then, as one, obeying their leader's signal, they clapped their hands over their ears in one lightning-fast motion and began screaming at the top of their lungs!

Pompeius Jaburek looked questioningly at His Lordship, then raised his rifle: the bizarre actions of the crowd suggested imminent attack. But what happened next sent his heart straight for his throat. A trembling, swirling gas cloud began to gather about His Lordship, somewhat resembling the fumes they had walked through earlier. Sir Roger's shape began to blur, to grow indistinct, as if its contours had been eroded by the whirling funnel. The man's head seemed to elongate to a point, the entire mass collapsing onto itself as if... *melting*. And on the very spot where only moments before the Englishman had stood was a pale violet cube, about the size and shape of a small sugarloaf.

The deaf Pompeius shook with a terrible rage. As the Tibetans kept up their screaming, he squinted to focus on their dancing lips and read whatever it was they might be saying. It was always the same word, over and over again. At once the leader came forward, and the rest left off screaming, took their hands off their ears, and rushed toward Pompeius. At this, he commenced firing wildly at the crowd with his repeating rifle, which halted them momentarily.

Then instinctively he shouted the word back at them, the word he had read off their lips: Ämälän–"Ämälän!" He yelled it so loudly that the ravine trembled as with an earthquake. Dizziness overcame him; he saw everything as if peering through thick glasses, and the ground heaved and swayed beneath him. This lasted just a moment, and then he could see clearly again.

The Tibetans had disappeared, just as His Lordship had. Before Pompeius only countless purple cones lay scattered.

The leader still lived. His legs had already transformed into blue mush, and even the torso was beginning to shrink. It was as if the whole man were being digested inside some transparent being. Instead of a red hat, the leader's head was covered by a thing shaped like a bishop's mitre in which golden, living eyes moved.

Jaburek smashed the leader's skull with his rifle butt, but he was not in time to prevent the dying man in his last moment stabbing him in the foot with a sickle. Then he surveyed the scene around him.

Not a living thing far and wide. The acrid scent of amberia blossoms had intensified and was almost stinging. It seemed to emanate from the purple skittles, and these Pompeius now investigated. They were all exactly alike, composed of a pale violet gelatinous mucus. As for the estimable Sir Roger Thornton, he could not now possibly be distinguished among the field of purple pyramids.

Pompeius gnashed his teeth and ground his heel in what remained of the dead leader's face. Then he turned and ran back along the way he had come. At a distance he beheld the copper helmets gleaming in the sun. Gaining them, he lost no time pumping his diving canister full of air and made his way across the gas zone. *Oh God, Oh God, His Lordship was dead! Dead, here in remotest India!* The ice-capped mountains of the Himalayan range yawned at the heavens: after all, what cared they for the suffering of one tiny beating human heart?

Pompeius accurately wrote down, word for word, everything he had experienced and seen, although he was still far from beginning to comprehend it. Then he sent his account to the secretary of His Lordship in Bombay, in 17 Adheritolla Street. The Afghan promised to ensure its delivery. Thus assured, Pompeius Jaburek died, the result of the poison with which the Tibetan's sickle had been smeared.

"There is no God but God and Muhammad is his Prophet," mumbled the Afghan, touching his forehead to the ground before the corpse, which the Hindu servants had strewn with flowers and now proceeded to cremate atop a bier, to the accompaniment of customary hymns.

Ali Murrad Bey, the secretary, receiving the horrible news, blanched and immediately sent the letter to the editorial office of the *Indian Gazette*. The Deluge broke out from there. The paper, which published "The Downfall of Sir Roger Thornton" the very next day, issued the morning edition a full three hours later than usual. A strange and indeed horrifying incident was blamed for the delay. It seems that Mr. Birendranath Naorodjee, the editor of *The Indian Gazette*, along with two assistants, was abducted without a trace from the closed work room where they sat reading the galleys around midnight. All that stood to mark their places was a trio of blue gelatinous cylinders, with sheets of freshly printed newsprint scattered between them. The police announced with pompous bluster that they had concluded their protocols and declared the case closed, albeit an insoluble mystery.

But that was only the beginning. Dozens of gesticulating men, who had only moments before been quietly perusing their newspapers, simply disappeared before the eyes of the terrified crowd which thronged the streets. In their places countless little violet pyramids stood about, on the steps, in the marketplace and side streets, everywhere the eye could see.

Before evening, Bombay had lost half its considerable population. An official health edict mandated that all ports be closed at once and that Bombay be sealed to all traffic with the outside world in an effort to contain the new epidemic. Only such drastic measures, it was thought, could hope to stem the tide. Meanwhile, telegraphs and cables were going day and night, sending the frightening report, including of course the entire transcript of the Thornton case, syllable for syllable, across the oceans and throughout the world.

By the very next day, the quarantine, imposed too late, was lifted.

From countries all over the world came the horrible news that the "Purple Death" had broken out everywhere simultaneously and threatened the population of the entire world. All lost their heads, and the civilized world looked like a teeming anthill into which some farm boy had thrust a burning tobacco pipe. In Germany, the plague broke out first in Hamburg. Austria, however, where they read only local news, remained impervious for weeks.

The first case in Hamburg was especially shocking. Pastor Stuhlken, a man whom advanced age had rendered practically deaf, sat down to an early breakfast surrounded by his beloved family: Theobald, his eldest, with his long-stemmed student pipe, Jette, his devoted wife, Michen, Tinche, in short, everyone, all fourteen members of his family. The graybeard had only just opened the newly-arrived English newspaper and begun to read to the others the report of "The Downfall of Sir Roger Thornton". He had just gotten past the strange word *Ämälän* when he paused in his reading to fortify himself with a sip of coffee. Just then, to his horror, he discovered that the breakfast table was circled with naught but purple blobs of slime. In one of them was stuck a long-stemmed pipe.

All fourteen souls had been taken by the Lord. The pious old man fainted dead away.

One week later, more than half the population was dead.

It was left at last to a German scholar to shed some light on the situation. The fact that only the deaf and the deaf-mutes seemed to be immune sparked the accurate theory that the epidemic was not a biological but rather an acoustic phenomenon. In the solitude of his study he had written a long scientific paper on the matter, then scheduled a public lecture, advertising it with several slogans.

His explanation was based on his knowledge of a very obscure Indian religious text which described the creation of astral and fluid tornadoes through the speaking aloud of certain words contained in spells. This apparent superstition, the savant claimed, could now be made sense of through the modern sciences of vibration and radiation theory.

He held his lecture in Berlin and was required to employ a megaphone to read the long sentences of his manuscript, so great was the crowd of the interested public.

The memorable speech concluded with concise words: "Go now to the audiologist and have him render you deaf, and so protect yourselves from the spoken word 'Ämälän'."

A second later, the scholar and his entire crowd of listeners were nothing more than slime blobs, but the manuscript remained behind. Over the course of time it became widely known and spared mankind from complete extinction.

A few decades later, about 1950, a new and universally deaf population inhabited the globe. Customs and habits were different, rank and possessions all rearranged. An audiologist ruled the world. Musical scores were relegated to the same dustbin with the alchemists' formulas of the Middle Ages; Mozart, Beethoven, Wagner, all as laughable as Albertus Magnus and Bombastus Paracelsus. Here and there in those torture chambers called museums a dusty piano bears its yellowing teeth.

(Author's postscript: The esteemed reader is hereby advised against a public recital of the forgoing.)

MISTS OF DEATH

BY RICHARD F. SEARIGHT & FRANKLYN SEARIGHT

PneephTaal waited.

Patiently.

For over four billion years PneephTaal had patiently waited, biding its time. It knew that one day, conceivably five or ten or fifteen million years or more in the future, its opportunity would come.

It would wait. It would be ready.

PneephTaal had come to earth while the youthful planet was still recovering from the titanic shock of cosmic birth, and since that time its sentient awareness had not dimmed. Although sealed within a cavernous rock-hewn vault by the authority of the Elder Gods—a force which even it could not overthrow—its life essence existed in a dormant state fired by an alien intellect which could never accept its own conquest. When it first had arrived, the planet had barely begun its primordial existence, being little more than some 500 million years old, still a fiery mass of unsolidified, molten rock.

Billions and many more millions of years passed as the land cooled and the atmosphere evolved to a state wherein life, shocked into nativity by a majestic flash uniting certain elementary molecular particles, could be sustained. And when this new life demonstrated its uniqueness by splitting into equal and identical units, PneephTaal regarded the embryonic creations with disinterest.

It paid little heed to the evolving, many-celled animals that swam in the salty seas and eventually developed a primitive intelligence; it sensed with total indifference the mutating life forms that later ventured forth to conquer the land. Nor was PneephTaal bored with its captive existence for its perceptive faculty was able to span the vastness of interstellar space probing the secrets of distant galaxies and individual star systems, invading in thought the inhabitants of a nearly endless array of tenanted planets that held even the tiniest shred of interest for it. There was little in the entire cosmos it did not know—except how to escape its bondage imposed by the Elder Gods. Millions upon millions of years continued to elapse and gigantic reptiles thundered over the earth, dimwitted creatures whose lives were spent in satisfying their never-ending need for sustenance to feed their ever-empty stomachs.

PneephTaal knew how they felt.

It waited, as man first began to tread the earth. And it brooded, as civilizations leaped to flaming heights, then perished. And it hungered with a craving that could have devoured galaxies! It thought of what it would do when once again it regained the freedom it once had known, when again it could feast throughout the star-flecked universe.

Paraphrased from the Eltdown Shards

With shocking suddenness, this sentient entity—mighty, seemingly indestructible, quasi-immortal—was aware of an amazing truth which momentarily stunned its intellect with a blinding flare. It was no longer imprisoned!

ALAN HASRAD, REPORTER FOR THE ARKHAM *DAILY NEWS*, sat in his book-lined study reading the afternoon mail. He rubbed thoughtfully at his large nose and pondered the curious letter from B. C. Fletcher he had just finished reading for the second time.

An indefinably sinister undertone ran through it, although the nature of the menace at which Fletcher hinted was not disclosed, and Alan was left with the haunting impression of some unnamed but very real evil affecting the writer. A genuine dread—not terror, for the man wrote with perfect calmness—seemed to raise a spectral head from behind his apparently casual words.

Fletcher was a complete stranger to Alan. He wrote in a rapid, scholarly script with diction and construction suggesting a man of more than average attainment. The letter explained how he had read of different arcane exploits in which Alan had been involved, events savoring of the fantastic and bizarre, and for this reason, along with Alan's standing as a respected journalist, regarded him as a possible source of help in the problem confronting him. He mentioned briefly that he had retired nearly a year ago to a small and semi-isolated cottage on Shadow Lake near Bramwell, a region of Massachusetts with which Alan had some familiarity. His next paragraphs spoke with ambiguous restraint about an inexplicable phenomenon which was causing the neighboring countryside great alarm, but suggested it would be inadvisable to attempt details by mail, believing an interesting and convincing demonstration would be witnessed by Alan if he would come in person.

The letter was an odd mixture of old-fashioned formality coupled with an obvious bewilderment and deep-seated uneasiness, which doubtless combined to produce the impression of dread on the part of the writer. He concluded with a rather formal invitation to visit him, with full directions for reaching his cottage near the lake should Alan drive and a promise to meet him if he came by train.

Scrawled beneath the closing was the flourishing signature of B. C. Fletcher.

Ordinarily, such a letter would have evoked little enthusiasm in Alan. As a journalist and minor participant in certain unusual phenomena which tended to escape the notice of most, he had grown accustomed to receiving all sorts of communications from cultured cranks, and had come to pay little attention to most of them. But this was different from the usual run of such letters. Its sincerity was undeniable and the sanity of the writer did not seem to be in question.

He reflected about Shadow Lake and the nearby town of Bramwell. Alan had several relatives living in the area, whom he visited from time to time, and was casually acquainted with some of the local town folks. Come to think of it, he considered, hadn't there been recent mention of that locality in the papers? Something to do with a killing which had some very interesting features? Alan seemed to think this was the case and spent the next few minutes examining back issues of the *Arkham Daily News* before locating the account he had recalled.

Slowly, with much more care than he had given to his first hasty perusal a week ago, he reread the article. It told of the death of Moss Kent, a farmer who had lived out on the Somersville Road a half mile east of Shadow Lake. Kent had been an old bachelor and hadn't been missed till one of his neighbors found him sprawled in the yard before his unpainted shack.

There was more, but no further information of practical importance was offered other than the notion that unnatural features were still being investigated by the authorities. It was a curious article, thought Alan, not because of what had been stated, but because of the provocative nature of that which had been left unsaid.

Alan debated the advisability of snatching a day or two to investigate. What finally decided him against it was the fact that Fletcher had declined to even suggest the nature of his trouble, and Alan felt slightly piqued to be called upon in such a manner. He wrote briefly, saying he was interested but busy and invited Fletcher to come to Arkham to discuss the matter or else write full details.

Fletcher's second letter arrived five days later. In part it read:

I cannot blame you for not wishing to come to Bramwell without full information. However, I have few tangible facts to offer you. It was with the thought that if you accepted my invitation you would see and perhaps understand and explain these terribly unnatural happenings...

Even as I write, the *Mists* are rising again from the swamp in back of my cottage. Each night between dusk and darkness I see the same sight as I sit at my library window, and it is not a pleasant one. More and more it suggests to me the steady, purposeful advance of an army. First comes the vanguard, stray scouts swirling and spiralling upwards from the dank marsh nearby, to feel the way for the dense murky phalanxes that follow. The advance does not take long. Soon the main body closes in, and my little cottage on its knoll between the swamp and the lake is besieged by the chill, writhing dampness which blots out the dim lights of Bramwell beyond the marsh like a stone wall.

Mr. Hasrad, *the mist is sentient!* Oh, I know how it sounds, but I'm not crazy; I know I'm not having hallucinations. Do you wonder that I hated to write this? Why my first letter was intentionally so vague? I wanted you to see for yourself—to look at these vast banks of lazily twisting vapor, slowly writhing and turning in chill, unnatural convolutions, encircling my dwelling with a living wall of frightfulness. Then you would understand and be convinced. When on a windless night you heard the timbers of the cottage creak and give beneath a hideous, external constriction, *you would know!* And if you sat through the long hours till dawn and watched their sullen retreat before the anemic rays of the pale watery sun...

The mists are all I claim them to be, Mr. Hasrad, and more. They are evil, and threaten mankind with a danger perhaps unequalled in the history of his evolution! About three weeks ago the farmers began finding their stock killed in a most peculiar manner, which I *attribute to the mists,* and two weeks ago it took the life of an old farmer—at least I'm nearly positive it was responsible, although I couldn't prove it in a court of law. The nature of these attacks I prefer not to describe on paper lest you put me down as a mildly interesting lunatic and suggest I seek psychiatric help. But join me here at Shadow Lake, and I will give you full details.

This letter was signed: "Bayard C. Fletcher".

Alan's eyes moved to the nearby bookshelves in his study after he read the signature, strayed and paused on a tall volume in red leather bearing the gilt words along its spine: *Before the Stone Age*—Bayard C. Fletcher. The writer of this letter was more than likely the very same Bayard C. Fletcher, a renowned paleontologist and author of sundry technical works of which *Before the Stone Age* was the last and most exhaustive and regarded by his colleagues as a rare contribution to the progress of their science.

Alan felt his doubts as to the sanity of the writer dissolve as salt does in water. If this were indeed *the* Bayard Fletcher, it might well be that something strange *was* haunting the vicinity of Shadow Lake. Alan knew Fletcher by reputation to be a man along in years, possibly sixty-seven or -eight, but certainly not far beyond the prime of his mental faculties. As Alan recalled, he had only recently retired from his Miskatonic University curatorship to gain more time for writing and private research. Known as a quiet man, with little social contact among other scientists, Fletcher had only recently dropped from sight completely. Probably only his publishers, intimate friends, and museum officials knew of his whereabouts.

Mists that were sentient? Alive? Capable of intelligent action, perhaps? A vague suspicion began to stir in Alan's mind, prompted by shuddering passages he recalled from midnight readings of the *Necronomicon*. But, no; the thought crossing his mind was unworthy of further consideration as it simply could not be possible.

Originating from almost any other man than the reserved, levelheaded old scientist, the thought of sentient mists would have been too preposterous for comment. And even so, Alan certainly did not believe for one moment that Fletcher's flamboyant assertion was correct. He merely paid Fletcher's genius the tribute of assuming that he had stumbled onto something decidedly abnormal and markedly outside and beyond the ordinary. And, in his lonely isolated quarters, the manifestation had probably gripped his mind and prayed upon his imagination until he had come to unreservedly admit to an impossible condition. But Fletcher still needed help; and, if a visit from Alan would cheer and reassure him and perhaps find an obvious, easily overlooked explanation for these unnatural happenings, he decided he could do no less than go.

Alan prepared to leave, with the grudging approval of his editor, for Shadow Lake the following afternoon.

The drive from Arkham, that festering, witch-cursed community squatting along the Atlantic, led southeast to Bramwell and was one he had always enjoyed. Something in his own restless nature responded to the wild primitive call of old, nearly impenetrable forests that stood sentinel along his route, barren meadowlands stripped of their harvests that undulated into the distance, stone fences falling into disrepair, and dilapidated farms and barns that tottered and rotted on the brink of irrestorable decay. Alan marveled at the hills and woods arrayed in their autumn colors of assorted golds and oranges and crimsons.

The slanting rays of a late afternoon sun were throwing shadows across the main street of Bramwell as Alan came to a stop at its single traffic light. He turned his car to the right, crossed the railroad tracks, and drove to the pumps of the town's only filling station. A sign above the door indicated the owner of this establishment to be Harold Webber, a round-faced middle-aged man whom Alan had met before.

Out of the gas station, with leisurely strides, stepped the proprietor. As he approached the car, wiping his hands on torn and grease-smeared overalls, he recognized its driver; he squinted and the grim line of his mouth curved in the suggestion of a smile.

"Afternoon. Mr. Hasrad, ain't it?"

Alan nodded. "How you been, Hal? Fill it up, please."

Harold retreated to the pumps. Inserting the nozzle into the gas tank and setting it to automatic, he ambled over to where Alan waited with window still rolled down.

"Haven't seen you in a spell," he said idly, beginning to wash the windows.

"No, I haven't been out this way for a few months. Bramwell seems to be about the same."

"Well, it ain't!" was Howard's terse, unexpected assertion. He rubbed briskly at a few insect specks then drew his squeegee across the window, wiping it dry.

"Oh?" Alan looked at him curiously. "Something new? Story in it for me?"

"Well, now, I don't know. You might think so." The gas station attendant shifted uneasily from one foot to another and the level of his voice dropped.

"We've had two extremely queer killings—any killing hereabouts would be queer, of course—within a mile of the village; not to mention the loss of considerable livestock in the same—ah, manner."

"I heard about one of the deaths—fellow named Moss Kent?"

"Yup. That was the first un. We had another just three days ago."

Webber shifted his gaze, looking up and down the street, as though he were about to reveal something that perhaps he shouldn't. "Well, this time it was the Widow Fisher. She was found dead 'bout ten o'clock at night in her own rear doorway. She lived just down the road from here. She'd gone out back for fire wood, and when she didn't return her children thought she'd dropped in at one of the neighbors. So it was a couple of hours before she was found."

"Certainly strange," Alan commented.

"I'll say it's strange! I don't suppose the deaths themselves would seem startling to a city man like you, especially a newspaper feller, but they've surely created one big excitement in this county; most people around here are getting to be afraid for their lives when it comes to going out after dark."

"As bad as that?"

Webber nodded. "There was no outcry—no noise of any sort." He leaned closer, his head almost inside the automobile. "But she had been crushed and was found limp and cold, lying across her own back steps! No one here 'bouts is anxious to go out after dark—especially with that damned mist that seems to invade Bramwell every night—if it can be avoided!"

"I can understand why. But you said she was crushed?"

"Yes, sir, crushed she was; just like Moss Kent. That's about all I know, and them that does know more don't seem to be saying much about it to anyone."

This was indeed news of a startling nature, and Alan could not help but wonder if the strange occurrences in the village were connected in some way with the uncanny activities occurring at nearby Shadow Lake. Leaving the station, he drove down the darkening street. Already, lights were beginning to glow from the forlorn huddle of houses. He turned at the general store at the crossroads onto a dusty gravel road which he knew led to Shadow Lake and picked up speed. Webber, he reflected, had seemed almost morbid with his unexplained inferences.

Dreary fields passed before his gaze, their harvests taken in, and dismal second growth accompanied the mile of gravel road. The scene was not more depressing than Alan's thoughts as it shaded them with a subtle, insidious aura of gloom. Fletcher's suggestion that some unknown dread was stalking the countryside was certainly confirmed by the words, although emotionally tainted, of Hal Webber. All sorts of possibilities occurred to him which before had not hitherto presented themselves. At first he had feared the letters might turn out to be the hoax of someone pretending to be Bayard Fletcher, or that Fletcher himself had somehow lost his reason. But now he strongly entertained the notion that the unnamed and unknown menace was not purely imaginary at all but perhaps very genuine. Not what Fletcher thought it to be, of course, but still something very real and noxious and deadly.

Could it be that his earlier suspicions were not so untenable after all?

And what was that ahead of him? He had been driving parallel to a meadow when something decidedly strange leaped into his vision, causing him to slow down for a closer look. Leaning motionless against the fence, obviously dead, was a cow looking as though it had been tossed there like a rag doll discarded by an irked child. But the proportions of its body seemed to be all wrong. It looked as though it had been deflated, like a basketball from which most of the air had leaked, much thinner and flatter than one would expect.

Alan shook his head, absently noting another huddled, unmoving mass much farther away in the meadow, and continued to Shadow Lake.

Presently he reached the narrow, winding lane which had been described by Fletcher, leading off to the left of the road. He carefully maneuvered through an aisle of rotting leaves carpeting the shallow wheel ruts; above, naked branches whipped the roof of his car.

His keen blue eyes searched the gathering dusk intently as the car wound through the clustering trees down the narrow gravel road to the lake and along the shore. Occasionally he passed cottages which were dark and unoccupied. Shadow Lake's long narrow expanse, as seen through a break in the trees, stretched cold and somber and still. Alan could just make out a gray barrier beyond the sullen surface of the water which was the tree-shrouded heights of the opposite shore. The lake was certainly desolate and lonely in the autumn after the departure of the summer residents and the closing of the few isolated cottages. But its very solitude probably appealed to Fletcher as a welcome contrast to the unpleasant features of big city life. Fletcher, he thought, would probably have the lake to himself from now until the following summer.

The cottage on the knoll, which presently came into view, was long and low. It appeared to be a late Victorian dwelling, spacious and in reasonably good repair, but looking somewhat bleak and desolate behind a wild tangle of uncut grass and bushes.

Alan turned into a clearing hemmed in by patches of unkempt

shrubbery and small trees, parked the car, and started to the cottage. Dusk continued to settle about the quiet countryside and the pine-fringed cleft in the knoll at his left was already shadowy and indistinct as was the narrow tree-screened path. Alan walked faster through the somberly rustling leaves, piled by the early autumn winds and seemingly undisturbed by human feet.

Fletcher opened the door at Alan's knock. He seemed to be almost painfully glad to see him and led him to his rustic study, a long, booklined room tastefully paneled with dark oak. They sat before a small fire pleasantly burning in a huge fireplace and talked.

Fletcher was tall and lean and slightly stooped, but still handsome and distinguished in bearing, with snowy hair and precise eyeglasses. His voice, cordial and controlled, gave little hint of the strain under which he had been living.

"I'm delighted that you could come, Mr. Hasrad, " he assured his guest after drinks were mixed and they were comfortably seated. "This thing I wrote of in my letters is so utterly at variance with anything normal and understandable that I almost believe I'd have pulled out rather than remain here alone much longer." His voice trembled momentarily and Alan had a flashing glimpse of the iron fortitude and determination of this man who would not run when retreat would so easily have solved his problem.

"I've heard talk in Bramwell that life has been threatened," Alan observed carefully.

Fletcher nodded confirmation.

"Yes." With slender, symmetrical hands he began to load a blackened briar. "This morning I found one of my neighbor's cats on the front porch. It had been crushed to a shapeless, furry pulp, just like a goat I saw on the road the day before, and flung there. Terror has struck this area, Mr. Hasrad, a terror which most people couldn't even begin to understand. In the past two weeks two people have been killed."

"I've heard of their deaths, " Alan said, "although only sketchy and incomplete accounts of what had occurred."

Fletcher, sprawled in his comfortable chair, drew lazily at his pipe. "I can probably fill in some of the details; I must, in order to convince you that the trouble here is very real. It's a terrible business that is getting worse all the time. Those in charge are being very careful as to just what news they release. I suppose they think people will believe a hoax is being perpetrated upon them. But I can tell you some of the facts, as I was present at the autopsies—county Medical Examiner's my cousin—and what I'm going to tell you just might be the strangest thing you've ever heard."

Fletcher leaned forward and peered through his spectacles, his gaunt face a study in earnestness.

"Now here's the really strange part. I saw the bodies myself, and there didn't seem to be a scratch on them anywhere. But they were limp as rags; the bones, subjected to some terrific pressure, had been crushed and splintered and broken to pieces. I could hear crepitation in a dozen places before my cousin started to cut.

"I suppose explanations, remote and far-fetched, could account for such conditions, but something else was discovered which makes it even more unbelievable if that could be possible. It seems that in both cases the cells of most organs of the bodies had been somehow drained of nearly every trace of their enzymes, hormones, and antibodies; in fact, nearly all the amino acids which make up these complex substances are gone! This has resulted, in terms a layman might better understand, in most of the protein matter being missing from the interior tissues! Protein, you might know, makes up a large part of each body cell, so you can imagine the incredible scene we viewed after a few simple incisions!"

Alan gazed at the professor nonplussed, and sipped from his glass.

"Yes," Fletcher nodded. "It's unbelievable but true. With the exception of certain organs and the skin, which seems in both cases not to have been touched, it would appear as though the bodies had been robbed in some inexplicable manner of nearly every molecule of protein within them! As you can imagine, there was little left to examine but flimsy husks!"

Alan, remembering the cow he had earlier seen, was thoughtful for a time. Finally: "And what does your cousin the Medical Examiner have to say?"

Fletcher smiled weakly. "What can he say? The only possible explanation that he and his colleagues can offer is that the countryside is being terrorized by an animal that swallows its prey, ingests the bodily matter its diet requires, then spits out or otherwise eliminates the carcass!"

Alan's lips tightened but he offered no comment.

"That, of course," Fletcher continued, "is the most absurd rubbish that one could hypothesize! And yet... I have no better theory myself to offer. To compound one's incredulity is the utterly impossible condition of the intact, unbroken skin."

Alan was thinking swiftly. "But, Doctor Fletcher—really, there must be a reasonable explanation for all of this. One of the constrictor snakes could have crushed them," he feebly offered, realizing as he spoke the unlikelihood of such a reptile being found anywhere near Bramwell.

Fletcher waved his hand. "Certainly," he returned quickly, a hint of disparagement in his voice, "and so could a steamroller; but a snake would have swallowed its prey. And explain a conceivable way in which it could extract most of the protein from the bodies. No," Fletcher shook his head with positive conviction, "obviously snakes don't feed that way." He fell into a troubled silence while he pondered his next words.

"But these killings were not the beginning," he finally continued, relighting his briar. "It started about a month ago with the destruction of the insects in this area; and within four or five days it was nearly impossible to find an insect or a spider of any sort. Fed upon in the same manner, countless numbers of their broken remains lay scattered about. Within a week the small rodent population was in the process of being decimated; and it wasn't long before dogs and cats and other small mammals that remained outdoors at night met with the same fate. Farmers then began to find livestock killed with all the same attributes, and these losses continue to increase. There's no doubt about it, Mr. Hasrad, this thing is strong enough now to attack humans and even the larger animals and anything else unfortunate enough to be outside after dark. In all, I know of at least a dozen full grown cows and four or five sheep that have been found—and there are probably many more—crushed and drained of the sustenance this... this, *whatever it is*, craves!

"No," he concluded, "we may as well face the fact that it's *not* a natural happening susceptible of an ordinary explanation." He rose and crossed to the bay window. "It won't be long now," he stated cryptically, "before you can see for yourself."

After a sketchy meal cooked on the gas range, they retired to the living room. Fletcher fed the small blaze in the fireplace with pieces of dried driftwood, and shadows danced and jerked over the paneled walls, bringing into momentary clearness the pastoral paintings suspended about, then hiding them in a shadowy background that was vague and indistinct.

Alan could hear the faint sounds of the wind outside grow louder as the autumn darkness deepened. Across the sky it whipped gray storm clouds, sending them scudding before its wild breath. He studied Fletcher seated in his chair beneath the probing rays of a nearby floor lamp which highlighted his face in shocked relief as he stood before one of the windows facing the swamp.

Alan smiled discreetly. A wind such as this would make short work of any mists should they present themselves.

But he was wrong.

The night was dark and clear; the wind blew even stronger with a keening cry, whipping the shrubbery and bending the long grasses beneath its blasts. Alan chose a chair and sat quietly by the window, watching where Fletcher told him the vanguard of the mist would appear.

And then, beneath the few faint and newly visible stars, long writhing streamers of fog appeared from over the brow of the hill above the marsh. Faint, white and utterly loathsome in their inexplicable defiance of natural laws, they moved toward the house *against the wind!* Alan watched the grass bend nearly flat by the whistling blasts which should have torn the fog to shreds, and knew that he was indeed witnessing something that completely opposed the laws of nature.

Darkness was soon complete—the utter lonely dark of the countryside unrelieved by street lights or homely reflections from house lamps. But there was still light enough to discern indistinctly the writhing mists slowly approaching till they stretched forth damp, clammy arms and caressed the window panes in a loathsome embrace—a nebulous, vast grayness with misty, armlike tentacles that moved and writhed and poked curiously at each nook and corner of the building although the main body seemed immobile. The thought flashed into Alan's mind that Fletcher's likening had been inaccurate. Instead of an army with scouts, it seemed more like a huge, gray, smoky octopus that squatted before them, moving ghastly tentacles in threatening gestures.

Fletcher finally broke the spell of silence that had settled over the interior of the cottage. He spoke quietly.

"You have seen, Mr. Hasrad. What do you make of it?"

Alan tore his gaze from the window. His figure was tense, his face engraved with lines of worry and haunting doubt which was foreign to his eager, enthusiastic nature. "I don't know what to think of it—yet," he confessed. "In view of the apparent strength of the wind, this has to be the most amazing thing I've ever seen. What would happen if I were to go out?"

Fletcher's frail, pale face looked anxious. He stroked his white hair uneasily and his thin lips twisted grimly. "Don't try it. Remember Kane and the widow and the livestock. It would make short work of a man. But, if past experience is any guide, we're safely enclosed in here." He moved to the windows and pulled down the shades, blotting from view the blindly crawling tentacles.

"When did this first begin?" Alan asked when he had resumed his chair.

"As best as I can determine, about five weeks ago," Fletcher answered, his keen face haggard and drawn in the revealing rays of the light.

Alan fell into a troubled silence. Finally: "I hardly know what to tell you, Dr. Fletcher, although my first inclination, after seeing that deadly mist, is to urge you as strongly as I can to leave this area until something can be done."

"That's precisely my feeling. And I would probably have left a couple of weeks ago..." Suddenly his voice reflected a vehemence unusual to his normally quiet tones. "...But the fact is I have strong reason to believe that I myself might be responsible for what has been happening. My infernal, prying curiosity has, I suspect, loosed this terror on the countryside—this ominous dread of whose real nature no one yet has any conception. That's why I'm so reluctant to leave. And I hesitate to take the legal authorities into my confidence, even if it would do any good. They'd confine me in an observation ward if I were to tell the truth, even the little I know, of this hideous *death* that stalks the vicinity at night. It's too bizarre, too utterly incredible, for any normal person to accept as factual.

"But I'm going to tell you all about it. I have read accounts of strange encounters you have had with hellish entities, and you are one of the very few people I know who might be able to advise me about the problems here. I've had it on my mind for five weeks now, and it'll do me good to tell it to someone I can trust. You see, I gave a hint or two to my cousin the Medical Examiner, and the way he looked at me made me quit right there and pass it off as a joke. And even then he suggested I take things easy and not let my imagination work overtime."

Fletcher stared silently into the dancing flames for a while before continuing.

"Mr. Hasrad, I'm anxious to hear your views when I tell you of my conviction that a horror, possibly dormant and unsuspected since the dawn of recorded history, has emerged to prey upon humanity—a foul and terrible thing which must have lain in a sort of suspended animation for untold eons, only to be released by the poking curiosity of a fool like me. You'd think I was batty, wouldn't you?"

Alan smiled faintly at the unexpected colloquialism used by the professor.

"But it's the only answer. Part of it is deduction, of course—I don't actually *know* anything about its past—but I can testify to the conditions under which I found it and, to my great sorrow, released it."

He stared into the glowing coals left by the nearly consumed wood, his briar now dead in his hand, then tossed another small log onto the dwindling fire. A faint chill seemed to be in the dwelling.

"You ask what I think about all of this," responded Alan, shifting his eyes from the glowing embers to the gaunt face of the professor, "and I must reply that your analysis is possibly correct."

It had come to Alan that the fantastic idea which had occurred to him earlier might not be so impossible as he first had judged. Now, it seemed to him, it was a very real, very deadly possibility.

"I've seen enough to know that something utterly beyond the knowledge of man is on the loose. But... tell me more. Just what is this mist and just how did you come to be responsible for its presence?"

Fletcher stuffed tobacco into the minute orifice left by the carbon in the pipe's bowl and began to pace the carpet restlessly.

"I don't know what it is, but I'm sure it's something utterly unnatural, a form of life created perhaps when the earth was in its infancy which should have perished long epochs before the stone age; certainly, it is nothing of which archaeology or paleontology could offer any hint!"

"Perhaps," mused Alan, "it is not even of this earth, but rather some unspeakable cosmic malevolence from an another, unknown section of the universe."

Dr. Fletcher stopped and nodded slowly. "That, too. After what I've seen I'm willing to believe nearly anything. I just don't know. But I can tell you how I found it, discovered it under conditions which make it seem that it *must* have been sealed in its rocky prison long, long ago, to be held there until I unintentionally broke in and left the way open for its escape.

"It happened a little more than a month ago, on the afternoon of one of those drowsy Indian summer days we were enjoying here at the time. I've always maintained an interest in geology; made it a sort of spare-time hobby when I wasn't tied down with strictly paleontological pursuits. Well... on this particular day, I'd knocked off work on my latest book—it was such lazy weather I thought I'd do myself more good outdoors—and gone for a ramble with my hammer.

"I'd circled about half the marsh behind us and was climbing the shrub-tangled bluff which overlooks the Miskatonic River on the other side, when I tripped on a root and rolled back halfway down the incline. That started things! I crashed through a growth of bushes into the mouth of a cave which they concealed. It's typical of the formations one sometimes finds around here; they're not uncommon, but because of its natural concealment I'd never known of this one.

"If only destiny had grabbed my ankles and prevented me from entering that cave! But no such intervention occurred and I pressed through the opening into a hidden cavern that perhaps had not been entered by man for many thousands of years—if ever! I took a large flashlight from my knapsack and played its rays over the ceiling and floor. Presently I advanced still further, making my way to the rear wall, tapping occasionally at projections of the rough rock as I examined it. It was only a very common variety of granite, but it was incredibly old—very, very ancient rock.

"Water, oozing from a spring in the rock above, trickled down the face of the blank wall at the back and dropped to the cavern's floor with an endless drip-drip-drip. I'm mentioning this to explain what happened next. I took another step towards the wall and, in the uncertain footing of the slippery, pebble-covered floor, I slipped. My ankle turned; I teetered wildly for balance, twisted half around, and crashed against the rear wall. And my elbow went through that rock as if it had been a pane of window glass! The water, evidently dripping for eons, must have eroded the stone to paper-thinness.

"The flashlight was fortunately undamaged. I got up with a throbbing ankle and elbow and played the light on the hole I had made in the wall; it was as big as my head. Extending the light through it, I saw beyond a cell-like chamber, perhaps ten feet square, from which dead, musty air seeped into the larger cavern.

"I stood back for a minute or two until the air in the smaller enclosure had improved. Then I inserted the light again and moved its rays over the uneven walls and rubble-covered floor. I was viewing a place which I now confidently believe had been sealed for perhaps countless thousands of years.

"And then I saw, almost at once, a huge flat stone, shaped—if you can credit this—in the perfect form of a conventional five-pointed star! The circular part I judged to be approximately three feet in diameter and lay on the floor near the center of the inner chamber. Mr. Hasrad, you can understand my astonishment and my determination to investigate more closely.

"I went outside and after a little search returned with a thick branch that made a fairly effective crowbar. With the leverage it provided I broke down the rotting wall 'till I could squeeze through the opening. Inside, I found myself in a naturally vaulted chamber; and just a few feet away was that star-shaped stone I mentioned. God, how I wish I had left it alone! Even now I don't know what prompted me to move it. Just a sudden inspiration, I guess. Well, I had been studying some curious symbols engraved on its surface which I suspected might be ancient writing of some sort—though I could not even begin to identify it let alone decipher it—when it occurred to me to turn it over to inspect the other side. And that, of course, fool that I am, is just what I proceeded to do. I found the slab, however, too heavy for me to lift, but during the attempt managed to slide it over a little. Mr. Hasrad, that star-shaped stone was covering a pit!

"I moved the covering over until more than half the opening to that nightmarish shaft was exposed! I knelt at its edge and, as though I were looking down a well, peered at smooth walls that descended as far as the light would reach. It was nearly three feet in diameter, and from my vantage point I could see the walls run down and down in a manner suggesting the inside of a telescopic tube, which lost itself at a lower level, giving no hint as to just how deep it was.

"As I lay on the rock floor peering over the rim it occurred to me that the smooth polished roundness of the sides was at odd variance with the crudely hewn walls and ceiling of the chamber itself. My next observation was that the sides of this shaft were not made of rock at all but were composed of what might be a metallic substance which I was unable to identify.

"But speculation was purposeless. I selected a good-sized stone, tossed it over the brink, then waited second after second 'till a faint thudding noise was returned to me. Judging from the time elapsed by the fall, that hole was incredibly deep! I don't believe the sound would have been audible at all had not the walls of the pit magnified it and carried it upwards to me. That shaft, I decided, must be hideously deep, and I backed away from it.

"At that point, my curiosity far from satiated, I resumed my inspection of those insane scribblings on the slab, unaware that the stone I had dropped had *disturbed* something that lived far below. Several minutes passed before I again felt the urge to examine the shaft, and as I did so my eyes focused upon a most astonishing sight."

Alan shifted his position in the easy chair. "And just what was it you saw, Dr. Fletcher?" he asked.

"What I saw, far down in the depths, was *movement* where none should have been. Up into the glare of the light came a swirling whitish mass that filled the pit from side to side. It seemed as though amorphous pseudopodian filaments stretched forth cautiously, writhing insanely; incredible feelers that contracted and heaved in a curiously obscene manner as they rose higher and higher. They were still far below, understand, and I had plenty of time to replace the stone slab had the thought occurred to me; but instead I knelt there watching its rapid ascent with an awe and fascination which seemed to render me immobile.

"Can you understand, Mr. Hasrad, how fantastic and incredible a phenomenon it was to see in such a place? There was something indefinable and utterly unnatural about the sight that chilled me. Hitherto I had been actuated by pleased curiosity; now I began to feel an intense fear, and I actually trembled at the sight of what I thought to be rising smoke or fog. But I continued to wait, crouching at the edge and peering down at the depths where the flashlight rays seemed to tenderly caress and melt within the ascending horror.

"It kept on and on, stopping for a few seconds now and then, not behaving at all as would rising smoke. I don't know how I had the brainless, unthinking audacity to crouch there and watch that *thing* inch its way up the passage in the glare of my flashlight. Suddenly I was trembling through and through, my heart was pounding as though it would smash through my chest, and my mouth was dry. Such was my response to the masses of matter composing that *thing*.

"Then, something seemed to click in my mind and I realized I must somehow halt its advance. I picked up assorted rubble littering the floor with my free hand and hurled it down on the pulsating mass. This had no effect, as the stones passed right through it, plunging down that seemingly bottomless shaft. The horror continued upward, and like a crazy old fool I waited, bent over the pit, my flashlight spraying into the depths as I watched that incredible monstrosity rise ever closer."

Alan barely stirred, his attention riveted upon the professor whose voice began to quiver as he became more troubled and unsettled.

"And then it reached the rim of the shaft. Nonplussed, I remained frozen at the spot, watching small tendrils poke up tentatively into the chamber and begin to probe and undulate about. With them rose an unexpected odor of mustiness which soon became overpowering in that narrow space. My hand was but inches away from one of the reaching tentacles, and when at last it touched me I finally moved. No longer was I stricken by the paralyzing fear which had seized me. I remember screaming once; then, squeezing through the opening to the chamber I had made, I dashed through the outer cave and into the sunshine. I scrambled up the embankment and ran till I lost my breath and fell to the ground, panting as though I had just run the marathon! A few minutes passed before I finally realized I was out of immediate danger."

Fletcher stopped abruptly and stared at Alan. His jaw muscles stood out with tension as he relived in memory the anxious moments he had described.

"And that, of course," Alan prompted, "was not the last you saw of it?"

Fletcher pulled his gaze away from the flames and began to reload his briar once again. His mind seemed to suddenly be preoccupied. "Eh? Oh, yes. I learned of the mysterious depredations about the countryside and I knew—I realized with a terrible certainty just what was behind them."

Alan gazed upon the gaunt, angular countenance of his new acquaintance and reflected as to just how much he should tell him of the awful suspicions that had been crowding into his own mind. Was Fletcher bordering on the brink of insanity or total collapse, as Alan at first had feared, or was there a hidden strength present that would sustain him when he learned of the awful suspicion Alan held?

Alan decided, relying on his intuitive judgment, that the fortitude of this man would probably endure the strain of the esoteric knowledge it was in his power to relate.

"Dr. Fletcher, you were right to invite me here, and I do believe I can assist you. Unless I am greatly mistaken, we are dealing with an intelligence far older than mankind—indeed, older than planet earth itself. Although it has never been an active force within the history of man, its existence is mentioned in various ancient volumes, the most notable of which is the *Pnakotic Manuscript* brought down to us from ancient Hyperborea by a secret cult; and the *Necronomicon* of the mad Arab, Abdul Alhazred, devotes brief passages to it. It is from this son of the desert whom I happen to be descended. I've also read of this entity in various translations, inexact as they might be, of the *Eltdown Shards*; also, mention of them is made in the *De Vermis Mysteriis* of Ludvig Prinn and the *Sigsand Manuscripts* which Robert W. Chambers consulted so frequently. The *Cuites des Goules*, written by the Comte d'Erlette, makes brief mention, and laconic notations in von Junzt's *Unaussprechlichen Kulten* gives us even further hints. From some place in space this hellish entity was spawned and, after traveling from galaxy to galaxy, reached earth when our planet was but a seething, bubbling, coalescing mass.

"In the elder books it is written as to how this presence, which you know to be inimical to mankind, was imprisoned deep within the ebony bowels of the earth by several of the Elder Gods. Now, it seems, that which held this entity imprisoned has been removed, and a new horror is now free to terrorize the lives of mankind."

"But its purpose, Mr. Hasrad?" Fletcher interjected with a nervous query. "If it is intelligent, as we both believe, surely it has a reason for its nightly presence."

Alan smiled firmly at the noted paleontologist. "Of course it has a purpose. It is feeding."

"Feeding?"

"Exactly. My guess is that it is still very weak, having remained dormant for countless millions of years, and needs nourishment—an attribute of all life forms. Since being released, unfortunately by yourself, it has gradually been building up its mass and strength by suitable repasts, keeping in hiding during the process, starting with the smallest of creatures and progressing each night to the larger. In some inexplicable way it must be gaining sustenance from the protein it has consumed during its nightly foraging. It seeks to grow, to expand, to regain the mountainous strength of near galactic proportions it once had. And then..."

"And then?" Fletcher urged.

"And then—for mankind—it will surely be too late. Earth would be devastated, totally stripped of life, before it moved on to other planets in distant galaxies."

Fletcher's face was a study in stunned consternation as the magnitude of Alan's revelation registered in his thoughts. "Is there nothing to be done?"

Alan wondered. If they acted now, while this intelligence was still in a state infinitely weaker than that which it once had known, perhaps it would not be too late. Then again, it might already be invulnerable to anything man might do to stop its advance. If only...

"We can try," he returned. "We must try, and hope, and not consider the consequences if we should fail. By tomorrow morning it will hopefully have returned to its lair. If it still considers itself weak it will probably continue to seek sanctuary during the day until it is strong enough to openly find its sustenance. To its lair then we will go and somehow attempt to render it harmless."

An amused smile played over the features of Dr. Fletcher. "Much in the manner one would destroy a vampire, eh, Mr. Hasrad? Strike while it is dormant!"

"Exactly. But this is no vampire, Dr. Fletcher, and the tools to be used will be different and far older than the traditional mallet and stake."

"Tomorrow then," agreed Dr. Fletcher, rising to his feet. "Let us retire for what remains of the night and pray to God or whatever guides the fortunes of mankind that tomorrow sees us reach a successful ending to this atrocity."

"Amen," affirmed Alan, rising to his feet and following his host to the guest room which had been readied for his use.

It was still dark outside, with just a hint of dawn emerging out of the east, when Alan awoke from a restless sleep and aroused his slumbering host. Together they looked out the window. The deadly mist had already begun its retreat before the coming light. No longer was the house enshrouded by its ghostly essence. Much still remained about the cottage, but no longer enough to pose the threat it had but a few hours before.

Alan and Fletcher stood on the wooden porch of the cottage, breathing deeply the crisp air and appraising the view offered to them of Shadow Lake visible through the stand of trees that pushed toward its edge. About the house, stray wisps of mist lingered but were departing slowly in a direction that led toward the nearby marsh.

"As I thought," remarked Alan. "The mist is not dissipating in the air as one would expect; it actually maintains its nebulous form as it makes its retreat."

"Precisely," returned Fletcher. "I've contended all along that it's not a material mist that dissolves into the air as unseen vapor."

"Well, if we are to learn more, it's obvious we must follow it, although there's little doubt in my mind—nor yours, I'm sure—as to where it's going."

Leaving the porch, the two men followed the vaporous trails around the cottage, away from the lake, towards the decline that led to the swampy area. Long strides carried them through the tract of hardwood trees along the heights overlooking the dismal marsh. The air was crisp and clear, but mist could still be seen in faint, wispy trails.

Soon they stood upon the crest of the rise overlooking the marsh, where it seemed as though they were on the rim of a gigantic soup bowl. Below, the mist seemed to be more compact, appearing as might a soft, gray carpet moving away from them. It massed together in impregnable shrouds, flowing and converging toward a distant point.

"It's almost," observed Fletcher, "as though someone pulled the plug in a gigantic circular bathtub and everything is going down the drain."

"An apt simile," agreed Alan.

Stray wisps constricted harmlessly about their ankles as they walked along the embankment circling the marsh, imprinting a temporary path on the dew-moist grasses that stretched across the side of the knoll.

"I don't think I've noticed it before, Mr. Hasrad, but it seems to me the mist is thicker... more compact, perhaps... no longer the flimsy, silky wisps we've been following. Now it's so thick we can't see the ground beneath it."

"You're absolutely right," Alan agreed, "and I think I can venture an explanation. It's my guess that this entity had, at one time, a solid body that was probably miles in length and width and height—but it has not fed, has literally been starved for many, many millions of years and has, as a result, lost a considerable portion of its bulk. Rather than shrinking in size, its dimensions have remained the same, but the atoms composing it are so wide apart that it has this hazy, unsubstantial mist-like appearance."

"Are you suggesting that it thickens as it feeds?"

"Exactly! And I further believe that if nothing is done to stop it, if it is left to continue unchecked, it will one day be a solid mass large enough to cover the entire countryside for miles around!"

Minutes passed and each step took them further away from the cottage on the knoll closer to the other side of the swamplands. They did not enter the marsh itself, as this was unnecessary, but traveled along its clearly defined edge, high above the patches of stagnant water and silently waiting ooze.

"It's headed toward the cave, all right," Fletcher exclaimed, beginning to breathe more heavily, following Alan as he led the way around a fallen log. "It's not very far ahead now."

A hundred feet further along found them at a point overlooking the cave to their right; off to their left they could see the sun advance over the distant horizon and delicately touch the leaden-colored Miskatonic River, winding serenely on its way in the far distance. Returning their gaze to the right, they could see the gray mist converge from all over upon a single point in the hillside. What they saw came not as a surprise, but the shock of realization that they had been correct held them spellbound for some moments.

"We were right, Alan... Mr. Hasrad," affirmed Fletcher very softly. "It's draining right into the cave."

"And it seems," Alan observed, "we haven't arrived too soon. In a couple of minutes it will all be gone—all funnelled into that horrible cave, down the shaft you unwittingly opened, to its prison created eons past by the Elder Gods—if certain ancient writings speak the truth. Do you realize, Professor, that beneath us, down incredibly far, is probably a hollow chamber that must stretch for miles in each direction, large enough to contain all the mist that has been covering the countryside?"

Fletcher nodded. "I suppose so... but come," he urged, "while there is still time to see what happens."

Most of the mist had disappeared into the hillside, and only stray, tattered remnants remained pursuing the main ranks, as the two scrambled and slipped in haste down the incline. There was no need for Fletcher to point out the precise location of the hidden cavern for the mist was guide enough. As water spirals down a basin drain, so did the mist appear to swirl into the concealed opening of the hill. Moving the branches aside that concealed the entrance, several of them broken, they peered through the ancient maw.

With no hesitation they parted and passed through the remaining bushes into the cool, dank blackness of the cave; inside, they snapped on the large flashlights they carried. They stood near the entrance and surveyed the cavern which ran back perhaps thirty feet into the hillside, ending in a blank wall broken by a shadowy opening. Along the floor and through this aperture flowed the remaining tendrils of fragile, hazy mist. Alan guided his light about the low-vaulted roof that pressed downward and along the irregular rock walls and rubble-covered floor. All in all, it was a wildly unnatural aspect that met their gaze.

Slowly they advanced to the back wall where gaped the forced entrance made by Fletcher more than a month ago. Alan led the way, scrambling through the opening into the small chamber it once had concealed, closely followed by his companion. Their lights revealed the pit, half-covered by a large, flat star-shaped stone. Above them, the cavern formed a low arch, hardly high enough to permit them to stand erect. Little of the mist now remained, but what was left was making its way into the opening.

"No doubt about it now, Dr. Fletcher. This is where it retreats during the daylight hours after its nightly feed is ended."

Fletcher slowly nodded. "Indeed, yes. The question now is how to keep it down there... permanently!"

"That hopefully will not be as difficult as you might imagine," ventured Alan, kneeling at the edge of the shaft. He moved his light about the smooth tube-like opening into the earth and watched the thinly dispersed mist flow over the edge and make its descent. Abruptly, Alan had a thought and withdrew from his pocket a tiny medicine bottle all but empty. He shook from it a few capsules, which he placed into his pocket, then held the open bottle near the shaft.

"Just what," Fletcher wanted to know, "are you doing?"

Alan gazed up at him with a strained grin. "Oh, just indulging an idle fancy. Silly, eh?"

"And what did you mean by suggesting there might be no problem in sealing this horror up again?"

"I meant that we can return things to the condition they were before you first entered this place." As Alan spoke, he carefully examined the rock slab that had covered the opening of the shaft. It was obviously not a formation created by nature, and he was equally certain it had never been constructed by man. Radiating points gave it the unquestionable form of a star. It was only about four inches thick, relieving it of what might have been considerable weight, and its circular diameter of at least three feet was more than enough to effectively cover the hole. Alan's light licked over the covering, which he dusted off, revealing curious lines etched onto the surface of what he took to be a seal.

"This," said Alan, pointing to the curlicue formations, "is writing of a kind, and I think I can assure you it is prehuman—certainly it was never made by man."

Fletcher nodded his agreement. "After what I've witnessed this past month, I certainly would not question your judgment."

As he finished, the two noticed the last of the mist had flowed into the shaft.

"The *Necronomicon* tells of such cryptic signs as this, used by the Elder Gods millions of years ago to restrain and virtually immobilize the enormous power of some of the Old Ones to which this mist is reputed to be directly related."

"Surely you're not implying that this stone can imprison the terror down there, are you? Anything strong enough to crush a cow isn't about to be stopped by a barrier such as this. Even I was able to move it!"

"I'm willing to wager it will. Not the stone itself, of course, but what has been written upon it. This script, whatever it might read, enforces an inexplicable cosmic spell, incredibly potent, that has been able to restrain the mist for what might have been many millions of years. You must realize, Dr. Fletcher, this is not a slab which someone had carved into the shape of a star and engraved with curious symbols. No, it is far, far more. Mystic incantations of towering proportions attended the creation of the runic inscriptions you see. I myself have seen similar star stones, most of them small enough to hold in my hand. This is by far the largest I've ever encountered, but its size is no doubt necessary to confine the actual bulk, as tenuous as it is at present, of the actual Old One. No, Doctor," Alan concluded. "I think I can assure you that the nocturnal feeding of this nightmare is at an end."

Dr. Fletcher was doubtful, but during the short duration of his acquaintance with Alan Hasrad, he had become so impressed with his sense of competence and sagacity that he had no reluctance in placing the matter solely in his hands.

"Well, then," he reflected, "I bow to your knowledge in this field of arcane matters, but I would feel better if something further could be done."

"Such as?"

"That I do not know. So... I am content simply to follow your advice. Let us cover the shaft now before *it* decides to come out again."

"A moment more, Professor," Alan said, continuing to kneel and examine the ancient writing. "All the mist seems to have disappeared in here, but you'd best check the cavern and outside area just to be certain. I'll stay here and cover the opening if it should decide to come back up."

Dr. Fletcher returned shortly and assured Alan that, to the best of his knowledge, all the mist had descended the shaft; he could detect none in the larger or smaller chamber nor outside. Satisfied, it took but a few moments, with their combined strength, to shove the star-shaped seal over the opening. They stood up, nodded firmly at the completion of their task, and gripped hands in silent recognition of this new friendship that had returned the deadly mist to captivity.

Outside, they spent some minutes sealing the small entrance with large boulders that lay scattered about with the conviction that no one must ever again discover this cavern. It was nearly eleven o'clock before they had finished and began their return to the cottage.

Alan stayed on for the remainder of the day and night, enjoying the company of Dr. Fletcher and the quiet serenity of the area. That first night the countryside, from all accounts, slumbered undisturbed, no longer troubled by the horror, and Alan left the following morning satisfied that the destiny of mankind was no longer threatened.

Two weeks later Alan Hasrad sat in his library examining the afternoon mail. His eyes seized upon one envelope in particular which bore the return address of Dr. Fletcher. Deftly, he slit it open and withdrew the contents, a single sheet of paper which relayed the happy message that all was well and serene at Shadow Lake and vicinity. The mist, Dr. Fletcher concluded, was surely laid to rest and the countryside had already returned to its usual tranquility.

Alan smiled and glanced over to a tiny bottle which adorned his desk. Inside, a gray cloud-like material seemed to squirm and struggle to free itself from its glass confinement. Continually in motion, constantly changing its formless shape, it charged and retreated from side to side and top to bottom of the imprisoning vial.

Alan continued to smile as he watched with total fascination this fragment from the stupendous whole of the primordial depravity he had captured within the cave before it could follow the larger mass into and down the shaft. Was it sentient, as was the parent body? Alan could not be certain, but he suspected a diminutive portion of the immeasurable intellect struggled to regain its freedom. And it amused him to know that his souvenir was none other than a part—an infinitesimal part—of the quasi-god itself.

Pneeph Taal waited.

Patiently.

It brooded over the irrational stratagem it had followed of returning to its prison while gaining bulk and strength, only to find itself once again effectively restrained. But one day, perhaps years or centuries or millenniums in the future, its fetters would once again be lifted and it would satisfy its consuming, cavernous appetite. That day, it knew, would surely come; and the same mistake would not be repeated.

SHOGGOTH'S OLD PECULIAR

BY NEIL GAIMAN

BENJAMIN LASSITER WAS COMING TO THE UNAVOIDABLE conclusion that the woman who had written the *Walking Tour of the British Coastline* book he was carrying in his backpack had never been on a walking tour of any kind, and would probably not recognise the British coastline if it were to dance through her bedroom at the head of a marching band, singing "I'm the British coastline" in a loud and cheerful voice while accompanying itself on the kazoo.

He had been following her advice for five days now, and had little to show for it, except blisters, and a backache. *All British seaside resorts contain a number of bed and breakfast establishments, who will be only too delighted to put you up in the "off-season,"* was one such piece of advice. Ben had crossed it out and written, in the margin beside it, *All British seaside resorts contain a handful of bed and breakfast establishments, the owners of which take off to Spain or Provence or somewhere on the last day of September, locking the doors behind them as they go.*

He had added a number of other marginal notes, too. Such as *Do not repeat not under any circumstances order fried eggs again in any roadside cafe* and *what is it with the fish and chips thing?* And *No they are not.* That last was written beside a paragraph which claimed that, if there was one thing that the inhabitants of scenic villages on the British coastline were pleased to see, it was a young American tourist on a walking tour.

For five hellish days Ben had walked from village to village, had drunk sweet tea and instant coffee in cafeterias and cafes, and stared out at grey rocky vistas and at the slate-coloured sea, shivered under his two thick sweaters, got wet, and failed to see any of the sights that were promised.

Sitting in the bus-shelter in which he had unrolled his sleeping bag one night he had begun to translate key descriptive words: *charming* he decided, meant *nondescript, scenic* meant *ugly but with a nice view if the rain ever lets up, delightful* probably meant *we've never been here and don't know anyone who has.* He had also come to the conclusion that the more exotic the name of the village, the duller the village.

Thus it was that Ben Lassiter came, on the fifth day, somewhere north of Bootle, to the village of Innsmouth, which was rated neither charming, scenic nor delightful in his guidebook. There were no descriptions of the rusting pier, nor the mounds of rotting lobster-pots upon the pebbly beach.

On the seafront were three bed and breakfasts, next to each other, *Sea View, Mon Repose* and *Shub Niggurath,* each with a neon *Vacancies* sign turned off in the window of the front parlour, each with a "closed for the season" notice thumbtacked to the front door.

There were no cafes open on the seafront. The lone fish and chip shop had a closed sign up. Ben waited outside for it to open, as the grey afternoon light faded into dusk. Finally a small, slightly frog-faced woman came down the road, and she unlocked the door of the shop. Ben asked her when they would be open for business, and she looked at him, puzzled, and said, "It's Monday, dear. We're never open on Monday." Then she went into the fish and chip shop and locked the door behind her, leaving Ben cold and hungry on her doorstep.

Ben had been raised in a dry town in northern Texas: the only water was in backyard swimming pools, and the only way to travel was in an air-conditioned pick-up truck. So the idea of walking, by the sea, in a country where they spoke English of a sort, had appealed to him. Ben's home town was doubly dry: it prided itself on having banned alcohol thirty years before the rest of America leapt onto the Prohibition bandwagon, and on never having got off again; thus all Ben knew of pubs was that they were sinful places, like bars, only with cuter names. The author of *A Walking Tour of the British Coastline* had, however, suggested that pubs were good places to go to find local colour and local information, that one should always *stand one's round,* and that some of them sold food.

The Innsmouth pub was called *The Book of Dead Names* and the sign over the door informed Ben that the proprietor was one A. Al-Hazred, licensed to sell wines and spirits. Ben wondered if this meant that they would serve Indian food, which he had eaten on his arrival in Bootle, and rather enjoyed. He paused at the signs directing him to the Public Bar or the Saloon Bar, wondering if British Public Bars were private like their Public Schools, and eventually, because it sounded more like something you would find in a Western, going into the Saloon Bar.

The Saloon Bar was almost empty. It smelled like last week's spilled beer and the day-before-yesterday's cigarette smoke. Behind the bar was a plump woman with bottle-blonde hair. Sitting in one corner were a couple of gentlemen wearing long grey raincoats, and scarves. They were playing dominoes and sipping dark brown, foam-topped beerish drinks from dimpled glass tankards.

Ben walked over to the bar. "Do you sell food here?"

The barmaid scratched the side of her nose for a moment, then admitted, grudgingly, that she could probably do him a ploughman's.

Ben had no idea what this meant, and found himself, for the hundredth time, wishing that the *Walking Tour of the British Coastline* had an American-English phrasebook in the back. "Is that food?" he asked.

She nodded.

"Okay. I'll have one of those."

"And to drink?"

"Coke, please."

"We haven't got any Coke."

"Pepsi, then."

"No Pepsi."

"Well, what do you have? Sprite? Seven-up? Gatorade?"

She looked blanker than previously. Then she said, "I think there's a bottle or two of cherryade in the back."

"That'll be fine."

"It'll be five pounds and twenty pence, and I'll bring you over your ploughman's when it's ready."

Ben decided, as he sat at a small and slightly sticky wooden table, drinking something fizzy that both looked and tasted a bright, chemical red, that a ploughman's was probably a steak of some kind. He reached this conclusion, coloured, he knew, by wishful thinking, from imagining rustic, possibly even bucolic, ploughmen leading their plump oxen through fresh ploughed fields at sunset, and because he could, by then, with equanimity and only a little help from others, have eaten an entire ox.

"Here you go. Ploughman's," said the barmaid, putting a plate down in front of him.

That a ploughman's turned out to be a rectangular slab of sharp-tasting cheese, a lettuce leaf, an undersized tomato with a thumb-print in it, a mound of something wet and brown that tasted like sour jam, and a small, hard, stale roll, came as a sad disappointment to Ben, who had already decided that the British treated food as some kind of punishment. He chewed the cheese and the lettuce leaf, and cursed every ploughman in England for choosing to dine upon such swill.

The gentlemen in grey raincoats, who had been sitting in the corner, finished their game of dominoes, picked up their drinks, and came and sat beside Ben. "What you drinkin'?" one of them asked, curiously.

"It's called Cherryade," he told them. "It tastes like something from a chemical factory."

"Interesting you should say that," said the shorter of the two. "Interesting you should say that. Because I had a friend worked in a chemical factory and he *never drank cherryade*." He paused dramatically, and then took a sip of his brown drink. Ben waited for him to go on, but that appeared to be that: the conversation had stopped.

In an effort to appear polite, Ben asked, in his turn, "So, what are you guys drinking?"

The taller of the two strangers, who had been looking lugubrious, brightened up. "Why, that's exceedingly kind of you. Pint of Shoggoth's Old Peculiar for me, please."

"And for me too," said his friend. "I could murder a Shoggoth's. 'Ere, I bet that would make a good advertising slogan. '*I could murder a Shoggoth's.*' I should write to them and suggest it. I bet they'd be very glad of me suggestin' it."

Ben went over to the barmaid, planning to ask her for two pints of Shoggoth's Old Peculiar and a glass of water for himself, only to find she had already poured three pints of the dark beer. Well, he thought, might as well be hung for a sheep as a lamb, and he was certain it couldn't be worse than the cherryade. He took a sip: the beer had the kind of flavour which, he suspected, advertisers would describe as "full-bodied," although if pressed they would have to admit that the body in question had been that of a goat.

He paid the barmaid, and maneuvered his way back to his new friends.

"So. What you doin' in Innsmouth?" asked the taller of the two. "I suppose you're one of our American cousins, come to see the most famous of English villages."

"They named the one in America after this one, you know," said the smaller one.

"Is there an Innsmouth in the States?" asked Ben.

"I should say so," said the smaller man. "He wrote about it all the time. Him whose name we don't mention."

"I'm sorry?" said Ben.

The little man looked over his shoulder, then he hissed, very loudly, "H. R Lovecraft!"

"I told you not to mention that name," said his friend, and he took a sip of the dark brown beer. "H. P. Lovecraft. H. P. bloody Lovecraft. H. bloody P. bloody Love bloody craft," he stopped to take a breath. "What did he know? Eh? I mean what did he bloody know?"

Ben sipped his beer. The name was vaguely familar; he remembered it from rummaging through the pile of old-style vinyl LPs in the back of his father's garage. "Weren't they a rock group?"

"Wasn't talkin' about any rock group. I mean the writer."

Ben shrugged. "I've never heard of him," he admitted. "I really mostly only read Westerns. And technical manuals."

The little man nudged his neighbour. "Here. Wilf. You hear that? He's never heard of him."

"Well. There's no harm in that. I used to read that Zane Grey," said the taller.

"Yes. Well. That's nothing to be proud of. This bloke—what you say your name was?"

"Ben. Ben Lassiter. And you are?..."

The little man smiled; he looked awfully like a frog, thought Ben. "I'm Seth," he said. "And my friend here is called Wilf."

"Charmed," said Wilf.

"Hi," said Ben.

"Frankly," said the little man, "I agree with you."

"You do?" said Ben, perplexed.

The little man nodded. "Yer. H. P. Lovecraft. I don't know what the fuss is about. He couldn't bloody write." He slurped his stout, then licked the foam from his lips with a long and flexible tongue. "I mean, for starters, you look at them words he used. *Eldritch*. You know what eldritch means?"

Ben shook his head. He seemed to be discussing literature with two strangers in an English pub while drinking beer. He wondered for a moment if he had become someone else, while he wasn't looking. The beer tasted less bad, the further down the glass he went, and was beginning to erase the lingering aftertaste of the cherryade.

"*Eldritch*. Means weird. Peculiar. Bloody odd. That's what it means. I looked it up. In a dictionary. And *gibbous*?"

Ben shook his head again.

"Gibbous means the moon was nearly full. And what about that one he was always calling us, eh? Thing. Wossname. Starts with a *B*. Tip of me tongue..."

"Bastards?" suggested Wilf.

"Nah. Thing. You know. *Batrachian*. That's it. Means looked like frogs."

"Hang on," said Wilf. "I thought they was, like, a kind of camel."

Seth shook his head vigorously. "S'definitely frogs. Not camels. Frogs."

Wilf slurped his Shoggoth's. Ben sipped his, carefully, without pleasure.

"So?" said Ben.

"They've got two humps," interjected Wilf, the tall one.

"Frogs?" asked Ben.

"Nah. Batrachians. Whereas your average dromedary camel, he's only got one. It's for the long journey through the desert. That's what they eat."

"Frogs?" asked Ben.

"Camel humps." Wilf fixed Ben with one bulging yellow eye. "You listen to me, matey-me-lad. After you've been out in some trackless desert for three or four weeks, a plate of roasted camel hump starts looking particularly tasty."

Seth looked scornful. "You've never eaten a camel hump."

"I might have done," said Wilf.

"Yes, but you haven't. You've never even been in a desert."

"Well, let's say, just supposing I'd been on a pilgrimage to the Tomb of Nyarlathotep..."

"The black king of the ancients who shall come in the night from the east and you shall not know him, you mean?"

"Of course that's who I mean."

"Just checking."

"Stupid question, if you ask me."

"You could of meant someone else with the same name."

"Well, it's not exactly a common name, is it? Nyarlathotep. There's not exactly going to be two of them, are there? 'Hullo, my name's Nyarlathotep, what a coincidence meeting you here, funny them bein' two of us,' I don't exactly think so. Anyway, so I'm trudging through them trackless wastes, thinking to myself, I could murder a camel hump..."

"But you haven't, have you? You've never been out of Innsmouth harbour."

"Well... No."

"There." Seth looked at Ben triumphantly. Then he leaned over, and whispered into Ben's ear, "He gets like this when he gets a few drinks into him, I'm afraid."

"I heard that," said Wilf.

"Good," said Seth. "Anyway. H. P. Lovecraft. He'd write one of his bloody sentences. Ahem. 'The gibbous moon hung low over the eldritch and batrachian inhabitants of squamous Dulwich.' What does he mean, eh? *What does he mean?* I'll tell you what he bloody means. What he bloody means is that the moon was nearly full, and everybody what lived in Dulwich was bloody peculiar frogs. That's what he means."

"What about the other thing you said," asked Wilf.

"What?"

"Squamous. Wossat mean, then?"

Seth shrugged. "Haven't a clue," he admitted. "But he used it an awful lot."

There was another pause.

"I'm a student," said Ben. "Gonna be a metallurgist." Somehow he had managed to finish the whole of his first pint of Shoggoth's Old

Peculiar, which was, he realised, pleasantly shocked, his first alcoholic beverage. "What do you guys do?"

"We," said Wilf, "are acolytes."

"Of Great Cthulhu," said Seth, proudly.

"Yeah?" said Ben. "And what exactly does that involve?"

"My shout," said Wilf. "Hang on." Wilf went over to the barmaid, and came back with three more pints. "Well," he said, "what it involves is, technically speaking, not a lot right now. The acolytin' is not really what you might call laborious employment in the middle of its busy season. That is, of course, because of his bein' *asleep*. Well, not exactly asleep. More like, if you want to put a finer point on it, *dead*."

"'In his house at sunken R'lyeh dead Cthulhu lies dreaming,'" interjected Seth. "Or, as the poet has it, *That is not dead what can eternal lie*–"

"*But in Strange Aeons*–" chanted Wilf.

"–and by *strange* he means *bloody peculiar*–"

"Exactly. We are not talking your normal Aeons here at all."

"*–But in Strange Aeons even Death can die.*"

Ben was mildly surprised to find that he seemed to be drinking another full-bodied pint of Shoggoth's Old Peculiar. Somehow the taste of rank goat was less offensive on the second pint. He was also delighted to notice that he was no longer hungry, that his blistered feet had stopped hurting and that his companions were charming, intelligent men whose names he was having difficulty in keeping apart. He did not have enough experience with alcohol to know that this was one of the symptoms of being on your second pint of Shoggoth's Old Peculiar.

"So right now," said Seth, or possibly Wilf, "the business is a bit light. Mostly consisting of waiting."

"And praying," said Wilf, if he wasn't Seth.

"And praying. But pretty soon now, that's all going to change."

"Yeah?" asked Ben. "How's that?"

"Well," confided the taller one. "Any day now, Great Cthulhu (currently impermanently deceased), who is our boss will wake up, in his undersea living-sort-of quarters."

"And then," said the shorter one, "he will stretch and yawn and get dressed–"

"Probably go to the toilet, I wouldn't be at all surprised."

"Maybe read the papers."

"—And having done all that, he will come out of the ocean depths and consume the world utterly."

Ben found this unspeakably funny. "Like a ploughman's," he said.

"Exactly. Exactly. Well put, the young American gentleman. Great Cthulhu will gobble the world up like a ploughman's lunch, leaving but only the lump of Branston pickle on the side of the plate."

"That's the brown stuff?" asked Ben. They assured him that it was, and he went up to the bar and brought them back another three pints of Shoggoth's Old Peculiar.

He could not remember much of the conversation that followed. He remembered finishing his pint, and his new friends inviting him on a walking tour of the village, pointing out the various sights to him. "That's where we rent our videos, and that big building next door is the Nameless Temple of Unspeakable Gods and on Saturday mornings there's a jumble sale in the crypt..."

He explained to them his theory of the walking tour book, and told them, emotionally, that Innsmouth was both *scenic* and *charming*. He told them that they were the best friends he had ever had, and that Innsmouth was *delightful*.

The moon was nearly full, and in the pale moonlight both of his new friends did look remarkably like huge frogs. Or possibly camels.

The three of them walked to the end of the rusted pier, and Seth and/or Wilf pointed out to Ben the ruins of sunken R'lyeh in the bay, visible in the moonlight, beneath the sea, and Ben was overcome by what he kept explaining was a sudden and unforeseen attack of seasickness, and was violently and unendingly sick over the metal railings, into the black sea below...

After that it all got a bit odd.

Ben Lassiter awoke on the cold hillside with his head pounding, and a bad taste in his mouth. His head was resting on his backpack. There was rocky moorland on each side of him, and no sign of a road, and no sign of any village, scenic, charming, delightful or even picturesque.

He stumbled and limped almost a mile to the nearest road, and walked along it until he reached a petrol station.

They told him that there was no village anywhere locally named Innsmouth. No village with a pub called The Book of Dead Names.

He told them about two men, named Wilf and Seth, and a friend of theirs, called Strange Ian, who was fast asleep somewhere, if he wasn't dead, under the sea. They told him that they didn't think much of American hippies who wandered about the countryside taking drugs, and that he'd probably feel better after a nice cup of tea and a tuna and cucumber sandwich, but, that if he was dead set on wandering the country taking drugs, young Ernie who worked the afternoon shift would be all too happy to sell him a nice little bag of homegrown cannabis, if he could come back after lunch.

Ben pulled out his *Walking Tour of the British Coastline* book and tried to find Innsmouth in it, to prove to them that he had not dreamed it, but he was unable to locate the page it had been on, if ever it had been there at all. Most of one page, however, had been ripped out, roughly, about halfway through the book.

And then Ben telephoned a taxi, which took him to Bootle railway station, where he caught a train, which took him to Manchester, where he got on an aeroplane, which took him to Chicago, where he changed planes, and flew to Dallas, where he got another plane going north, and he rented a car, and went home.

He found the knowledge that he was over 600 miles away from the ocean very comforting; although, later in life, he moved to Nebraska, to increase the distance from the sea: there were things he had seen, or thought he had seen, beneath the old pier that night, that he would never be able to get out of his head. There were things that lurked beneath grey raincoats that man was not meant to know. *Squamous.* He did not need to look it up. He knew. They were squamous.

A couple of weeks after his return home Ben posted his annotated copy of *A Walking Tour of the British Coastline* to the author, care of her publisher, with an extensive letter containing a number of helpful suggestions for future editions. He also asked the author if she would send him a copy of the page that had been ripped from his guide book, to set his mind at rest; but he was secretly relieved, as the days turned into months, and the months turned into years and then into decades, that she never replied.

ABOUT THE EDITOR

ROBERT M. PRICE is the editor of the journal *Crypt of Cthulhu* and is one of the most acclaimed Lovecraft scholars and editors in the world. As a prominent American theologian, he brings a unique perspective to the works of H. P. Lovecraft, drawing in authors from a wide spectrum of styles and backgrounds.

BLACK WINGS OF CTHULHU

TWENTY-ONE TALES OF LOVECRAFTIAN HORROR

EDITED BY S. T. JOSHI

S. T. Joshi—the twenty-first century's preeminent expert on all things Lovecraftian—gathers twenty-one of the master's greatest modern acolytes, including Caitlín R. Kiernan, Ramsey Campbell, Michael Shea, Brian Stableford, Nicholas Royle, Darrell Schweitzer and W. H. Pugmire, each of whom serves up a new masterpiece of cosmic terror that delves deep into the human psyche to horrify and disturb.

"[An] exceptional set of original horror tales... [*Black Wings*] will delight even horror fans completely unfamiliar with Lovecraft."
Booklist

"Cumulatively creepy studies of Lovecraft-style locales where inexplicable supernatural phenomena suggest an otherworldly dimension intersecting our own."
Publishers Weekly

"Joshi's tribute proves there's still plenty of life in the Elder Gods yet— and plenty of highly talented writers penning dark fiction these days."
Fantasy Magazine

BLACK WINGS OF CTHULHU 2

EIGHTEEN TALES OF LOVECRAFTIAN HORROR

EDITED BY S. T. JOSHI

In the second volume of the critically acclaimed Black Wings series, S. T. Joshi—the world's foremost Lovecraft scholar—has assembled eighteen more brand-new and imaginative horror tales, inspired by the twentieth century's greatest writer of the supernatural, H. P. Lovecraft.

Leading contemporary horror authors, including John Shirley, Tom Fletcher, Caitlín R. Kiernan, Jonathan Thomas, Nick Mamatas, Richard Gavin, Melanie Tem, John Langan, Jason C. Eckhardt, Don Webb, Darrell Schweitzer, Nicholas Royle, Steve Rasnic Tem, Brian Evenson, Rick Dakan, Donald Tyson, Jason V. Brock, and Chet Williamson, will draw upon themes, images, and ideas from the life and work of the master of the genre to deliver a rich feast of terror.

SHADOWS OVER INNSMOUTH

EDITED BY STEPHEN JONES

Under the unblinking eye of World Fantasy award-winning editor Stephen Jones, sixteen of the finest modern authors, including Neil Gaiman, Kim Newman, Ramsey Campbell and Brian Lumley contribute stories to the canon of Cthulhu. Also featuring the story that started it all, by the master of horror, H. P. Lovecraft.

"A fine assembly of talented writers... A superb anthology for Lovecraft fans."
Science Fiction Chronicle

"Horror abounds in *Shadows Over Innsmouth*."
Publishers Weekly

"Good, slimy fun... There are a number of genuinely frightening pieces here."
San Francisco Chronicle

WEIRD SHADOWS OVER INNSMOUTH

EDITED BY STEPHEN JONES

Including the unpublished early draft of 'The Shadow Over Innsmouth,' by H. P. Lovecraft, this extraordinary volume features twelve stories by some of the world's most prominent Lovecraftian authors, including Ramsey Campbell, Kim Newman, Michael Marshall Smith, John Glasby, Paul McAuley, Steve Rasnic Tem, Caitlín R. Kiernan, Brian Lumley, Basil Copper, Hugh B. Cave, and Richard Lupoff.

"H. P. Lovecraft fans will revel in this fine follow-up to Jones' *Shadows Over Innsmouth*, a World Fantasy finalist."
Publishers Weekly

"Jones has brought together some of the industry's top-notch authors... strongly recommended for Mythos fans."
Hellnotes

"Fascinating and recommended."
All Hallows